SO-AFE-759

"[A] celebration of the purity of the sport."
—*Fort Worth Star-Telegram*

"For a young man or woman, the twenty-first-century onslaught against purity and potential offers very few havens, but John L. Parker, Jr.'s lovely novel *Racing the Rain* reminds us that within amateur sports, especially a good footrace, all of us, athletes and spectators alike, might find what is most valuable in any life—the spirit to accomplish impossible things."
—Bob Shacochis, National Book Award winner
and author of *The Woman Who Lost Her Soul*

"Much of the intrigue of the book lies in discovering how Cassidy developed into the elite runner he became, when and how his talent revealed itself, and how he came to recognize his extraordinary ability to focus, train, and endure pain with purpose. But *Racing the Rain* offers myriad other delights, not the least of which is the friendship Cassidy strikes up with a (real-life) swamp man named Trapper Nelson. . . . [The book is] loaded with elegance and evocative writing. . . . A worthy, compelling, and satisfying conclusion to the Quenton Cassidy trilogy."
—*Paste Magazine*

"In *Racing the Rain*, John L. Parker, Jr., not only creates the indomitable Quenton Cassidy but perfectly captures the world that teaches him to be so enduring. From diving the Atlantic deeps to paddling the intracoastal waterways, young Cassidy develops the metabolism of a champion. Parker shows that the wilds of his beloved Loxahatchee River are just as good a cradle for a miler as the Colorado mountains or the Oregon woods. I was with him all the way."
—Kenny Moore, former senior writer, *Sports Illustrated*,
and 1968 and 1972 Olympic marathoner

ALSO BY JOHN L. PARKER, JR.

Once a Runner

Again to Carthage

Runners & Other Dreamers

Uncommon Heart (with Anne Audain)

Marty Liquori's Guide for the Elite Runner (with Marty Liquori)

Run Down Fired Up and Teed Off

And Then the Vulture Eats You (editor)

Heart Monitor Training for the Compleat Idiot

RACING

THE

RAIN

- A NOVEL -

JOHN L. PARKER, JR.

Scribner
New York London Toronto Sydney New Delhi

Scribner
An Imprint of Simon & Schuster, Inc.
1230 Avenue of the Americas
New York, NY 10020

First Scribner trade paperback edition September 2016

SCRIBNER and design are registered trademarks of The Gale Group, Inc., used under license by Simon & Schuster, Inc., the publisher of this work.

For information about special discounts for bulk purchases, please contact Simon & Schuster Special Sales at 1-866-506-1949 or business@simonandschuster.com.

The Simon & Schuster Speakers Bureau can bring authors to your live event. For more information or to book an event, contact the Simon & Schuster Speakers Bureau at 1-866-248-3049 or visit our website at www.simonspeakers.com.

Interior design by Jill Putorti

10   9   8   7   6   5   4   3   2

The Library of Congress has cataloged the hardcover edition as follows:

Parker, John L., Jr.
Racing the rain : a novel / John L. Parker. —First Scribner hardcover edition.
   pages ; cm
Prequel to: Once a runner.
1. Runners (Sports)—Fiction. 2. Running—Fiction. 3. Sports stories. I. Title.
PS3566.A679R33 2015
813'.54—dc23   2015016535

ISBN 978-1-4767-6986-8
ISBN 978-1-4767-6988-2 (pbk)
ISBN 978-1-4767-6987-5 (ebook)

One chapter of this book was published in much different form in the October 2006 issue of *Runner's World*.

For Ramsey W. Dulin, Esq., and Caldwell W. Smith, MD,
Friends of My Youth, who were there . . .

It's a treat, being a long-distance runner, out in the world by yourself . . .

—Alan Sillitoe, *The Loneliness of the Long-Distance Runner*

AUTHOR'S NOTE

Some characters and situations in this book were inspired by actual people and historical events, though I have used (and perhaps misused) them in entirely fictional ways. Seemingly, the most obviously "made-up" character in the book would have to be Trapper Nelson, of course. Rest assured, dear reader, that this amazing being lived and breathed and walked upon this earth.

RACING

THE

RAIN

CHAPTER 1

THE VERY EDGE OF THINGS

The first- and second-fastest kids in the second grade stood at the end of Rosedale Street in the early June heat, their bird chests heaving, asphalt fumes stinging their noses. They were so thin a mesh of blue veins showed under brown skin.

"It's cuh-cuh-coming," the smaller boy said, nodding toward the angry purple smudge on the horizon behind them. His skull was slightly elongated, somehow giving him a studious air.

"Couple minutes," said the other, taller but just as brown and skinny, scrunching his bare toes into the sun-softened tar.

It would have been difficult for an adult to appreciate their boundless sense of possibilities as they stood waiting: the vastness of the coming summer, the endless expanse of school years ahead, the insignificance of their tiny lives when measured against any grown-up conception of time.

But for now they were simply oblivious to everything but the dark specter approaching Rosedale Street.

The sky darkened suddenly, and from nowhere a chilly wind began whipping through the Spanish moss in the live oaks across Bumby Avenue, raising goose bumps on their forearms. The boys leaned into a half crouch with hands on knees and waited.

The first fat drops splatted on the roadway, making little hissy puffs of steam, and as they began landing on the boys' skin, a crack of thunder split the sky. They took off down the street in a blur of spindly legs and arms.

They were fairly evenly matched but were not really racing each other as much as simply trying to stay ahead of the deluge at their heels.

This moment always seemed magical to them: a bright tropical day loomed in front as a purple monsoon came on from behind. And they were thrilled as only children can be thrilled to exist for a moment at the very edge of things, at the buzzy existential margin of all possibilities. One might go fetch a Popsicle or be struck by lightning or live to a well-tended old age with golf clubs in the trunk. Whirl was king and all was in play.

All they knew was that for this moment in time they were racing the rain, and they were laughing laughing laughing.

CHAPTER 2

ANTS

The skinniest of the boys was named Quenton Cassidy. The year before, in the first grade, he had marched up to his gangly bespectacled best friend Stiggs at recess and announced: "I'm the fastest kid in first grade."

"No, you aren't," Stiggs said. "*He* is."

He was pointing to Demski, a spindly creature with an oblong skull and a crew cut so severe as to make his hair invisible. He was squatting in the roots of a huge live oak next to the jungle bars, enthralled by a very active colony of red ants. Demski lived on Homer Circle two blocks from Cassidy, and because his mom wouldn't let him play pickup football, no one had paid him much attention. When they marched over, Demski didn't look up.

"Whatcha doin', looking at ants?" Cassidy said.

Demski nodded.

"What are they up to?" Stiggs said.

Demski shrugged. "Buh-buh-buh-building stuff, I guess."

Cassidy and Stiggs leaned over to get a better look.

"There sure are a lot of them," Cassidy said.

Demski nodded.

"He wants to race you," Stiggs said. "He says he's the fastest kid in first grade."

"Okay," said Demski without enthusiasm.

Several other kids had gathered around because three people watching ants apparently constituted some kind of quorum.

"Race, race!" they chanted.

"Monkey bars to home plate on the first diamond," said Stiggs, assuming authority as usual. "I say, 'Ready, set, go,' and you take off. Randleman, you go stand at home in case it's close, which it won't be."

Randleman, a sturdy, good-natured kid, loped off.

"Ready. Set. Go!" said Stiggs. Demski took off, but Cassidy was holding his hand up.

"Time out!" he said. "Kings X! I need to take my shoes off. I have to run barefoot." Demski circled back, eyeing Cassidy dispassionately as he removed his Thom McAns and the ridiculous argyle socks his mother made him wear because they were a Christmas present from his great-aunt Mary and she had diabetes.

"All right, dammit," said Stiggs, who was just learning to cuss. "Take your damn shoes off. Anything else you need? Want to change your clothes or have a little snack?" The small crowd laughed. Stiggs, everyone agreed, was the wittiest kid in first grade.

When Cassidy was finally ready and he and Demski were crouched side by side, Stiggs held his arm in the air dramatically.

"Ready. Set. *Go!*" Apropos of nothing, he added another "Dammit."

Ed Demski really was the fastest kid in first grade, so it wasn't much of a contest, though Cassidy surprised everyone by making it close.

Stiggs was standing by the monkey bars, arms folded smugly across his chest, as Cassidy came back to get his shoes and socks, still panting.

"What do you say now, big mouth?" Stiggs said as the bell rang.

Cassidy sat on the ground with spindly legs crossed, vigorously shaking sand out of a shoe. He looked up at Stiggs and brightened.

"Hey, Stiggs," he said, "guess what? I'm the second-fastest kid in first grade!"

CHAPTER 3

PARCHED

They were always thirsty.

It would be ninety-two in the shade by midmorning and they would stop their front yard ball game and disperse to houses known to serve Kool-Aid, returning with faint clown smiles of various flavors. Or they would gobble plasticky water from the hose after running it for a while to get all the hot out. At the school gym they'd take a break from the shirts-and-skins basketball game to crowd around the rumbling old watercooler, urging the guy in front to goddamn hurry *up*! Hey, spaz, leave some for the fish! Hey, ya big jerk, you're not a camel!

Sometimes they'd see the edges of a little grin protruding from either side of the pencil-thin stream of frigid water, and they'd go thirst crazy.

"Dammit, Stiggs!" And a writhing body would be pulled away from the fountain and briefly pummeled.

If anyone had money, they would race their bicycles through the wavy afternoon heat to the A&W, where the root beer mugs were frozen so solidly they gave off smoke in the afternoon heat and at some point a perfectly round medallion of ice would detach from the bottom and float majestically up through the bubbles to bob around in the foamy surface before being crunched by little teeth. Sometimes they'd pedal to Palm Drugs for a five-cent Pepsi, which the soda jerk would have to mix manually and which they would nurse for a half hour or more, not leaving the blessed air-conditioning until they had pried the last melting morsel of ice from the bottom of the glass with a straw.

Food mattered little to them and they tried not to waste too much time at their Formica kitchen tables, but their thirst was another matter. It would make them so desperate they would sometimes gulp water right from the lake or the river they were swimming in, despite admonitions from adults.

He and Stiggs and Randleman were on Rosedale Street; Joe and Johnny Augenblick, proprietors of a decent backyard basketball court, were one street over on Betty Drive, as were Buddy Lockridge and Billy Claytor. Demski was two blocks away on Homer Circle. The girls were playmates of last resort, but some of them were okay: Libby Claytor, Patty Robertson, Bonnie Johnson, and of course the adorable Maria DaRosa. They even knew some kids from six and seven blocks away, all the way up to Chelsea Street and Christy Avenue, though they seemed a bit foreign and exotic.

Cassidy was vaguely proud that his own roots went deeper than most of the others', whose families came after the war, pouring back down to the sunny reptile farms and honky-tonk beaches dad had discovered in boot camp or flight school. Many were among the new breed of electronic warrior more at home with soldering irons, capacitors, and resistors than with guns and tanks. They worked on Air Force radar at Fort Murphy or Navy sonar at Lake Gem Mary or on one of dozens of cold war projects up and down the state, some as civilians, some still "in." Others came down to start businesses or to take jobs in the newly awakened economy. No one had heard the term "baby boom," but they were all nonetheless in the business of producing offspring, herds of skinny young'uns who grew up in baking pastel cinder-block houses in those wondrous days when air-conditioning was just a cruel rumor.

Cassidy would never forget endless summer nights perspiring on damp sheets, the faint hope of sleep just a fever dream. The droning arc of the rotating fan would bring a few seconds of blessed relief before sweeping past and lingering uselessly for a moment at the far end of its cycle.

Most of the children around Rosedale Street had never hurled a snowball, but they had flung many a rotten orange. That was one reason they loved winter, when the heat would finally back off, and abundant ammunition lay all around on the ground, courtesy of the remnants of the old citrus groves their houses were built among.

Most of the year they lived like simians, sometimes sitting right in the trees while munching on the flora. Or they would pull fruit from limbs as they ran by: loquats, a kind of sweet yellow plum with a single big seed; Brazilian cherries, which were miniature red-orange pumpkins that grew on hedges and were sweet but had a slightly nasty aftertaste; pink-fleshed guavas and red-yellow mangoes; fat little fig bananas; and of course citrus of all kinds, most of which dropped unnoticed from ignored trees. After a few days the oranges were mushy and fermented, perfect for rendering friends and enemies sticky, smelly, and spoiling for revenge. Mothers did a lot of laundry.

They got sandspurs in their feet, sunburns on their backs, and boils all over from the sandy soil. They were bitten by mosquitoes, chiggers, and occasionally each other. They were as at home in water as they were on land, and by the age of twelve many of them had landed their first sailfish or marlin. Most could throw a cast net, paddle a canoe, and handle a gaff.

In the happy midpoint of the twentieth century, Quenton Cassidy and the other kids on Rosedale Street grew up this way in Citrus City, a pebble toss away from the Atlantic Ocean, in the southern part of a coral peninsula the Spaniards named for flowers.

CHAPTER 4

NUCLEAR OBLIVION

By third grade, softball had become Cassidy's second-favorite sport, so there was nothing unusual about being still sweaty from a before-school game of scrub. This morning it made his iron-hard desk seat even more uncomfortable than usual, not helped by the fact that he'd picked up some well-placed grains of sand in his underwear sliding into home for no particular reason.

A determined bumblebee was trying to bump his way through one of the window screens, and Cassidy watched it with interest as he desperately maneuvered his itchy butt cheeks around.

Mrs. Chickering, whose elaborately rhinestoned eyeglasses lent wings to her pretty dark eyes, was going on and on about the exports of Paraguay. She stopped in midsentence, marking her place with a forefinger and lowering her book. She focused her lovely eyes on Cassidy with ill-concealed exasperation.

"Quenton, do you need the hall pass?"

"No, ma'am."

"Then will you please stop squirming?"

"Yes, ma'am."

The class tittered, as it always did when someone got in trouble. Mrs. Chickering went back to discussing "hardwoods," a mystery to

Cassidy. It seemed to him that wood in general was hard (his satanic desk seat being a case in point), and if it wasn't, then what good was it anyway? What use could possibly be made of soft wood?

Such are the diversions of a lively child stunned by humidity and boredom. Trying to take his mind from his inflamed backside, he surreptitiously kept track of the relentless bee.

At long last Mrs. Chickering put her book away and picked up a mimeographed sheet from her desk.

"All right, children, we have art after lunch, so Miss Baskind will be here. I expect that you will be well-behaved ladies and gentlemen and that no one will have to come fetch me from the teachers' lounge," she said. An excited murmur swept through the room. Everyone liked art.

"All right, settle down. In a few minutes we will be heading to assembly. As always, there will be no talking once we are in line, and no talking while we are marching to the auditorium. Does everyone understand that? Carl Wagner? Olivia Lattermore? Quenton Cassidy?"

The class chatterboxes dutifully muttered assent, but Mrs. Chickering paused for an interminable few seconds to emphasize her point. Not before everyone was suitably uncomfortable did she continue reading from the sheet.

"This morning in the auditorium we will see a movie from the United States Office of Civil Defense featuring Bert, the civil defense turtle. After assembly we will spend fifteen minutes practicing the duck-and-cover drills that we learn about in the movie."

More murmuring now. This was shaping up to be a pretty good day. Any event that broke the monotony of memorizing the exports of South American countries was entirely welcome. No one really knew what civil defense was, but Bert was apparently a cartoon turtle of some kind, and anything having to do with cartoons, even a government turtle, was good.

It was the most natural thing in the world to Quenton Cassidy, his classmates, and everyone he knew, to be living in a booming, vaguely militarized postwar America that went to bed dreaming not only of Amana freezers and Mohawk carpeting, but also of mushroom clouds and foreign paratroopers.

The current boogeyman was the Union of Soviet Socialist Republics, commonly referred to as "the Russians," a theoretically Marxist operation that in actuality was an entire society organized around the guiding principles of the United States Post Office.

The Soviets couldn't for the life of them produce a decent pair of Levi's or a grade of toilet paper that didn't actually draw blood, but they at least knew how to make big old scary rockets, and so that's exactly what they did.

Their counterparts on our side did likewise, and so, thanks to the world's grown-ups, Cassidy and his classmates were obliged to drill for the apocalypse.

The eerie wail of the air-raid siren would send them scrunching up under their desks and placing their tiny hands on top of their barely closed fontanels, ostensibly safe now from instant incineration, shock wave trauma, and a general hosing down with gamma rays.

From this position Cassidy once spotted Ed Demski across the row, arms folded dutifully over his asymmetrical noggin, eyes bulging from either terror or strain, Cassidy couldn't tell which. When he was sure he had Ed's eye, Cassidy widened his eyes and placed the tips of his index fingers into his ears and made the universal kid noise for a massive explosion.

Ed immediately went into head-thumping paroxysms under his desk, silenced only by the sudden upside-down appearance of a narrowed pair of winged eyes belonging to a very cross Mrs. Chickering. The two were unceremoniously dispatched to Principal Fravel's office in the care of a smirking hall monitor.

Mr. Fravel tried to make himself seem appropriately stern and authoritarian but understood at some deep and fundamental level that it was something of a miracle these two waifs were even capable of mocking one of the most fundamental and sacrosanct principles of education in mid-twentieth-century America: that there was to be no talking or horseplay during a nuclear holocaust.

CHAPTER 5

CHURCH

School desks were one thing, but church pews seemed ever harder to small children with no personal padding where it counted. Surely they were made from a kind of hardwood Paraguay would be proud to export. Thus, some of Cassidy's most torturous and mind-numbing moments on earth were spent on the rock-hard pews of the un-air-conditioned Reeves Memorial Methodist Church. This was despite his mother furiously fanning them both with a wooden stick–handled cardboard oval displaying an advertisement for Anderson's Dry Cleaners on South Orange Blossom Trail ("For Your Sunday Best—and All the Rest!").

Stiggs went to the same church as Cassidy, but Randleman was—in Stiggs's words—a "half-assed Catholic"—i.e., an Episcopalian, and went to St. Matthew's downtown. Demski was, however, an almost unheard-of real Catholic, and it was on his account—and that of two others—that they all ate fish sticks on Friday.

But every Sunday, pious little Cassidy, suffocating in his clip-on bow tie and starched short-sleeved white shirt, listened dazedly to some deluded or cynical mountebank go on and on about the Annunciation, the Holy Trinity, or the Ascension. Cassidy was besotted for a while by the airy nuances of Protestant theological doubletalk, but then Demski showed up at school one Monday morning spouting authoritatively about "t-t-t-transubstantiation." Cassidy didn't think the Methodists had any ecclesiastical terms with that many syllables, so for a while he was pretty sure he was a Catholic. Seething at the idea that she had unknowingly raised a little papist under her own roof, his mother bit her tongue for the three Sundays in a row Cassidy attended Mass with the Demskis.

Little Cassidy, though he was truly entranced by the Latin gobbledygook and the profusion of robes, miters, crucifixes, and other fabulous pagan paraphernalia, soon returned to the fold, however, pronouncing that his knees just couldn't take it.

It wasn't until years later, in his freshman comparative religion class, that he read a chapter from a book called *Religion from Tolstoy to Camus* titled "The Dark Side of Religion." One paragraph read, "The Protestant Calvin burned [at the stake] the scholarly Servetus for holding that Jesus was 'the eternal son of God,' rather than 'the son of the eternal God.'"

It seemed to Cassidy fairly harsh punishment for the misplacement of an adjective, even if the point were granted. Perhaps Servetus had made a typo.

But that, as far as Cassidy was concerned, was just the icing on a frightening cake of apostate immolations, witch torturings, and child sacrifices that Christianity had proudly authored in its early days.

His mother, however, made no exceptions for budding heretics, so he attended church and Sunday school regularly, messed around with Stiggs in the Fellowship Hall, and never missed the potluck suppers. No one ever made baked beans as well as the ladies at Reeves Memorial.

CHAPTER 6

REGGIE HARRIS

Cassidy lolled in the grass in Carl Wagner's front yard, waiting to fight Reggie Harris.

Now in the sixth grade, he was used to being picked on because of his small size and big mouth, but this animosity from Reggie was a surprise. They had been friends in the second and third grades, trading comic books and playing at each other's houses. They drifted apart but were still more or less friendly. Now all of a sudden it was, "Hey, let's fight."

"How come?" Cassidy said.

Reggie just shrugged. "See you at Carl Wagner's after school," he said, going back to his disheveled desk as the bell rang.

So Cassidy sat with Stiggs and Randleman and Stiggs's freckle-faced little brother, Timmy, who was, pound for pound, tougher than all of them, and who was now all but vibrating in anticipation. He would have gladly taken on Reggie Harris by himself.

"You stay out of this or I'll kill you," Cassidy told him. And to Stiggs: "Watch him, okay?"

"Here they come," said Stiggs. "I'll go get Carl Wagner."

"He's in his bedroom working on his P-51. He's putting the decals on today but he said to come get him."

"Did he get the Revell or the Aurora one?"

"I don't know. The cool British one."

Carl Wagner had been working on it all week, showing up in Miss Leydon's class every morning with dried Testors cement on his fingertips. The dark-complected Carl Wagner, whose parents were Lebanese immigrants, was an important personage at Fern Creek Elementary because his house was right across the street from the school. Also, both his parents worked, so many important after-school events were staged at his house. No one knew why he was always referred to by both names, never just "Carl" or "Wagner."

"Tell him Reggie's coming and he's bringing his brothers," Cassidy said.

Randleman did a rolling back flip to his hands and knees and hopped up as the shirtless Reggie and the two older boys sauntered up. Timmy glowered at the three of them but sat still.

"You ready?" Reggie said.

"I guess," said Cassidy, climbing to his feet and starting to take his shirt off.

Reggie tackled him around the waist and drove him back to the ground, his buzz-cut brown head buried under Cassidy's sternum. When they hit the ground, it felt like Reggie's thick forehead proceeded on down to tap the inside of Cassidy's spine, forcing every molecule of air out of his body.

Tears of shock welled in his eyes and he tried to push Reggie's head away so he could get his breath back, but Reggie kept flailing at him, keeping him pinned and helpless. He began to panic when he couldn't loosen his diaphragm enough to take a breath. He was vaguely aware of Dickie Harris urging Reggie on, but he also heard Carl Wagner's voice saying, "Let him up, this isn't fair." Stiggs was already holding his squirming little brother around the waist.

Fairness was a big thing in their world.

They were both undersized, wiry as lynxes, skinned-knee tough and a little on the grimy side even before the fight began. But with

Reggie it looked more worked-in, with several layers of kid soil not often disturbed by enforced bathing. He was already showing traces of the deep-seated resentment and sullenness that would almost certainly one day blossom into full-blown sociopathy.

He came by it honestly, however, growing up in a low-income housing area called Sunrise Estates, where he shared a run-down cottage with his cigarette-sneaking brothers and a permanently hair-rollered, TV-obsessed mother. Their father had gone back to upstate New York to paint barns, and their mother's life now centered around *The Guiding Light*, S&H Green Stamps, and the very same comic books her children read.

Some algorithm deep in Reggie Harris's frontal lobes had apparently worked out that he was doomed.

For the time being he was merely nursing a mean streak that Quenton Cassidy suddenly found himself on the business end of. Down the road waiting for Reggie would be a succession of defeated teachers, outmanned social workers, and bored cops who would form the conduit through which Reggie and his mean streak would be processed through the elaborate drainage system of the Republic. Much of this even an innocent like Quenton Cassidy somehow understood on a primal level, but it availed him not a whit at the moment.

In desperation, he began rocking Reggie from side to side until he got him off balance enough to dump him over. Then he got to his hands and knees and tried to draw that impossible first breath. Reggie was instantly on his knees beside him, holding him in a headlock and swinging uppercuts at his rib cage.

The deep, noisy first breath came at long last, ragged and painful but quelling his panic. He might live after all, but he was still so shaky and desperate for air that he was having to will himself not to start bawling out of frustration and self-pity. It would have been, really, the worst thing he could do. His friends would be humiliated and everybody in school would know about it the next day. In their little society there was precious little sympathy for a crybaby.

He began to feel real anger toward Reggie Harris for the first time. This was something new. Most fights were semi-lighthearted scuffles more like his losing wrestling matches with Stiggs and Randleman. This felt different.

"Work the body! Work the body!" cried Donnie Harris. Cassidy wasn't sure what that meant exactly, but it was obvious Reggie was getting more than encouragement from the peanut gallery, and it finally dawned on Cassidy what this was all about: his siblings had been trying to toughen Reggie up for the coming Rat Wars, and the undersized Cassidy must have seemed a good early palooka.

Cassidy looked over at Reggie and saw him winding up to deliver the coup de grâce. Everything seemed to be happening in slow motion now, and Cassidy easily ducked under the roundhouse, feeling the air whiffing above him as the blow sailed over.

He realized something else as he scrambled to his feet and turned to face his tormentor: Reggie wasn't that good at this. Cassidy knew that he was not only quicker than Reggie, but he wasn't breathing as hard. Maybe Reggie had already picked up some of his brothers' bad habits.

Now Reggie was huffing and puffing just as Cassidy was getting back to breathing normally again. Yes, he remembered, this is how it goes.

Reggie let go another roundhouse right so far off the mark Cassidy didn't even bother to duck. No wonder Reggie needed his brothers to egg him on. Cassidy felt something almost like pity for him and his squalid little life, but anger still gripped him.

When Reggie got ready to try the right again, Cassidy saw an opening and stepped in and hit him hard in the midsection with his left hand, sinking his little knot of a fist into the declivity under Reggie's sternum that Cassidy's cousin Henry called "the solar plexus, your opponent's secret off switch."

Reggie's face lost its sneer and turned into a comic aggregation of circles, round eyes, and round mouth inside a round face. His hands dropped as he grabbed his knees and began struggling for breath, just as Cassidy had. Red faced now, he looked up at Cassidy almost in disbelief, and for a very brief moment Cassidy saw in his eyes something he was not expecting: a look of the old rapport they had had in their comic-book-trading days.

Cassidy lost a lot of his anger then, but not his will to finish this. As he stepped toward Reggie, thinking to get him in a headlock and wring the rest of the fight out of him, Reggie's middle brother, Dickie, stepped between them.

"All right, round one. Time-out," he said. He had an unfiltered cigarette behind his left ear, and he was barefoot. He had a ballpoint "tattoo" on his biceps of a cross overlaid with a dagger dripping a single drop of blood.

"Huh?" Cassidy said.

"It's round one. Now we go to our corners and rest."

"What corners?"

"It's just what they call it. You seen the Friday Night Fights, ain't you? Brought to you by Gillette blue blades in the handy dispenser? What'll ya have, Pabst Blue Ribbon?" He was helping Reggie over to where the oldest brother, Donnie, sat in the grass, smoking a cigarette and looking disgusted. He was in high school and had a work-study job at a gas station.

"My dad drinks the beer that made Milwaukee famous," Cassidy muttered to no one in particular. But maybe Dickie had a point. None of the fights at Fern Creek Elementary ever had "rounds," but Cassidy had to admit he had seen them on TV.

Fingering several sore places on his face, he trudged over to where Randleman and Carl Wagner were lying in the grass poking at some kind of woolly caterpillar with a twig.

"Pretty neat!" said Carl Wagner. "You really pasted him good!"

"Why didn't ya clean his clock when ya had the chance?" said Randleman.

"I don't know. I guess we're doing rounds," Cassidy said.

"Rounds?" said Carl Wagner.

"Like boxing, on TV."

"Aw, those old guys. Some of them are even bald! They don't look tough to me," said Randleman, hard to impress as usual.

"They don't hit each other all that much," Cassidy admitted. "They just kind of stand there and hug each other for a while and then the referee comes in and makes them stop. My dad likes it though."

"Mine, too," said Randleman. He had finally coaxed the caterpillar onto the twig and was holding it up for Cassidy to see. Carl Wagner reached over to run his finger down the bug's furry back and everyone shivered in disgust.

Cassidy flopped on his back, watching the low clouds sliding across the blue summer sky. He was still breathing hard.

"I have to go finish my decals," said Carl Wagner, chewing dried cement from his forefinger. "Are you guys going to fight any more?"

Cassidy shrugged.

Stiggs helped him up, and he and Cassidy walked over to where the Harris brothers were sitting. Randleman stayed to hold Timmy back, and Carl Wagner was given custody of the caterpillar.

"Okay, Reggie," said Cassidy. "Ding goes the bell."

Reggie looked up at him, glanced at his brothers, then looked away. Cassidy couldn't believe it. He looked to Dickie, the apparent ringleader, for an explanation. Dickie looked away, too. The disgusted Donnie was already getting up to leave, rolling his pack of Luckies into the sleeve of his T-shirt.

"I'll be ready in a minute," said Reggie, trying to salvage something.

"I'm ready now," said Cassidy.

Reggie didn't say anything. Dickie was sitting cross-legged, looking down at the grass between his knees.

"I'm going to count to ten, then screw you guys, I'm going home," said Cassidy. "One, two, three . . ."

Reggie wasn't going to get up, any fool could see that. But Cassidy felt he had to do something to give this nonevent some kind of arguable conclusion, so no one could ever say he chickened out.

When he finished counting and Reggie hadn't moved—hadn't even looked at him—Cassidy returned to the others. Carl Wagner was showing the caterpillar to his little sister, Suzie, who had wandered over with her so-called babysitter, Maria DaRosa, who wasn't much older than she was.

"What are you going to do with him?" Suzie asked.

"Well, we thought about eating him for dinner," said Randleman.

Her eyes widened and she studied the others, ever on the alert for teasing. "You wouldn't!"

"They might," said Maria DaRosa. "Boys are pretty stupid, you know."

"Why not?" said Randleman. "Course, you have to skin them first." More wide eyes.

"Cut it out, Randleman," said Cassidy. "They're not going to eat him, Suzie." Randleman was just trying to impress Maria, who was almost as good an athlete as most of the boys. But Cassidy knew she didn't impress easily.

"We could," said Carl Wagner defensively. "My uncle Cliff said they eat bugs in survival school. He's a Ranger. And they had to drink water out of a stream that had green stuff growing in it!"

They all made noises of disgust. Citrus City had lots of lakes, but they were mostly clean. It was hard indeed to imagine how gross it would be to drink green slime, though they would have gladly watched someone else do it.

"Besides eating caterpillars, what are you all doing?" asked Maria DaRosa.

"Having a fight," said Cassidy.

"With who?"

"Reggie Harris."

"Where is he?"

Cassidy gestured behind him, but when he looked, Reggie and his brothers were gone.

"Come on, Suzie," said Maria DaRosa. "Boys are stupid *and* boring."

CHAPTER 7

WILD MAN

Cassidy stopped paddling with a nicety of judgment that allowed the canoe to glide the rest of the way, finally scrunching up onto the small beach on the intracoastal near the mouth of the Loxahatchee River.

His first love was now basketball, but he was small and skinny and regularly got trounced by the likes of Stiggs and Randleman, both of whom won much admiration on their junior high team. Cassidy, on the other hand, had had to skulk shamefacedly away from the list pinned to the bulletin board in the gym. He had not even made the first cut.

What he *was* good at was holding his breath underwater, at first a worthless skill until he found useful tasks to do while submerged, such as procuring various forms of dinner. He learned that grown-ups would shower him with high praise and rewards when he returned from water sports with one or more interesting entrées. He had become expert in the use of different kinds of pole spears and spear guns, but his favorite weapon was the Hawaiian sling, a sort of underwater slingshot.

Cassidy stowed the paddle in the back and took in the silence, resting in effort-induced contentment. The only sounds came from lapping wavelets and the light metallic scraping of a half dozen orange spiny lobsters in the front of the boat. Shirtless and barefoot, he got out carefully and—tides being second nature to him—pulled the boat up until it mostly lay on dry white sand, wrapping the painter round and round a cypress root. Fetching his net equipment bag from the boat, he dragged it over to a hurricane-felled palm tree and sat.

This was a good spot for mangrove snappers, but because they would be small, he decided against the Hawaiian sling he had been using all morning and instead began putting his pole spear together.

He didn't hear the slightest sound, but when he looked up from his task, he was staring straight into the eyes of the largest and scariest-looking creature he had ever seen, either in real life or in the movies. And he had seen an angry hammerhead shark in real life.

Cassidy's mouth dropped open, and though every molecule of his being was poised to flee, he didn't move. He stared wordlessly at the apparition.

It was obviously a man of some kind but unlike any he had ever seen. Cassidy's father was over six feet tall, but this man would have dwarfed him. And he was so muscular he looked like a caricature from the weight-gain comic book ads. The man was shiny from sweat and river water and was deeply tanned. Swamp muck coated his bare legs up to his knees. Cassidy was horrified to see a huge red leech attached to his thigh. He wore only cutoff army fatigues, dilap-idated combat boots, no socks, and greasy burlap bags tied around his ankles. A sweaty reddish bandana circled his forehead. When he moved, Cassidy could see every strand of muscle gliding beneath taut skin.

Over one shoulder he carried a pair of wire animal traps, and over the other a live alligator that looked to be about four feet long, mouth neatly taped shut with electrical tape and feet bound together by pieces of clothesline. Tucked into his waist was a burlap bag full of something wiggling.

"Mind if I have a drink?"

The apparition dropped the traps where he stood, gesturing at Cassidy's canteen, which he handed over wordlessly. In one long gulp the swamp man all but drained it before handing it back without comment. Cassidy noticed the man's eyes held no malice, just intelligence and mild amusement, and he slowly let out some of the air he'd been holding.

The man placed the alligator gently under the shade of a palmetto bush, pulled the burlap bag from his belt, and tossed it down next to Cassidy before sitting matter-of-factly on the log beside him.

"You're that Cassidy kid," he said.

Cassidy stared, still wide-eyed, before noticing movement at his feet. He looked down to see a small head poking tentatively out of the burlap bag. He involuntarily jumped when he saw it was a snake.

"Just black snakes," the man said. He was holding a handful of powdery sand against the big leech on his leg, drying it out. After a few moments he carefully peeled off the now white-coated creature and tossed it out into the water.

"Darn things," he said. "Must have picked him up setting traps in Otter Creek. But I guess even leeches gotta make a living."

Cassidy sat back down next to the burlap bag, peering at the little creature now trying to slither out. He reached down in one motion and caught the snake behind the head and pulled it smoothly out of the bag, holding it up in front of him to admire. The swamp man watched him, saying nothing.

"He's pretty small, just a baby," Cassidy said. The snake coiled around his wrist. Its skin was a beautiful greenish-black in a beam of strong sunlight.

"Found a whole nest of them about a mile upriver."

Cassidy nodded, held the snake up again, then opened the bag and dropped it back in, twisting it several times and wrapping the top back up under the bottom to prevent more escape attempts.

"I see you got some bugs this morning." The swamp man gestured toward the canoe, where the lobsters were still noisily scraping at their aluminum jail.

"Yes, sir."

"They say you can go to forty feet and stay awhile. That true?"

"I guess maybe by the end of the summer. Can't right now. These were only at twenty feet or so, right along the inner reef line."

The stranger looked at him, and Cassidy had the distinct impression he was being appraised.

"I know your dad," the man said finally. "And your uncle Joe. You don't have to be afraid of me, son. I'm Trapper Nelson."

Cassidy had been hearing about Trapper Nelson since he was little, and the stories were all so mythic, so gilded with hyperbole and heroic imagery he hardly knew what to make of them. Trapper Nelson was supposedly bigger and stronger than Paul Bunyan, had more powers than Superman, knew more about animals than Tarzan; he wrestled alligators for fun, laughed at poisonous snakes. He disliked civilization and lived back in the swamp way up on the Loxahatchee River, hunting and trapping for a living. He would supposedly eat just about anything that walked, swam, or crawled. No one knew more about the ocean, the swamp, or the river than Trapper Nelson. His purview encompassed both the creatures that dwelled in them and the tastiest methods for their preparation. That included possums, turtles, alligators, snakes, sharks, oysters, stingrays, conchs, manatees, catfish, and of course the more standard fare of snapper, grouper, mackerel, and snook. And it apparently included, Cassidy surmised from the man's frank and continuing interest, spiny lobsters.

Cassidy's older friends snickered that rich and beautiful ladies from Palm Beach would leave their oceanside mansions to come visit Trapper in his primitive compound on the river, and some reportedly spent the night. Famous and powerful men were brought around, men like Jack Dempsey and Babe Ruth, who would become giddy and childlike in his presence, awed by his strength and obvious mastery of the Florida wilds.

And here he was, sitting next to the larval Quenton Cassidy like they were waiting for a bus! Trying hard to keep his voice casual, Cassidy gestured at the alligator lying placidly in the shade.

"What are you going to do with him?"

"It's a her, I think. Haven't checked yet. They asked for a female. She's headed to a zoo outside St. Louis."

"That's kind of sad."

"Is it? She'll get fed regularly, be warm in the winter and cool in the summer. And she won't get eaten by some hungry twelve-foot cousin of hers. Sounds like a pretty good deal to me."

"Well . . ."

"But the best part of it is I'm going to get seventy-five American greenbacks for her!" He laughed so loud that a pair of pelicans erupted from a nearby cypress and flapped away up the river.

Cassidy couldn't help but laugh, too, but he still felt bad for the little gator, destined to be ogled and hooted at by a bunch of white-kneed Yankees.

"You play sports, Youngblood?" Trapper asked.

"Yes, sir. Well, try to. Basketball, mostly. Haven't made the team, though."

"Lot of good players at your school. Pretty big boys, too."

"Yes sir. I know I'm not that big."

"Have you tried track?"

Cassidy looked down. "I'm not fast enough," he said.

"Hmmm. Other ways to skin a cat."

"Sir?"

When Trapper Nelson talked about skinning something, he might not be speaking figuratively.

"Just an expression. Tell you what, you know where my place is, up the Loxahatchee, where the rope swing is? You come by sometime. I got a bunch of critters around you might find interesting. Just be sure to ask your parents first. It's up the river a good bit, just past the bend at Cypress Creek, if you're in the mood to paddle that far."

"I don't mind. I've been down the intracoastal almost to North Palm before," said Cassidy.

"Good! Means you've got some stamina! We'll have to go for a run sometime. You ever run on the beach?"

Cassidy looked dubious.

"No? It's fun. I used to do my road work on the beach at Singer Island back when I was training for boxing."

Cassidy couldn't imagine being hit by one of those huge hands.

"Well, better get a move on," said Trapper, slapping his knees. "Got critters need feeding. Thanks for the drink, Youngblood." He stood and started assembling his load, then looked back toward Cassidy's canoe.

"Say, you wouldn't want to trade for a couple of those crawfish, would you? Looking at them has made me hungry. I don't have much with me. Would you have any use for a black snake or two?"

"I already have a couple, and my mother said if I brought another one home I'd have to live on the carport with it."

Trapper Nelson smiled.

"But you don't have to trade me anything, Mr. Nelson. You can have some crawfish. I can get more."

"If you can go to forty feet, I bet you can," he said, ambling over to the canoe where he stood appraising the creatures for a moment before nonchalantly grabbing the two biggest ones by the base of their antennae. He came back and wrapped the top on the burlap bag around them so he could carry both in his right hand. Then he threw the little alligator over his right shoulder and balanced it there while he picked up his traps with his left hand. He smiled and nodded to Cassidy before starting back upriver in water halfway up his shins, his shrugged shoulder pinning the little gator against his tilted head.

"Hey," Cassidy called, "I can paddle you back upriver if you want!"

"My canoe's just past Moccasin Gap. Thanks for the lobsters! I owe you one."

Cassidy watched him walking down the river for a few moments, then stood up suddenly and called out, "Two! You owe me two!"

Trapper's right arm, snakes, lobsters, and all, shot into the air in agreement, and Cassidy could hear the laughter booming down the river corridor.

CHAPTER 8

POT ROAST

Dinner tonight was one of the few grown-up dishes Cassidy actually liked, so he was not engaged in his usual squirmy charade of pushing food around his plate until enough time had passed so he could politely abscond.

The timing was crucial. If his escape bid was premature, some mysterious grown-up sense of propriety would be offended and he'd be told: For goodness' sake, we just sat down. At least eat some of your squash casserole.

This was the most dangerous kind of injunction, focusing attention on a single undesirable item, which might then take on a significance wholly out of proportion to its ostensible nutritional value. The situation could escalate into a regular casus belli, with an outcome much worse than a shortened play session. Tears, confinement to quarters, even corporal punishment were all in the offing. In such a case it would be impossible to neutralize the item in question by the usual mangling, clever plate distribution, or sleight of hand.

"You might as well just eat the damn stuff," his uncle Henry once advised. "The collard greens probably won't kill you, though come to think of it, the turtle patties might."

But Cassidy considered pot roast perfectly edible, in part due to his mother's singular obsession with her pressure cooker. He couldn't

imagine what strange alchemy was going on inside that hissing, rattling contraption, which seemed to dominate the kitchen all afternoon with its implied threat of detonation. But he certainly couldn't
argue with the results. The succulent cubes of beef parted at the touch
of a fork, the potatoes and carrots emerged tender and tasty in the
plentiful gravy, and the occasional half-moon of limp celery was easily separated out and pushed to the edge of the plate to wither and
molder until the expiration of the known universe.

His father had no such scruples when it came to icky items. Himself a big proponent of pot roast, he had come to the table still in
his Air Force khakis, incongruously stiff with starch in those places
where rings of perspiration hadn't soaked through. The master sergeant's stripes and the metal insignia over the breast pocket always
fascinated Cassidy, triggering some deep patriotic impulse.

The old man simply wolfed it all down, never bothering to separate out clearly objectionable items. Celery was no problem for
him whatsoever. A chunk of turnip from some strange stew would
go right down the hatch. Even those rare and possibly toxic bits
of flotsam and jetsam—bay leaves, cloves, parsley sprigs—were
blithely countenanced by his father. But when Cassidy found such
an item, he would disgustedly and accusingly hold it up on the end
of his fork. Stop making that face, his mother would say, it's just
for flavor, for heaven's sake. No, you don't have to eat it, just put it
under the edge of your plate. Don't look at me like that, it wouldn't
have killed you!

Cassidy had pretty much cleaned his plate save for the celery and
a large and disgusting bay leaf and was preparing to make his break
when his father suddenly became interested in conversation. Cassidy's heart sank.

The sun had dropped low enough in the western sky that it now
penetrated the thin cotton print curtains of the jalousied side door,
filling the tiny kitchen with a harsh glare and almost unbreathably hot

afternoon air. In such circumstances Cassidy couldn't help squirming like a defendant without an alibi.

"I hear you met Vince down at the river yesterday," the old man said. Cassidy looked puzzled.

"That's Trapper Nelson's real name, honey," said his mother. "Vincent Natulkiewicz. He made up the name Trapper Nelson because when he first showed up here, no one could pronounce his real name."

Cassidy was amazed. "Where did he come from?" he said.

"Originally from New Jersey. He came down during the Depression. He and his brother Charlie and a friend were riding the rails down to Key West. They just hopped off here to take a break, see if they could find some work. They set up a beach camp down at Jupiter, and he just never got around to leaving."

His father was spooning blackstrap molasses onto his plate, mashed a pat of butter into it, and spread it onto a slice of Merita white bread. Cassidy had seen this humble dessert so many times it no longer disgusted him.

"The trapping and fishing were pretty good in those days. That was back in the thirties, and it was still pretty wild around here. Those boys were making a pretty good go of it. It was a real shame—"

His mother shot his father a look.

"John," she said. Cassidy knew this signal, and his ears perked up.

"What happened?" he said.

His father was looking at his mother, who steadily held his gaze. His father looked as if he was actually thinking of ignoring the signal.

"Oh," he said, looking back to Cassidy, "there was a disagreement. It got out of hand. There was—"

"John."

His father fell silent.

"It was a long time ago," he said. "Vincent . . . *Trapper* was hardly even involved. It was between the other two, Charlie and this John Dykas fellow."

"Who?"

His father looked over at his mother, who sighed and looked away.

"Fella they knew from New Jersey. They'd been bummin' around together for years. Spent some time in Michigan, then out west, hunting and trapping. They'd get odd jobs when they could, but there wasn't much work in those days. Eventually they caught a freight out of Jacksonville and headed down this way, the three of them."

"What was the argument?"

"Charlie said it was about how to divide up the money they had made. Vincent supposedly was out trapping, not even there when it happened. But there are still some folks around here who won't have anything to do with Trapper because of it. Think he got away with something," he said.

"I didn't know Trapper had a brother," said Cassidy.

"Sure did. Older stepbrother, Charlie. Not as big as Trapper but three times as crazy."

"What happened to him?"

"Judge Chillingworth sent him to Raiford for a long long time," his father said, gazing out the back window at the royal palm tree blowing in the afternoon sea breeze. He fell silent.

"And the other one, the friend . . ."

His mother got up suddenly and began to clear the table. Cassidy could see that she wasn't happy, but she didn't say anything. His father leaned over. Cassidy could see the nearly skinned oval in the center of his military flattop.

"Dykas. John Dykas. He's down there at Roselawn to this day, deader than Kelsey's nuts."

CHAPTER 9

UP THE LOXAHATCHEE

Very little light was coming through the cypress canopy as Cassidy paddled up to Trapper Nelson's dock. It was early Saturday morning, but Trapper apparently was an early riser. Wet clothes hung on the line, several baskets of freshly picked vegetables and citrus sat on the porch. A nervous lynx cowered in the back of one of the wire pens and a bobcat lay stretched out in a sunbeam in another. A pit next to the garden held turtles, and a flock of noisy guinea hens fluttered around in the lower branches of a live oak, ruled over by a yellow-crested Amazon parrot who intimidated the bolder hens with a fierce-looking open beak if they got too close.

Another boat was pushing off from the dock, a fast-looking open-fisherman with an Evinrude 100 on the back. Cassidy waved at the man at the wheel, Jim Branch, a friend of his father's. He was easy to recognize from the battered straw Panama hat he always wore. A stern-looking man wearing wire-rimmed eyeglasses sat in front of the center console, but Cassidy didn't recognize him. He might have smiled a little at Cassidy, but it was hard to tell.

Trapper Nelson was busy at the cleaning station on the dock, working with a wooden-handled fillet knife.

"Hello and good morning!" he called out, holding up a slimy hand in greeting.

"Hello!" yelled the parrot. Then: "Willie! Cut that out!" An unholy screech followed.

"Yeah, exactly right! Cut that out, you betcha," said Trapper Nelson, squirting the hose at him. The bird, hoping for a real shower, fluffed up the feathers on his head and turned it sideways, holding his wings out like an eagle. The startlingly beautiful red and purple showed on his shoulders and Cassidy stared, transfixed.

"Well, Youngblood, I didn't expect to see you today. You been in a fight or something?"

"Sort of," Cassidy said.

He sat in the canoe next to the dock with the paddle across his lap, taking in Trapper's compound. There was the main cabin by the river, but there were also pens and cages, outbuildings, woodpiles, a water tower, fruit trees, and a garden.

"I hope the other guy looks worse," said Trapper pleasantly.

Cassidy shrugged. "Billy Claytor said you paid kids a quarter each for box turtles," he said.

Trapper looked up from his fish. "True enough," he said. "You got some?"

"Yes, sir. A couple. And I know where there are more."

"Good! I'll take all you can get."

"Whatcha do with them? Are they good to eat?"

Trapper laughed. "Only in a pinch. Now, gopher tortoise stew is another story. There's a whole pit full of them over there. We used to call them 'Hoover chickens.'"

"Yuck."

"Don't knock it till you've tried it. And don't try it until you're good and hungry."

Cassidy made a face. His grandfather caught snapping turtles from a river. He had once paid Cassidy a quarter to eat a sliver half the size of a thimble. It wasn't worth it.

"But box turtles, buncha folks want them for pets, put them in their gardens," Trapper said. "They like the yellow designs on them, I guess. I don't know why they don't just go out in the woods and look at one when they want to, but then there's a lot of things people do I don't understand."

He was working the sharp thin blade flat along the spine of a large gray grouper, removing a fillet from each side of the fish. He placed them flat on the cutting board and used his thumbnail to pin the tough skin to the board, then ran the flattened blade horizontally between the flesh and the skin to remove it, holding the pearly white meat up to the sunshine and flicking the skin into the river. It floated for no more than a second before there was a swirl of motion and something got it. He picked up the skeleton of the fish by the gills and held it up to Cassidy. It looked like nothing so much as what a cartoon cat pulls out of a garbage pail.

"Twenty pounder, at least," Trapper said.

"Where'd you catch him? Off the wrecks?"

"Don't know where he came from exactly. Jim Branch and Judge Chillingworth said they were fishing the outer reef line, but that's all they'd say. They got ten or so and brought me these three before heading back to West Palm."

Trapper tossed the grouper carcass into a beat-up zinc pail that already held several others.

"Going to make fish stew?" Cassidy asked, gesturing at the pail.

"Oh, yeah. Best part of the fish, in my opinion. Can't beat grouper throats and cheeks. You like fish chowder?" Trapper was hosing fish slime off the rough planks.

"I could eat the lips off a fish chowder," said Cassidy.

Trapper laughed so loud Willie the parrot flew to a higher limb.

"Well, come on up. And bring your turtles. There won't be any fish chowder for a few hours yet, but scrambled eggs with chanterelles will only take ten minutes."

"Shanty who?"

"Ah, city slickers. Well, after this morning you'll have one entirely reliable mushroom in your repertoire," he said, taking the burlap bag from Cassidy and wrapping the canoe's painter around the dock post. He picked up the zinc pail with the other hand and started for the cabin, motioning for Cassidy to bring the fillet knife and the stack of unused rags.

Cassidy sat lazily swinging his legs off the edge of Trapper's deck, trying to talk to Willie the parrot, who ignored him. Cassidy had washed the dishes while Trapper did some paperwork at his desk. When he started getting ready to leave, not wanting to overstay his welcome, Trapper handed him a handful of peanuts.

"Just sit with these in a pile next to you for a few minutes," he said. "When Willie sees you have them, he'll be a lot friendlier. Just don't be too obvious about it. Let him think it's his idea. I've got a little more work to do, then we can talk a bit."

Sure enough, as soon as he saw the peanuts, Willie flew over and landed on a perch mounted to the deck rail. Cassidy could tell the bird spent a lot of time there because the deck underneath the perch was all white and green with his droppings.

Cassidy turned his back to the bird and watched the river, where every few seconds a meaty projectile of a fish would launch itself into the air and land with a robust splash. Out of the corner of his eye, Cassidy could see the bird hop down to the deck rail and take a few pigeon-toed steps in his direction. *That's right, Willie. Just watching some mullet. Nothing going on here. Just me and my peanuts watching the fish jump.*

He reached down and picked up a peanut, bringing it to his mouth and biting down on the shell so that it made a crunching sound, immediately getting the bird's attention. The feathers on Willie's head flattened as he stretched his neck up into the air like an ostrich. He took a few more awkward steps in Cassidy's direction.

Cassidy pretended to grab another peanut and crunch it, which brought the bird closer, though still well out of reach. He was getting close enough to the peanuts to try for a quick grab, so Cassidy slid the pile closer to himself. This irritated the bird, who started pacing and grumbling. Trapper was now at the door, watching.

When Cassidy pretended to eat another peanut, the bird flapped his wings and yelled, "Cracker!"

"Okay, that's his word for food. He's almost ready to be friends," said Trapper. "Hold one out to him, but act like you don't care if he takes it or not."

When Cassidy did so, the bird retreated a few clumsy steps.

"Cracker?" the parrot said.

"That's good. He's getting used to you. And he wants to make friends before all the nuts are gone, so pretend you're eating another one."

Cassidy crunched another one. The bird held his wings up in the eagle pose again. "Willie! Cut that out!" he yelled.

Trapper chuckled. "Okay," he said, "offer it to him again."

Cassidy held the peanut out while concentrating his attention on the river. The bird edged closer, carefully craning his neck out toward the nut.

"Take it back some. Make him trust you a little," said Trapper.

When Cassidy did so, the bird sidestepped a little closer to him, craning his neck out ridiculously. He had all but toppled over when Trapper said, "Okay, let him have it." Cassidy handed the peanut over. The bird snatched it from his fingers and immediately flew back to his perch, cackling evilly.

"What do you say, Willie?" Trapper called.

"Cut that out!" the bird screeched, then bit into the peanut, pulling one of the pink nuts expertly out of the shell with the sharp tip of his beak.

"I guess it's going to take some work to get 'thank you' into his vocabulary," said Trapper, sitting down next to Cassidy with a paper plate of what appeared to be strangely shaped flowers.

"Next time he'll treat you like a long-lost buddy, especially if you have peanuts. You might even get him on your hand, but probably that'll be the time after that. Willie, come here!"

The bird flew over and landed on Trapper's forearm. His head fluffed up and turned sideways and Trapper rubbed the yellow spot over his beak and all around his fuzzy green cheeks. Then he gave the bird one of Cassidy's peanuts, which he quickly snatched and flew back to his perch.

"You're welcome," Trapper said.

The bird cackled.

"You recognize these?" Trapper held up the paper plate to Cassidy.

"They're like the ones you chopped up in the eggs?"

"Right, chanterelles. They're what make ordinary scrambled eggs into food for the gods. You've seen them in the woods, right?"

"I think so. Sometimes the baby ones are bright orange?"

"Well, those are a little different. They're cinnamon chanterelles. They're edible, too, but it takes a thousand of them to make anything. These are golden chanterelles, the ones the chefs want. Even chefs in Paris, France. Hold one up to your nose and see if you smell anything."

Cassidy sniffed. "Don't think so," he said.

"Try again. It's kind of subtle."

"Oh, yeah. Kind of nice, like a flower or something."

"Right," said Trapper. "Like a gardenia, maybe, something like that. Very faint, but it's there. No other mushroom I know of smells anything like that. So that's one clue. Now turn it upside down and look at the underside of it. What do you see?"

"Just the gills, I guess." Cassidy studied the fungus.

"Right, but with a chanterelle they're not gills but ridges. About the only thing out there you might confuse a golden chanterelle with is a jack-o'-lantern, because the colors are similar. It would be a bad mistake, because it's a completely different species and poisonous as all get-out. The gills are the best way to tell them apart. I wish I had a jack-o'-lantern so you could see them side by side."

"I think I've seen them," said Cassidy.

"Probably. They grow in big bunches, usually right on a piece of wood. Chanterelles grow separately on the ground. But the big thing is, jack-o'-lanterns have actual gills, not ridges. They also have a different smell. Pleasant, but not like a gardenia. You can really tell them apart at night because the jack-o'-lantern's gills glow in the dark. That's a jack-o'-lantern for you, and of no use to man nor beast. In fact, it'll make you sick as three dogs."

"Maybe I'll just stick to plain eggs."

"No need. You can learn to tell the difference. But if you ever run into any and want to try them, just bring them by here first. I'll check them out and make sure you don't poison yourself."

"Okay."

"I've checked out your turtles and they look fine. Got a male and a female there, in case you were wondering. The female has a really nice pattern. Remind me and I'll show you how to tell the difference."

"Sure," said Cassidy.

"Now, here's your fifty cents, and you've got to scat. If you want to do a little run some morning, I'll meet you at the inlet. Right now I have to get my chowder started and get this place ready for guests."

"Guests?" Cassidy couldn't tell if he was being put on.

"I kid you not. Dave Brooker brings a boatload of tourists up from Jupiter twice a week. Calls it Trapper Nelson's Jungle Cruise. I dress up like Tarzan, wrap a black snake around my neck, feed them a bowl of chowder, sell them some trinkets, and send them on their way."

"What kind of trinkets?"

"Oh, a rattlesnake rattle or a conch shell, almost anything carved from a cypress knee. Amazing what city people will buy."

"Like maybe a box turtle?"

"Hmmm." Trapper scratched his chin. "Maybe."

"And about how much would a city person pay for a box turtle?" asked Cassidy.

There was the big laugh again. Willie flapped his wings and screeched.

"Whatever the market will bear, Youngblood! Whatever the market will bear!" said Trapper Nelson.

CHAPTER 10

CHIP NEWSPICKLE

Chip Newspickle was famous for having a hilarious name. He shared this distinction with a sad little girl named Amarylis Character and the irrepressible Richard "Dick" Hertz, the designated class clown since kindergarten.

But Chip Newspickle, in addition to his compelling moniker, was famous for being a fast runner. Astoundingly fast.

By the time he got to junior high school, Cassidy had gradually relinquished his illusions about being truly fleet of foot. Even Demski now found himself surrounded by kids who could leave him behind with ease. Cassidy turned his attention to basketball, at which he had shown some meager neighborhood-level ability, and Demski, lacking any kind of coordination whatsoever, was now much taken with model airplanes.

But everyone in school knew about the phenomenon that was Chip Newspickle. He was very low-key about it, but then again he could afford to be; he had newspaper clippings.

Despite being only an eighth grader, Chip held the school and county records for the fifty- and hundred-yard dashes. He was such a star on the track team people had forgotten how funny his name was; it now just seemed cool.

Quenton Cassidy had taken his share of grief over his own name and was envious of anyone who had done something noteworthy enough to make the transition from funny name to cool name. But he had a hard time believing Chip Newspickle had actually run that fast. Cassidy had seen him ambling along the sandy hallways of Glenridge Junior High, and while he seemed maybe a little cocky—who wouldn't be?—he looked altogether mortal.

All of Cassidy's friends knew their times for the fifty-yard dash. Cassidy's was exactly 7.2 seconds, which had been one of the best in his gym class, though two of the ninth graders had gone under seven. To Cassidy, a time of 6.9 or 6.8 was comprehensible, but just barely. He had run enough time trials in phys ed to become familiar with what a tenth of a second meant on a running track, and he knew just how flat out he had had to run to get that 7.2. Moreover, when he ran it again at the end of the semester, he ran exactly the same time again, despite trying so hard he almost lost his Pop-Tarts on the infield.

Huffing and puffing, he walked back to where Coach Bickerstaff was studying the stopwatch.

"Seven point two. Good job, son," said Bickerstaff, who had no idea why Cassidy walked away so unhappy.

For the first time in his life he was coming up against the cold, hard judgment of the stopwatch, and he now knew that his 7.2 represented the outer limits of his ability. It was disconcerting to think that some other mortal, some kid more or less his own age, could finish the same distance in "six something," could simply fly on up ahead of him so many yards in such a short distance. But then he heard about Chip Newspickle and had to get his mind around the idea that there were human beings who not only ran in the sixes, but in the fives!

Chip Newspickle ran the fifty-yard dash in 5.8 seconds!

And now, this morning, in second-period gym class, there was Chip Newspickle in the flesh, sitting there doing butterfly stretches as Coach Bickerstaff took roll. He was dressed out, too, even though this was not his gym class. He wore red-and-green-plaid gym shorts and a Glenridge T-shirt, like nearly everyone else, but also something Cassidy had never seen before: tight-fitting bright white kangaroo-skin track slippers with wicked-looking long spikes and three perfectly spaced black stripes slanted on the sides. They were the most amazing shoes Cassidy had ever seen.

Coach Bickerstaff finally looked up from his clipboard. "All right, gentlemen, this morning we're gonna be doing 440 time trials," he said. "This is part of President Kennedy's fitness program, like the sit-up and pull-up tests we did last week. We'll do all this again at the end of the year, and your times will be recorded and compiled in a report that will go to the superintendent's office, then to Tallahassee, and eventually on up to President Kennedy in Washington, D.C."

That sobered everyone. No one wanted to let President Kennedy down. He had been on a PT boat that got sunk.

"Everyone will line up at the starting post and we've got two watches so we'll run two at a time like we did last time. If you don't already have a partner, Coach Burke will pair you up with someone close to your speed so you'll have some competition."

There was nervous grumbling. A 440 was a whole lap, and everyone could see what a long way that was. Even a 100 seemed like a fairly long race compared to the 50, and a 220 was way beyond that. Twice a 220 was hard to imagine.

"Oh, and before we get started, y'all probably noticed Chip here. He needs to get his 440 done this period because he has a dentist appointment this afternoon. So, who wants to run with Chip?"

Everyone laughed. Exactly nobody wanted to run with Chip Newspickle.

"All right, settle down. Hohlmeister, Castleberry, you're the fastest guys in class. How about it, one of you?" They were the two ninth graders who were under seven seconds. They were both on the football team, but neither of them wanted any part of Chip Newspickle in a foot race.

"Uh, we're running with each other." Castleberry pointed to Hohlmeister sitting next to him. Hohlmeister nodded vigorously. "We already decided," he said.

Bickerstaff looked at the group and suppressed a sigh. He couldn't really blame them. He was about to announce that Chip would run by himself when he heard a thin voice from the back of the throng.

"I'll run."

Everyone turned to look. Bickerstaff smiled. Of course. The skinny kid who kept trying out for the basketball team. Everyone was craning around to look, and the laughter was starting already.

"All right, fair enough, Mr. Kissam Building Supply," he said, referring to Cassidy's T-shirt, a freebie from last weekend's Bargain Days Lumber Sale his father had taken him to. "The rest of you, shut up. At least he has some gumption. Now, up and at 'em. Two lines at the start. Coach Burke will arrange you into pairs if you haven't already found somebody. I'll be in the middle of the field so I can give you the split at the 220 mark. Coach Burke will give you a three command start. He'll say 'Ready, set . . . ,' and then the whistle. Okay, that's it. Start lining up. Chip, you and your opponent go first so you can get changed and go meet your mom." Most were already clambering to their feet.

"And boys, one more thing. The 440 is a long race. I repeat, a *long* race," Bickerstaff said. "It's a whole lap, one quarter of a mile around. Do yourselves a favor and pace yourselves. Do not, I repeat, do *not* blast out and think you can run full speed the whole way. I promise you that you can't do it." He began walking toward the middle of the field.

As they were all milling around the white starting post at the middle of the straightaway, Cassidy noticed that Chip Newspickle—who had hardly even looked at him—was about his same height, not very tall, and though he was a bit more muscular and moved with an athlete's slightly pigeon-toed grace, there didn't seem to be anything special about him, nothing to hint at the 5.8 that he was supposedly capable of.

Maybe I'm crazy, Cassidy thought. Certainly his friends told him he was. But Cassidy knew something the rest of them didn't. Most days after school he and Stiggs and Randleman had been biking or running over to their old elementary school, Fern Creek. There they played basketball and did fifty-yard dashes until they got bored. Stiggs and Randleman always got bored before Cassidy did, so he would do a few more while they horsed around on the jungle bars. After a while, Cassidy noticed a pattern. On the first sprint, he would finish five yards ahead of Randleman, who would be a yard or two ahead of the gangly Stiggs.

By their fourth or fifth repeat, when the other two would usually quit, Cassidy was finishing ten or fifteen yards in front. Cassidy accused them of goldbricking, which just made them mad.

And after several weeks, when they would jog the mile and a half to Fern Creek, Cassidy would have to stop several times to wait for them. This would tick them off, particularly when Cassidy called them "lard asses" or "Mother Hubbards."

One Friday afternoon as they were huffing and puffing to keep up, he began to literally run circles around them, which he kept up all the rest of the way to the school. He ended up regretting it because it was much harder to do than he thought it would be, and also because after they arrived at the playground and rested a few minutes they pounced on him and administered a red belly.

It finally dawned on Cassidy that the longer the distance, the better he did and the worse everyone else did. In gym class he got killed in the 50 by the fastest guys, but he was at least among the top handful in the 220.

He had never raced a 440 before, but the prospect didn't intimidate him in the least.

Still, it was a long way around. Even now as they lined up he had a hard time taking in the entire quarter-mile oval at once.

Coach Bickerstaff stood in the middle of the field, his red brush cut visible beneath a battered Red Sox baseball cap. He held up his clipboard to signal to Coach Burke that he was ready.

"Go get him, skinny," someone called. More laughs.

"Eat me," Cassidy muttered. Hell, they were all skinny except for Billy Parish. What did that have to do with anything?

Coach Burke smiled sympathetically at Cassidy and told them to get ready. Chip Newspickle dropped down to his hands and knees, digging the beautiful spikes into the clay, right foot slightly in front of the left, fingertips spread flat against the chalk line. He looked like he knew exactly what he was doing. Cassidy didn't have a clue about a sprinter's crouch, so when Coach Burke rather sharply reminded him again to get ready, he nervously toed the line with his left canvas tennis shoe, leaning forward loosely from the waist, the way he always did. Chip Newspickle, he saw, was poised like a cat.

"Get ready . . . set . . ." The blast of the whistle was so shrill Cassidy actually flinched. When he gathered himself and pushed off from the starting line, his left tennis shoe slipped and his first three strides were so off balance he thought he was going to go right down on his face. More hoots from the crowd.

Getting control of his panic, he concentrated on the ground a few yards in front of him and finally felt his familiar stride settling in beneath him. But when he looked up, he saw Chip Newspickle's backside all but disappearing up the track.

He could hear the growing glee behind him as the knot of humiliation grew in the pit of his stomach. He now understood that the 5.8 was no myth and that Chip Newspickle was in fact some kind of freak of nature. And this also occurred to him: most likely, Quenton Cassidy was an ordinary fool with some very silly ideas.

He tried to put Chip Newspickle out of his mind and simply concentrate on running smoothly. He didn't have anywhere near that amazing leg speed, but he was still running well. His stride was longer than Chip's and the ground was passing quickly beneath him. More than that, he was feeling comfortable despite running almost flat out. It occurred to him that he was merely doing something he was used to and that he in fact enjoyed.

He consciously loosened his shoulders and relaxed the rest of his body and noticed that he actually began to go a little faster.

Something else was odd. As they neared the middle of the turn at the 110 post, Chip Newspickle was no farther ahead than he had been at the end of the first fifty yards. He had fifteen yards on Cassidy, which seemed like a very long way, but at least he was not gaining anymore. Was the laughter from the crowd subsiding a little?

When Chip hit the straightaway at the end of the first curve, Cassidy was now matching him stride for stride, though still far behind. For the first time it seemed to Cassidy that he was not really flat out yet. He was probably at ninety percent, but that felt reasonable. He was keenly aware of how much ground his strides were eating up.

At the 220 mark, halfway through the back straightaway, Bickerstaff called out, "Twenty-*seven*! Twenty-*eight*! Twenty-*nine*! Thirty *flat*, thirty-*one*, thirty-*two* . . ."

Chip Newspickle was just under twenty-eight seconds, Cassidy three seconds back, but he had gained five yards. And he could see something familiar happening up ahead. Chip Newspickle's back and shoulders were slightly arched and he was carrying his arms wider and more stiffly, like he saw Stiggs and especially Randleman do. Chip was still moving fast but no longer looked invincible. A shiver ran up Cassidy's spine and tingled the hair on the back of his neck, and he thought, *I can beat him.*

He concentrated on his stride and tried to imagine himself floating over the track, eating up the yards as effortlessly as he could. At the 330 post, Cassidy had gained back another five yards. It was obvious to everyone now that they were watching a real race. There was no laughter from the crowd, just a single pleading call: "Come *on*, Chip!"

But Chip's form continued to degenerate; he began to arch backward and his arms and shoulders were now moving as a solid unit, rotating awkwardly around his trunk instead of pumping up and down like pistons.

Sensing the other boy's vulnerability, Cassidy bore down around the final curve, pulling him back with every stride. He kept his eyes fixed on those beautiful spiked shoes flashing in front of him and concentrated on relaxing and extending his stride.

As they came out of the turn with fifty-five yards to go, he was just off Chip's shoulder and Cassidy saw his quick, panic-stricken glance. Chip turned grimly back to his task, bore down as he had been trained to do. At the finish line he willed himself into a lean.

That lean saved Chip Newspickle from the ignominy of losing a race to a skinny nobody in second-period gym class.

"Sixty flat point three!" shouted Coach Bickerstaff, hurrying over in his stiff-legged gait. "Dead heat!" He looked at Burke, who nodded, a tight smile on his face.

A stunned group milled around the finish line, looking at each other and at the runners in disbelief. The laws of the universe had been turned upside down before their eyes, and they were still trying to make sense of it.

Bickerstaff and Burke began shooing them back onto the track, trying to get them organized.

"All right, all right, knock it off!" said Bickerstaff. "Get ready, the rest of you. And let's see more of the kind of effort we just saw there!" But no one was paying much attention. They were still wandering around and gawking at the two red-faced, completely blown-out runners.

Bickerstaff walked back to the infield where Cassidy and Chip

Newspickle were still wobbling, bent over at the waist, hands on knees, elbows touching in a kind of sympathetic camaraderie, rasping in the air with a desperation that bordered on panic.

"What's your name, son?" he asked.

"Cass . . ." he said. "Cass . . . Cassidy."

"After you've changed, come on by my office."

CHAPTER 11

COACH BICKERSTAFF

The office was a fascinating hodgepodge of sporting paraphernalia and coachly miscellany.

There was a diploma on the wall from Eastern Kentucky State College, dated June 6, 1949, awarded to one Robert Leroy Bickerstaff, a bachelor of science degree in physical education. There was a basketball team photo with the legend "Maroons Basketball—1947." In the photo, second from the far right, standing next to the slightly taller equipment manager, was a crew-cut sprite of a boy wearing number 13. If it hadn't been for the Dumbo ears, Cassidy would not have recognized Coach Bickerstaff at all. The telltale red hair did not register in black and white. It was a strange thing to contemplate, that Coach Bickerstaff had played sports in his youth, that he had had an actual boyhood of his own.

Cassidy sat, hair damp, books in lap, taking it all in: the pair of nested low hurdles needing repair in the corner, the shelves filled with books on basketball, football, weight lifting, calisthenics. There was one called *Doc Counsilman on Swimming* and another called *Modern Interval Training* by someone named Mihály Iglói. There were stacks of correspondence from other coaches and athletic directors seeking to schedule games and meets. There were stopwatches and coaching whistles hanging from hooks on the side of the bookcase, along with baseball caps, clipboards, sunglasses, and windbreakers. There was a dusty glass-fronted case filled with trophies from days gone by.

He noticed one small black-and-white photograph on the wall, almost hidden among the rest. It showed a group of eight young boys squinting into the sun from the steps of an old-timey brick schoolhouse, accompanied by an older gentleman in a three-piece suit. Their names were listed below the photograph, along with the caption: "Cynthiana Junior High track team, 1940." It didn't take Cassidy long to spot the telltale ears of the elf-boy standing next to one Oley Fightmaster, a young brute holding a shot.

"We were undefeated that year," said Coach Bickerstaff, hurrying through the door. Cassidy jumped back in his chair. The coach tossed his clipboard on top of the messy desk and sat down heavily in the ancient swivel chair.

"Of course, size of our school, everybody did practically every event. A couple of those boys were pretty fast, including yours truly," said Bickerstaff, putting his ripple-soled coaching shoes up on the corner of the desk. He leaned his head back and closed his eyes with the momentary relief of a man who spent most of his day on his feet. "And Oley there was third in the state in the shot. But the competition wasn't all that tough back then, at least not in north-central Kentucky."

"Yes, sir," Cassidy said. Coach Bickerstaff had played basketball in college! He was from Kentucky! It never occurred to Cassidy that coaches and teachers were *from* anywhere.

"It's okay, Quenton, relax. I just wanted to talk to you for a minute. Coach Burke says you've tried out for the basketball team . . ."

"Yes, sir, I practice a lot. And I'm growing."

Bickerstaff's smile was sympathetic.

"Well, son, lots of boys are after those twelve spots. You've surely noticed that most of them are a lot bigger than you."

"Yes, sir," said Cassidy glumly. This was not new information.

Stiggs and Randleman were constantly reminding him what a shrimp he was.

"Have you ever considered track?"

"No, sir."

"Why not?"

"Too slow, I guess."

"Well, there's more to track than the fifty and the hundred. It takes a lot of stamina to run a good quarter. And it takes even more to run the 880."

Cassidy looked puzzled.

"Yes, that's right. In track there are races longer than the one you ran this morning. The 880—a half mile—is two laps around. It's a tough race."

"Yes, sir."

"Now, I don't want to mislead you. You tied in a race with a very good sprinter today. But Chip's no quarter-miler. In fact, he's not as good in the 220 as he is in the 100 and the 50."

Cassidy wondered what motive Bickerstaff could possibly have for downplaying the greatest near triumph of his life.

"But still, he's no slouch," Bickerstaff said, taking his feet off the desk and sitting up straight. "He's full of fight and he wouldn't have let you get anywhere near him if he could have helped it."

"He ran pretty hard," Cassidy said.

"You didn't give him much choice."

"Yes, sir."

"Now, Chip's never run anything longer than a 220 in a meet, but a 60 flat quarter mile would win some of our dual meets. And if you can push beyond that a bit, you might just give Demski something to think about in the 880. He's just getting started, but he's getting to be pretty darned tough. I want you to think about that. If you came out for track at the end of March, I think you might do very well."

Cassidy wasn't sure what to think. He had always pinned his hopes for glory on basketball. Other than Chip Newspickle and Ed Demski, the track team was notorious for being a scut bucket of misfits and rejects.

"I really want to play basketball," he said.

"I read you. Your prerogative entirely. But it's not an either-or situation is all I'm saying. I just want you to think about it. Will you do that for me?" Then he actually smiled. Cassidy had never seen him smile before.

"Yes, sir! I will."

"Okay, go ahead and take off. You're going to be late to third period. If you get any grief, tell them you had a conference with me."

Bickerstaff started taking papers off the top of the stack on his desk, reaching for his reading glasses.

"Yes?" he said, looking up. Cassidy was still by the door.

"What's the school record for the 880?" Cassidy asked.

"You probably shouldn't be too concerned about—"

"I just wanted to know," Cassidy said.

"Son, it's 2:07.3. That's a tick under two sixty-four-second quarters back to back. I know that sounds awfully—"

"I can run faster than that," Cassidy said, and left.

Bickerstaff stared at the door. What was it with this kid? He started reading the first letter but stopped after the first paragraph and took off his glasses.

What the hell, he thought, *maybe he can at that.* Bickerstaff looked over at the small black-and-white photograph of himself and his teammates from all those years ago. There was a fierce and familiar look of determination on the face of that strange-looking, Dumbo-eared child.

CHAPTER 12

STATUS OF A SORT

They were shooting at a netless hoop at their old elementary school, and Stiggs and Randleman were acting more than a little pissy.

They had seen people smiling at Cassidy in the hallways. A couple of guys had actually stopped by their table at lunch to make some wisecracks and it was obvious they were including Cassidy in their ribaldry. Stiggs and Randleman, as starting forwards on the basketball team, were accustomed to tolerating Cassidy as a goofy sidekick. They allowed him in their pickup games because he was a warm body and he was always available. *They* were actual stars, whereas he was a mascot. This new status of his was not sitting well.

"I heard Chip had a charley horse in his leg," said Stiggs, shooting up a brick that clunked in the dead spot between the back of the rim and the backboard before rolling forward into the basket. Their attempts at ego deflation had been going on for some time.

"Yeah," said Randleman, driving to his left, faking a jump shot, then reversing and making a short hook. "Or a side stitch or something."

"Somebody said he was sick. His mom had to take him to the hospital," Stiggs said.

"Funny he didn't mention it," said Cassidy. "And he came back from the hospital with braces on his teeth." He knew better than to rise to the bait, but couldn't help himself. He dribbled out to the foul line, turned, and heaved up a hopeless brick of a two-handed set shot that missed everything.

"Swish!" he proclaimed. "Jerry West scores again!"

"Yeah, right," said Stiggs. "More like an air ball. He snagged the ball out of the air and started his own voice-over: ". . . Bill Russell with the rebound and he's bringing it up the court himself."

Randleman lunged at the ball and got a fingertip on it, but Stiggs recovered and kept up his banter as he turned at the top of the key and headed back toward the hoop.

"Time running down with the score tied ninety-five–all. Twenty seconds left and Cousy is covered, K.C. is covered, Russell takes it himself down the key . . ."

Cassidy swiped at the ball as he went by, but Stiggs did a smooth crossover dribble and left him flailing at empty air as he laid the ball gently on the backboard for an easy bucket.

"The crowd goes . . ." Stiggs began.

". . . wild . . ." said Cassidy, grabbing the ball, ". . . but maybe too soon, because Jerry West takes the inbound pass and is bringing it up the floor with just five seconds left . . ." Cassidy was dribbling back to the foul line, dodging nonexistent opponents.

"But it's *too late* because . . ." said Stiggs.

". . . *Almost* too late as he shoots his famous jump shot from the top of the key . . ." said Cassidy.

The "jump shot" was the same two-handed set shot but with an added little hop at the end. Again, it touched nothing, but it was much closer than the last one and may have even gone in.

"Swish!" said Cassidy.

"But the referee ruled the shot was not in time . . ." said Stiggs, chasing the ball as it bounced under the basket and off the court.

"But then the *other* referee overruled him and said the shot was good and the game was over and the Lakers win! The end, and good night!" Cassidy grabbed the ball out of Stiggs's hands and thrust his face up at the bigger boy.

"Drive carefully, folks," Cassidy said.

Stiggs slapped the ball away from Cassidy and began dribbling back toward the foul line.

"But then the *other* other referee put two seconds back on the clock and . . ." Stiggs was not giving up yet.

"NOOO!" said Cassidy and Randleman together. Randleman, like Cassidy, was a Lakers fan, plus he maintained that these imaginary contests should adhere to a few very basic laws of physics.

". . . and Russell does his world-famous hook shot . . ."

"No, he already got you," said Randleman.

". . . and it's up and it's . . ."

But Cassidy and Randleman were already fetching their T-shirts.

". . . just short," said Stiggs, conceding finally. He undid the strap from his black Buddy Holly glasses and wiped the sweat from his eyes with his shoulder as the other two raced to the water fountain.

After they had thoroughly waterlogged themselves, they sat on the picnic table by the monkey bars and contemplated their tight, water-balloon bellies. Still a little red faced, Stiggs was lying on his back on the tabletop, his skinny legs dangling off the end, watching the fast-moving orange clouds moving across the south Florida sky.

Randleman tried to interest them in the dingy cigarette stub he had salvaged from his dad's ashtray, but no one was in the mood. All three felt the palpable stillness of stopped kid time that comes at twilight, when the day is over but night hasn't quite begun. Those in-between moments seemed to exist separate and apart from the rest of time; they sensed this intuitively and always tried to make them last.

So now they lolled about, putting off the moment they would have to collect themselves and pedal the mile and a half back to Rosedale Street.

No one wanted to be the one to call it, though. Randleman slouched backward on one bench, studying his old sixth-grade classroom, where Mr. Meredith had once awakened him from a sound midmorning nap with a well-aimed eraser. Stiggs was still on his back but no longer watching the clouds. Stiggs's eyes were almost shut, as if he were dozing off. But then he said, softly:

"Imagine that. I bet ol' Chip Newspickle was *surprised as hell.*"

CHAPTER 13

THE JUPITER HILTON

The sun was just climbing out of the ocean beyond the far end of the Singer Island bridge. The fat tires of Cassidy's old Schwinn buzzed pleasantly on the heavy metal grating of the drawbridge as he pedaled across, using a splay-footed style to keep from banging his knees on the zinc bucket hanging from his handlebars.

He wasn't concentrating particularly well and thus whacked a knee every now and then. The warmth of the early sun was nicely balanced by the salty breeze from the intracoastal waterway, inducing a kind of numb-brained kid euphoria. It was Saturday and midwinter was finally beginning to leaven the tropical misery. The sandy halls of Glenridge Junior High seemed a million miles away.

Air Force beach was deserted. He left his bike and trudged laboriously through the powdered sugar of the dunes to the top, setting his bucket down and looking out across the glittering panorama of the Atlantic Ocean. The bottoms of his feet were tough, but the soft sand was already hot around the edges as he stood there, feeling a little thrill of greed as he peered through the cattails and saw water dappling with life in the shallow tide pools. Today he would be a successful capitalist.

He removed the little cast net from the bucket and waded into the shallow tide pool, biting down daintily on one salty fold as he untangled the lead weights and separated the folds of netting.

He blew the first cast as usual. The net flattened in the air, forming a nice oval momentarily, but the timing was off and it bounced back into an inefficient hourglass shape before it landed. Only a few of the unluckiest fish were under it. He frowned in distaste as he tugged in his meager haul.

Sitting by the edge of the pool, he scooped some water into the bucket and began picking the jittery fry out of the netting, making his hands form oval pincers to avoid the dorsal fins. It was perfect kid work, requiring a modicum of skill and a lot of patience. The downtown businessmen, lawyers, and doctors who would later purchase these little fish for bait were probably capable of getting them themselves but mostly couldn't be bothered. Cassidy considered himself lucky to have found one of those happy interstices in the economy where an alert underage entrepreneur could actually make a buck.

Though it was still cool, he could already feel the sun cranking up across a thousand miles of Atlantic. Its place in the sky told him he had time for only a few more casts before he had to meet Trapper.

The next cast was much better, forming a fairly symmetrical oval before dropping onto several dozen glittering creatures. A few escapees nevertheless managed to strand themselves on dry land, where they lay panting and flopping next to the very bucket they were trying to avoid. Their narrow bodies flashed like quicksilver in the sun. Cassidy licked the salt off his lower lip, pulling the net in, satisfied this time with his cast.

The Jupiter Marina was not much more than a shack on stilts. It sat on a rickety dock where the Loxahatchee River emptied into the intracoastal waterway. Everyone called it "the Jupiter Hilton," which the locals deemed the height of sardonic wit.

The irony was lost on Cassidy. To him it was one of the epicenters of his life, the place where all the fishermen and divers sooner or later ended up on any given weekend. It was where you got fuel if you were rich enough to be gas-powered, where you got lunch if you were not too far out in the Gulf Stream, and where you went to deal in baitfish if you had some to buy or sell.

Cassidy, a seller this morning, rode up with the heavy bucket swinging on his handlebars, noticing as he dismounted two rough-looking men at the dock—one white, one black—pumping fuel into the battered red can on their grungy skiff. He had seen them around before, but they had never paid him any attention. This time the white one nudged the other and gestured toward Cassidy. He ignored them and leaned his bike next to the ice cooler. There was another man, nicely dressed in clean khaki shorts and a spotless white bass fishing shirt, sitting in the back of the skiff rather imperiously, reading the *Palm Beach Post*.

Cassidy went around to the back of the building to use the hose, shivering from the cool water as he washed the salt away. By the time he got back to the front, the bucket was gone. He looked around and saw it sitting on the green bench between the two men at the front of the store. The black one was sitting next to it, the other standing with his knee cocked up on the bench, looking at Cassidy and smiling a not particularly friendly smile.

Taking a deep breath, Cassidy walked over to them and reached for the bucket. The white one pushed his baseball cap back on his sunburned forehead and placed the bucket on the ground, pushing it with his toe under the bench.

"Hey!" Cassidy said.

"Hey yourself," said the white one.

"That's my—"

"Your bucket?" said the white one. "Dogged if it didn't look exactly like our bucket, didn't it, Bobby?"

The black man didn't answer. In fact, he didn't seem to even be listening. When he finally looked over, Cassidy saw something so completely dead behind his bloodshot eyes that a shiver ran down his spine. Cassidy looked over to the boat where the nicely dressed man continued to read his paper, paying them no attention.

The white man was talking again in his false-friendly way. "You're that little diver people talks about," he said.

His smile wasn't reassuring. The man was fair-skinned but clearly spent so much time in the sun he seemed to be in a permanent state of sunburn. Anywhere on him that wasn't already peeling was red and getting ready to. He wore cutoff jeans, incredibly worn Docksiders, and a sleeveless Walker's Cay Marina staff T-shirt with LUCKY embroidered over the pocket.

"Got the little skiff with a old Evinrude Handitwin three on it?" the white man said.

Cassidy shrugged.

"Sometimes a little aluminum canoe? Have to use that trick where you use a little rope ladder to come in over the bow?"

Cassidy was surprised. He'd never noticed anyone watching him out there.

"You like to dive off the lighthouse on Frazier's Reef, 'bout a half mile out."

He was no longer asking questions; he was making statements.

"Bobby," said the white man, "this is that little Cassidy kid. You remember, the one old man Branch said got his anchor up from sixty feet? Said he was straight up and down over it and damn if the kid didn't go down and work it out of the rocks. Sixty feet down. Went home and measured the wet rope."

Bobby was looking out at the intracoastal, bored. He spit into the broken shells of the parking lot.

The white man's smile disappeared like a light going off. His eyes weren't dead like Bobby's, but overly active, jumping around like he was barely in control of himself. Cassidy didn't know which one of them was scarier.

"This right here's the reason, Bobby, the reason we ain't been able to find a eating-size lobster around Frasier's Reef in more'n a year! What do you think about that?"

Bobby sat up straight, and for the first time seemed to look at Cassidy with interest.

But then the white man's attitude seemed to change abruptly. His smile came back and he casually nudged the zinc bucket out from under the bench toward Cassidy.

"Anyway, the name's Floyd, people call me Lucky, and this here's Bobby Lincoln from over to Riviera Beach. We just wanted to say howdy in case we ever happen to run into you out there on the salt salt sea," he said.

Cassidy sensed a trick and didn't reach for the bucket yet. When he glanced at the ground, he saw the big shadow coming from behind him.

Trapper Nelson stood there, arms akimbo, looking huge and not happy.

"Go on and take your fish inside, Quenton," he said. "I'll help Floyd and Bobby get on their way."

Cassidy grabbed the bucket and pushed through the screen door. Glancing back, he could see Trapper Nelson stepping closer to the two men, who stared up at him.

"Aren't you supposed to be in school, young man?" said old man Tolbert, almost hidden behind the counter, sitting back in his ancient metal office chair, reading a tattered issue of *Harper's Magazine*.

"No, sir. It's Saturday," said Cassidy, hoisting the bucket onto the table beside the bubbling bait tank. Dave Tolbert knew what day it was, and Cassidy knew that he knew.

"So it is, so it is. What do you have for us today?"

"Ballyhoo mostly. A few greenies and menhaden that got mixed in with them."

The old man rose from his seat and peered into the bucket, pushing his reading glasses up to peer through them.

"Where'd you get 'em?"

"Tide pools off Air Force beach."

"Hmmm. Very nice. I count about thirteen ballyhoo, plus about a half dozen of the other. That what you figure?"

"I thought it was only eleven, sir."

"Well, they are moving around pretty good in there. We'll call it thirteen. Okay, they're going for a dime, threads and pogies get a nickel each, making it a buck eighty, right?" he said, punching up No Sale on the ancient cash register.

"Uh, I believe that's a dollar sixty, sir," said Cassidy meekly.

Tolbert pretended to do some figuring on the margin of his newspaper with the stub of a golf pencil.

"Right as rain," he said. "Never was good at the higher mathematics." He ceremoniously placed a dollar bill on the counter with one hand, and two quarters and a dime on top of it with the other.

He smiled at Cassidy. "It's been a business doing pleasure with you."

Cassidy laughed again. "Thanks, Mr. Tolbert," he said, folding the bill into a small square with the coins inside and tucking it into the pocket of his bathing trunks. He turned toward the door.

"Say, Quenton."

"Sir?"

"I saw you talking to Floyd and Bobby out there." Old man Tolbert lost his smile briefly, then found it again.

"Yes, sir," said Cassidy.

"You didn't hear it from me, but they are two people it's a good idea not to get to know too well."

"Yes, sir."

Mr. Tolbert brightened suddenly. "You going fishing with Trapper Nelson this morning? If so, perhaps you'd be interested in some excellent baitfish. I just happened to get a fresh shipment in earlier today. Let you have some awful cheap. Ballyhoo a buck each, greenies and pogies two bits!"

Cassidy giggled again. "We're supposed to go for a run on the beach," he said.

"You're going to run with Trapper?"

"Try to, I guess," said Cassidy. "We're going to cross over in the boat and then run down toward Juno."

"You know he runs all the way down to the other inlet sometimes, don't you? Must be over twelve miles. He used to do a lot of road work out there back when he boxed."

"Yes, sir."

"Well, take it easy on him. If I'm not mistaken, I just heard him bid Lucky and Bobby a fond adieu. Here, don't forget your bucket."

Trapper was helping the other two, handing down another full gas can and some other gear from the dock. They seemed to be engaged in a serious discussion for a few minutes and finally Trapper shook hands with the one called Floyd and returned to his boat, where Cassidy was waiting.

"All set for a nice morning canter?" he said.

Trapper didn't say much as they crossed the inlet. He just sat in the back tending his ancient Schnacke Mid-Jet outboard as the skiff bounced over the confused chop of the flooding inlet.

"I thought my Evinrude was old," said Cassidy, gesturing at the engine.

"Wouldn't trade it," said Trapper. "It's like an Erector set. You can see how everything works just by looking at it. I actually stopped by to see Old Man Schnacke in Evansville one time."

"What'd he say?"

"Oh, not too much. It was on a weekend and he was in his workshop behind his house, working on a new impeller idea. Said he was tickled to see a satisfied customer. Wanted to know all about the fishing down our way. All he knew was crappies and dogfish."

Cassidy was squinting against the sun, enjoying the occasional spray of salty water coming over the gunnel. The money from his morning labors was tucked safely in his buttoned bathing suit pocket. The bouncing of the boat was rhythmic, almost hypnotic, and he caught himself starting to nod off.

He snapped wide awake as they came up on a kind of whirlpool in the middle of the inlet, where the outflowing river struggled against the encroaching ocean, forming a treacherous bowl of confused water. It looked scary, but Trapper skillfully skirted around the upper lip on the seaward side of the bowl, and they were quickly on the other side of the inlet skimming along in placid water by the white sand of Jupiter Beach Park.

"Listen, Quenton," said Trapper, "I want to tell you something, okay?"

Cassidy looked back, surprised to see Trapper Nelson looking unusually serious.

"Okay," he said.

"Those two guys you were talking to back there, their names are Floyd Holzapfel—they call him Lucky—and Bobby Lincoln. I don't personally know for a fact what kinds of shenanigans they're up to, but nothing I heard would surprise me."

Cassidy nodded, not exactly sure what this was all about.

Trapper saw his confusion.

"I do know that they can be lively company, but they're both bad to go to the bottle, and they're not too particular how they make a dollar."

"Okay," Cassidy said.

"Look," Trapper said, "when I first came down here years ago with my brother Charlie and a friend named John Dykas, we had some trouble at our camp. Serious trouble. The law was involved. Maybe you heard something about it?"

Cassidy shrugged. He remembered what his father said but had finally concluded that the Trapper Nelson he knew just could not have been involved.

"Well, it was serious. A man named John Dykas ended up dead. For a while some people thought I had something to do with it. All of a sudden I didn't have many friends around here. Floyd and Bobby, though, they became long-lost cousins. It took me awhile to convince them I didn't want any part of their tomfoolery."

Cassidy still wasn't sure what this was all about, so he studied the reef line moving slowly beneath them in twenty feet of clear water.

"What I'm saying is that it would be best to steer clear of them. No need to be rude or anything, just keep your distance. They try to talk to you, just say yes, sir and no, sir and politely make your excuses."

"Yes, sir. That's what Mr. Tolbert said."

"Right. And a smarter gentleman you won't find on this whole coast. Okay, then, here we are. Hop on up and let's pull the skiff up. Then we'll get loosened up."

"What about the other man, the one in the back of the boat, dressed kinda like a tourist?"

"That was Joe Peel."

"Is he a businessman? He didn't look like he belonged with the other two."

"Business? Yeah, if you count monkey business. Nah, he's a municipal judge and an attorney in West Palm, and he's had problems of his own. He'd be another one to steer clear of."

"Yes, sir."

Cassidy rarely got down the coast this far, so Trapper Nelson told him about the history of the area. The coast south of Hobe Sound was a particularly desolate stretch of beach. In 1696, a hurricane-wrecked party led by a pious Quaker named Jonathan Dickinson straggled up that same beach in the dead of a particularly chilly winter. The hardscrabble Native Americans who lived along the coast were so destitute they happily stripped the survivors of everything they had, including their clothes. Even Dickinson's young nursing wife and child were left with hardly a stitch. But at least the locals grudgingly kept them alive as they painfully made their frozen way north to St. Augustine, where the Spanish took pity on them.

Most of the people who lived in the area knew about Jonathan Dickinson, and they knew this barren stretch of beach. Even those with poor imaginations could empathize with the half-starved castaways who'd passed this way centuries before.

But for Cassidy, this barefoot run was a different kind of trial. He had jogged and run with his friends, but he'd never encountered a fit adult who actually knew how to run. Trapper Nelson not only kept up a good pace, he kept up a steady stream of chatter while Cassidy concentrated in silence just to keep up.

At first Cassidy had tried to chat back, but he soon found himself gasping from the effort. He went back to running and listening. The sand was too soft for comfortable running in most places, so he concentrated on staying parallel to the edge of the water where the waves always pounded a solid strip along the beach. It took a lot less energy to stay on that strip, but he noticed that Trapper didn't even bother. He slogged along quite happily in the looser sand and kept chattering away. They were both barefoot and shirtless, moving along steadily down the deserted strip of coral sand, and after a mile Cassidy began to feel a little exhilarated, despite the effort.

There wasn't much in the way of buildings along here, just a few fishermen's shanties and an occasional sun-bleached weekend cottage. When they got to a place where they could hear traffic from A1A, Trapper veered off into the water, woo-hooing and high stepping as far out as he could get before diving headfirst into the surfless green water.

Cassidy followed along, if not quite as enthusiastically.

Trapper surfaced, huffing and blowing and shaking water off like a dog, then looked at Cassidy with a big grin.

"Turnaround time. I always have a little cooldown splash before heading back."

Cassidy couldn't believe they had come two miles already. He had never run that far in his life. He and Stiggs and Randleman had once done a mile and a half, but the other two complained so much they had never run farther than a mile since.

"Okay," said Trapper, beginning to trudge back toward shore, "back to the real fun. Are your feet holding up?"

"Yeah," said Cassidy. "My toes are a little sore, though."

"Right. They're tender under your toes where you try to grip the sand. It's like sandpaper. You better try to stay in a little bit of water going back. Tide's about dead high, so there should be some good footing in the shallows."

They started back up the beach, this time with Cassidy running pleasantly in the edge of the surf.

"Try not to step on any fish," said Trapper.

Cassidy laughed, but Trapper was perfectly serious.

"It happened to me once," he said, "and it wasn't pleasant. I thought he just jabbed me in the heel, but it was still bothering me a week later. I got to messing around with a pair of tweezers and finally pulled out about an inch-long dorsal spike."

Cassidy looked dismayed.

"Don't worry, kid. What are the chances it would happen to both of us?" His laugh boomed up and down the empty beach.

CHAPTER 14

REEKS & WRECKS

All winter Cassidy sat in the stands and watched Stiggs and Randleman in their glory on the Glenridge Junior High hardwood. Stiggs was developing into a deceptively agile forward, and Randleman, whose nickname was now "Moose," had become a sturdy rebounder. Cassidy had to be content with the vicarious satisfactions of the enthusiast, but he was wounded to the core when John Ayers, one of the equipment managers, got mono halfway through the season and Stiggs suggested Cassidy apply for the job.

"At least you'd be with the team. You'd make the trips," said Stiggs. Cassidy just looked at him.

"Goddamn, Stiggs," said Randleman, before walking away.

Cassidy couldn't wait for spring and the start of track season. He had things to prove.

But on the first day of practice, there didn't appear to be much glory in the offing. With the exception of Chip Newspickle, Ed Demski, and two or three other actual athletes, the track team turned out to be the usual collection of castoffs and ne'er-do-wells.

"Paste eaters and pencil necks," pronounced Stiggs, whom Cassidy had dragged along to try the high jump. Randleman tagged along to try the shot and discus. They jogged out to the infield and began, as Stiggs put it, "scoping out the asylum."

Near the high-jump pit, Demski was sitting next to another runner named Lenny Lindstrom, who was just getting up to go jog. Cassidy and Stiggs plopped down next to Demski.

"W-w-what are you g-g-guys doing here?" asked Demski.

"He's going to run, I'm going to high-jump," said Stiggs. "Randleman's going to throw stuff. Coach said it would keep us in shape for basketball."

"Y-y-yeah, I guess it would," said Demski dubiously.

"Who the heck are these guys, anyway?" asked Cassidy, gesturing at a motley trio jogging by very slowly.

Demski laughed. "T-t-track's kind of like p-prison," he said. "Some guys just kinda end up here." He went down the roster of those he knew.

There was Dewey Kuster, who fancied himself a pole-vaulter. He had the same aerodynamically interesting ears that Coach Bickerstaff had sported in a younger day. A severely beeswaxed flattop and a really cool silver front tooth brought him much more fame locally than his debatable athletic skills. He could barely clear his own height but was tolerated on the team because his uncle, an irrigation contractor, had bought him a top-of-the-line bamboo pole that he was persuaded to let the other boys use.

There was Frazier Ravenscraft, III, scion of what passed for Citrus City aristocracy, an incredibly good-looking boy who was actually a decent high hurdler. He might have been even better were his energies not so diverted by more licentious pursuits. Frazier could always draw a rapt audience on those occasions he was persuaded to share his tales of sexual derring-do, real and imagined. He had been hot and heavy with Henrietta Delvechio since the fifth grade, and it was said that they'd gone "most of the way." Cassidy had no idea what that could possibly mean, but he paid rapt attention to stories redolent of popcorn, mosquito-coil smoke, and passionate grapplings backlit by heavily spliced fourth-run drive-in movies.

Albert Nutgrass, Jr., was a runner of sorts and considered to be of a piece with the rest of the Nutgrasses, generations of whom were skilled at poaching, moonshining, and helping themselves to the bounty of other people's traps and trotlines. The family had actually made a considerable amount of money during the glory days of Prohibition, running bonded booze in from Bahamian-based mother ships and up into the labyrinthine channels of the St. Lucie River. The current generation of Nutgrasses were known for their elaborate taste in pickup trucks.

Rufus Pulliam was an erstwhile discus thrower who was always injured, which prompted Frazier Ravenscraft's waggish designation: "Rufus Pullyhim Hamstring."

There were also Miley Tharpe, Derwood Garr, and Jarvis Parsley. No one knew for sure what their events were supposed to be. There were a few others Ed knew nothing about, including their purported specialties.

Where do they find such individuals?" Stiggs sniffed. "Did they drain the swamps?"

"Everyone knows Frazier," said Cassidy. "Dewey's in my science class. But I don't think I've ever seen the rest of them in my life."

"A lot of them take shop and m-m-m-mechanical drawing and stuff. Some of them do some kind of work-study p-p-program."

"What do they do in practice?"

"They m-m-mostly just kind of jog around," said Demski. "Sometimes they do intervals, but n-n-not with us. Coach gives them a workout and tells them to stay out of the way."

"What's intervals?" said Cassidy. Demski looked at him.

"Y-y-you'll find out."

Find out he did. Cassidy ended that day's set of 220s with needlelike pains on the tops of his thighs. He thought they would go away, but the next day when they were still there, he went to Coach Bickerstaff.

"Son, you're just having growing pains," the coach said.

Demski noticed something was wrong even as they were jogging a warm-up mile the next day.

"Y-y-you're running funny," he said.

"The top of my legs hurt, I can't lift my knees up. You ever have that?"

"N-no. It'll pr-pr-probably go away."

But it didn't. Instead, it grew more painful by the day until mercifully the weekend arrived and Cassidy gratefully left his running shoes alone and picked up his paddle.

CHAPTER 15

MOCCASIN COVE

The air was worthy of Bombay as he paddled north, but his sore legs felt better from diving that morning; pushing the big rocket fins through the water had loosened them up some.

It had been dry for months, so the Loxahatchee was low, fed mostly by cold sweet springs.

If it were August, he thought, *people would call these "dog days."* Cassidy figured that had something to do with the way the dogs laid around with their tongues lolling out. Days not fit for dogs, days that made dogs suffer, dog days, it sort of made sense. Anyway, people seemed to know what you meant when you said it.

He should have made this trip long before now. He had felt a vague guilt every time he walked by his little canoe in the backyard, all but abandoned, strapped facedown on its bike trailer, ready to go but ignored. But for the first time in his life he had been feeling the tug of forces pulling him away from the water. With his still new status as an almost-athlete, the anticipation of the start of track season, and a first budding interest in girls, he just hadn't been on the water in a while. With the casual solipsism of the young, Cassidy just naturally assumed Trapper Nelson had missed him terribly.

But now that he'd spent the morning on the ocean and river, Cassidy realized that he would always return to the water. The salt sea could sting, but it could also heal. Near it, in it, or especially under it, a nameless delight always made his sternum tingle.

This was the time of year his submerged staying power would start to build. Late in the summer he would stay down several minutes, busy the whole time. That was when he would begin to think of himself as a sea creature. On really hot days he would put five or six pounds of lead on his weight belt and just lie on the bottom in twenty or thirty feet in the ocean or river. He was so relaxed he almost felt he could fall asleep.

Right now, though, despite the shade from the mangroves, paddling was sweaty work. He was daydreaming about the first plunge off the dock at Trapper's.

Trapper would surely be happy to see him for at least one reason: the front of his boat was alive with snapper and small grouper he'd gotten that morning with his pole spear. He'd even gotten a hog snapper, which they didn't see all that much anymore. Even better was the large clump of plump-looking oysters he'd dredged up, a happy discovery made when he'd retrieved his anchor in the shallows of the intracoastal waterway and it had come back with a cluster of bivalves lodged in the flukes.

He tried to remember whether Trapper liked oysters, but upon a moment's reflection it seemed a silly question. He didn't know many organisms Trapper wouldn't eat.

When he reached the halfway point, a little clearing called Moccasin Cove, he saw Trapper's dark green canoe pulled up by a mangrove stand. Next to it was Trapper, gesturing vigorously at him.

"S'matter, cat got your tongue?" Cassidy said, pulling in next to his boat.

"No voice," Trapper half whispered, pointing to his throat. "Had a cold, gone now. Feel fine, but I still got this."

"Whatcha doing with the traps? I thought Saturdays were 'make-and-mend' days."

"Usually is. I just had a few to check back up in Cypress Creek, and they weren't doing any good so I thought I'd bring them down this way a little."

"They got some kind of bait in them? Something smells funny."

"Yeah, they're baited, but that's not what you're smelling. It's the mocs. They get all riled up this time of year and start giving off their musk. And they get all aggressive on you, too. Best to keep an eye out around here. There's a reason they call this Moccasin Cove, you know."

"I was with my dad one time one tried to bite the pontoon on our boat," Cassidy said. Trapper nodded.

"Whatcha got there?" he asked.

Cassidy brightened. "Mostly little snappers. One hog. But look at this!" He proudly held up the big clump of oysters.

"Whoa! Where'd you find those?"

"Intracoastal just north of the Sanderson place, maybe a hundred yards offshore. Some came up with my hook. I thought it was just a rock until I rinsed them off a little. I jumped out and grabbed a bunch and threw them in the boat. Pretty good, huh?"

"Oh, boy, I love a good raw oyster with a dash of Tabasco sauce! Haven't had any since that bed Joe Kern and I found got wiped out by a hurricane. Any idea how big the bed is?"

"I couldn't tell. Water isn't very clear in there. I put my sandals on and felt around with my feet, but I never came to the end of them. Must be pretty good size. I can find it again easy. I have it triangulated," Cassidy said.

"Good boy!" Trapper croaked. "Mother Nature sometimes makes it hard to find dinner. She wants to make sure you want it bad enough."

"She can't fool me. But I don't like raw ones much. I like them roasted on the fire with melted butter. And lots of crackers."

"That works, too," Trapper rasped, rubbing his bare belly.

Cassidy nodded. "Hey, you need help with those?" He gestured at the pile of traps.

"Naw, just take a few minutes," he whispered, picking up a pair of traps. "You headed up to the camp?"

"Yes, sir. Thought I was due for a visit."

"You bet you are. Due and overdue. Well, good. We'll fire up some of those oysters. I'll see you upriver."

As Cassidy eased back into the river and pushed his paddle against the bottom to get his canoe pointed upstream, Trapper saw something dark fall from a tree limb at the water's edge into the back of the boat. He thought it was just a dead branch until he heard the meaty thunk it made when it landed. Cassidy didn't notice.

"Quenton!"

Trapper called as loud as he could, but only a squeak came out. He picked up a rock and slammed it against the side of his wooden canoe, but the sound wasn't loud enough to be heard over Cassidy clanging around with his paddle. Slamming the rock against a mangrove tree was even less effective. Banging it against one of the metal traps made a louder noise, but by now Cassidy was twenty yards up the river.

Trapper's mind was racing. He didn't have his shotgun with him and there was nothing else he could use to make a noise loud enough. He took off running down the path that paralleled the river.

One of his untied combat boots came off right away and he soon kicked the other one off. The path veered away from the river for sixty or seventy yards around a swampy area before rejoining it at a bamboo stand. It then paralleled the river all the way back to his camp, a mile upriver. The trail was studded with roots and rocks, but Trapper's feet were tough from all the time he spent barefoot around the camp and on the beach. He was fast and in good shape, but he didn't know how much time he had.

"Quenton!" he squeaked, trying to make his voice work. His eyes welled in frustration.

As he came around the last bend before the path rejoined the river, he could hear a thin voice singing a Bahamian folk ditty: "*Now

de fishing's good near your island, dat's why I come back for more . . ."
Trapper knew that Cassidy hadn't been bitten yet, but he was clearly
oblivious to the danger.

Trapper ran to the first break in the bamboo stand just as Cassidy
was passing. He could see the moccasin making his way up from
the back of the boat. Trapper had been hoping it was a brown water
snake, but the muted banding and the girth of the thing were all too
obvious.

Trapper thought the snake was probably just after the fish, but
that wouldn't really matter in the end. Trapper grabbed a handful of
bamboo shoots and shook them furiously. Cassidy paddled on, singing: *"But when you swim me boat 'round naked, I follow you back to de
shore . . ."*

"Quenton!" This time it was barely a whisper. He ran back to the
path and sprinted twenty yards to the next gap in the bamboo, just as
Cassidy was passing. Gasping now from the effort and the tension,
he waved his arms frantically, looking around for something to throw
at the side of the boat.

To his horror, he saw that the snake was now almost underneath
the seat. The kid was kneeling on a life preserver in front of the seat,
blocking the snake's path to the fish. Trapper knew that as soon as the
snake started to go around him, assuming he didn't just attack first,
the kid would no doubt reach down to see what was brushing him,
and that's when it would happen.

The next gap in the bamboo was just a few yards away, and when
he reached it he launched himself into a flat dive directly at a wide-
eyed Cassidy, who looked up just in time to see a looming humanoid
projectile coming right at him. He thought his life was over, ended by
some huge bird of prey. It was the second time Trapper Nelson had
nearly scared him to death, and it wouldn't be the last.

Trapper landed half on the canoe and half in the water, reaching
his left hand out to the middle of Cassidy's chest to thrust him out of

the canoe like a child flicking over a toy soldier with his finger. The canoe nearly capsized, Trapper fell back into the water, and Cassidy came up sputtering and gagging.

Cassidy now knew it was Trapper Nelson who had attacked him but could not for the life of him think why. Trapper was known for a lot of things, but not for pulling pranks.

"Are you bit?" Trapper rasped, dragging Cassidy into the shallows. Then he had him by the shoulders, shaking him, trying to get his attention. All Cassidy could do was gag and sputter. He tried to say something but couldn't make words. He shook his head. He didn't think he was bitten by anything but he had no idea what Trapper was talking about.

"Are you sure?" Trapper tried to yell. This time the first word came out in his normal voice, but the other two words were squeaks. Cassidy wiped water from his eyes and face.

"By what? By what? What's the . . ." he sputtered.

Trapper pulled him up on the bank and began searching up and down his legs and feet for the two dreaded puncture holes. He saw none, and at last took a deep breath and let it out slowly, looking dourly at Cassidy. He pulled him close and gave him a hug. *Good grief, he's never done that before*, Cassidy thought.

"What's going on, Trap?"

Trapper Nelson, panting, hung his head between his knees, exhausted. He looked up at Cassidy, then gestured with his chin at the canoe, almost half full of water now, where it had drifted into some reeds at the edge of the river. As Cassidy watched, a four-foot-long cottonmouth moccasin made his way up and over the gunnel and into the river, carrying one of Cassidy's mangrove snappers in his mouth. Paying them not the slightest attention, the snake turned downriver and swam past them, his fat, buoyant body riding high in the water, the fish held up triumphantly in front of him.

Cassidy looked at Trapper Nelson and burst out laughing.

"It's . . . not . . . funny," Trapper said, fighting for air. "The hospital in Citrus City. Good *forty-five minutes* from here. *If* my Jeep started. Martin Memorial almost as far."

Cassidy sighed. "I would have *given* him a fish," he said.

Trapper Nelson, still panting, looked at his feet for the first time. He slipped them into the cool water and watched as the current carried the muck and blood away. Finally, he looked over at Cassidy with a sheepish grin.

"Hope we didn't lose any oysters," he said.

CHAPTER 16

TRACK DISASTER

The needlelike pains in the tops of Cassidy's quadriceps never completely went away. When he took a weekend off from training, they were much better by the next Monday. But Coach Bickerstaff always started off the week with hard intervals, and by Tuesday he was limping. He complained to Bickerstaff again, to no avail. The man had ears of stone when it came to the aches and pains of thirteen-year-olds.

To survive the afternoons, Cassidy adopted a strange running style that involved the barest minimum of knee lift and a big back kick. He looked like a man running while carrying a large box in front of him. Demski had a field day teasing him about his "flamingo gallop," but it was the only way he could get through the workout.

Their first competition was at home, a dual meet with Pompano, a junior high farther down the coast. Cassidy was put in the half mile, along with Demski and Lenny Lindstrom. Pompano had a runner named Mizner, tall, dark complected, and reed thin. He was all business, too, jumping out to the lead at the gun. Demski fell in behind, with Cassidy behind him. Everyone else just let them go.

They ran that way for a sixty-nine-second first lap. As they came by the starting post, Demski tried to make a move to pass Mizner, but the taller runner was having none of it. Demski fell back in behind again before the first turn. Cassidy's frustration grew with every step. He had no trouble with the pace, but his ridiculous man-carrying-a-box running style all but hamstrung him. Every time he tried to bring his knees up a little bit higher to produce some speed, his rebellious thighs screamed.

Throughout the second lap, he watched with increasing misery as Mizner and Demski battled it out up ahead. It wasn't just that he was behind, but more from the knowledge that he wasn't at all tired. He knew that without this handicap he would be right up there mixing it up with Demski and Mizner.

As it was, Demski finally got around Mizner before the last turn, and they battled all the way down the final straightaway, with Demski winning by a yard in 2:21. Cassidy galloped in awkwardly, fifteen yards back, but ahead of Lindstrom and the two Pompano runners.

Walking around in circles, trying to catch his breath, Cassidy was muttering and trying to spit, but failing at even that. He had so little saliva that his tongue was sticking to the roof of his mouth. His invective was therefore unintelligible.

Coach Bickerstaff seemed annoyingly jubilant.

"That's hanging in there, Quenton! You got us a point!"

"Craff!"

"Beg pardon?"

But Bickerstaff was off to congratulate Demski on his great kick, leaving Cassidy bent over, grabbing his knees, and sucking air. The frustration boiled over again when Demski gave him a big grin and a high sign. Cassidy gave him a wave then bent back over, pounding on his inflamed thighs with his fists.

It didn't help.

CHAPTER 17

LONG WEEKEND

The torture continued through April, and Cassidy didn't know which was worse, the pain or the frustration. Or maybe the fact that Coach Bickerstaff was actually pleased with his piddling performances. The more fourth and fifth places he suffered through, the more Bickerstaff seemed to think he was the king bee!

But Cassidy now knew something was seriously wrong with him, and that if he could just stop training long enough for it to heal, he would have been fine. He begged Bickerstaff to let him try taking a few days off, and got a "nice try" chuckle in response. Bickerstaff had spent much of his ten coaching years listening to goldbricking kids.

The first week in May, a teachers' planning day on Monday gave them a long weekend. With no scheduled meets, Cassidy purposefully didn't run a step for three days in a row. Instead, he and Stiggs and Randleman hiked in to Trapper Nelson's camp on the rugged Jeep road, packing in supplies for a weenie roast. Trapper already had the fire going and the table set when they got there, so they spent a pleasant hour on the rope swing, dropping into the cool river and trying to splash Willie the parrot, who was far too smart to stay in range of teenagers.

They had brought two packages of hot dogs, one for them and one for Trapper. Trapper ate the whole package save a single hot dog. The boys had two hot dogs each, and thus two were left over. Trapper was eyeing the remaining three weenies on a paper plate at the end of the picnic table, but finally declared a truce.

"There was a time when I would have finished them off and been looking for more. I guess I'm slowing down a bit," he said.

"I wish I could slow down like you," said Randleman, flexing a biceps. He had lifted weights for years trying to develop a physique like Trapper's.

"Yeah, well, don't wish your life away, Youngblood. You've got plenty of time. Hey, looks like your ride's here. All day-campers to the dock!"

"To the dock!" cried Willie the parrot.

The twenty-two-foot Aquasport was just pulling in from downriver with Randleman's dad at the wheel. He was a retired Air Force officer who now sold insurance, and sold a lot of it, judging by the little tricked-out boat with its bimini top, outriggers, dive platform, and front canopy. There was another man on the boat sitting very erect in the back. It took Cassidy a moment to place the judge.

"All aboard!" Captain Randleman called out.

"How you doing, Pete?" Trapper called. "You guys do any good today?"

"Hey, Trap. Got one sail. The judge had another one on for half an hour but lost it at the gaff. Trolled the ledges a bit and picked up some rock hinds. Leave you a few if you want. Not a bad day for a late start."

Trapper was helping Stiggs and Randleman get their gear down to the dock. Cassidy had gotten permission to spend the night and, stuffed from dinner, was content to watch the activity from the deck.

"You okay, Quenton?" someone called from the boat.

Cassidy peered out over the rail. It was Judge Chillingworth calling to him. He gave Cassidy a little wave.

"Hi, Judge. Doing fine, sir. Hello, Captain Randleman."

"Coach Bickerstaff says you're tearing them up on the track," said Captain Randleman. For some reason this made Cassidy's heart sink.

"I don't know about that," he said, hoping his chuckle didn't sound forced.

After they'd cleared away the dinner things and cleaned the little groupers, Cassidy and Trapper sat on a homemade bench by the fire. It wasn't exactly chilly out, but the warmth felt good anyway. Trapper was slicing up a pair of lusciously ripe Hayden mangoes from his own tree, handing some pieces to Cassidy and some to Willie, who would fly down to the table, snatch a piece of fruit, then return to his limb to eat it.

"So, what's been going on with you, anyway? I can tell something's up," said Trapper.

With only a little prodding, Cassidy told him about his wounded thighs and the misery they had been causing.

"This has been going on for how long?"

"Since the start of track, back in March."

"Hmmm."

"I've thought about asking my parents if I can go to the doctor."

"Well, you could do that. In my experience, though, most regular doctors don't know a lot about sports injuries and it sounds like you have a sports injury."

"Coach Bickerstaff thinks I'm just trying to get out of doing the workouts. He says I've got growing pains. But Trapper, I *like* to run."

"I know you do. And this has gone on way too long for growing pains."

"That's what I thought. But I don't know what to do. I'm so tired of running with this ridiculous stride like a waterbird just to get through the workouts. Then, on the weekends when we have meets, I barely hang on in races I think I could win! All I want to do is be able to run like I know I can."

"I don't blame you for being upset, Quenton. Coach Bickerstaff is a good man, but he's pretty much overworked with all the different sports they have him doing, in addition to teaching phys ed and doing the administrative stuff. I believe he mostly played basketball in college, didn't he?"

"Yes, but he ran sprints in track. I think he was pretty fast. He has some trophies."

"Okay, sprinters are a different breed. Tell you what, all I know about running is doing road work for boxing. Let me talk to Dennis Kamrad at the high school about this. They finally hired him over there to teach civics and coach the varsity crew full-time. Rowing is an endurance sport. He's a smart guy. I'll bet he'll have some ideas."

"That would be terrific, if you would."

"I've also got this friend out in Kansas, guy I worked with one summer when Charlie and I were on the road. He hurt his leg really bad as a kid, got run over by a truck. They wanted to amputate it, but the kid put up such a fuss they let him keep it. They were pretty sure he would never walk again. But he not only walked, he became a great—and I mean *great*—runner. We got to be pretty good friends that summer. I'll write to him. Better yet, I'll call him up, long distance, next time I get into Stuart to pick up my mail. If anybody can help, he can."

"Trapper, that would be . . . I just . . . Thanks, Trap, thank you."

"Save it till we see how it goes. May not pan out at all. But I'd put money on my guy. He was really a terrific athlete in his day."

"What event did he do?"

"The mile."

"What's his name?"

"Archie San Romani."

"Never heard of him."

"That's funny, he speaks highly of you."

It took Cassidy a few seconds to get it.

CHAPTER 18

FAINT GLORY

When Monday afternoon arrived hot and still, Cassidy was amazed to find that his thighs barely hurt at all. He jogged the warm-up mile like a normal human being and even had no trouble sprinting the straights and jogging the curves for another half mile.

"Wh-wh-where's the fl-fl-fl-flamingo today?" said Demski.

"Flew the coop," said Cassidy. "Better watch out, Ed."

Ed grinned.

"Okay, jumpers and throwers meet with Coach Burke at the high-jump pit, sprinters get with Mr. Ayers on the infield for stretching, the rest of you over here with me," said Coach Bickerstaff. "All right, listen up," he said, after he had the runners grouped up. "We've got more than a month under our belts and we're looking toward the *big* meets now. It's gettin' around to no-foolin' time around here, boys."

Bickerstaff's Red Sox cap already had a dark sweat ring, and he was holding his clipboard out away from him to keep from dripping onto the mimeographed workout sheets.

"The workout today is eight times 440, with a—"

He was interrupted by the groans.

"All right, settle down. Eight quarters with a 220 in between, and,

Demski, I want you to try to keep them as close to seventy-five as you can, the rest of you just do the best you can. Any questions? Yes, Lenny?"

"Who's going to notify our next of kin?"

"Hardee har har har. Any other wisenheimer comments? All right, let's do some striders back and forth on the straightaway. We'll start in about five."

Cassidy couldn't believe how great it felt to be actually running again! He had a hard time restraining himself even on the little sprints they were doing.

"Whoa, hoss!" said Demski, as they finished a strider, barely able to keep up. Cassidy just grinned. This was what it was supposed to be like.

Demski had a very good sense of pace, and he finished the first quarter in seventy-four, with Cassidy and Lindstrom a step behind.

"Good, Ed!" said Bickerstaff. "Len and Quenton, way to hang in there. The rest of you were about eighty-two."

Cassidy was thrilled. He barely felt the effort and didn't stop for even a second to grab his knees. He just jogged on toward the far starting post, waiting for everyone else to catch up. Bickerstaff walked to the middle of the infield to be closer to the next start.

Demski came up to Cassidy ten yards before the starting line, gave him a funny look, then raised his arm as they approached the white post. He dropped his arm as they took off and they ran side by side the whole way. Demski pushed it a little over the last fifty yards, but Cassidy matched him and they finished exactly even.

"Seventy-two!" called Bickerstaff from the other side of the track. "Lenny seventy-eight, the rest of you about eighty-three."

"Uh-oh," said Demski, as they slowed to a jog, "Parsley is going to ralph."

Sure enough, one of the slower guys, a small kid with a comical cowlick, ran to the outside of the track and let go, keeping his feet wide apart in a vain attempt to avoid splashing his shoes.

"I f-f-forgot Monday was spaghetti day," Demski said, still jogging,

Demski and Cassidy were both breathing hard but not gasping. Cassidy was elated. The tops of his thighs merely tingled, nothing like the needle stabs that had tormented him for weeks. He could feel them more acutely now than during the warm-up, but it wasn't bad at all.

Cassidy expected to get shut down by Ed eventually, so he figured he might as well earn a little credibility while he could. *No way I can keep this up, but I can have some fun in the meantime,* he thought.

On the next interval he blasted away at the post just as Ed dropped his arm. Cassidy got five yards on him and was surprised that Ed didn't come right back. In fact, he didn't make up the deficit at all. Cassidy concentrated on his long stride, stretching out on the back straight and just letting it rip all the way around the final curve. He expected Ed to come back on him at any moment, but he never did. Though he could now feel the sharp little stabs of pain in the tops of his thighs starting up again, it was nothing like before and nothing he couldn't handle.

Bickerstaff was waiting at the white finish post, giving Cassidy a puzzled look as he blew past, ten yards in front of Demski.

"Sixty-eight," said Bickerstaff, his voice soft. He collected himself somewhat before Demski came by.

"Seventy-two, Ed. Good one, you guys. All right, all the way through, the rest of you. Seventy-six, Lenny. Seventy-seven, seventy-eight, Miley. Okay, eighty, eighty-one, and eighty-two, Derwood, Jarvis. Good work, men. Keep moving. Number four coming up."

Well, I've had my fun, Cassidy thought, *and now I'm in for it. Ed's gonna be ticked, and I've probably shot my wad.*

But the next one went much the same. He finished in sixty-eight again, with Ed a full three seconds back this time.

Cassidy wasn't sure what was going on. His little show of bravado had been intended as a kind of a joke, a quick grab for a snippet of glory before Ed and the others caught on and lowered the boom on him. But he had run with little pain and some very real joy at last, and no one else was to match him. In fact, they seemed to be falling behind. The rest of them were eyeing him curiously during the rests, even Demski.

Ed seemed to recover a little bit on number five and actually led most of the way, but Cassidy could tell the pace was getting to him, and he slipped past Demski in the last fifty yards and led by a second with another sixty-eight.

This time Ed stopped and grabbed his knees just past the finish line, and Cassidy did the same.

Coach Bickerstaff had grown strangely silent. After giving the stragglers their times, he walked over to where Cassidy and Demski were still bent over, gasping. He swatted their fannies with his clipboard.

"Okay, you guys," he said. But it wasn't the usual command to keep moving, just a gesture of encouragement.

Demski really came alive on the number six, and Cassidy had to admire the fight in him. He took the lead from the start, led all the way around the first turn, and then fought Cassidy off twice on the back straight. Cassidy thought he heard Bickerstaff call out a split time of thirty-three seconds at the 220, but figured he heard wrong.

Though the tops of his thighs were once again on fire, Cassidy drove down the final straightaway, leaving Ed struggling a full second behind.

"Sixty-seven," Bickerstaff read from the watch as Cassidy went by. Again he said it in a normal voice, kept studying his watch, seeming surprised by what he was seeing.

The rest of the runners were now strung out so far that it was taking longer and longer to get them organized between intervals. Cassidy and Demski were grateful for the extra time provided by the stragglers, some of whom were now taking more than ninety seconds to finish.

They themselves could jog only a few yards before they had to walk again. When they started number seven it was obvious they were still blown out, and Bickerstaff had no doubt they were also trying to save a little something for the last one.

But still they finished number seven in seventy-two seconds, coming across the line almost neck and neck. They stopped for a few seconds before jogging on, but they were the only ones capable of doing that. Everyone else staggered around in random clumps. Jarvis Parsley was collapsed on the infield, and Bickerstaff sent him to the locker room in the care of a manager.

Bickerstaff watched Cassidy and Demski jogging along with little slow, prancing steps all around the turn, sweat flying off them on every stride. *Now*, he thought. *Now we shall see what we shall see.*

But if he thought the anomaly of the earlier intervals was now going to be corrected and that the world would thus be set aright, he was in for one last surprise.

Cassidy sprinted away from Demski from the start and simply ran away from the rest of them. He telescoped his lead over Demski up to twenty yards before the end. Stiggs and some of the other jumpers were standing on the infield yelling themselves hoarse as he went by. Even some of the weight men joined in. The tops of Cassidy's thighs were screaming at him again, but he didn't care; he could endure anything for a few more seconds. He finished gasping, body frozen into a solid block of lactic acid, but many full seconds in front of Demski, who, anyone could easily see, was absolutely balls-to-the-wall flat out.

Bickerstaff studied his watch as Cassidy went by. If he called out a time, Cassidy didn't hear it. He slowed to a straight-legged stagger, then halted, grabbed his knees, and wobbled around, working so hard to get air into his lungs he sounded in his own head as if he were shrieking. Demski and the rest were finishing now and doing likewise.

With a strange look on his face, Coach Bickerstaff walked over with the split timer held faceup in his right hand, the lanyard dangling. He held it down to where Cassidy was bent over, gasping.

It took a moment to focus, but when his vision cleared he was able to read the watch: 64.8.

"Do you still think you're a basketball player?" Bickerstaff said.

CHAPTER 19

NO QUARTER

"This friend of mine," said Trapper, "he's pretty knowledgeable. You know the last thing on my mind is to interfere with your team, but I thought you'd want to hear what he had to say." He was a little uncomfortable, having put on a clean shirt and long pants, rare for him. Mr. Kamrad sat in the other chair, across from Coach Bickerstaff.

"What'd you say his name was?"

"San Romani. Archie San Romani."

Bickerstaff emitted a low whistle.

"You know him?"

"Criminy, Trapper. Everybody knows Archie San Romani. Everybody who knows anything about track and field. Kid had his leg mangled under a truck, then grows up to be a national champion."

"Right, right. That's him. They thought he was going to be the first four-minute-miler there for a while, I guess."

"I remember. I actually saw him run once, at the Mason-Dixon Games." Bickerstaff shoved his baseball cap back on his head and rocked back in his swivel chair.

He turned to Kamrad. "And what is your interest in all this, Dennis?"

"Just a friend of the court. I've talked on the phone with Archie, and I'm generally in agreement with his point of view."

Bickerstaff turned back to Trapper Nelson. "And how do you know San Romani, anyway?" he said.

"We worked at the same place one summer in Michigan. He was going to some college in Kansas and was working over the summer. I was on my way out west. The company was called Crown Cork & Seal, manufactured bottle caps, cans, mason jar lids, and such. Noisiest place you ever heard. We worked on the same production line, got to be pretty good friends. He weighed about a hundred and forty pounds, but he could work circles around any three of the rest of us."

"And you say you've stayed in touch with him?"

"Just Christmas cards and such. But when young Quenton mentioned the trouble he's been having with his legs . . ."

"And you know Quenton how?"

"We're just friends. Fishing and whatnot."

"Okay, well, I don't think those growing pains are bothering him anymore, not after what I saw on Monday."

"Oh?"

"We've got this kid, Demski, eighth grader like Quenton, ran for me last year. Showed a lot of promise, but he was still young. Well, he shows up in March this year in pretty good shape and it wasn't long before he was winning everything in sight. No one could touch him in the half mile, and he was almost as good in the 440. Cassidy, meantime, is doing okay, too. He can't keep up with Demski, but he's holding his own, picking up thirds, fourths, fifths—"

"Yeah, that's what I wanted to talk to you—"

"Let me finish. This past Monday we've got this bear of a workout scheduled. Eight quarter miles with a 220 jog in between. I wanted them in seventy-five seconds or so, knowing Demski's probably the only kid that can hit that, but, you know, giving them all something to shoot for—"

"Let me guess what happened," Trapper interrupted.

Bickerstaff looked at him.

"Quenton walked all over them."

Bickerstaff studied him. "How'd you know that?"

"I'm right, aren't I? What did he average?"

"A tick over sixty-nine. Demski was seventy-one flat."

"That's what I thought. You just saw the real Quenton then."

"What are you talking about? I've been coaching him straight through since the first of March. He's never shown me anything like that before."

"That's what I've been trying to tell you, Bick. The kid's been about half injured the whole time."

Trapper Nelson took a sheath of folded notebook paper out of his back pocket.

"I made a few notes here from talking with Archie," he said. "He knew exactly what I was talking about when I described Quenton's injury to him. I said it was needlelike pains in the tops of the quadriceps that keep him from getting any knee lift. Archie said they're caused by too much speed work too early. You get these small tears in the muscles on the tops of the thighs. Archie said *he's* had them before, usually early in the season. But he says they're easy to get rid of, you just have to take a little time off."

"What time off? The big meets are just coming up now! How's he going to be ready if he's sitting on his heinie?"

"They just need enough time to heal, and the kid'll be fine," said Mr. Kamrad. "We get the same thing in rowing with the shoulder muscles, caused by pulling too hard too early. There's no way around it, you just have to let them heal."

"Well, let me tell you something, Trapper, Dennis. I've been coaching track and field for more than a decade and I've never heard of this so-called injury. Plus, from what I saw on Monday, there is nothing whatsoever wrong with his quadriceps, his biceps, his triceps, or his any other kind of 'ceps. This kid is *over* his little episode of growing pains and he's ready to take on the world, I tell you what. Otherwise, how do you explain what I just saw?"

"Easy to explain, Bob. He just had a three-day weekend rest, finally giving him a chance to heal up a little bit. I'll bet by now he's right back to where he was before," said Mr. Kamrad.

Bickerstaff made a dismissive gesture. Trapper Nelson sighed.

"Archie also had some workout suggestions," Trapper said quietly, holding up his notes. "I don't suppose you'd be interested in seeing those."

"I'm pretty much all set on that score," Bickerstaff said coldly. "But thank you for the offer. And thank Mr. San Romani when you talk to him."

The two got up to leave.

"And, Dennis, I appreciate the concern," said Bickerstaff.

Mr. Kamrad paused at the door and gave Bickerstaff a tight smile.

CHAPTER 20

PAIN AND HUMILIATION

"Uh-uh-uh-oh," said Demski. "The fl-fl-fl-fl-fl, waterbird is back."

Cassidy was miserable. They were still jogging the warm-up and already his legs were excruciating. On Monday he was invincible, and now, on Friday, he was right back where he had been before. Maybe worse.

He knew Trapper Nelson and Mr. Kamrad had failed in their intervention attempt, and with that failure Cassidy saw his dreams of glory on the track blowing away like spindrift. He tried to assure Trapper that everything would be fine, that he appreciated his efforts, but Trapper was not to be consoled. He offered to talk to Cassidy's parents, but Cassidy declined. He figured it would only complicate things further and Bickerstaff already had his back up. As Cassidy's performance declined steadily during the week, Bickerstaff became convinced that he was putting on a show for his benefit, trying to convince him that Trapper Nelson's diagnosis was correct. This seemed to anger him further, this battle of wills with one of his charges.

The workout of the day was twelve times 220 with a two-minute walk between. He wanted them to shoot for thirty-six seconds, which meant he expected Ed and Cassidy to duke it out at that speed and the rest of them to hang on as best they could.

"Y-y-you okay?" asked Ed as they lined up.

"Not really," said Cassidy. After a horrible long run the day before, he was dreading this.

Ed finished the first one in thirty-five and Cassidy was five seconds back, his face twisted in pain. Lenny Lindstrom and Jarvis Parsley finished in front of him.

"All right, Ed, good going," said Bickerstaff. "Len, Jarvis, thirty-eight. Good. Walk it off. Quenton, come here a second."

Still gasping for air, Cassidy walked stiff-leggedly over to the coach.

"I know what you're doing," he said quietly, holding up his clipboard to the side of his face for privacy. "It's not going to work. You might as well straighten up and fly right."

Cassidy walked back to the runners assembling at the starting line. The others were surprised to see him almost in tears.

"All right, runners. Number two, still shooting for thirty-six. Set and go!" called Bickerstaff.

For Cassidy it just got worse. He finished the workout, coming in farther and farther behind. Bickerstaff didn't say anything, but Cassidy could see the look of disgust on his face. By the time he finished the eighth repetition, there were real tears rolling down his cheeks. He couldn't help it. While the others jogged the two-lap cooldown, he walked stiff-leggedly to the gym. When he got to the stairs to the second-floor locker room, he had to turn sideways and climb them by throwing one leg straight out in front of him and rotating it over to the stair, then standing up straight on it and repeating the process with the other leg, using his arms to haul himself up.

He was showered and nearly dressed by the time the others started wandering in. He sat for a few moments in front of his locker, staring at the clean white singlet folded neatly atop the matching shorts on the upper shelf. His racing uniform. It felt as if everyone was tiptoeing around him. He knew his face was still red, but he wasn't even embarrassed about it.

Finally, he stood and retrieved the singlet, unfolding it and holding it in front of him. It was spotlessly white, with a red satin sash running diagonally across the chest and a small winged "G" for Glenridge over the left breast. He remembered the incredible pride that welled up in him the first time he put it on. And every time thereafter, for that matter.

He couldn't believe what he had to do.

Bickerstaff had his reading glasses on, going over the numbers on his clipboard from the day's workout.

"Come in," he said.

Cassidy walked in, tears now falling freely from his eyes. He laid the singlet, red sash up, on the coach's desk.

"All right," said the coach.

CHAPTER 21

ALL-COMERS COMEUPPANCE

After a few days of inactivity, Cassidy's legs were sufficiently healed that he could go out and shoot baskets, then jog around the court a little with very little pain. A few days after that, his legs were perfectly fine again. He could hardly believe he'd ever had the injury at all. Fixing it was so simple.

Stiggs was still high jumping, but Randleman had given up the shot put as too boring, so Cassidy was happy to have a basketball partner back. Randleman and Cassidy started working out together, doing drills and playing one-on-one. Cassidy wasn't nearly big enough to keep Randleman out of the key, so they had to make adjustments to the rules to make it more fair. That in itself was a little humiliating, but Cassidy got his revenge when they went running. He could tell he was still in terrific shape despite running hurt all those weeks.

He and Randleman were playing one-on-one at the public courts on Singer Island when Trapper Nelson's Jeep pulled up. Trapper sat on a courtside bench, watching them while drinking a huge Icee from the Dairy Queen.

"Hey, Trap, come on and play some. We'll get somebody else and go two-on-two," Cassidy said.

"No thanks, I'll keep what little dignity I still have," said Trapper, toasting them with his drink.

Randleman was taking the ball out.

"Okay, ten–nine me, win by two. You ready?" He checked the ball to Cassidy, who tapped it back.

Randleman drove powerfully down the left side of the lane, but Cassidy managed to get ahead of him and take a good thumping before stopping the big forward. Randleman immediately pivoted away from Cassidy and began backing him into the key.

"Three dribbles!" called Cassidy, jogging toward the backcourt and calling for the ball. That was the rule. To keep Randleman from posting up on every play, he was allowed only two dribbles with his back to the basket. With a sour look on his face, he flipped the ball to Cassidy and assumed a defensive position. Cassidy took a false step to his right and when Randleman responded he went straight up into a reasonable imitation of a jump shot. It hit the back of the rim and rattled in.

"Tie ball game!" he said.

Randleman was perturbed, but this time when he drove and turned his back to the rim, he was so distracted counting his dribbles that Cassidy slipped around him and snaked the ball away. He quickly returned the ball back to the top of the key, then turned before Randleman could get organized and shot the same jump shot from the foul line. Again it went in.

"My ad," he said.

Randleman tried a jump shot of his own, but it was way off, slamming against the backboard and coming right to Cassidy, who had the bigger boy boxed out.

Cassidy took it out, turned, saw that Randleman was right on top of him, gave a little pause that brought Randleman up on his toes to stop the jump shot, then blew by him in a flash and put up the easy layup.

"The crowd goes wild!" Cassidy raised his arms in triumph. Trapper was clapping. Even Randleman was grinning. This happened once in a blue moon, the skinny kid prevailing like that with a little luck. He was entitled to his fun.

Randleman had to take off, so he secured the ball in a net bag on his rear luggage rack and pedaled off toward the mainland. Cassidy sat next to Trapper Nelson, still breathing hard, shiny with sweat.

"Pretty impressive, boy-o," said Trapper. "Teaching some tricks to the big boy."

"Nah, he usually kills me," said Cassidy.

"Still, that was pretty good shooting from where I sit."

"I've been back practicing most afternoons. Since . . . well, since I don't have . . ."

"I know. I've been thinking about that. I probably shouldn't have stuck my big nose into the middle of it."

"No, Trap, don't say that. It was worth a try. You were right about everything. I got completely over those pains in just a few days. I even thought about going to talk to Bickerstaff about it, but . . ."

"Why don't you? Might be worth a try. Heck, he might even admit he made a mistake."

"I don't think so. I saw him in the hallway one day and he just looked at me and shook his head," Cassidy said.

"Sorry to hear that."

"Yeah . . ."

"So, want to hear my plan?"

"Plan?" said Cassidy.

Trapper pulled a sheath of notebook papers from his back pocket. It was his notes from talking to Archie San Romani. He smoothed them out on his knee, where Cassidy stared at the strange notations:

1 m warm-up

10 x 100 striders

1 x 110 goal pace

1 x 220

1 x 330

1 x 440

1 x 880

jog 440

repeat

warm-down 880 jog

"What's all this?" Cassidy tapped the paper.

"It's called a ladder. He gave me some others called 'stepladders.' Archie said it's a good way to do intervals without getting hurt. You sort of ease into them. It builds slowly, and then either backs down or repeats. He swears by them."

"Yeah, but, Trap, I'm not on the track team anymore," Cassidy said. Just saying it made him sad.

"I know that, Youngblood. That's what the plan is about. 'You have to have a plan, even if it's wrong.' Isn't that what you say?" He cracked up.

Cassidy hadn't heard Trapper's laugh in a while. It startled him.

The county track meet was held three weeks later on a balmy Friday evening at Twin Lakes High School in West Palm Beach. Cassidy sat in the stands with Stiggs, Randleman, and Trapper Nelson, watching the officials setting up the high hurdles for the first event.

"Gotta go warm up," said Stiggs. He was a co-favorite in the high jump.

"Go get 'em, Stiggs!" said Cassidy.

"Yeah, you too, man. Give 'em hell out there." And Stiggs was gone. Cassidy looked at Trapper Nelson.

"Are you sure they're having this?" he asked.

"Positive. What do you think we've been doing all this for? Now, right before they run the high hurdles off, I want you to start warming up. Archie said it's almost impossible to warm up too hard for a distance event, so don't leave anything out. How do you feel?"

"Fine, I told you. Have you seen Bickerstaff?"

"No, but don't worry about him. He doesn't have anything to do with this."

"Okay."

Sure enough, just as Cassidy was starting to jog around the outside of the track before the first heat of the hurdles, the announcer came on the PA system:

"Ladies and gentlemen, welcome again to the Tri-County Junior High School track meet, featuring the best track athletes from every school in the three-county area. We're also pleased tonight to welcome athletes in several open events, including the 100-yard dash, the 180-yard low hurdles, the pole vault, and the 880-yard run. These athletes will compete immediately after each regular championship event. These are athletes who are out of school or otherwise ineligible to compete officially, but they're here tonight to do their absolute best. So let's hear a big hand for all of our all-comers athletes tonight!"

Cassidy heard a few whistles and catcalls. No one cared a fig about a handful of rejects and losers out for a few moments of secondhand glory. He left the track and jogged a full mile around the outside of the stadium, keeping an eye out for Coach Bickerstaff, whom he really didn't want to run into.

He took off his dowdy gray cotton sweat suit after the first mile, feeling that he was more than warmed up already. He could hear them lining up the sprinters for the hundred-yard dash inside the stadium as he started the first of the many striders he had agreed to do.

It was a strange feeling, warming up all alone out here in the dark, no teammates around, no lights or crowd to distract him. Upon reflection, he realized that he preferred being by himself. *I've done most of the running alone,* he thought, *so why not get ready to race alone?*

He was shiny with sweat as he put his sweat suit back on and climbed up in the stands to sit with Trapper.

"What did I miss?"

"Chip Newspickle ran away with the one hundred. Ten eight, I think. Stiggs cleared the first two heights. I think they're up to 4-10 now, don't quote me," said Trapper.

"How long until the 880?"

Trapper looked at his mimeographed program. "Right after the sprint medley, which is coming up. Don't sit here too long and get stiff. Go down to the infield and keep jogging while they run off the regular heat of the 880."

"But Bickerstaff is . . ."

"I told you, he has nothing to do with this. You are officially entered as an open athlete in the all-comers 880 event. You are not in his jurisdiction."

"Okay, if you say so."

Cassidy couldn't help the way his heart was pounding as Demski jumped out to the lead in the 880, just a step ahead and inside of Mizner, who looked even fitter today than he did the last time.

"All right, ED!" yelled Cassidy as they swept by him on the far straightaway. The other five runners were already hopelessly strung out.

Cassidy was startled to look up and see Coach Bickerstaff, clipboard in hand, Red Sox baseball cap on his orange crew cut, staring straight at him. Cassidy thought he detected a scowl from the coach as he went back to writing Demski's splits on his clipboard.

Just before the starting post at the end of the first lap, Mizner jumped Demski and was leading as they went into the final lap. The gun went off and Cassidy jumped as he usually did. Mizner expanded his lead all the way around the first turn and had seven yards on Demski by the time they got to Cassidy on the back straight.

"Hang in there with him, Ed," called Cassidy. He thought he got just a split second of eye contact from Ed, who looked amazingly calm going into the last 220.

Ed caught back up before going into the last curve, and Mizner seemed to be struggling. Demski didn't try to pass. He didn't even come up to Mizner's shoulder. He ran directly behind him in the first lane, biding his time. When they came out of the turn, Demski went into overdrive and just ran away from the taller runner. Cassidy had forgotten about his own race and was jumping up and down in excitement. He looked up in the stands to Trapper Nelson and saw him looking back, sternly shaking his head. Cassidy got a grip. It wasn't good to lose focus like that. Cassidy jogged around on the infield, waiting for the official results.

"Ladies and gentlemen," said the announcer. "We have the finish of the 880 finals: Fifth, from Glenridge, Parsley in 2:15.6; fourth, from Riviera Beach, Pearlman in 2:14 flat; third, from Palm Beach Gardens, Dulin in 2:13.8; second, from Pompano Beach, Jerome Mizner in 2:08.2; and the winner, from Glenridge Junior High School, Ed Demski in a new county record, 2:07 flat!"

Cassidy was so proud of Ed he was almost in tears. Grinning like a hyena, Ed jogged over to where Cassidy was stripping off his gray sweat bottoms.

"Way to go, Ed! Great race. Great kick. Just plain all-around great!" Cassidy was hopping on one foot, trying to get the bulky sweats off.

"H-h-hey, go get 'em," said Ed, still grinning through the copious sweat on his face. They slapped hands. Bickerstaff, Cassidy noticed, was scowling at them.

"O-k-k-kay. Time to focus," said Ed, taking Cassidy's sweats from him. "Hey, you want to borrow my spikes?"

Cassidy didn't have real track shoes. He was wearing black Converse track flats that Trapper had found in an equipment room at the base gym.

"You mean it?"

Ed sat down immediately and started peeling off the white kangaroo-skin Adidas, identical to the ones Chip Newspickle wore. They fit perfectly.

Cassidy jogged up to the starting line, feeling like his legs were filled with helium. The spikes weighed nothing at all.

"Last call for the all-comers 880," said the announcer.

Cassidy could see Coach Bickerstaff on the infield arguing with one of the officials. The official kept shaking his head and pointing to his clipboard. Bickerstaff finally slammed his own clipboard against his thigh and stalked off.

Cassidy walked onto the track. There were only two other runners.

"In the open division, in lane one, from Glenridge Junior High, but running unattached, is Quenton Cassidy . . ."

There was polite applause, but Cassidy mostly heard Trapper's booming cheer.

"In lane two, formerly of Hialeah but running unattached, is Dan McKillip . . ."

More polite applause. He looked too muscular for a distance runner but seemed entirely at ease, wearing a white singlet with green piping. Cassidy was embarrassed by his own Kissam Building Supply T-shirt, which he had almost outgrown.

"And finally, in lane three, formerly of Dunedin, a former runner-up in the Pinellis County high school mile run, running unattached tonight, is Del Ramers!"

He must have brought his own fan club, because Ramers got considerably more response from the crowd than the other two had. His uniform was maroon with gold piping. Cassidy was alarmed to see the uniform was from Florida State. Was this guy a *college* runner?

What have I gotten myself into? Cassidy thought. Then he noticed that Ramers, although fit looking, seemed to have a little bit of extra padding around the waist, like maybe he was just coming back from an extended injury break.

Cassidy looked up in the stands, and Trapper Nelson was giving him the clenched-fist sign. Cassidy nodded.

When the gun went off, he couldn't believe how fast the other two took off. It was as if he were still standing at the starting line. They had ten yards on him going into the first turn, the powerful McKillip leading, with Ramers on his outside shoulder. *It doesn't make any difference how big that guy is*, Cassidy thought, *he can flat out* run.

Cassidy did his best to relax and loosen his stride, and he seemed to be matching the other two through the turn and starting down the back straight. There was a coach at the halfway post reading off split times, and as the pair went by up ahead Cassidy heard: "Twenty-*eight*, twenty-*nine* . . ."

They were running under a two-minute pace! Cassidy went by in thirty-one seconds, feeling like a fool in his old T-shirt and his borrowed shoes. Still, this was faster than he had ever run in a race and he had to admit he felt pretty good. *Of course I do,* he thought. *It never felt bad until the first lap was over.* Trapper had put him through two solid weeks of those horrendous ladder and stepladder intervals. Trapper had written down all his times and had even called Archie San Romani again to get last-second advice.

Cassidy ran as evenly as he could all through the turn, and when they got back to the starting post again, he was only five yards behind. McKillip was still leading as the timer began reading: "Sixty-*two*, sixty-*three*, sixty-*four* . . ." And that's where he was, two seconds back.

Now Ramers was fighting his way around McKillip going into the first turn. Though they had clearly slowed down after their blazing first 220, they were both full of fight. Cassidy found himself watching the duel up ahead when the *crack!* of the gun—going off late for some reason—brought him back to reality and he realized that he had less than a lap to run in this race. And he realized something else: *he still felt okay*. There was no telling how good his conditioning really had been all that time he was injured, and now that he had healed and been put through some paces designed by an Olympic miler, Cassidy realized, for the first time in his life: *I am a real runner*.

He slowly worked his way back to within striking distance of the other two. *Tell him not to make moves too quickly in a race*, San Romani had counseled Trapper. *It wastes energy*.

When they reached the halfway post, Cassidy was drafting directly behind them. McKillip had retaken the lead but Ramers was right on his shoulder. Just before they reached the post, Cassidy saw Ramers look back, surprised to see Cassidy, who was just striding along, studying the heels of the other two.

"One thirty-*four*, one thirty-*five*," and that was it, they were all past the post. The crowd was getting into it now, and Cassidy could hear Demski's voice screaming—without a stutter!—as he ran across the infield toward him. Now Cassidy started really paying attention to the older runners. The big guy, McKillip, was clearly beginning to struggle. Ramers was running smoothly, but Cassidy saw him looking back nervously once more. Finally, just as they came out of the final curve, Ramers made his move and went by the struggling McKillip, who began to tie up and slide to the outside of the first lane.

Cassidy had been getting ready to try to pass him and go after Ramers, but now the lane was open directly in front of him. Not only that, Ramers hadn't bothered to move back to the inside lane, so the path was open all the way to the finish line.

When he finally launched into an all-out kick, Cassidy was amazed at how much he had left. He went by the slowing McKillip in an instant, and—as the crowd shrieked in his ears—pulled up on the inside of Ramers without the other runner even knowing he was there. Ramers took one more look over his outside shoulder as Cassidy made a final lunge to get past him. He broke the yarn with his chest and was grateful when someone caught him and prevented him from going right into the asphalt.

He grabbed his knees, gasping, dizzy but completely elated. He had never felt so wonderful in his life. When he straightened up, Ramers was standing beside him, arm around him, panting.

"Who. Are. You?" Ramers gasped.

"H-h-h-his name's Cassidy!" said Demski, taking his other arm, "and he just ran 2:03.7 for the h-h-half-mile."

"Ed," Cassidy said, "these shoes. Haven't. Lost. Tonight!"

CHAPTER 22

FIRST CUT

Cassidy was surprised when Coach Bickerstaff came up to him in the hallway the next day and shook his hand.

"Congratulations, Quenton, that was a fine effort. Because your race was unofficial, Demski will still have the county record, but you might want to know that I am submitting both Ed's 2:07 and your 2:03.7 to the athletic director as new school records. I have no doubt they will both be approved, though yours, of course, will be the one that counts from now on," he said. "I hope you will consider coming out for track again next year."

But Cassidy—though he didn't say anything to Bickerstaff—was already starting to think about basketball again. It was great to win races, but he had finally realized how little everyone cared about track. Basketball was different; the whole school was crazy about it.

Over the last weeks of school, Bickerstaff remained cordial to him, despite a decided coolness. On the other hand, Cassidy really liked Coach Burke, the basketball coach.

All that summer Stiggs and Randleman seemed to gain height daily. They were both pushing six feet by the start of their ninth school year. Even Cassidy was no longer such a runt.

"Five feet nine and a half inches!" pronounced his father, measuring the highest mark on the kitchen doorjamb, while his mother made the appropriate oohs and ahhs. He was now taller than his mom.

He still couldn't hold a candle to his two friends on the basketball court, but every now and then when the giants let their guard down, he struck a meager blow for the little people of the world.

He ran some on the beach, occasionally with Trapper, and he sometimes did one of San Romani's workouts just to stay in shape, but basketball became his thing again, and he played nearly every day throughout the summer.

When school started, his whole world—like that of around fifty boys in the school—was focused on making the first cut.

Even if you never made a team in your life, if you made the first cut you would *be* somebody. You would carry a mark of distinction that would forever set you apart from the teeming throngs of beautiful dreamers. "There goes Cassidy," they would say. "Last year he made the first cut."

At the bigger schools in the county, there might be up to a hundred wannabes "coming out." For many of them it would be an act of blatant hubris, offering themselves up for certain ridicule. Everything would be decided by a single afternoon's ad hoc scrimmage, the coaches watching and making notations on their ever-present clipboards. On this first go-round, one scrimmage was all they needed to eliminate the obvious chaff. That was all the first cut did. It said to about thirty boys: you're not so awful that we can eliminate you at a glance.

The next morning they'd post The List outside the gym and a knot of boys would form around it. A few confident ones would glance at it quickly before trundling off to class. A few shamefaced ones would break out of the knot and hurry off, hoping no one saw their brimming eyes.

The coaches didn't enjoy crushing young dreams, but they needed to get an uncluttered look at the handful that might amount to something. Among them would be the sure things, the boys who had previously made the team, along with some others who had come close and would thus be remembered. In a practical sense, the whole process really boiled down to which three or four additional boys would be selected from among the throngs of earnest strivers.

To anyone who hoped to become an athlete, making the first cut was a requisite milestone. Making the second cut was almost as good as making the team, at least as far as your reputation went. You would have been a boy or two from being an anointed one.

Coach Burke had a completely neutral look on his face as he made his way through the small throng of boys to the bulletin board. He avoided all eye contact as he thumb-tacked the single page to the board and closed and locked the glass door before making his way back out, still avoiding all eye contact.

Cassidy was right up front and found himself crushed against the glass. He leaned back away from the case so he could clearly read the notice:

Coach Blythe and I want to thank all the boys who came out for basketball this year. We are sorry that we are able to select only 12 players from this group, as there are many talented athletes among those we saw. The following 25 players please report to the gym tomorrow afternoon at 4:00 p.m., dressed out and ready to scrimmage:

Joe Walton
Ralph Erickson
Phil Jameson
Kent Stewart
Samuel Stiggs
Erich Randleman
Quenton Cassidy . . .

Cassidy could read no farther. He stumbled out of the crowd and wandered aimlessly down the hall, vaguely aware that Stiggs and Randleman had come running by on their way to class, pounding him on the back and hooting. A few other guys gave him friendly slaps, too. Cassidy, walking along in a kind of trance, didn't speak.

It was several minutes before he realized he had walked to the end of the corridor in Building A, and his homeroom was all the way at the other end of Building B.

Shaking his welling eyes clear at last, he chuckled and turned and hurried back in the opposite direction. It almost seemed like a miracle, or something he had just imagined, but there it was in black and white—others had seen it too: Quenton Cassidy had made the first cut!

Nothing so wonderful could last, of course.

The second-cut list did not include the name Cassidy. Stiggs and Randleman were on it, but not him. Again that winter they would be among the favored few whom everyone else, Cassidy included, would get to watch from the bleachers.

He wasn't so deluded as to allow this turn of events to get him down. He'd known his chances were slim. Besides, he couldn't help feel that things were turning around for him. He was no longer this skinny little nerd with delusions of grandeur, no longer just Stiggs and Randleman's mascot. He was distinctly aware that people seemed to know who he was in the hallways and people he didn't know said hi. It had never occurred to him how nice that would be.

At long last it began to dawn on him that he might actually *be* somebody. He was, after all, the school record holder in the half-mile! And he had made the first cut!

CHAPTER 23

RON LEFARO

It was an unusually cool, bright Saturday morning, and Cassidy was biking back across the Blue Heron Bridge when he heard the distinctive bleat from Trapper Nelson's beleaguered Jeep. He hadn't seen him in more than a month. As soon as they were off the bridge, he pulled over and Trapper idled up beside him and turned off the ignition. The engine dieseled for a few seconds before finally coughing to a halt.

"Whatcha doin'?" said Trapper.

He had to talk over the traffic noise. He was dressed in his usual quasi-military garb: army fatigue cutoffs, with half-laced-up combat boots and no socks.

"Shooting hoops over by the Colonnades," said Cassidy. "I was going to go in the inlet to look for gray grouper, but it seemed too cold and I just didn't get around to it." He gestured to the Hawaiian spear and diving gear bungeed along his top tube.

Trapper nodded. "Should be about time for them to come in," he said, scratching his chin. "Haven't seen any yet. Lots of snook around the dock pilings, though. Got three nice ones the other day."

Cassidy nodded.

"What's going on with basketball?" asked Trapper.

Cassidy looked down. "Well, I made the first cut, but that was it. I haven't decided if I should go out next year or not."

"What gives? I thought this was going to be your bag now."

"I don't know. I've tried every year since fifth grade. It's getting to be a kind of joke."

Trapper looked at him as if trying to decide something. Cassidy finally got embarrassed and looked away.

"Hey, where are you headed right now?" asked Trapper.

"Just home. Stiggs and Randleman are gonna come over to mess around."

"Those two scalawags can wait. Throw your bike in the back and come for a ride. Somebody I want you to meet. I'll drop you off at home afterward, save you a few miles of pedaling."

Cassidy liked riding with Trapper, who was constantly tapping his horn, responding to beeps and waves as they went through town. He regaled Cassidy with fishing and trapping stories, as well as anecdotes about recent visitors, some quite famous, who had come by his camp on the Loxahatchee. Cassidy really wanted to ask about the strange events that led to his brother going to prison, but he couldn't think of a way to broach the subject. It reminded him of something else.

"What's going on with your friends from the dock?" he asked finally.

"Who?"

"Those two guys, Lucky what's his name and that guy Bobby. And their fishing client, that judge guy."

"Listen, those are no friends of mine. His name is Holzapfel. He may think I'm a fan of theirs, and that's just what I want them to think, but believe me, I don't have anything to do with those guys and you shouldn't either."

"How about the judge? He's all right, isn't he? He looked okay."

"Between you and me—and I mean it, no talking out of school— Peel's in trouble, too. He's mixed up with betting and 'shine and all kinds of stuff, just like you'd expect for a friend of Lucky's. Judge Chillingworth's getting ready to lower the boom on him."

"I thought *Peel* was a judge."

"Just a city judge. Judge Chillingworth's the head of the whole circuit. They used to be friends, but he's about fed up with Joe right about now. This is between you and me now, you understand?"

"Yes, sir."

Trapper was rattling on about how he taught the great Babe Ruth how to use a bait-casting rod. He made a right-hand turn off A1A and headed out the long, straight road that went west to Camp Murphy.

"We going to the base?" Cassidy asked.

"Yep."

"How do you get in if you're not military?"

"Got a sticker. I was stationed here during the war. When they found out what I did in real life they made me an MP and a critter-getter. Gators in the ponds, snakes in the toilets, ducks on the runway, I was the guy they called. Believe me, wild and woolly as it was back then, I got called a lot. I still help them out now and again. They even pay me! Can you imagine that? I take home a critter I can sell, plus I get a U.S. government check in the mail. I guess that makes me a government contractor!" His laugh boomed in the trees.

Sure enough, at the guard station the MP didn't even get up from his chair, just leaned out the door and waved them through. Trapper ignored the signal and pulled over.

"Hey, Frank, is Lieutenant Lefaro at the gym this morning?" asked Trapper.

"Yeah, he came through about a hour ago. I guess that's where he was going. He was dressed in sweats anyway."

The exhaust fans were beating away up in the rafters and the gym was empty save for two young captains playing badminton and one short, stocky, dark-haired guy shooting set shots from the top of the key. He looked to be of Mediterranean extraction. Cassidy recognized him as one of the guys he always saw playing in the really good afternoon pickup games. Games he was never invited to join.

He came over with a head-wagging, jaunty stride, a big smile on his face. The leather ball was tucked casually on his hip. Despite the heat, he wore white cotton sweat bottoms, a black singlet, and some kind of gold chain around his neck with a small gold medallion. Cassidy thought he was the most confident-acting person he had ever met.

"Hey, Trap," the man said. "This the kid?"

"This is him. First Lieutenant Ronald Lefaro, meet freshman Quenton Cassidy."

Lefaro stuck his hand out and when Cassidy took it, he was surprised how small and soft—almost dainty—it was.

"You wouldn't know it to look at him, but Lieutenant Lefaro is arguably the best one-on-one basketball player on this base, now that Al Smith has mustered out," Trapper said. "Ron started all three years at Colby, and in his senior year, this officer and gentleman was an all-American."

"*Little* all-American," Lefaro corrected.

"Still," said Trapper.

Cassidy's eyes were as big as sand dollars.

"Okay, kid," said Lefaro, "I've seen you a few times in pickup games with your buddies. You handle the ball good and you've got a decent shot. You leaving us, Trap?"

"Got to run some errands on base. Quenton, I'll be back to pick you up in one hour. Pay attention to this man. It could change your life."

Lefaro was already walking out onto the court, motioning to Cassidy to follow. The other officers had finished their badminton game, so the gymnasium was quiet except for the big exhaust fans beating away at the warm air.

"Okay, here's the first thing you need to work on. And keep in mind, this won't be as much fun as playing pickup games with your friends. This is more like real work. But if you want to get better, this is what you need to do."

Lefaro stood on the foul line, facing away from the basket. He motioned for Cassidy to go to the top of the key. He bounced the ball to him.

"Okay, let me show you how I would defend you," he said. "Go ahead and drive on me. Give me your best move."

Cassidy took the ball and, as he had been taught, first looked at the rim as if he might shoot. Lefaro's knees were bent slightly, but otherwise he almost looked as if he were standing around waiting for a bus.

Cassidy gave a quick jerk with his head and the ball as if he were indeed looking to shoot, but then brought the ball down and in an instant began driving to his right, thinking that he would blow by this way-too-casual older man for an easy layup.

Lefaro quickly sidestepped to his left, and before he knew it Cassidy was making contact, his progress toward the rim now subtly altered. He put his head down and drove wider to the right, trying to get around the man, but the more he veered out the more Lefaro rode him farther out. Finally, it got ridiculous and Cassidy realized that the man was not going to let him go right. In fact, he was overplaying Cassidy so much that the path straight to the basket lay wide open in front of him. All Cassidy had to do was stop his futile effort to drive to his right and just head straight for the hoop.

To accomplish this he retreated a half step, did a crossover dribble from right to left, started to dribble with his left hand, and . . .

The ball was gone. Lefaro was at the top of the key, dribbling casually, doing that little arrogant head wag, and looking at Cassidy with raised eyebrows that said: *See?*

He had simply reached down and tipped the ball away as soon as Cassidy switched to his clumsier left hand. As Cassidy continued to the rim, Lefaro had slipped behind him and scooped up the ball. Cassidy ended up dribbling air.

"Know what happened?" he asked.

"Yeah, you stole the ball," said Cassidy.

"Okay. But more basic than that?"

Cassidy shrugged.

"You can't go to your left," Lefaro said. "Neither can most of your friends—well, except for the lefty. And he can't go to his right. If a guy can't go one way or the other, he's easy to guard. You give him the way he doesn't want to go, and overplay him the way he wants to go. You take away seventy-five percent of his game before he makes the first move. Try again." Lefaro bounced the ball to Cassidy and assumed the defensive position.

Cassidy took the ball at the top of the key, did the quick shot fake, took one dribble to the right, and quickly crossed over to his left as Lefaro called, "Good!"

Lefaro stepped over to Cassidy's left to cut him off, but Cassidy now found himself with a half-step lead, which he tried to exploit by driving down the left side of the lane, dribbling with his left hand. For a thrilling split second he thought he was going to get an easy layup on this arrogant man, but Lefaro's incredibly quick feet had brought him back up against Cassidy, forcing him once again to the outside. Every dribble down the key he took, Cassidy was being driven farther from the basket.

When he was even with the rim, not knowing what else to do, Cassidy picked up his dribble and began trying to find a way to take his free step around Lefaro. It was impossible. Lefaro was right on top of him, and whenever Cassidy gave him any look at the ball at all, his hands were flashing out, slapping at it, clipping the ball, twice nearly dislodging it altogether.

Finally, out of desperation, Cassidy turned his back to the rim, took one step away, and shot a fairly decent hook shot with his right hand. Lefaro didn't block it, but he was in Cassidy's face the whole way, and Cassidy was almost proud that the ball actually caught the front of the rim before bouncing away. It wasn't really that close, but it wasn't an embarrassing attempt, either.

"Okay," said Lefaro, who was at least breathing harder now. "You had a good fake and a good first step. Then what happened?"

"You were on me."

"Right, but what happened?"

"I took a hook."

"You took a *desperation* hook," said Lefaro.

Cassidy said nothing but had to admit it was true.

"You went left because I gave you left. That's all well and good. But then when push came to shove, you didn't have anything to finish with. I've seen your pull-up jumper on the right. I've seen your driving hook on the right. What do you have on the left?"

Cassidy shook his head.

"Basketball, like most sports, is a game of action and reaction. If I overplay you to your right, knowing that's where you want to go, I'm trying to make you pay for your weakness. So what do you do in response?"

"Go left?"

"Not just go left, but go left *successfully*. Make me pay for overplaying you. The only way to do that is to learn how to score going left, just like you do going right. Learn to dribble better with your left hand, get yourself a reliable left-handed layup, a left-handed hook that you're not afraid to shoot in a game. Practice other tricks, your crossover move, or that inside-out hook you tried, but practice them until they're natural moves that you actually *like* to do, not ones you use when you have to."

Lefaro noticed that Cassidy looked a little glum.

"Sorry, kid, none of this will be much fun until you do it in practice and then start seeing it work in games."

"I don't mind practicing," said Cassidy.

"I know that. I've seen you. That's why I'm here right now. But you've spent a long time practicing the things you do best. It's always more fun to work on strengths rather than weaknesses. The problem is that a smart opponent will make you pay for it. The way you beat him is to not have any weaknesses."

Cassidy was in a kind of shock. The simple truth of what Lefaro was saying stopped him completely. He had thought he was playing the game of basketball all this time. What he was really playing was half a game of basketball.

"All right, let me show you one more thing," said Lefaro, heading back to the top of the key. "You guard me now."

He checked the ball to Cassidy, who tapped it back. Cassidy assumed a defensive stance a half step to Lefaro's right, but staying ready to adjust, figuring Lefaro would have some good moves to his left.

Lefaro took the ball, looked at the rim, brought the ball up in shooting position . . .

And shot the ball! It cut the net cleanly and with enough backspin that it bounced right back to them.

"All right," said Lefaro. "Don't forget: that's the third option. I can go left, I can go right, or I can shoot. Those are your three options in one-on-one. Let's try again."

Cassidy checked the ball back to him and again assumed a slight overplay position to Lefaro's right.

Lefaro brought the ball up, faked the shot, pulled the ball back down, and started to his left. Cassidy did a quick sidestep to his right to cut off the drive as Lefaro straightened up and shot the ball again, this time catching the back of the rim and deflecting straight down through the net.

Jeez, thought Cassidy, *I'm getting drilled here.*

"Once more," said Lefaro, checking the ball to Cassidy again.

This time Cassidy was primed. If Lefaro tried the little one-hander again he'd be eating some leather. Cassidy tapped the ball back and assumed a defensive position a half step closer to him. Lefaro took the ball, did a little halfhearted fake to his right, then started to bring the ball up into shooting position. Cassidy shifted his weight to his toes and got ready to spring. When Lefaro went into the first motions of his shot, Cassidy began to elevate, the toes of his Converse low-cuts now barely on the floor.

In the blink of an eye Lefaro was gone, quick-stepping around him and casually laying the ball up softly against the glass backboard. He hadn't gotten Cassidy quite into the air, but he had rendered him nearly weightless, and therefore helpless, before bringing the ball down and zipping by him.

Cassidy sighed and hung his head. He was just plain beaten. As his father would have said, no two ways about it.

"I don't get it," he said. "What am I doing wrong?"

"Nothing really," said Lefaro, walking back with the ball tucked on his hip, head wagging outrageously. "I've shown you three ways I can beat you, and you know you can't discount any of them. You have to be ready to counter all three, and it's just more than you can handle right now. That's the position you want to put *your* opponents in."

"But how can I stop you?"

"You can't."

"But . . ."

"You'll get bigger and quicker and better. I'll get older and slower. Time will even things out, believe me. What you can do right now is get smarter. And better. You do that by practicing what you need to practice. By working relentlessly on what I showed you today."

Out of the corner of his eye, Cassidy saw Trapper just coming in the back door. He looked back to Lefaro. "When can we get together again?" Cassidy said.

"Don't worry about that," said Lefaro.

Cassidy lost the grin. "But what . . ."

"I'm not taking you to raise. I'm just pointing you in the right direction. This is all stuff you're going to have to work on yourself. I'm talking hours and hours of practice, every day if you can. For weeks and weeks, months and months. Sorry, but that's the hard truth. Most guys won't do it. They'd rather just come out and play three-on-three, couple games of horse, have a few laughs with their buddies, and go shoot pool at the service club. You notice how many people are out here this morning, working on their weak sides?"

"Yeah," said Cassidy. "It's empty a lot when I'm practicing."

"I know," said Lefaro. "I've seen you. Like I say, it's why I'm here. That, and that big galoot over there."

Trapper was jingling the keys to his Jeep as he walked to the edge of the floor.

"Lieutenant Lefaro," said Cassidy, "thank you, sir . . ."

"Call me Ron. And don't worry about it. Just keep working and I'll see you around the campus."

"Yes, sir."

"We'll play some horse or something. Just no one-on-one. Not for a while, anyway."

"Lord, no." Cassidy laughed.

"Hey, you guys," Trapper said, "what's so funny?"

"This kid has a helluva move to his right," said Lefaro.

CHAPTER 24

HOUSE, SATCH, AND DEE-TROIT

In World War II, the cavernous building that became the gym where Cassidy played had held a massive sand table where they planned the invasion of Normandy. If some bright OSS cartographer had had the foresight to glue on some tough little HO-scale hedgerows, it might have helped the Allies win the war quicker.

A corporal named Lafollette, whose maternal grandmother lived in Sainte-Mère-Église, tried to tell his superiors about the "gnarly-ass hedges" he knew only too well (he had visited her in the summers and spoke French fluently). But they had bade him shut up and ordered him back to gluing down miniature trees and church steeples. They thought the big problem was going to be finding recognizable landmarks, not a bunch of bushes big enough to stop tanks.

Thus the allies found themselves "bogged down in the hedgerows," and a few thousand more American boys would now remain forever teenagers slumbering under white crosses, row on row, in the quiet fields of Brittany.

The sand table was many years gone now and the building had been turned into a gymnasium where the Air Force officers came to play badminton or take a steam, and the enlisted men and "dependents," children of servicemen, would play pickup games on the gleaming hardwood floor. This floor, with its splendid glass backboards, was Cassidy's home court.

They were soon to be sophomores in high school, and Cassidy had grown in the past year. He wasn't over six feet like Stiggs and Randleman, but he was closing in on it. And while the other two could now—with a little run-up—touch the rim, he could with great effort get to the third or fourth row of knots in the net. He was far too skinny to be very effective under the backboard like the other two, but he occasionally got his timing just right and snagged a surprising rebound that would have Stiggs staring at him in exasperation.

He had been at the gym since ten that morning. After lifting weights, he played some pickup games with a couple of airmen who weren't very good, then rode his bike over to the cafeteria for lunch. Cheeseburgers were twenty cents; for less than half a dollar you could walk out pretty much stuffed, a condition that might last an hour. In no time he was back in the gym working on left-handed layups.

Stiggs and Randleman showed up midafternoon. Randleman and Cassidy were official "dependents," but Stiggs had no military status at all. Still, he hardly even slowed down his bike at the gate. He was so familiar to the guards they just waved him through. For dependents the base was a paradise. They could swim at a lake at the officers' or NCO club, go to a movie, shop at the BX, even play a round of golf. Sometimes when they were feeling brave they would shoot pool at the service club until someone noticed they weren't old enough to be servicemen, and they were booted out. But the gym was where they lived.

The three played horse until some of the better players started straggling in.

"You gennamin like a lil' friendly game a' three-on-three?" a lanky black player asked Randleman.

"Sure, House," he said. "Shirts and skins?"

House laughed. "Don't make no difference. You all too white to mix up. Go 'head and take it out."

The black guys all went by nicknames. Cassidy had played with "House" and "Satch" plenty of times, but he didn't know the little guy they called "Dee-troit." The first two were over six feet and could both jump, but neither one could throw a ball in the ocean from more than five feet away. Dee-troit was quick as a mongoose, however, and had a deadly short jump shot. He got by Cassidy at the top of the key and nailed three in a row before the game was barely under way.

"That's okay," Stiggs said to Cassidy. "Three to zip. Let him shoot whenever he wants."

"*You* want him?" Cassidy asked. Stiggs thought about it, shook his head.

Cassidy tossed it in to Randleman coming up into the high post and then broke right around Dee-troit and flared for the basket, calling for the ball back. Randleman ignored him and backed House down into the key before wheeling into his famous hook shot, which House immediately spiked like a volleyball.

Cassidy had anticipated this and had circled out to the backcourt to watch Randleman's humiliation. It so happened that House spiked the ball right to him.

House was still doing his victory dance in the key, shaking his finger in Randleman's face and making his usual catcalls. "In yo' face, baby!" he said. "Man got *nuffin'*! Try *hook shot* on the House-man, sheee-it!"

Cassidy stood, ball on hip, giving Randleman an inquiring look he could hardly misinterpret. It said: *Are you ready to play ball now?* Randleman nodded grimly.

Cassidy leaned around Dee-troit and one-handed a bounce pass to Randleman back in the high post, and this time cut left to the basket, again leaving Dee-troit flat-footed as the man watched the ball instead of Cassidy. Stiggs saw Cassidy coming and cleared out along the baseline, taking his man with him and leaving the hoop open.

Randleman backhanded a no-look bounce pass to Cassidy, who laid it up softly with his left hand.

The play was so quick and professional looking that it almost shut House up momentarily. "Man right-handed but shoot left," he muttered, calling for the ball. Dee-troit lobbed it in to him at the top of the key. He turned to face Randleman, looking to take him to the hoop. But Dee-troit hadn't broken for the basket and instead just floated back out in the backcourt, leaving Cassidy to loiter around the top of the key, seemingly ignoring House.

House made a clumsy head fake left and started right, just as Cassidy anticipated, and when the ball hit the floor for the first dribble, Cassidy's fingertips were already there, flicking the ball up to Randleman, who pivoted and laid the ball in.

There followed a huge argument over whether the basket counted because they didn't take it "out" first, which in turn depended upon whether they were playing "possession" or "backboard." It was settled, as always, by counting the basket "this time" but agreeing that on all future changes of possession the ball would have to be taken back beyond the top of the key before it could be advanced toward the goal by the opposite team.

But some kind of threshold had been reached, and from then on the airmen took the high school kids more seriously. Still, to their shock, they lost the first game 11–8. In the second game, Dee-troit again left Cassidy twice at the top of the key, first hitting his short jumper and next time dumping off to Satch, who had enough momentum and clearance from Stiggs to cram a thunderous two-handed dunk down the pipe.

So overjoyed were the trio by this stark put-down, they seemed not to notice that they lost again, this time 11–9. When the kids won the third game 11–6, the airmen walked off to the showers, high-fiving and celebrating like they had just won an NBA division title. Cassidy, Stiggs, and Randleman stood there sweating, hands on hips, looking at each other in amazement.

"What just happened?" asked Stiggs. His socks bunching up on his ankles made his calves look even skinnier. "Unless they changed the Arabic numeral system, we won every game, didn't we?"

"All they care about is Satch jamming on Randleman. Far as they're concerned, that's better than winning," said Cassidy.

"They wouldn't be sayin' that if there was another group in the stands ready to play winners," said Randleman. "Then they'd have plenty of time to celebrate sitting on their asses."

"Aw, it was a pretty good dunk, you have to admit," said Stiggs, retrieving his sweatshirt from where it was tucked into the top of the safety pad under the basket. He and Randleman were drenched and still breathing hard.

"You guys want to stay and do some drills?" said Cassidy. He was standing on the foul line, shirt off, breathing lightly, a sheen of perspiration on his skinny brown chest.

Stiggs and Randleman, as usual, looked at him like he had three heads.

The tall windows on either side of the court were darkened now as Cassidy drove the full length down the floor at his best under-control speed, flicking the ball out in front of him, dribbling with his head up and eyes downcourt scanning for approaching defenders or streaking allies, though the gym was empty.

The slapping of taut leather on varnished oak echoed in the far rafters of the huge place. The sweat-blackened leather ball smelled of pennies and the gym smelled of varnish and piney sawdust.

He reached the top of the key dribbling with his right hand, gave a quick glance at the rim, and brought his left hand up as if to pull up for a shot. Instead, he took a quick stutter-step, crossed over his dribble, and drove down the left side of the key, launching himself off his left foot and going up with his right hand to flick an improbable-looking reverse layup up toward the painted white square on the glass. On the way up, the ball appeared to have been overshot, landing too far inside the square and destined to cross the rim and tick off the right side and out, but there was just a hint of backspin on it, and when it kissed off the glass, its arc changed subtly. Instead of going all the way across the rim, the ball pitched slightly upward, stopped in its arc altogether, hung for a moment, and dropped gently through the net.

Breathing hard and sweating profusely, he landed and turned a hundred and eighty degrees so that his back slammed into the protective wall pad with a *whack*. He used the rebound effect to reverse direction, catching the ball as it dropped from the net and flicking it back down the court toward the other end, where he started the process all over again.

Though it was decidedly cool in the gym now, he was glistening under the lights, and sweat flew from his fingertips on every dribble.

He had already done his jump shots from around the top of the key, using a portable volleyball judge's tall stand as a substitute defender, driving toward it as if coming off a screen, pulling up into his jump shot directly in front of the wooden stand, arching backward into a slight fadeaway, and launching the ball toward the rim twenty feet away. He took care that the ball always left his fingertips with just a hint of reverse English, and that his hand flopped over into the perfect swan's neck follow-through. He had made eighty-eight out of one hundred.

Then there were the hooks, fifty on each side, using the left hand on the left side, right hand on the right side. Next there were the baseline jumpers and then the free throws.

Now he was at the end of the routine, the full-court layup drill, as hard as he could go, at least twenty of them, and some nights as many as forty. He never walked off the court without being utterly exhausted. He had made up this routine himself and he had intentionally made it so physically punishing that he was sure no one he knew would want to do it regularly, if at all. Stiggs and Randleman had tried it one night and had walked off the court halfway through, laughing at him.

His rasping breath and the sound of slapping leather were the only sounds echoing in the rafters as he drove himself down the court on the last one. He had pushed himself so hard he felt his thighs catching occasionally as if wanting to spasm, but he didn't ease up. He went the length of the court, this time stutter-stepping and veering to the right, laying the ball up perfectly at the top of his jump, trying without success to nick the bottom of the backboard with his fingertips on the way down.

This time when he slammed into the end pad, he did not bounce off. Leaning back against his own indentation in the damp canvas, he reached down and grabbed his knees and squeezed his stinging eyes shut against the sweat pouring down his face, desperately gasping as much air as he could get into his lungs.

He tried to take a few steps toward the locker room, but his vision went all hazy and he had to stop. He grabbed his knees again and gave himself a few more minutes of desperate gasping before stumbling off to the showers.

The gym manager, a corporal named Don Spacht, was making his closing rounds. His dog tags jangled against his sleeveless GI olive-drab undershirt as he picked up the ball where it had rolled up against the bleachers. He looked at Cassidy with a sympathetic smile.

"You are either going to kill yourself or you're going to be all-state, Cassidy," he said.

Cassidy gave him a tired little wave as he stumbled toward the locker room. He would have a long bike ride across a spooky old World War II airfield to get home, and his dinner would be in the oven, barely warm but still waiting for him. Some nights he could barely eat it.

Outside in the chilly night air as he mounted his beat-up ten-speed, Cassidy felt his quivering thighs protesting. They did not want to go back to work so soon. He knew from experience that they would be all right in a few minutes.

In the middle of his ride across the dark, abandoned airfield, he would look up at the clear panoply of winking stars and feel like the last person on the planet. It was a biting kind of loneliness that had surprised and almost frightened him as the days became shorter. Now it was familiar, almost comforting.

And too, before leaving the gym that night he realized that he had finally become comfortable with the most forlorn sound in athletics: a solitary dripping showerhead in the far corner of a deserted locker room late at night. It was, he realized finally, the answer to the question: *What does excellence sound like?*

He was fifteen years old, he could touch the third row of knots on the net, and though he had not yet made a single basketball team he had tried out for, he was never the last one picked anymore.

CHAPTER 25

THE BLEACHERS

It was not even midmorning, but it was already stifling as the second-period gym class waited in the bleachers for Coach Stoddard to waddle out in his squeaky ripple-soled coaching shoes to take role. It was their first day of high school and as hot as any day in the summer had been, but even the heat couldn't suppress the ambient excitement.

They were not "dressed out" today. This class would merely be a somnambulant orientation session ("You will be required to bring with you on Monday of every week the following: one pair of clean cotton gym shorts, red in color; one clean jock strap of the appropriate size . . .").

Cassidy sat next to a faintly unpleasant kid he had known since second grade, Gary Castleton, a redheaded, fox-faced creature who perpetually looked as if he had just smelled something distasteful.

"Are you going out for basketball?" Gary asked.

Cassidy, trying not to show too much enthusiasm, said that he was.

"You won't make it," Gary sneered dismissively.

Cassidy was surprised at his own visceral reaction to this pronouncement. The fine hairs on the back of his neck stood on end. His scalp actually tingled at this casual prediction of failure.

Somehow he knew it wasn't personal. As far as he knew, Gary Castleton had never even seen Cassidy so much as pick up a basketball.

His prediction of unavoidable failure was generic in nature. Cassidy wouldn't make the team because nobody Gary Castleton knew would make it. Those twelve spots were reserved for a handful of extraordinary beings, and Gary Castleton wanted Cassidy to understand that he was anything but extraordinary, just like Gary himself.

His was the voice of the real world, issuing a stinging denunciation of a foolish dreamer.

The all-purpose negativity of people like Gary was loathsome to Cassidy, and he realized later that the reason he resented them was that, statistically speaking, such people were usually right. And if Gary was right about him, it meant that Cassidy was a fatuous idiot, throwing away his life in empty, smelly gymnasiums, running laps around hardscrabble tracks, busting his gut in claustrophobic weight rooms, choking down ridiculous mail-order protein pills. And for what?

For the chance to prove sniveling naysayers like Gary Castleton spectacularly correct in the most public, the most final, the most humiliating manner possible: a typed list on a bulletin board at the bottom of the stairs in a high school gymnasium. A list on which his name was, simply, not.

Cassidy readily understood that most dreamy high school thespians would not become international movie stars; most tots prancing across stages wearing rhinestone tiaras would not become Miss America; most ROTC standouts would not become heroes or astronauts.

But at the same time he was pretty sure that a few would. He had to believe in his heart that some of them would do these things. He understood that, even if Gary Castleton did not.

What he really blamed Gary for was his almost joyful renunciation of The Possible. Gary would not even acknowledge some tiny sliver of one percent of humanity actually *would* wear an Olympic garland; actually *would* be handed an Oscar by a smiling and envious colleague; actually *would* fly a rocket to the moon and whack golf balls into orbit.

That night at the gym, the thought of Gary Castleton's sneering dismissal would drive Cassidy through an extra fifty jump shots from the top of the key, an extra twenty hooks from each side, an extra ten full-court layups. All of it leaving him a pile of mush once more, leaning unsteadily against the safety pad, gasping for breath in the dank and empty gymnasium.

Stumbling to the locker room, he contemplated his long, dark bike ride home and the cooling dinner awaiting him. *Maybe Gary Castleton is right,* Cassidy thought, eyeing the sky full of bright stars over the deserted airfield. *But then again, maybe he isn't.*

Some have to be chosen. *Maybe I am one.*

CHAPTER 26

THUNDEROUS ASCENSION

The first clue that something was up was when they were stopped by the MP at the entrance to Fort Murphy. Accustomed to breezing through without slowing down, Stiggs and Cassidy almost wrecked their bikes when they heard the first angry blast from the guard's whistle. After that it was all "yes, sir" and "no, sir" to the black airman in full regalia, including leggings, white MP helmet, white cord epaulets, nightstick, and .45 automatic. They usually just wore fatigues and waved everyone through. But this one demanded their military IDs, and when they were produced, stuck them on his clipboard and began making notations. As he was writing, his attitude seemed to change and he no longer seemed so ticked off.

"Hey, what gives?" asked Randleman. "Nobody ever stopped us before."

"Yeah," said Cassidy. "There an inspection or something?"

The MP handed their cards back.

"What are you, kiddin' me?" he said. "Haven't you guys heard what's goin' on?"

Cassidy knew only that his parents had been strangely quiet, shooting glances at each other at dinner.

"We're just kids," said Randleman. "We can hardly find out the correct time."

"Well, how 'bout this. How about we're at Defcon three," said the guard, turning to deal with the cars stacking up. "If we go to Defcon two, no dependents allowed at all. So enjoy base privileges while you can."

"Yes, sir," said Cassidy.

"Yes, sir," said Stiggs.

"And you," said the guard, pointing his clipboard back at Cassidy, "stop shootin' so much."

Cassidy studied the guard's face.

"Dee-troit!"

"Yeah. Now get outta here. These other guys been waitin'."

"That was Dee-troit?" said Randleman as they pedaled toward the gym. "I never saw him in anything but those gross red shorts and black Converse high-tops."

"Yeah," said Cassidy. "Most people look different when they're armed."

Mr. Kamrad was more wound up than usual in civics class. It was known to some around school that while a student at Rollins College in Winter Park, Mr. Kamrad had hung out with people who wore beards. He had allegedly sat around drinking flavored coffees at a place called the Careera Room, where he discussed the conformist masses and the men in gray flannel suits who led them around like sheep. He was even rumored to be friends with a beatnik writer guy who lived in a little bungalow on Clouser Avenue in College Park with, of all things, his mother. The guy's name was Kerouac.

Mr. Kamrad these days was pretty straitlaced and his hair was shorn almost to military precision, as befitting a man who had started the only high school crew team in the southeastern United States, but he was said to still harbor some fairly exotic political views. This made for interesting discussions in this new kind of civics class that had recently been added by legislative fiat from Tallahassee. The class was actually called "Americanism versus Communism," which everyone had to pass before they could graduate in the state of Florida. It was Mr. Kamrad's last semester to teach it, so Cassidy got permission to take it early. Almost everyone else in the class was a senior.

"How many of you saw the president on TV last night?" Mr. Kamrad asked. Nearly every hand went up.

"Would anyone care to sum up what he said? Alan?"

Alan Mcree was the son of a full bird colonel, an honor student, a football player, and a shoe-in for an appointment to the Air Force Academy. He also, incongruously, did a pretty good rendition of the Kingston Trio's "Scotch and Soda" on a twelve-string guitar.

"The Russians are putting missiles in Cuba. We have photographic proof from spy planes. President Kennedy said they have to take them out and we've sent the Navy to blockade Cuba. We're on military alert."

"Okay, very good, Alan. Good, concise summary. Anybody else have a comment about what's going on?"

Cassidy thought about trying to make his and Randleman's encounter at the base into some kind of anecdote, preferably one in which he and Randleman would come off as perhaps brave or clever, but since the MP hadn't pulled his weapon—plus he was a guy they played basketball with—the incident really didn't seem to have the ingredients of a very exciting story.

A few people made comments, but they were of a piece throughout. There wasn't much controversy. Here were the Russians up to their old tricks again. What they were doing was simply unconscionable and the president had no choice but to take the steps he did. If the Russians refused to back down, then we would have to go to war.

"And what would that mean? Anyone?" Mr. Kamrad looked around the room. Everyone looked puzzled. They had always assumed it would be pretty bad, but that was as far as the thinking went.

"Why don't you enlighten us, Mr. Gravatt."

Ronald Gravatt, a pleasant-looking dark-haired boy in horn-rimmed glasses, sat up straight, a puzzled look on his face. He was probably the smartest kid in school, Harvard-bound, but against all odds was one of those clever kids who managed to be popular, too. This was probably because he was down-to-earth and funny, and he didn't carry a briefcase or wear a pocket protector.

"Sir?"

"Tell them about your primary extracurricular activity last year and specifically what you learned from it."

"Oh. Well, I was on the debate team last year, uh, with Susan, and our topic was nuclear weapons, so . . . Uh, how far do you want me to go with this, Mr. Kamrad?"

"Just give them the basics. How might an all-out nuclear exchange come about, and what would be the general outcome."

"Well, there are all kinds of ways it could happen, but the most likely scenario is where both sides have nukes, but one side has a big conventional advantage—like we do with Cuba, or like they do in Eastern Europe. See, there are these weapons called 'tactical nukes,' which are relatively small nuclear devices attached to artillery shells or supposedly even torpedoes. If a general or admiral gets in a situation where he feels he's going to lose a conventional war, he will likely resort to one of these devices. The command-and-control situation on these weapons is such that the officer in the field can sometimes use them on his own authority. In other words, he may not have to go back to his superiors for any kind of launch codes or passwords."

"So, say some general shoots one of these things off, what happens then?" asked Mr. Kamrad.

"Once the nuclear trip wire has been triggered, things will probably escalate fast. One tactical shell will be answered by two, or five, or a dozen. Then the first side decides to try to take out the other side's command and control with a larger device, then the other side responds to *that* . . . Well, basically, it's not long before there are dozens or hundreds of strategic megaton-level weapons in the air flying toward each other. At that point, each side will probably just let go with everything they have. No reason for restraint any longer, you see."

"And what does that look like on the ground?"

"Mr. Kamrad, I don't know how well I remember the details from last year . . ."

"It's okay, Ronald. Just do the best you can."

"Yes, sir. Well, the first thing that would happen is the most high-priority targets would get hit by submarine-launched missiles from just a couple hundred miles offshore, maybe closer than that. Russia has about seventy of those. We have twice as many. They would be aimed at taking out ICBM launch sites out west and our North American SAC bases, to stop the bombers. Also, some would be used for a so-called decapitation strike at Washington and a few key military facilities, as well as New York City and maybe a handful of other population centers."

"What kinds of defenses do we have for these weapons?"

"Well . . ."

"Come on, this is 1962, surely our scientists . . ."

"No, sir. There aren't any. None. We can't stop them, all we can do is retaliate."

"How much warning would we have?"

"Well, none really."

"None? But we have all these civil defense plans, evacuation routes, bomb shelters. We all know how to duck and cover. What do you mean, 'none'?"

"Those first weapons are launched from underwater from a few miles off our coasts. They can be set to fly in a low-arc trajectory to their targets. We're talking a matter of minutes from the time they're launched till they hit. That wouldn't be enough time to alert state or local authorities, or to issue any radio alerts or set off air raid sirens."

"So, our first indication that we were under attack would be . . ."

"A nuclear flash in the sky. That is, if you were close enough to the primary targets. If you were lucky enough to be far away, you'd just notice that a lot of stuff would just stop working. Network television and radio would go out, electricity in a lot of areas, most commerce and transportation would stop completely."

"Then what?"

"That would be the first wave. The next wave would be the ICBMs, the ballistic missiles. They take thirty to forty minutes to reach the U.S. from the Soviet Union, and vice versa. Some would be targeted at many of the same high-priority targets as the first wave, just to be sure they are taken out. Others would be aimed at regional and local infrastructure, power generation, transportation, and communication. And, of course, the population centers, most of them would be taken out by this wave."

"What kind of numbers are we talking about?"

"We believe the Soviets have about forty intercontinental ballistic missiles right now. Their guidance systems aren't very good, but realistically speaking, they don't have to be."

"And how many do we have?"

"Oh, we have at least a couple hundred, and they're much more accurate."

"So we've taken—and given them—a pretty good pounding, right? But still, at that point there ought to be quite a few people left to . . ."

"Mr. Kamrad?"

"Yes, Ronald? Am I forgetting something?"

"Yes, sir. The third leg of the nuclear so-called triad and the oldest one, the bombers."

Mr. Kamrad sighed theatrically and moved away from the blackboard where he had been writing the numbers as Ronald gave them. As if he were getting too tired to stand anymore, he walked to the front of his desk and half sat on the corner.

"The bombers. Okay, let's have it."

"This is all very iffy because it's impossible to tell how many of them would be left after the initial strikes on their bases. But there are a number of them in the air around the clock, so presumably at the very least those would survive. But we don't know how many would make it through whatever air defenses are left. But they think a significant fraction would make it and deliver their bombs on the remaining targets."

"And the numbers?"

"The Russians have around a hundred and forty strategic bombers and around four hundred warheads. We have more than thirteen hundred bombers and over three thousand warheads."

"And what would they be targeting?"

Ronald shrugged and made a funny face. Nervous laughter erupted from a few classmates.

"Whatever's left, I guess."

Mr. Kamrad went to the blackboard and in silence wrote the last numbers down: "Bombers: Them 140/400 vs. Us 1,300/3,000," then returned to his perch on his desk. The room was silent except for some coughs and the whir of the big oscillating fan at the front of the room.

"Okay," said Mr. Kamrad. "Everyone got that? Anyone have any questions or comments? Yes, Alan?"

"This all sounds pretty bad, but what if there isn't any choice and we have to fight or else end up becoming Communists?"

"Good point. Better dead than red, right? What about that, Susan?"

Susan Wiseman was Ronald's debate partner and academic nemesis. Her grade-point average was five hundredths of a point below Ronald's perfect 4.0, owing to a maddening B in sophomore phys ed. Like Ronald, she was popular. She was forgiven her brains simply because she was gorgeous and didn't seem to realize it. She made no attempt whatsoever to capitalize on it. She also didn't suffer fools—or anyone else—gladly. Cassidy and Stiggs were both madly in love with her. In Cassidy's case, second only to Maria DaRosa.

"I don't know, Mr. Kamrad. After a nuclear exchange like we're talking about, I don't think ideology would have any real meaning."

"Why is that, Susan?"

"We're talking about a hundred million dead on each side within hours or days, mostly from the initial blast and heat waves, plus the initial radiation. Then millions more within a few weeks or months. That's from lingering radiation and fallout, earlier injuries, infections and other diseases. Not to mention the sort of incidental deaths that would come with a complete breakdown of civil society. Anyone who gets a heart attack or a stroke would probably just die. There wouldn't be any functioning hospitals, no doctors or nurses. Very little or no law enforcement or other government help. Food and water would rapidly get scarce. Some scientists think that even the weather could be affected, maybe leading to a new ice age or at least serious long-term disruptions in the food supply."

"Good! And I don't mean 'good' as in 'this is a good situation,' I mean this was an excellent recitation of the facts. It's easy to see why Ronald and Susan were the runners-up in the state debate tournament last May in Tallahassee. By the way, what was the exact topic anyway, Ronald?"

Ronald looked at Susan with a tight, weary smile. Just the idea of it brought back the hundreds of hours they'd spent in the library, mostly making note cards with horrific quotations from books like Dr. Samuel Glasstone's *Effects of Nuclear Weapons.*

"'Resolved that nuclear weapons should be controlled by an international organization,'" said Ronald robotically.

"Yes, and good luck with that, right?"

"Yes, sir. Though we did prefer to argue in the affirmative."

"And why is that? Susan?"

"Because of everything we've just been talking about, Mr. Kamrad. Those are just facts and estimates and projections. There are some people—these are just opinions now, but informed ones—who go even farther in the direction of gloom and doom."

"Farther than a hundred million dead?"

"Mr. Kamrad, there are people who think that an all-out nuclear war would mean the end of our species."

The teacher let that sink in. The bell was about to ring, which normally would have meant a lot of hubbub, but now the class was silent.

"Okay," he said finally, getting up from his perch on the desk and walking to the blackboard. He picked up the eraser but then put it back down and turned back to the class.

"One more thing. What strategic advantage do these medium-range ballistic missiles give Cuba or the Soviets?"

The two debaters glanced grimly at each other, then looked down at their desks.

"Ronald?"

He looked up reluctantly. "That's the thing that doesn't make any sense, Mr. Kamrad. To either of us."

"What doesn't?"

"Well, the submarine-launched missiles would get to Washington a few minutes before these medium-range weapons would, and the ICBMs a few minutes after, but essentially . . ."

"Yes?"

"Mr. Kamrad, those missiles don't make any real strategic difference at all."

Mr. Kamrad seemed to be gazing over the heads of the students, through the windows into the palm-shaded courtyard between the school's two classroom wings. He was tapping the eraser against the knuckles of his left hand, making little clouds of yellow dust with each tap.

"Yes," he said quietly. "Exactly right."

The class sat perfectly still until the mechanical minute hand on the wall clock clicked straight up to the hour, and nearly everyone jolted upright when the shrill clanging of the bell split the air.

There was none of the usual fracas. Everyone—Cassidy included—left the room quietly.

His father was there when Cassidy got home, which hardly ever happened. He walked back to his parents' bedroom where his father, dressed in his flight suit, was packing a small duffel bag.

"Dad?"

He realized too late that there was enough of that whiney kid fear in his voice to shame him instantly.

"It's okay, son. I'll be out in a minute. Your mom's next door, she'll be back in a sec."

Filled with a vague dread, Cassidy sat on the floral-patterned wraparound couch that dominated the tiny living room. It occurred to him that he spent almost no time in this room except when some grown-up—like the preacher or some nebulous relative—was visiting, or when he was waiting for something faintly unpleasant, like church. This was a room that served mainly as a kind of limbo where as a child he was expected to sit still and not mess up his clothes.

His father came out and put the duffel by the door, then sat next to Cassidy. He was still dressed in his flight suit, which always meant that he was leaving immediately. It sometimes meant for a long time, months in one case. He put his hand on Cassidy's knee. This familiarity was also alarming.

"You know what's going on, right, son?"

"I know about the missiles. We had a class on it today. Is there something new happening?"

"We just had a jet go down. The pilot's missing in the Atlantic somewhere. You know the new system that I've been working on for the past two years, the one I can't say much about? Well, at least I can tell you that what it does is find people; people like this pilot. It's not really operational yet, but they want us to take our test units out and try to locate our man."

"But you're not . . ."

"I know. I don't usually do this kind of thing. But I'm still writing the training manuals. None of our search-and-rescue guys have even seen the equipment, much less know how to operate it."

He looked at his son with a tight smile. Cassidy tried to smile back but reddened when he realized his vision was blurred. He knew he wasn't supposed to be acting this way, and he expected his father to be angry with him. Instead, he just patted him on the knee.

"Look, it's going to be okay. We have complete air superiority out there, so no one's going to bother us. We're just going to go out over the Gulf Stream and find our guy and bring him back. Our guys do this kind of thing all the time. It's what they do."

"Yes, sir."

"I don't know how long I'll be gone. You'll be the man of the house. I expect you to look after your mother and take care of things around here."

"Yes, sir." He was horrified to realize how close he was to just out and out blubbering.

"Okay, here she is now." His father stood, gave Cassidy's shoulder an awkward squeeze, and headed for the door. His mother's face looked strained, but she gave Cassidy a quick smile.

"Cal was just on the phone with them and they're on the way," she said. Their neighbor and his father's best friend worked in the same squadron.

"Why are they . . ." Cassidy was puzzled. They never sent anyone to pick him up.

His father held the door open, looking at his mother.

"Okay," he said, and kissed her harder than Cassidy had seen before.

"Okay," she said, brushing at her eyes.

"Okay," he said.

They followed his father out the door. Cassidy was fighting to control his emotions now. He had watched his father leave on military trips before, but never like this. His dad walked right past the family station wagon and began heading down Rosedale Street on foot. Cassidy was confused.

"Mom, what's he . . ." he croaked.

She was crying openly now, making no effort to hide her tears. She didn't try to speak, just looked toward the east, from which direction they had been hearing a steadily increasing roar. It got louder and louder until, just as it became deafening, an apparition appeared over the tops of the live oak trees where Rosedale dead-ended into a big vacant field. Looking like a giant metallic dragonfly from some antediluvian nightmare, the Sikorsky UH-19B Chickasaw helicopter set down right in the middle of the sandy field where Cassidy and his friends played football. It was emblazoned with the Air Force star and a bold yellow vertical stripe right behind the cockpit. The side door in large letters said RESCUE. On the nose, in bouncing letters, was the word HOPALONG. The roar was almost overpowering and the small hurricane it kicked up made Cassidy's pants legs flap even as he watched from halfway down the block. Clouds of white sand flew up in gusts all along the street as children stopped their games and grown-ups gawked from their porches.

The side door was already open as the craft descended slowly, and his father tossed the crewman his duffel before the skids even touched down. With a helping hand, his father put one foot on the skid and was hauled inside the craft in an instant. Before the door was even closed, it was ascending and simultaneously doing a hammerhead turn to head toward the coast. It lifted in an obstreperous chorus, its roar no louder but somehow more earnest as it picked up height and speed simultaneously, and in a very few seconds it was a barely audible speck on the horizon.

Then it was gone, leaving a ringing silence so profound it precluded thought. There were still miniature whirlwinds winding down here and there, limbs trembling in the trees, bits of detritus settling back to earth. Some neighbors, only partially jaded by living next to a twentieth-century American Air Force base, still stood on their porches, shading their eyes and scanning the pale horizon for a last glimpse of the thunderous ascension.

CHAPTER 27

THE LIST

Cassidy stood in a kind of trance in front of the gym bulletin board. Others came and went, with a few guys giving him strange looks as they passed. He wasn't surprised to find his name on the list. That wasn't it.

He had improved vastly. Everyone knew that. And he had grown, too. Not as much as Stiggs and Randleman, who were both over six two now, but almost to an even six feet. And although he was still skinny as an egret, he had begun to fill out a little.

He no longer consistently lost to either of his friends in one-on-one. They weren't as fast as he was and couldn't shoot as well or from as far out. Both were regularly baffled when he produced a move they had never seen or when he finished with a left-handed shot from a position they were unprepared for.

His progress mystified some people, but not Cassidy. While his taller friends had been playing against other ninth graders, he had been at the base gym doing drills, lifting weights, and getting in games with servicemen, some of whom had played high school or college ball. Some were big-city black guys who grew up playing wild and woolly playground ball. His school was lily white and so was every school they played against.

Lieutenant Lefaro not only continued to hold coaching clinics with him, he occasionally picked Cassidy for his team in three-on-three. It was a rare day when Cassidy could not get into a game now.

As he stood in front of the list, feeling light-headed, his mind reeled with recollections of his heretofore failed basketball career. It amounted to years of disappointment and unrewarded striving, lasting right up until his brief triumph on the track had given him some hope that he wasn't completely doomed as an athlete. At least he could run.

And now, here was his redemption in black and white, proof for all to see that he was a basketball player, too.

He read the notice for the tenth time:

FINAL CUT

The following boys have been selected for this year's Edgewater High School junior varsity basketball squad:

Samuel Stiggs
Erich Randleman
Quenton Cassidy . . .

He turned to go to homeroom when something occurred to him he hadn't thought of in a long time. His sixth-grade teacher, Mr. Meredith, had been something of a polymath. He often gave interesting and unusual lessons that were unique to his classroom. One day he showed some slides from a recent trip to Europe.

Cassidy sat in the darkened classroom as the portable screen at the front of the room shone with Michelangelo's *David*, standing languidly in front of the Accademia Gallery in Florence in white marble splendor. The figure evinced an easy grace, almost an insolence, as David tarried momentarily before battling Goliath. The deadly sling with which he would make himself immortal draped casually over his shoulder. David gazed into the middle distance, wistfully pondering the impossible task before him.

Everyone else was tittering because they had never seen nudity in school before, even rendered in marble, but Cassidy was mostly struck by the familiarity of David's stance, the way he held himself, the powerful and graceful torso and legs.

Mr. Meredith was talking about how the statue was a wonderful example of the Renaissance mannerist style and of Michelangelo's genius for proportion and the human form and blah blah blah. Cassidy stared at the statue, fascinated.

"Notice the angle of hips," said Mr. Meredith. "Not many people realize that the reason it's done that way was the shape of the original block of marble Michelangelo was working with . . ."

It struck Cassidy that there was something familiar about the five-hundred-year-old statue that he couldn't put his finger on. Then he realized it was simply that Michelangelo's David was an athlete.

He had the same manner, a mixture of anxiety, confidence, and grace that Cassidy had noticed in athletes like Chip Newspickle, or the school's best football player, Harry Winkler. And yes, even in his own friends Stiggs and Randleman.

But the most remarkable thing, said Mr. Meredith, was that Michelangelo chose to render David not in a moment of triumph or in the midst of competition, but in the calm before battle, in that quiet moment of introspection before going out to meet his fate.

He doesn't know if he can win, but he knows that he will try. Perhaps he will be overmatched—his opponent is twice as big as him—but David's physical form tells you that, like all athletes, he has spent much of his life in preparation for this moment.

Quenton Cassidy realized that day in Mr. Meredith's class that he would give anything in the world to be like David, to be one of the exalted beings he saw every day ambling down the halls of their school. He longed to command that grace, power, and speed. But mostly he wanted to embody the spirit of that figure, the courage and the determination it took to accomplish impossible things, things that most others would not even attempt.

Up until now, most of his efforts had ended in disappointment. Being rebuffed time and again had brought him derision and self-doubt. He was the silly kid who didn't know when to quit.

Now, in his fifteenth year, he realized that seeing that image of David up on the screen in a grade school classroom all those years ago was the moment he understood what an athlete really was.

And it was the moment he decided that he would become one.

CHAPTER 28

UNFORGETTABLE DAY, 11/22/63

"Regular team practices start at the end of October," Cassidy wrote to his uncle Henry, in reality an older cousin. "I may not get to play much, but that doesn't matter. In fact, if I got struck by lightning tomorrow bream fishing on Lake Okeechobee, I would go to Valhalla a happy boy."

He meant it, too. His last growth spurt earned him a promotion out of the skinny shrimp club into the pond bird club, but making the JV team had really put him on the map. People were nice to him now for no reason, even girls he didn't know. Guys were vaguely respectful or, even better, envious. Teachers he liked, like Mr. Kamrad, now seemed to know who he was. Sometimes they wanted to chat.

It was so much better than being a dweeb!

Stiggs and Randleman, after getting over the shock, were sanguine about the whole thing. They were still the stars, of course, and he was just a bench-bound journeyman, but at least he was on the bus. The three were more of a trio than ever, which took Demski some getting used to. Now he was the odd man out.

It was Friday and Cassidy was looking forward to practice. Afterward, everyone was going directly to the football game. He was working on drills in Mrs. Abke's fifth-period typing class, trying his best to train his right index finger to distinguish between the "n" and the "m" on the bottom row of the maddeningly blank keys of the big Olivettis.

The PA system came on, and after some fumbling around, a male voice said: "This is Principal Fleming. This news bulletin is just coming in on the radio." There was more jostling as the microphone slid across the desk to the radio.

". . . in Dallas, Texas, three shots were fired at President Kennedy's motorcade in downtown Dallas. The first reports say that President Kennedy has been seriously wounded by this shooting . . . More details just arrived. These details about the same as previously: President Kennedy shot today just as his motorcade left downtown Dallas. Mrs. Kennedy jumped up and grabbed Mr. Kennedy. She called, 'Oh, no.' The motorcade sped on. United Press says that the wounds for President Kennedy perhaps could be fatal.

"Repeating, a bulletin from CBS news, President Kennedy has been shot by a would-be assassin in Dallas, Texas. Stay tuned to CBS news for further details . . ."

The same noise of the microphone sliding was followed by the resumption of the regular program, which sounded like a soap opera. Principal Fleming's voice sounded strained when he came back on.

"That's all we know right now. We will let you know when there is further news." Then, after a pause: "God bless America."

The typing class was mostly girls, and many were visibly shaken. Two were openly weeping. Mrs. Abke appeared distressed, absent-mindedly wringing her hands at the front of the room.

"All right," she said. "Those of you who do not feel like continuing with your exercises right now may sit quietly at your desks. You may put your heads down if you like. There are only twenty minutes left in the period. I'm sure Principal Fleming will let us know when there is more news."

Cassidy, dazed, tried to finish the exercise, as did several other students, though the usual steady clattering of their machines was now coming in fits and spurts.

Cassidy was working on a formal business letter in which he had to make up the names for the sender and recipient. He typed:

> . . . and, upon further reflection, it appears we will be needing another three (3) cases of your type L-24 aluminum brackets, and would be most pleased if you could reserve another two (2) cases for delivery before the end of next nomth. Our purchase orders for same will follow forthwith.
>
> I would like to relate to you how particularly impressed we are with the L-24, not only in its utility, but indeed in its aesthetic appeal as well. Congratulations on this most important innovation inthe field of bracketology.
>
> Sincerely yours,
>
>
> Robert Benchley
> Senior Production Manager
> Acme Steel Hanky Co.
> 307 Drudgery Street
> Pontiac, Michigan

But he made two typos and decided not to turn it in until he could retype it the next day. By the time the bell rang for next period, half the class appeared to be in a state of shock. The hallways were nearly silent as he made his way over to the B wing for sixth-period algebra with Mr. Cieplechowicz.

No one could concentrate in that class either, so Mr. Cieplecho-wicz didn't even try. This time, more than half the heads went down on the desks immediately. Cassidy was stunned, too. He looked at

Stiggs one row over, who just shrugged. He had been a big Kennedy fan, and he looked confused and miserable.

The PA crackled again, but Principal Fleming didn't say anything. He just moved the microphone over next to the radio. Cassidy now recognized the announcer's voice as that of Walter Cronkite, the CBS anchorman whom his father watched every night.

". . . From Dallas, Texas, the flash—apparently official—President Kennedy died at one P.M., Central Standard time, two o'clock, Eastern Standard time, some thirty-eight minutes ago. Vice President Lyndon Johnson has left the hospital in Dallas, but we do not know to where he has proceeded; presumably he will be taking the oath of office shortly and become the thirty-sixth president of the United States."

Basketball practice was canceled, as was the football game that night. Cassidy, Stiggs, and Randleman got a ride home with Phil Jameson, who drove a 1952 Ford Crestline and let everyone carpool with him for gas money. No one said much of anything except Stiggs, who occasionally uttered a muted, "Damn."

It seemed strange to be home early in the afternoon with nothing to do. Neither of Cassidy's parents were there, and the neighborhood seemed eerily deserted. He went to the backyard and hitched his canoe trailer to his bike and pedaled to the intracoastal. He wasn't sure exactly where he was going, he just wanted to be going somewhere. In half an hour he found himself passing the Jupiter Hilton and decided to stop for something to drink. Mr. Tolbert was in his usual chair behind the counter, reading *Harper's Magazine.* When he looked up and saw Cassidy, he smiled broadly and put down the periodical. He reached over and turned down the sound on the small black-and-white television beside him.

"Why, I believe it is one of our cage stars," he said. "I find it hard to believe he is playing hooky from practice. Coach Stoddard must not be the heartless taskmaster we had been led to believe."

"Hi, Mr. Tolbert. You been listening to the news?"

"Yes, son, I have," he said softly.

Cassidy nodded, then went to the drink cooler and located a big Topp Cola, his preferred brand.

"Can I ask you something, Mr. Tolbert?" said Cassidy, handing over a quarter.

"Of course you can, Quenton," he said, handing back his change.

"I guess I don't understand why anyone would want to kill President Kennedy," Cassidy said.

Mr. Tolbert sat back in his chair, thought about it a moment, then motioned Cassidy to come around the counter and pull up an empty wooden drink crate. They could see on the silent TV the same video clips and still photographs over and over from earlier in the day, the president and first lady in a convertible waving to the crowd as they went by the camera, then black-and-white shots of people panicking, flinging themselves to the ground, looking around in stark terror as the events unfolded. Then a homemade snapshot of Lee Harvey Oswald, standing in what appeared to be a backyard, proudly displaying a rifle.

"The short answer is, I don't know," Mr. Tolbert said, casting his eyes downward. "I do know that occasionally murdering our leaders is a trait that human beings have exhibited since the beginning of recorded history. It was happening even before that, probably, come to think of it. That is, if you can judge by the behavior of some of our primate cousins."

"Really?"

"Well, Julius Caesar was killed forty-four years before the birth of Christ, and Abraham Lincoln was shot right after the Civil War. Why, even the great Zulu warrior chief Shaka was murdered by his own brothers in the early 1800s. I'm afraid leader killing has been much with us as a species."

"I guess so," said Cassidy, "but why?"

"Lots of reasons," said Mr. Tolbert. "Others want their power, their influence, their juju. They want to substitute their own vision of the future for that of the departed. Sadly enough, it often works. And I can't even sit here and tell you that I think it always and forever ends in a terrible outcome. Why, Hitler's own generals tried to do away with him and darned near succeeded. Who knows how many thousands—hundreds of thousands or millions—of lives might have been saved, how many cities spared destruction, if that bomb had been pushed a little closer to the führer's hind end."

Paddling home, Cassidy reflected on that. Within hours of hearing that a much-beloved president had been gunned down in cold blood in an American city, the kindest and smartest man he knew proposed that the world would have been better off had the German chancellor's fanny been more directly seated over a satchel of high explosives.

CHAPTER 29

BASKETBALL JONES

Head high school basketball coach Jim Cinnamon was a no-nonsense taskmaster, though he typically paid little attention to the junior varsity. The JV coach was a huge, pear-shaped, flat-topped retread from the football team named Dewey Stoddard. Dewey claimed a degree from a dubious teachers' college outside Dothan, Alabama, and was renowned around Edgewater for his malaprops and mispronunciations. He was kind of a poor man's Yogi Berra.

Dewey had been a lineman in college but had also managed one year of freshman basketball, thanks to his six-foot-five-inch frame and the school's lack of scholarship money for any sport that didn't involve an oblong ball.

He was given his marching orders daily by Coach Cinnamon, and the practices ran smoothly enough, though they hardly seemed strenuous to Cassidy, accustomed as he was to his self-inflicted daily annihilations at the base gym. In fact, once he got a good sense of what would be expected of them, Cassidy took to dressing out early and running laps around the practice court. Sometimes, if the varsity was scrimmaging full court, he would put on his old gym shoes and do his laps outside on the asphalt track. He had promised Trapper Nelson he would keep up running as best he could through basketball, and in truth he was happy to have a way to burn off excess energy.

It was obvious right away that Stiggs and Randleman would be starters. Kent Stewart wasn't as maneuverable or as good a shot, but he was nearly six seven and strong as an ox, so he was clearly the third member of the starting front court.

The guards were Drake Osgood and Carroll Morgan, good ball handlers though erratic shooters. The first replacement guard was Stan Jenson, a tough little terrier of a player who liked nothing better than diving on the floor for loose balls. He also had a deadly accurate set shot, if he could ever get open enough to use it. Cassidy figured he was next in line after Stan, should some series of catastrophes incapacitate everyone else. Even then it was not a sure thing, as Dewey would sometimes take out one of the guards and put in Phil Jones, another big man, leaving either Drake or Carroll as a point guard.

Cassidy was still mostly a spectator. But at least he was in high school, he had left Bob Bickerstaff behind, and he was a certified basketball player. To make his joy nearly complete, Edgewater had hired Mr. Kamrad away from Glenridge to coach crew and teach psychology and sociology.

The varsity rolled over their first three opponents, Belle Glade, Pahokee, and Okeechobee, and the junior varsity won, though more modestly. In sheer size, the juniors' starting five actually averaged about an inch taller than the varsity, which was much commented on by sportswriters and the peanut gallery. Some were already making giddy predictions about future state rankings and possible tournament prospects.

Then came the Riviera Beach game, a local powerhouse, played at their little cracker box gym. The Riviera jayvees looked big and confident in the warm-ups. So much so that Stiggs and Randleman tried to loosen everyone up during their own drills by making wisecracks about "showing the big boys how it's done." It worked to some extent, but the mood was still pretty somber as they went back into the dressing room before the tip-off.

"All right, you probably already know what I know about these guys," said Dewey, studying his clipboard. "They're bigger than their size indicates. And they're undefeated with no losses, like we are. They've got this kid Stansfield, who's six four and pretty tough in the key. Randleman, I want you to take him, but Stiggs be ready to help out. Don't double-team him all the time, but both of you be ready to get all over him like a prom dress."

Stiggs and Randleman sat, sweating already, towels around their necks, staring down at their shoe tops. They both nodded solemnly.

"This guy Genchi at forward is six two and he can jump. He's also a decent shot. Stewart, you take him so Stiggs can take the weaker guy and help Randleman out with Stansfield. Drake, Houldsworth is a pretty good guard, I hear. He's yours. He's not afraid to shoot and he can get hot. He's averaging ten a game, second to Stansfield, so you can't lay off him too much. This other guy, Garret, is a good ball handler but that's all. Carroll, he's yours. See if you can slough off of him a bit and jam up the middle, make it tougher for Stansfield in there. Okay, I think everyone knows we've got our work cut out for us out there tonight, but Coach Cinnamon and I both feel like you guys can handle it. Just remember how lucky we are, boys, to be living in the greatest country in America! Let's get out there and show 'em what we can do!"

They all gathered up and did a hands-in huddle, breaking with a cheer and rushing to the door. Cassidy was at the back, waiting for the jam at the door to clear, when he heard his name.

"Hang back a sec, Quenton," said Dewey.

Cassidy was puzzled. He'd never been singled out by Dewey for anything before.

"Yes, sir?"

Dewey waited until everyone left.

"Stan hurt his ankle yesterday screwing around like an idiot with his brothers. Dr. Parr has given him a cortisone injection and Stan says it feels okay, but doc don't want him playing tonight. I know you haven't played much yet, but it looks like you're the first guard in if we need to substitute. If we stick to a two-guard front, that is," he said.

Cassidy nodded.

"It may not come up at all, but I just wanted you to be ready if you need to go in. Keep your head in the game and be prepared, okay? All right, get out there."

Cassidy was almost dizzy as he went back out for the last bit of limbering up before the tip-off. He could hardly believe he might actually get a chance to play in a game when it still mattered, and not just after the regulars had run up the score.

He jogged back on the court and started taking free throws. Stiggs and Randleman kept eyeballing him, obviously dying of curiosity. Finally Stiggs joined him on the foul line.

"So what's up? What did he want?" he asked.

Cassidy struggled to keep his voice casual. "Nothing, really. Stan's not full speed, is all. I might get in."

"No kidding? Really? Hey, Randleman, get a load of—"

"Shhhhh." Cassidy grabbed his arm. "Keep it down! Nobody is supposed to know."

The klaxon sounded for the opening tip-off.

After the last huddle, Cassidy returned to the bench without the usual resigned expression of a perennial sub. He would actually be paying attention to a game that he might be in.

Stansfield was for real. He outjumped Stiggs on the tip-off, tapping it to Genchi who immediately flipped it to Houldsworth streaking toward the rim. In an instant it was 2–0.

Cassidy glanced down at Dewey, who sat with his mouth agape. The play did not resemble any JV play he had seen before.

Carroll Morgan brought the ball down the floor and took it to the right side of Riviera's zone, holding up one finger to indicate the wheel offense. Stiggs cleared out along the baseline, and Randleman came up to the high post. Morgan faked him a bounce pass, then flipped it over to Osgood so he could whip it back around the horn to Stewart and then to Stiggs, who was setting up on the baseline for the shot.

But Houldsworth was anticipating the pass to Osgood, and he jumped out and deflected it over to the other guard, Garret, who picked it up at full stride and went the length of the floor with no one remotely close to him. In fact, he slowed down at the foul line and casually jogged the last few steps before laying the ball gently against the backboard. It was 4–0 and the game was less than a minute old.

Edgewater recovered somewhat and tried to adjust to Riviera's quickness and aggressiveness, but halfway through the eight-minute period, it was 12–4, and two of the four points had been free throws. They had a single bucket, and that was an amazing hook shot Stiggs managed to launch over Stansfield.

Dewey called time-out and made small adjustments to their offensive positions. He switched Morgan and Osgood's men on defense, and put Stiggs on their big man. It seemed to Cassidy almost beside the point, more like window dressing.

Sure enough, as the horn sounded at the end of the period, the scoreboard read 22–8. When Riviera grabbed a defensive rebound, Cassidy caught himself actually admiring the Riviera Beach style of play. It was fast, efficient, and aggressive, with little time or attention devoted to setting up elaborate plays or making multiple passes. When they grabbed a defensive rebound, they cleared it out to a guard and brought it up fast, looking for an open man. If a shot presented itself, they took it.

Even after Edgewater had scored on one play, Garret quickly took the ball out of the net and inbounded it to Houldsworth, who brought it straight up the sidelines, beating most of the Eagles back down the floor. Stiggs, the only one left between him and the basket, moved out to cover him, leaving the key completely open to Stansfield coming in from the right wing to make the easy layup.

Although he was disturbed at the bludgeoning his team was taking, Cassidy was also fascinated. There was something familiar in Riviera's style of play, something he recognized though it had little to do with anything his team had ever practiced. When Garret casually flipped Stansfield a no-look behind-the-back pass in the key, it struck Cassidy: these guys played like the guys at the base gym! They didn't need elaborate plays or meticulous passing to work their way around to a decent shot, they just made a quick pass, set up a screen, took a dribble, and then took the shot. They shot with confidence bordering on arrogance. They shot like they expected to make every single one of them, and they weren't far wrong.

Cassidy's reverie was interrupted by Phil Jones's nudging. Carroll Morgan had bumped knees with Houldsworth on a fast break and was limping toward the bench in obvious pain. Cassidy started to pull his warm-up over his head, but when Dewey barked out a name, it was not his.

"Phil!"

Jones, blinking in surprise, pulled off his warm-up and checked in with the scorer. They were going to go with one point guard. Dewey called an additional time-out to get them organized.

Cassidy, deflated, listened from the outer ring of the huddle.

"All right, we're going to a one-three-one. Stiggs, you move to the low post. Phil, you take his wing. Any questions?"

It was a disaster.

The Riviera coach had anticipated the change, and as soon as Edgewater brought the ball in, they ran into a full-court zone press. Osgood tried to dribble against it and was herded to the sideline, where he was trapped. Edgewater's big men had little experience handling the ball and they panicked. Osgood tried to throw a soft looping pass over the trapping guards to Jones, but it was easily intercepted by Houldsworth and laid up on the backboard for an easy basket.

This happened twice more before Dewey called time-out.

"Cassidy!" he called down the bench.

They went back to two guards. Dewey gave them all kinds of contradictory advice in the huddle, trying to diagram the way the trap worked on his green board. It occurred to Cassidy that their coach was essentially guessing.

"Take it toward the sidelines but kick it back to me before they put the trap on," Cassidy told Osgood as they walked back onto the court. "Then take off down the sidelines as fast as you can go. If someone comes to cover you after you get a pass back, look to the middle of the court for Stiggs."

Osgood wasn't accustomed to taking directions from a bench-warmer, but Cassidy could see from the look on his face that he was scared enough to pay attention to anyone who sounded confident.

Cassidy took the ball out-of-bounds and tossed it in to Osgood, who turned to face the three defenders spread across the court at the foul line. It was a classic 3-1-1 zone trap and almost impossible to dribble against if the defenders were good.

But Cassidy had the benefit of the advice of First Lieutenant Ron Lefaro, USAF, who had played ball at little Colby College, an undersized, scrappy, full-court-press terror of NCAA Division II basketball. He had shown Cassidy how easy it was to break the press with two guards and one halfway agile big man. Cassidy grabbed the front of Stiggs's jersey and told him to loiter at center court and break toward the ball if someone got trapped with it.

Osgood started to dribble upcourt and was immediately cut off and herded toward the sideline by the middle guard, Garret. Before the other guard, Houldsworth, could spring the trap, Osgood turned and flipped the ball back to Cassidy, who had not advanced at all. He was still very near the baseline and thus had not attracted any attention from the third man in the three-man front.

As Osgood took off down the sideline, and Houldsworth turned to herd Cassidy toward the opposite sideline, Cassidy took one dribble and lifted into the air off one foot. He hit Osgood with a leading baseball pass that the guard caught at full stride. Riviera was well coached, however, and Osgood was immediately picked up by the first 1 in the 3-1-1, who had left his spot at center court where he had been shadowing Stiggs. Osgood saw that Stiggs was now open at center court, and he hit him immediately. Stiggs turned and was amazed to see one lone Riviera defender at the foul line and two Edgewater forwards spread on the baseline. And Cassidy had been sprinting down the right sideline after his initial pass. They had gone from having a guard in a two-man trap to a four-on-one fast break. Suddenly the press didn't look so invulnerable.

Stiggs took the ball straight toward the hoop, pulling up just inside the foul line. When the lone Riviera defender came out to pick him up, he dumped it off to Randleman underneath, who took it up for the bunny shot, getting so high up he slapped the backboard on the way down.

The small crowd of Edgewater fans who had come early for the JV game erupted. It was the first thing they'd had to cheer about in a long while.

Just as they were quieting down, a shaken-looking Riviera guard was inbounding the ball to the other guard, Houldsworth, who casually waited for it just inside the foul line. Cassidy, appearing to keep his eyes downcourt, was actually watching them in his peripheral vision. He was more or less jogging in place, giving the appearance of heading upcourt with his teammates but without actually going anywhere. As soon as the inbounding pass left the guard's hands, Cassidy whirled around and stepped in front of Houldsworth and took the ball waist high. He tapped it once for a single dribble and laid it up high on the left side of the backboard with his left hand and, like Randleman, got so high up on the backboard that he lightly slapped the glass on the way down.

The guard who had thrown the careless inbound pass, seeking to quickly redress his error, rushed over just in time to foul Cassidy. His foul shot hit nothing but net.

But it was the next play that changed Cassidy's life forever.

Riviera tried to force the ball in to Stansfield and Stiggs got a hand on it and deflected it over to Osgood, who shovel-passed it out to Cassidy, already at full stride down the court. Houldsworth was defending, running backward, but when Cassidy got to the foul line, Houldsworth dropped back, expecting Cassidy to pass it to one wing or the other, since they had a three-on-one advantage. Instead, Cassidy went straight up into his pull-up jump shot. As he began to lift off the hardwood, he realized how easy it would be to miss this completely uncontested shot. And the reason for that was simply that he wanted so badly to make it. He had made the same shot hundreds—thousands—of times practicing on his own, but now that it really mattered, he felt the implacable forces of nature—of the universe—that wanted that shot *not* to go it. There were an infinite number of ways to miss such a shot but only a handful of ways to make it. He realized that the more he absolutely, positively, more-than-life-itself craved to see that ball drop through the net, the more likely it was he would miss it. Not by much, but miss it nevertheless. The sheer intensity of his desire would cause a tiny bit of extra lift, an imperceptibly more vigorous flick of the wrist, but *something*, some tiny flaw. And that would be that.

So as he rose for the shot he concentrated on trying to do something he had learned skin diving: not to care. Underwater he had learned to be detached, because to be in a constant state of concern was to be using oxygen. You have to make yourself not care, he would say when people asked how he did it. Not caring was why it was so easy to make these shots in practice when it didn't matter and so easy to *miss* them in games when it did.

So now, at this very moment, it mattered. It mattered a lot. He would have this one chance to make this shot and it would never come again. So as he lifted off the floor, he began willing himself not to care. This shot would go in or it would not, and the earth would still turn on its axis. Children would still starve in Africa and armies would clash by night. No matter what one skinny teenager's existential investment in it might be, nothing in the larger scheme of things was riding on this shot.

That freed his mind to deal with the important details: squaring his body to the rim, feeling the pebble-grain surface of the ball on his fingertips, getting the exact rhythm of the motion of whipping the ball up from his waist to a point just above his forehead, holding it there until the exact moment he reached the apex of his jump, launching it ever so softly into its perfect arc, with the ball spinning slightly backward, his hand and forearm continuing on and collapsing into the perfect "dying swan" follow-through of all good shooters. And, as with all good shooters, he knew the second the ball left his fingertips that it was a dead-center perfect shot. He knew it so completely that he could not help disobeying a cardinal rule of basketball: follow your shot. Instead, he simply bounced happily there in place, content to watch the arc of the ball as if it were a separate entity, a thing of beauty totally unrelated to himself.

The ball cut the net so cleanly that it popped through the cords and hung momentarily in space, still spinning backward, before dropping to the hardwood floor.

And, just like that, Cassidy understood the real secret of shooting a basketball.

Stiggs, who had been expecting the pass, had to change his tune in mid-invective. It went like this:

"Cassidy! What the hell . . ."

Swish.

"Nice shot."

* * *

The bus would have been pretty rowdy but for the varsity players, whose loss easily trumped the elation of the jayvees. They seemed particularly vexed at Cassidy, who had always been an object of special derision for them, either because he was too cocky, too skinny, or too uncool generally. That is, they acted that way when they acknowledged the existence of a JV player at all, which was rare.

Cassidy sat, alone as usual, in the seat behind Stiggs and Randleman. He would like to have felt bad for the varsity, but it was all he could do to suppress his joy. He had scored twenty-two points, leading both teams, but more than that, he had clearly engineered a five-point victory out of an impending drubbing.

Still, the varsity had lost, and Cassidy was obligated to project a glumness that he did not feel.

Coach Cinnamon came aboard last, trying to act chipper but not succeeding very well. He went down the aisle, saying a few words of encouragement here and there to the varsity players. When he got to the middle of the bus where Cassidy sat, he stopped for a moment. He stood and smiled at Cassidy, who finally looked away in embarrassment.

Coach Cinnamon put his hand on Cassidy's shoulder and, without saying anything, continued down the aisle.

CHAPTER 30

ARGUABLY A STAR

The most ardent cares of his former life fell away.

Worrying about being noticed in practice, or whether he would get any playing time, or whether he would, by some miracle, start a game—all of that went away. He left his reversible jersey red side out at scrimmage time instead of automatically turning it to the white side, the second-team color.

Dewey Stoddard still hardly spoke to him, but Cassidy detected a grudging respect instead of the usual studied indifference. Coach Cinnamon must have talked to Dewey, Cassidy thought, because Dewey was just dense enough to think that what he saw during the Riviera Beach game was some kind of fluke.

In the next game, Pahokee came to play the Edgewater jayvees in a solo afternoon game while the varsity was away at a holiday tournament in Fort Lauderdale. Forty-some people, mostly parents and siblings, showed up to watch in the stuffy Edgewater gym. The big overhead fans were going full blast as the late-afternoon sun streamed through the upper windows. Even December had some miserably hot days on the Gold Coast.

Drake Osgood started at one guard, Cassidy the other. Stiggs was jumping center against a smaller player, so when Cassidy got his attention he pointed to Stewart, the tallest guy on the team. Stiggs nodded. When Cassidy got Stewart's attention, he pointed to his left, letting him know which way he was going to break for the basket. Stewart nodded. It was the play Riviera had pulled on them.

It worked perfectly. Stiggs was a whole forearm above their poor opposing center, easily tapping the ball to Stewart, who flipped it nonchalantly over his shoulder to Cassidy, who was already halfway to the rim. Two dribbles took him too far under the left side of the rim, so he crossed under and did a reverse layup on the right side, laying the ball gently in with his right hand and turning in midair so his back would bounce off the safety pad when he landed.

It happened so quickly the Pahokee players had barely figured out which basket they were going for. Now they were down two points.

In their first game of the season, despite their smaller size, Pahokee had played them tough. They challenged the ball all the way up the floor and they were in constant motion on offense, trying to wear down their bigger opponents. Now they brought the ball down and started the same tactic again, working it around to the corner, then back out and around to the other corner, where their wing hit a nice shot from the baseline. Their guards immediately set up to contest the inbound pass.

Cassidy pulled the ball out of the net, but he and Osgood both stepped out-of-bounds simultaneously fifteen feet apart. Cassidy acted like he was going to throw a baseball pass downcourt, which got his man up in the air, then tossed the ball over to Osgood, who was still out of bounds, waiting. Not many players were aware that a pass between two out-of-bounds players was completely legal. Cassidy immediately stepped around his airborne defender and headed downcourt as Osgood hit him with a quick pass. By the time his man got back on terra firma, Cassidy had a five-yard lead on him, which he maintained all the way down the floor.

Pahokee's center and forwards were not set up when Cassidy got to the top of the key, but one of them turned just in time to see Cassidy getting ready to shoot. He immediately went to defend just as Randleman stepped over and turned sideways, setting a left screen on the guy at the foul line. Cassidy did a crossover dribble and went left around the screen, which now left him completely open down the key. Everyone else on the Pahokee team was busy trying to figure out whom they were supposed to be guarding, what the score was, whether their uniform jerseys were properly tucked in, everything but stopping the guy with the ball. It was the simplest offensive concept in basketball: get open and put the ball in the hole. Cassidy pulled up into his jumper and buried it.

Now the Pahokee guys looked at each other with real concern. In their first game Quenton Cassidy hadn't played at all, and little Pahokee had come within five points of beating Edgewater. That fact didn't engender a great deal of respect for anything about Edgewater except its size. Now this guy they'd never seen before had just breezily scored twice in less than a minute. Worse, it all seemed too casual. The guy wasn't in the least surprised, and neither was anyone on his team.

Cassidy was trotting back on defense when he heard a familiar jungle call among the noise from the little crowd. He looked over to the home side and was surprised to see Trapper Nelson sitting courtside. And by him, in civvies, was Ron Lefaro, giving him a pumping fist and a whoop. Cassidy gave them a happy little wave as he scurried down the court.

Edgewater ran the score up so high the reserves played most of the last quarter. For once Cassidy was happy to sit on the bench, cheering on the second team.

Pahokee was just the first in a long succession of one-sided victories. Dewey Stoddard still hardly had a word to say to him, but Cassidy started every game. After the games, Coach Cinnamon would sometimes offer a word of praise or encouragement, but Dewey said nothing.

In fact, Dewey was as clueless as everyone else about his own sudden startling success as a basketball coach. In reality, Cassidy and Stiggs had taken over the team, working out a system of hand gestures to indicate changing from man-to-man to zone, which out-of-bounds play to use, which offense to set up, and so on. Dewey was only vaguely aware that something was going on, but as long as it seemed to be working he didn't trouble himself about it. His coaching advice, when he had any to offer, was opaque and confusing: Don't take anything the defense doesn't give you! Cut off the passing lanes! Give and go!

When the JV team went 18–2 for the season, the conference coaches voted Dewey the junior varsity Coach of the Year. Cassidy told Stiggs and Randleman that everyone on the JV team should become professional magicians, because they had somehow turned Dewey Stoddard—who still thought a zone press was something you used to make Cuban sandwiches—into a basketball genius.

"Yeah, we were winning by fifteen a game until Dewey got the flu. Then we won by thirty-two and twenty-eight with Mr. Kamrad coaching. And Mr. Kamrad never played basketball in his life. If Dewey had just stayed at home every game, he'd have made Coach of the Century."

The irony of Dewey's award was not lost on the local sportswriters, who loved to report examples of "Dewenglish" in their columns:

"Sure, we've got some height. But what we don't have in height, we make up for in size," he told the *Orlando Sentinel*'s Bill Buchalter.

In a pep talk about sticking to training rules, he told his minions: "You can't just keep burning your bridges at both ends."

When explaining why he was resting a semi-injured player for two games, Dewey explained: "You've got to be careful not to kill the goose that laid the deviled egg."

Then there were the cryptic practice directives: "All right, men, line up alphabetically by height."

And: "Now I want everyone to pair up in threes and line up in a circle."

They could have given the credit to the ladies in the lunchroom for all Cassidy cared. He was on top of the world. Stiggs and Randleman told him he was becoming pretty obnoxious, but they were mostly kidding. Mostly.

Jim Cinnamon came by fifth-period study hall, which was held in the cafeteria. He talked to Mrs. Midyette, the monitor, then signaled Cassidy.

"Hope you don't mind me pulling you out of study hall like this," he said, his ripple-soled coaching shoes making little squeaks on the terrazzo hallway floor.

"No, sir. I've worked out enough quadratic equations to last the rest of the year. Is there anything wrong?"

"Not at all. I just wanted to talk to you about next season. That suit you?"

"Yes, sir!"

"I didn't think you'd mind. Say, are you growing again?"

"Yes, sir. I hope to be over six feet by next year," said Cassidy.

"Me too!" said Coach Cinnamon.

When they sat down in his office, Coach Cinnamon picked up a sheath of stapled mimeographed pages from a stack on the corner of his desk.

"This is the offense I'm thinking about running next year. It's basically a one-three-one, with a low post, a high post, and two wings. That essentially gives us two centers and two forwards. But the key is the last guy, the point guard. He has to be able to bring the ball up—under pressure sometimes—and he has to start the offense. He has to be able to hit from the outside so they can't sag on him and jam up the middle. He has to be able to penetrate so they can't just lay back in a zone. If he can manage all that, that lets us put a really big team on the floor: two inside big boys, two outside big boys—four tough rebounders on the boards on every shot."

Cassidy whistled.

"But it doesn't work without the point guard. He can't be a weak link. In fact, he has to be a strong link. If they can stifle him, they stifle the whole offense. He has to be aggressive and just . . . well, just active. He has to be in constant motion, a nonstop scoring threat, but always looking to penetrate the key or pass it inside to the big boys."

"Yes, sir."

"So. Think you can handle it?"

Cassidy could not pretend to be surprised. His JV team had often run much the same offense just because of the personnel they had on the floor and the fact that Cassidy didn't really need help bringing the ball up. They often found themselves with four big players and Cassidy. Dewey hadn't put in an offense that took advantage of that fact, so he just called one of the big men a "strong guard" and told them to run their regular offense. Stiggs and Cassidy quickly figured out how to use the extra forward, and they had basically come up with their own version of a 1-3-1.

Jim Cinnamon was now telling him that they were going to make that familiar formation their official offense for the next season.

"What I need to know, Quenton, is whether you think you can be our point guard?" he said.

After an 18–2 season and leading the JV team in scoring and several other categories, Cassidy had left his nerdy persona behind. Humility had never been his strong suit, and he was already developing an affinity for intentional mixed metaphors.

"Does a one-legged duck swim in the woods?" Cassidy said.

Coach Cinnamon gave him a strange look. "Afraid I don't follow."

"I mean, *yes, sir!*" said Cassidy.

CHAPTER 31

BAG BOY SUMMER

This was shaping up to be a pretty darned good summer despite the fact that Cassidy had what he thought was the most grueling and thankless job in Citrus City.

With no small amount of silent cussing, he got two heavily laden carts through the automatic doors and out into the ferocious heat and humidity of the commissary parking lot. It was payday and the place was packed with military wives and their squalling progeny, and the women always left the place with at least two grocery carts loaded to the scuppers with Pop-Tarts, Froot Loops, and Cheez Whiz.

Cassidy pushed one cart with his right hand while dragging the other one behind with his left. His customer, a young Filipina woman, had her hands full with a five-year-old girl who was blowing a steady stream of soap bubbles, and a three-year-old boy running around in a harness at the end of an honest-to-God leash.

Dog-boy eyed Cassidy suspiciously. He was wearing a little jumper embroidered with a happy-looking Dutch child and the legend BUSTER BROWN. Cassidy winked at him, causing him to widen his eyes with alarm and reach for the water pistol in the little plastic holster he wore around his nonexistent hips.

"Freddo, what did we talk about already?" said the mother.

Freddo pouted unhappily at his mother, whom Cassidy was just now noticing was actually pretty attractive. Freddo looked at him with narrowed eyes.

"What was it, Freddo?" she said. Freddo slumped in defeat, taking his hand off his six-shooter.

"NO 'QUIRTING!"

"That's right, baby, no squirting until we're in the backyard again."

"Thank you, ma'am," Cassidy told her out of the side of his mouth. Actually, he might not have minded a quick dousing, since he was sweating like a field hand as he maneuvered both carts through the blistering asphalt hell of the parking lot. Other bag boys whooped at him as they raced back to the store pushing empty carts. You had to go through a complete rotation, like a batting order, to get to be the lead bagger, the one who got the tip—if any. Everyone else pitched in and bagged like maniacs to help get their buddy out the door, not out of altruism or any sense of esprit de corps, but because the faster they got rid of the guy in front, the faster their turn came up.

Stiggs went flying by, riding his cart like a skateboard. He held up two dollar bills and waved them in Cassidy's face.

Damn, Cassidy thought. He had had just one cart, not even full at that, and he got two bucks! Must have been an officer's wife. Enlisted men's wives were the stingiest, but noncoms usually weren't too bad. Cassidy hoped his customer would pick up a hint from Stiggs's elation, but she seemed intent on reining in the dog-child, who was groaning mightily and straining at the end of his leash toward a parked 1932 Harley-Davidson seventy-four-inch flathead motorcycle that was still clicking and pinging as it dissipated heat.

"Don't let him . . ." Cassidy started, but it was too late. Dog-boy, completely helpless in the powerful spell of the machine, had fetched up at the end of his retractable leash but still had just enough room to reach out and touch the object of his fascination, the bright chrome exhaust of the elegant machine.

It took a second to register, but when the circle of synapses in

Freddo's little nervous system had finally completed the loop, the kid went wild.

"WAAAAAHHHHHHHHH!" He held his already blistering fingers up accusingly to his mother, crying so hard that for a moment he went completely silent as he tried to catch his breath for the next round.

Cassidy's heart sank as he tried to calculate how much extra time this was going to cost him before he could get back into the rotation.

The little girl was wholly unconcerned, happily tending her bubbles. The mom, at least, wasn't completely losing it. Apparently this was not Freddo's first experience with interesting objects that caused pain, and Cassidy was beginning to appreciate the undeniable utility of that harness.

By the time they got to the car, a de rigueur 1962 Ford Falcon station wagon, the woman had downgraded Freddo from panicky screaming to simple loud crying. Cassidy, dripping sweat now, had to clear out a space among the toys in back—Fanner-50 cap pistols, Etch A Sketch tablets, Little Princess coloring books, 112-color Crayolas, Slinkies, Silly Putty, Hot Wheels, Easy-Bake Oven, Doctor Who's Astro-Ray Dalek Gun, not to mention uncountable loose Lincoln Logs, dominoes, and Pick-up Sticks.

Goaded by Freddo's continued wailing, Cassidy loaded the groceries as fast as he could, and when he came to one heavy bag full of frozen stuff, he got a brainstorm and took the time to dig through the bag and locate a box of Popsicles. At his suggestion, the mom took a Popsicle and had Freddo hold it in his poor little burnt fingers. Whether out of real relief or mere distraction, he seemed somewhat mollified and the wailing was reduced to intermittent whimpering and finally to exhausted snuffling.

A favorite phrase of Cassidy's own mother's came to mind when she was especially exasperated with him: *I hope you have ten just like you.*

All loaded finally, the mother got behind the wheel and looked up at Cassidy with gratitude, then backed out and drove off. Cassidy stood, forlorn and unbelieving, watching the little station wagon pull away. A good solid half hour of blood, sweat, toil, and tears, and he had absolutely nothing to show for it.

Maybe she looked in the rearview and took pity on him. For whatever reason, the brake lights flashed on, the station wagon came to a stop. Slowly at first, then gaining speed, the car backed up all the way to where Cassidy stood with his two empty grocery carts.

His heart soared like a hawk!

The window rolled down, a brown, braceleted arm extended. Cassidy reached his hand out and she dropped the coins in. She drove off without a word as Cassidy looked down. Resting in his glistening palm were two shiny liberty head dimes.

The commissary itself was air-conditioned to a fare-thee-well, and since he worked there every day but Sunday, Cassidy suffered from a more or less permanent summer cold. On weekdays Randleman had a job as a fry cook at the Burger King on Dixie Highway, and Stiggs had lucked into a high-paying job with a plumbing contractor, soldering copper pipes. It was hard work, but he made real money, which his father made him deposit into an account at Citrus City First Federal.

But they all quit work at four P.M. and were at the base gym by four forty-five, about the time the servicemen started drifting in for their pickup games.

Stiggs was skinny as ever but had shot up to almost six six, and he had springs for legs. The weight room in the gym had a heavy-duty squat station, on which the three of them did three sets of half-squats every day after their games and drills. They did one set of eight or more reps with relatively light weight, one set of six reps with moderate weight, and one set of three or four reps with as much weight as they could tolerate.

Despite his thin frame, Stiggs could handle more than two hundred pounds on his final set. He could now stand flat-footed under the rim and dunk the ball one-handed. Randleman outweighed Stiggs by twenty pounds, but he could jump almost as high. And he was particularly good at maneuvering his sturdy frame underneath the boards.

Cassidy could now, with a running start, grab the rim one-handed and hang on like a monkey, though the coveted dunk still eluded him. He could occasionally slam home a volleyball, though, and that gave him great status in certain quarters.

Perhaps the best thing about coming into their own as ballplayers was the way the trio had slowly, almost imperceptibly, begun to be accepted by the gym regulars. They even had their own base nicknames.

"I pick Moose," said House, pointing to Randleman, who moved over to his side.

"I'll take the kid," said Ron Lefaro, pointing to Cassidy.

"Man choose Hot Shot," said House. "Got two shooters now. I take Stretch."

Stiggs joined House. They clearly had the rebounds. The rest of the candidates were divvied up. All three of the boys had been picked before any of the older players, but they weren't surprised anymore when that happened.

The games went on most of the afternoon, and to Cassidy's surprise, his team won most of them. Or more correctly, Lefaro *figured out* a way to win most of them.

"I don't get it," Cassidy said, resting in the bleachers during a break. "We got almost no rebounding whatsoever."

"Right," said Lefaro. "So what do you do?"

"I don't know," said Cassidy. "Punt?"

"No. You avoid creating rebounds."

Cassidy looked at him.

Lefaro slapped him on the knee. "You don't miss, Hot Shot! Just don't ever miss!"

Randleman had his mother's car, so they drove over to the cafeteria afterward. Cassidy got two cheeseburgers, two donuts, and two Cokes. Stiggs got a banana split, Randleman a tuna sandwich and potato salad. They inhaled it all so fast they sat at the Formica table afterward looking at each other and breathing hard, like they had just come off the court.

"Hey, I just realized something," said Stiggs.

"What's that?" Randleman said from under the table, where he was retying his Converse lowcuts.

"All three of us are going to start next year!"

"Shhh!" said Cassidy. "Don't put your mouth on it. Don't you dare put your mouth on it."

CHAPTER 32

GLORIOUS SEASON

All three of them started every game.

At the end of March they were 26–3 and ranked seventh in the state. They came back from the state tournament in Kernsville licking their wounds, but it had been an amazing season.

And because the first of April felt like summer already, Trapper Nelson proposed a tank dive trip in celebration; also, he had some people who had requested certain tropical fish—Trapper rarely did anything for pleasure alone. Jim Branch had loaned them his twenty-two-foot Aquasport with its commodious dive platform, so they cruised along for once in unaccustomed luxury.

Cassidy sat on the cushioned built-in seat in front of the center console while Trapper steered from behind. Cassidy looked down at his legs and was dismayed at how blindingly white they were in the morning sunshine. He tried to remember the last time he had done much of anything outside. Last summer? Basketball had rendered him a subterranean creature, peering painfully into the unfamiliar sunlight with pale vestigial eyeballs.

Beach houses and low-slung motels dotted the beaches of Singer Island before the larger structure of the Colonnades resort hove into sight.

"Wonder if Old Man MacArthur is at his favorite table in there counting napkins and salvaging catsup," Cassidy yelled back over his shoulder.

"Don't knock it until you've made a few million yourself," Trapper called back with a laugh. "I can tell you from personal knowledge he is a tough guy to do business with."

Strange, thought Cassidy. What kind of business a famously tight animal trapper would have had with the famously tight tycoon? He knew better than to ask.

They traversed the rough water at the opening of the Palm Beach inlet, where the sheltered waters of Lake Worth flowed into the wild Atlantic. They took a couple of chilly spray showers over the bow, enough to raise gooseflesh on Cassidy's fish belly legs, but in a few rough minutes they were past it.

"Sorry 'bout that," yelled Trapper.

Cassidy waved it off. *"No importa."*

More elaborate houses went by now, seaside "cottages" with eight or ten bedrooms and barrel-tiled roofs, the winter digs of America's generationally wealthy. They passed former ambassador to Cuba Earl E. T. Smith's place, then old Joe Kennedy's compound, perhaps close enough together, Cassidy thought, for the lovely Mrs. Smith to traipse across in a housecoat to trouble Rose for a cup of sugar.

When they got to the Breakers, Trapper took them close to shore, then turned and headed straight out into the Gulf Stream, looking over his shoulders for his landmarks. Cassidy stood up to help.

"What is it, the leftmost cupola of the Breakers and that church steeple?"

"Right, we've almost got it now. Then we veer off and pick up the TV antenna on that white house and the middle of the water tower."

It was a mysterious business, locating a precise section of sea bottom by triangulating points on land, but Trapper was good at it, and he never forgot his triangulation landmarks once he knew them. The water went from light aquamarine to dark aquamarine to, finally, the purple of the Gulf Stream.

"Okay," said Trapper, squinting landward under a shading hand, "that's it. Drop the anchor."

Cassidy tossed it overboard from the bow and watched the coiled line play out. They were in more than a hundred feet of water and the line buzzed out over the rub rail for a while. Finally it went slack. Cassidy fed thirty more feet into the water and cleated it off. The boat, which had seemed to be bobbing along in place, fetched up hard against the anchor rope and began riding into the current, which was fast enough to throw up a little wake under the bow.

"Enough scope?" asked Cassidy.

"Better give it another twenty feet or so. The tide is ripping pretty good. Last thing we need is to be dragging anchor out here. Jim Branch will make us swim to Jacksonville to fetch his boat."

Cassidy reset the anchor and joined Trapper in the back to suit up. The current flowing under them made it seem for all the world as if they were coursing along under power. Cassidy looked wearily at the pile of equipment at his feet: tanks, regulator, pressure gauge, weight belt, inflatable safety vest, dive knife, and wet suit top, not to mention the nets, prods, and jars they would need to catch tropicals.

"Now I remember why I like skin diving better," he said.

"Not to mention I hate the idea of paying someone for God's air. But you'll never catch any tropicals without tanks, unless you're in five feet of water with no current."

"Mmmm," said Cassidy, wiggling into the tight wet suit top. He wouldn't bother with the bottoms today. It wouldn't be that cold in the stream, even at 110 feet.

Trapper attached his regulator to the valve at the top of the tank, tightened it, opened the flow knob until he heard a hiss that instantly diminished to silence as the regulator hoses filled. He bit on the mouthpiece and inhaled, immediately getting a mechanical click and a rush of the cold, compressed air. He picked up the pressure gauge, saw that it read eighteen hundred pounds, then put the tank aside and started on the rest of the rigmarole.

"Well, I want to hear all about the game, of course. If it's not too painful, that is. In the regionals against Cocoa I thought I'd have a heart attack. I wanted to go up to Kernsville for the finals, but then Marcie and Nell were here with the kids and I just couldn't leave them alone at the camp."

"Sure, of course. You didn't miss much but the crushing disappointment. But for the first three quarters you would have been just like the rest of us, counting your chickens and looking forward to Tampa Hillsborough the next night."

"So who was it you lost to?"

"Jacksonville Paxon. Bunch of football players, mostly. They didn't even have a coach until right before the season started. Had to get a teacher to volunteer to take them. We weren't too worried about them, and it did seem like a cakewalk for a while. At one point we had them by thirteen."

"So what happened?"

Cassidy shrugged. "They put on a full-court press and we just experienced a sudden loss of cabin pressure. They kept chipping away at the lead and we kept forgetting how to play basketball until, with fifty-six seconds left, it was fifty-six to fifty-six. I'll never forget it, the scoreboard just read fifty-six–fifty-six–fifty-six straight across."

"Oooh. Tense."

"You said it. They stalled around with it and Stiggs damn near stole the ball when they tried to get it inside to this man-mountain named Clyde Israel. But Stiggs couldn't hang on to it and it went out-of-bounds on the sidelines. Okay, so now they get the ball out-of-bounds and there's like two seconds left."

"Gulp," said Trapper.

"Yeah, I know. So their guard throws it in to one of the football players, this guy Ron Sellers, a six-four wide receiver, who I'm guard-ing. He's about forty-five feet out and everyone in the gym knows he's going to shoot, right? But I've got four fouls, and I'm just assuming, like everyone else in the gym, that this game is going to overtime. And I'd be damned—pardon my French—if I was going to sit there and watch the most important period of basketball of my life from the bench. So I make sure there is discernible separation between us—I don't want to give some antsy ref any excuses—and I go straight up with him and get a hand right in his face."

"From forty-five feet still?"

"If it was an inch. So here I am, high as I can go, hand in his face, and this yahoo football player lets fly. The ball is in midflight as the buzzer goes off . . ."

"Let me guess."

"Oh, of course. Tore the *bottom* out of the net."

Trapper Nelson made a low, sympathetic whistle.

"Something, isn't it?" said Cassidy. "The SOBs were never in the lead at any time during the regulation thirty-two minutes of the game. Not from the opening tip-off until the final buzzer. But they darned sure won anyway."

"Sounds like one of those high school sports novels," said Trapper.

"Yeah, it does," said Cassidy. "Except it's the hero who's supposed to be shooting that last-second shot, not some football player from Jacksonville."

Trapper stood up and checked his equipment, then sat on the gun-nel, spitting into his mask and leaning back to rinse it in seawater.

"Well, I'm no expert, of course, but it seems to me that the defi-nition of the word 'hero' in the sporting context is just exactly 'the guy who hits the last-second shot,'" said Trapper, but his tone was sympathetic.

Cassidy, now ready on the opposite gunnel, spat and rinsed his own mask. The sun was high enough now that he could feel the reassuring warmth on his salty face. He was even starting to sweat inside his wet suit.

"Yeah, well, about seven thousand people in Florida Gym as well as every sportswriter in the state would agree with you there. Technically, I would too, but . . ."

He put on his mask and bit down on the mouthpiece of his regulator, then took it out and held it in front of his mouth.

". . . well, except gosh darn it, Trap, *we* were supposed to be the heroes of this story. I was sure of it." He stuck the regulator into his mouth and grinned around it.

Trapper nodded, still smiling. He could hardly believe this rangy near-man was the same barefoot waif he'd befriended on the Loxahatchee River so many years ago. Having had heartbreak in his own life, Trapper knew it wasn't easy coming to grips with those times when life didn't follow the Hollywood narrative. Trapper took the regulator out of his mouth.

"Okay, hero. Let's go catch some tropicals," he said, replacing it and flipping backward into the purple Gulf Stream.

Their world went silent as soon as they were under, and had to swim precisely like heroes to make it to the bow of the boat and grab the anchor line. From there they could relax and proceed hand over hand down through the surging current. On the bottom the flow would be slower and they could propel themselves along using handholds on the ocean floor, which was a lot more efficient than trying to swim against the current.

And handholds there were. As the bottom slowly coalesced out of the general bluish gloom, Cassidy at first thought that Trapper had made some kind of mistake. It seemed they were over nothing more than large rolling sand dunes, rippled on the surface but otherwise lacking feature or distinction. But then as they got within fifty feet of the bottom, Cassidy saw two of the largest groupers he had ever seen in his life, one Nassau, one spotted black, cruising lazily over the top of one of the dunes, disappearing down the other side.

Damn, thought Cassidy, *what a day to be after tropicals.* Then he thought of what a sixty-pound fish could do with his stainless steel Hawaiian sling shaft, and he decided it was probably better he didn't have it. Unless he was in good enough spear-fishing shape to get a clean head or spine shot, he would have to have a big gun with a corded spear, and even then a grouper of that size could drag him all over the ocean bottom.

And that bottom, he could now see, was not sand but mostly coral, pockmarked and riddled with fissures and apertures of all shapes and sizes. When they got within ten feet of the anchor itself, Cassidy was amazed to see that most of the holes and fissures exhibited a live face, some curious denizen peering out at him, wondering what was out there making all those bubbles.

Trapper clinked the handle of his dive knife against the bottom of his tank to get Cassidy's attention. He pointed to a clump of outcroppings upstream from where the anchor was lodged in a small crevice. The outcrops were coral, too. Just one kind of coral growing on top of another kind of coral. But as they approached them it was clear to Cassidy why Trapper liked this spot.

Though the depth of the water filtered out most color from the sun's spectrum, this bluish-tinted vault was full of creatures of almost every shape and hue, living ornaments that could swim. Some were so exotic they seemed a product not of the natural world but of some schizophrenic jeweler. All up under the coral heads and throughout the myriad passages you could see them by the thousands: squirrel-fish, sergeant majors, beau gregories, top hats, Cuban hogfish, baby triggerfish, royal grammas, queen angels, rock beauties, French angels, and countless varieties of tangs, damsels, grunts, and wrasses. They roiled in the surging current like an explosion of neon confetti.

Trapper particularly wanted to get a rock beauty, a gorgeous species of angelfish with a black body and a golden face and tail. Its face was fatter and more expressive than most of the angels, and that gave them, to Cassidy's way of thinking, not only more personality but also an air of intelligence and curiosity.

Trapper motioned to one that was about the size he wanted, and they both took up a position near the fish's territory to observe him. Holding on to the coral with one hand to avoid being pushed away by the current, Trapper used a small probe to chase the fish from his preferred lingering spot. The fish left his hole and rushed to another three feet away. When he was flushed from there, he left and went to a third hole, and when flushed again, he returned to his original home. Most of the tropicals maintained that kind of three-cornered evasion pattern, and it worked well enough to evade most of their antagonists but was scarcely sufficient to baffle the single curious vertebrate on the planet capable of recognizing a triangle.

Trapper handed Cassidy the restaurant-size mayonnaise jar that had been carefully cleaned of all traces of paper label and glue and was thus all but invisible to the fish. Cassidy lined up the mouth of the jar directly in the pathway between the rock beauty's second and third hidey-holes. Trapper prodded the fish from spot one to spot two, then from two to three. The fish bumped into the rim of the jar's spout, thought it over for a second, then went around. Cassidy scooched the jar over two more inches, then took his hand away so as not to spook the little beauty. This time around he swam directly into the mayonnaise jar and bumped into the bottom of it before he figured out that something was wrong. By that time, Trapper had the top on and was giving Cassidy a thumbs-up.

Then they got two French angels, a top hat, and another rock beauty before Trapper held up his gauge and showed Cassidy that he had only two hundred pounds of air left. Cassidy checked his and saw that he had nearly twice that. But it was always the hard breathers who dictated the length of the dive, so he nodded to Trapper and pointed up. Trapper nodded. They gathered up their things into the net bags and attached them to the weight belts. Their prizes had all been herded into one of the large mayonnaise jars, with its lid screwed down finger tight, to allow the pressure to escape as they rose.

They crabbed along the bottom to the anchor, where Trapper indicated to Cassidy to go up the rope first.

Once on the surface, the boat was still bouncing through the current like it was in a race. The dive platform on the back slammed up and down in the waves until Cassidy thought it would tear the hinges off. Swimming to the height of their ability with the rocket fins, they began dropping equipment over the gunnel, leaving their fins on so they would still have maneuverability in the water. Trapper took his tank off first. This was the tricky part. Even empty, the tank was heavy and awkward to deal with in the water. Together, they both swam upward as hard as they could and finally shoved the tank over the gunnel and into the boat. Trapper then pulled himself up on the dive platform, where he removed his fins and swung his feet around into the boat. He could now take Cassidy's tank and help him onto the platform and into the boat with little trouble.

Trapper immediately began searching up under the console until he found a nylon zip-up case of small tools. He removed a needle from a small vial while Cassidy hurriedly unscrewed the mayonnaise jar and started removing the fish, each of which now looked like he had a small balloon attached to his underside. Trapper took them one by one and carefully inserted the needle into their swollen air bladders. The tropicals, now rid of all the compressed air they brought with them from the depths, swam around calmly in their new temporary home.

Trapper held them up admiringly, their colors now startling and fully saturated in the sunshine. The first rock beauty, the larger of the two, was especially elegant. It swam around serenely, ignoring its fellow captives, staring out through the glass walls at a strange waterless world it had never seen before and could not have imagined.

They had not taken any lunch with them, and by the time they got back to Trapper's camp on the Loxahatchee they were both ravenous.

"There's some smoked amberjack in the icebox," said Trapper. "See what else you can find in there. I've got to get these little gems into the holding tank."

"How do you keep that thing aerated? I thought you didn't have any electricity."

"I don't. Got an old pump mounted to a concrete block out on the river bottom. It just blows a stream of bubbles through this hose here. Everything else in the place runs on propane, including that refrigerator that you're standing in front of letting all the cold air out of."

Cassidy fetched a jar of homemade tartar sauce and a tub of dill pickles and closed the fridge.

"Amberjack sandwiches okay?"

"Sounds good to me. I could eat a horseshoe crab." Trapper was carefully transferring the tropicals into the big tank at the end of his living room. He watched the fish for a few moments to make sure they were not in shock from all the handling, then washed his hands at the sink and began to help Cassidy.

"Jeeminy, how tall are you getting to be anyway? I believe you've about caught up to me." Trapper put his flat hand on top of Cassidy's head and moved it across to his own head, where it came near the top of his forehead.

"About six one, maybe a little more. I hope I'm over six two by next season. That'll make me the tallest guard in south Florida."

"I don't doubt it. How about Stiggs and Randleman? They must be about seven feet by now."

Cassidy put the thick sandwiches onto paper plates and, after fetching two glasses of sweetened cold tea from the refrigerator, they sat down on the screened-in porch overlooking the river.

"Well, they're both about six six, but I think they may be about done. But they're both getting letters from college coaches. Stiggs got one last week from Lefty Driesell at Davidson."

"Oh yeah? What'd it say?"

"It said, 'Oh, Mr. Stiggs, we think you are so wonderful and we just won twenty games this year and we'd just *love* to have you come help us win twenty-one next year.'"

"How about you? You must be hot property yourself."

"Not really. Got a note from the guy at Florida Presbyterian and a postcard from Glenn Wilkes at Stetson."

"Yeah?"

"Said he had to save his scholarships for big guys, but if I was interested, he would try to get me some loans and stuff."

"Well, that's something."

"I don't think anyone's getting too excited about a barely six-foot-tall, skinny guard. Maybe if I have a really good year next year they'll come knocking."

"How about track? Are you running any?"

"I thought about it, but they've hired coach Bickerstaff from Glenridge to replace Blackwelder as track coach. He still acts kind of squirrelly around me. Besides, they've had two meets already and I'm in terrible running shape. It was weird, I was in such good shape at the end of the summer that I think I could have done pretty well at cross-country. Then once basketball started, I just slowly got out of shape. And I even ran laps around the gym every day before practice."

"Well, I know you love basketball and all, but . . ."

"What?"

"Oh, it was something Archie San Romani said back when you were doing those workouts of his before the all-comers meet. I was going to tell you, but then you made the basketball team and I just . . . Well, I probably shouldn't even say anything now."

"Come on, Trap."

"Well, he said that considering the progress you made in those few weeks, that he had never seen a runner your age do anything like that. He said . . ."

Trapper, lost in thought, was watching a pair of mullet jumping almost in tandem right next to his dock.

"Trapper! What'd he say?"

"He said that you were a natural-born runner, and that it would be a shame if you didn't pursue it."

"Really?"

"He said you were given a gift. That you were one in a million and you shouldn't squander that."

CHAPTER 33

DEWEY STODDARD

Third-period History of Western Civilization was taught by the pear-shaped, flattopped Dewey Stoddard, Cassidy's former JV basketball coach, who had since been promoted to offensive and defensive line coach on the football team.

Dressed in enormous red canvas coaching shorts, a white cotton polo shirt with a flying eagle over the pocket, tube socks, and black ripple-soled coaching shoes, Dewey in a classroom was as incongruous as a brown bear at Tiffany's. His teaching style was a thing of his own invention. Leaning back against his desk, licking his thumb, and leafing languidly through the textbook, he would read more or less random passages while a buzzing fan blew warmish air back and forth across the heat-stunned students. He would occasionally attempt to interpret certain historical events with a modern sensibility, particularly as they might pertain to, say, football. The fan would have drowned out a lot of teachers, but Dewey's practice field voice boomed off the walls of the stuffy classroom.

This morning it was already warm although only ten o'clock. Air-conditioning was a blessing found only in movie theaters, drugstores, and a few homes of the well-off. There weren't even any official electric fans in the building either, but a few teachers like Dewey purchased them and brought them to school on their own. The school board wasn't even embarrassed.

Cassidy still had very little posterior cushioning, so the hard desk seats were uncomfortable even under the best of conditions. On steamy spring mornings like this, his cotton underwear and thin pants would fuse itchily to his skin, and when he squirmed, the oak veneer seat would grind into his meager tuber ischiadicum. Every now and again he would lean forward and, as surreptitiously as he could, peel the irritating fabric away from his inflamed coccyx and try to remain in that awkward vulture-leaning position long enough for the fabric to dry out a little.

But worse than cheek itch were these lectures.

"All right, people, let's take a look at this fella, the Emperor Charlemagne," said Dewey, holding up his open text to the appropriate chapter in case anyone might think he was just making this up. He pronounced it, believe it or not, "Empra Charlie Mange."

Dewey was a big fan of conquerors, whom he considered to be the progenitors of modern football coaches, and as far as Dewey was concerned, much of the ebb and flow of Western civilization could be explained in gridiron terms. Cassidy had come to believe that Dewey was an undiscovered comedic genius, and when he came out with a good one, Cassidy would roll his eyes at Ed Demski in the next row.

"Now, if you Charlie Mange, you look around your territory and you get to frettin' about what you see," said Dewey. "You got your defenses and all, but you look out across your borders, and whatcha got?"

Dewey's unique style of pedagogy was to personalize the subject matter by figuratively placing the student right in a historical epoch in order to make the past "come alive." This he learned at a Division III land grant institution near Dothan, Alabama.

"Why, you're a Christian and all you got is pagan opponents. You got your Saxons, you got your Goths. Heck, you got your Slavs and your Basques, too. You throw in a few Moors and Huns and, why, next thing you know you completely surrounded by heathens! And you about to get sacked in y'own backfield!"

Cassidy knew where this was headed. He tore a corner off a sheet of notebook paper, folded it in half, and wrote, "Charlie Mange is going up the middle. Probably off-tackle," and slipped it to Ed Demski, who had been going to a speech therapist twice a week and hardly stuttered at all anymore. He glanced at the note, turned beet red, put his chin in his hand, and started studying the Map of the Ancient World hanging on the side wall.

"So he says to hisself, 'Hey, I got a army. I got horses and catapults and whatnot. I bet I could whip them others!' Mr. Dinsky, is there somethin' a'matter with you, son?"

Demski swallowed hard, looked up briefly at Dewey, and shook his head, his bulbous eyes glistening.

"No, sir," he croaked.

Ed managed to keep himself more or less under control by looking anywhere but directly at Dewey. A Mexican standoff of several seconds' duration took place as Dewey glared at him and Ed kept his eyes carefully trained on the big rotating Breeze King fan. Dewey was about to return to A.D. 768 when Ed let loose a loud, involuntary snort, quickly covering his mouth and turning his head aside. The class tittered.

"Listen up, Mr. Dinsky. You had better straighten up and fly right, son. Is there somethin' you find amusin' about the Empra Charlie Mange?"

Cassidy coughed. Demski shook his head, choking and red faced.

"Well, then, I . . ."

"I think I s-swallowed a gnat!" Demski croaked. For some reason, he had always pronounced it "guh-nat." It brought the house down.

"Well, hellfire, son, go get a drink a' water or somethin'! Don't let a little inseck innarrup everbody else's education here!"

"Yes, sir!" Demski blurted, absconding in a flash, even taking his books with him. *Damn*, Cassidy wondered, *how did that happen?*

Cassidy sighed. Now that Ed had escaped, this class was going to be worse than church. He looked around for other victims, but the only potential target was in the desk behind Ed's, Maria DaRosa. Cassidy had known her since they were tiny and knew she was nowhere near as easy as Demski. What's more, she was perfectly capable of cracking *Cassidy* up, in which case he'd be the one in trouble.

She smiled sweetly at him. "Let's go, big boy," she mouthed silently. Cassidy crossed his eyes and stuck his tongue prominently into his left cheek: no response.

"Jesus H.," said Dewey, glaring at the door closing behind Demski. "All right, people, settle down. It was just a little gnat. No need to fly off the handle. Now, let's get back to . . . What is it, Mr. Cassidy?"

"Coach Stoddard, if I swallow a guh-nat, can I leave, too?"

Pandemonium ruled for thirty seconds while Dewey glowered. Fortunately, Cassidy had a certain amount of limited immunity, being a member of one of the two "revenue" sports.

Besides, Dewey was a little amused himself, though he dared not show it. Instead, he focused his red-faced football death ray on him until Cassidy looked properly contrite and the rest of the class finally quieted. In his peripheral vision Cassidy noticed with satisfaction that he had finally gotten to Maria DaRosa.

"Mr. Cassidy, you cruisin' for a bruisin'. Do you read me, son?"

"Yes, sir," said Cassidy meekly. Maria winked at him.

"All right, then. Now, Charlie Mange, people. Pay attention . . ."

Unfortunately, his ad-libbed introductory summation had exhausted his knowledge and unique take on the subject matter, so Dewey returned to his primary teaching technique of reading from the textbook.

"Charlie Mange, also known as Charles the Great, was borned in either . . ."

The business with Cassidy, Ed, and Maria had been going on for some time but had really picked up the year before in Miss Ameison's Spanish class when a standard-issue funny face from Cassidy caught Demski by surprise and brought the rather mild wrath of the dainty Miss Ameison descending upon his asymmetrical noggin. *That was too easy*, Cassidy thought.

The next day the class was silently taking the weekly multiple-choice vocabulary test, and Cassidy was concentrating mightily: was *pollo* apple or chicken?

He heard a fake cough and looked over at the unsmiling Demski, who had removed his jacket and was working intently on his test in a three-sizes-too-small T-shirt with a graphic of a huge baseball with crossed bats and the bold legend JUNIOR MAJOR LEAGUER. In a ring around the baseball were circular mug shots of a number of the biggest stars of the American and National Leagues: Mickey Mantle, Roger Maris, Clete Boyer, Joe DiMaggio, Jackie Robinson, Sandy Koufax, Ernie Banks, Willie Mays, Yogi Berra, Whitey Ford, and Peewee Reese.

Cassidy lost it and was promptly banished from the class. As he was being escorted to the door with a note for the principal, written by the actually quite pissed-off Miss Ameison, he had to admire how calmly and methodically Ed had simply slipped his jacket back on, leaving most of the class—as well as Miss Ameison—thoroughly confused about the source of the ruckus.

Not everyone had missed it. Maria DaRosa gave Demski a thumbs-up. It was shortly after that that she and Cassidy started occasionally going out "as friends."

After Dewey's class, a grinning Demski was waiting by the water fountain.

"Hey, thanks for giving me the royal shaft, ya big spaz," Demski said, mock-frogging him on the deltoid.

"You kidding me?" said Cassidy. "You had it made in the shade, buddy. You got to skip most of Charlie Mange and . . . Say, how did you come up with that 'gnat' thing, anyway?"

They started making their way down the crowded hall toward Mr. Kamrad's class.

"I d-didn't come up with anything, man. *I actually swallowed a guh-nat.*"

CHAPTER 34

BOB BICKERSTAFF REDUX

Coach Jim Cinnamon pushed his reading glasses toward the end of his nose so he could read, for perhaps the two hundredth time, the brass plate on the large trophy sitting on the end of his credenza:

> 1963–64 Class 4-A Region 4 Champions
> Citrus City Edgewater High School
> Jim Cinnamon, Coach

He could still barely believe it. They had beaten Cocoa 51–49 in a wild back-and-forth battle that had seen three of his starters foul out, including Stiggs and Randleman. But Cassidy had hit seven for nine from the floor and Stewart's two free throws at the end had clinched the game.

The state semifinal in Kernsville had been just as wild, but this time without a happy ending, and the bus ride back to South Florida had been long and quiet. With all but one of the starters returning next year, though, the sportswriters were already talking about next season. Not bad work for someone in just his fifth year of varsity coaching.

Cinnamon shook his head clear and got back to work. He was

writing out in longhand some formations he wanted to give the players to study over the summer.

Pressing hard with his ballpoint pen to cut the stencil, he wrote:

Diamond I Zone Press

This press is not designed to steal the ball every time, but to constantly harass a team and force it into mistakes. In this particular defense it is possible for us to overplay our opponents for the interception and still have them covered in case they break the press.

Each player must always be alert and on his toes in order to cut off an attempt to pass to his man—this pass must never be completed. The inbound pass must be a long one, at least to the back of the foul circle. Several steals, interceptions, or turnovers of any type will break down the morale of any team.

His big men had good hands and decent speed down the court. It would shock everyone in the conference next year if they came out in a full-court press. It was counter to all traditional wisdom of the game. Big teams were supposed to hang around the rim and take utmost advantage of their height. Small teams were supposed to keep you from getting the ball upcourt without a battle. They nipped at you like little terriers, biting at your ankles, trying to provoke mistakes by sheer obnoxiousness.

Cinnamon used a ruler and compass to draw several court diagrams on the page, crosshatching the areas of responsibility for each man, identified as X1 through X5. Thirty minutes later he wrote the concluding paragraph:

After we have scored, X5 must turn and run down the floor as hard and as fast as he can. He must get back in order to release X1. If this release of X1 is too slow, it gives the opposition time to find an open man.

The primary objective of this defense is to pick off the first pass, and if everyone carries out his assignment, this objective will be accomplished.

He went back over the four pages, making sure he had not left anything out. He paper-clipped the pages together, along with a note to the mimeo clerk about the number of copies he needed and when he needed them, along with a little pretend begging to get them earlier, if possible.

He was just finishing up when Dewey Stoddard stuck his large flattopped head in the door.

"Hey, Dew, what's up?" said Cinnamon.

"Denise says you have a call on line one. Someone named Doug DeAngelis from Miami Senior."

"Okeydoke. Probably wants to schedule us. Hey, if you're going that way anyway, can you drop these off at the mimeo room?"

The article on the front page of the *Citrus City Sentinel Star* read:

CINNAMON SIGNS ON WITH STINGAREES
By Al Whitmarsh
Sentinel Sports Staff

Jim Cinnamon, who led the Edgewater Eagles to the state semifinals this year, is heading south.

The Metro Conference Coach of the Year has been hired to lead one of the oldest and most consistently dominant basketball powerhouses in the state, Miami Senior High School, said Stingaree athletic director Douglas DeAngelis at a press conference in Miami yesterday.

"Coach Cinnamon has shown the kind of innovative and inspirational leadership in his career that we have always prized at Miami Senior, and now that Al Blanchard is stepping down after 22 years and seven state championships . . ."

Stunned, Cassidy sped through the paragraphs of boilerplate coach-speak. It was all blah blah "He'll have some pretty big shoes to fill . . ." (DeAngelis) and blah blah "Hate to leave such an outstanding group of young men . . ." (Cinnamon) and "I can't think of a better man to take over . . ." (Blanchard) and "Just too great an opportunity to pass up . . ." (Cinnamon again).

Finally, in the last paragraph, he found what he was looking for:

Edgewater principal Howard Fleming announced at the same press conference that Bob Bickerstaff, who was an all-conference guard in his college playing days at Eastern Kentucky, will take over the top hoops job. Bickerstaff is currently Edgewater's track and field coach. Fleming said that Dennis Kamrad, the current crew coach, will now assume the track and field duties as well.

Cassidy, still in a daze, went to the phone on the kitchen wall and, with the greatest of difficulty, after three tries managed to successfully dial a number he had known almost his whole life.

"Stiggs?" he said. "What is . . . I mean . . . Stiggs . . . *what the hell?*"

CHAPTER 35

CHANGING OF THE GUARD

Summer doldrums had already arrived in the hallways of Edgewater, though it was only the end of April. Everyone called it spring fever. Students strolled slack-jawed down hallways in the direction of classes they'd had the year before. They dozed in Western Civ after lunch and studied passing clouds through the windows in Trig. Shop teachers carefully chaperoned the use of any type of machine capable of removing digits. Couples made out behind opened locker doors, and other mating rituals could be seen. Who says the semitropics are seasonless?

The shock of Jim Cinnamon's announced departure was almost matched by Jim Cinnamon's actual departure. He had said he was eager to get started in Miami, and everyone agreed that it was such an awkward situation that it would probably be best if he'd just go ahead and go. The bastard.

Bob Bickerstaff wasted no time in calling for a team powwow. For privacy's sake and the lack of any better place—the football team had the varsity locker room for spring practice—it was held after fifth period in the tiny weight room at the end of the gymnasium. Everyone sat around on different kinds of apparatus and benches, moody and subdued. Cassidy lounged on a stack of evil-smelling wrestling mats.

Finally, Stiggs got bored waiting for Bickerstaff to show up and began entertaining everyone with his imitation of Dewey Stoddard giving a pregame talk.

"These Riviera boys are not only big and quick, but they're also very, uh . . . quick!" For a prop, he held up and pretended to be reading from an upside-down clipboard.

Bickerstaff looked mildly perplexed at the guffaws as he entered but quickly surmised that the culprit was Stiggs, who was just taking his seat, carrying, for some reason, the weight room workout clipboard. Bickerstaff took off his ever-present Red Sox cap and ran a hand through his red crew cut.

"Boys, I know the events of the past few days have come as a real big surprise. They have been real upsetting for a lot of us. Coach Cinnamon has been a force to be reckoned with at Edgewater for the past five years, and I think I speak for everyone when I say that he will be greatly missed . . ."

Negative rumbling in the ranks indicated that he did not speak for everyone.

". . . and that we certainly wish him all the best in his new, uh, endeavor."

More rumbling. Rather than all the best, some apparently wished him all the worst. Some wished him to be stranded in the Everglades on his way south, to be found weeks later, his rib cage providing refuge for pollywogs. Aw, who were they kidding? They loved the guy. They just couldn't believe he would up and abandon them like that, particularly after the amazing season they'd had. Miami Senior was a '50s-era juggernaut; their old coach still thought the two-handed set shot was just swell. They hadn't even made it out of their group last season.

"Some of you only know me as the track coach or possibly a driver's ed instructor," Bickerstaff said. "Some of you know me from Glenridge. Well, I just want you to know that I've seen most of your games—home games, anyway—and I understand what kind of spirit and pride this team has, and what kind of success you achieved this past season. I don't intend to come in here and upset the apple cart. Or as Coach Stoddard says, 'I won't kill the goose that laid the deviled egg.'"

That got a good laugh. A Dewey reference was always good for a tension breaker.

The mood proceeded to lighten considerably, particularly as Bickerstaff praised the team's accomplishments and pledged to keep things "on an even keel." He said that what he most highly prized was "hustle and teamwork" and that as far as he was concerned the secret to success in basketball as well as in life was "just plain hard work."

No one was about to quarrel with the kind of good old American Calvinist boilerplate that had been drummed into them since they had first set foot on a court or playing field years ago as larval athletes. Everyone seemed fully in accord, except Cassidy, who was thinking to himself, *How about just putting the ball in the hole? Surely they still award two points for that?*

But generally speaking, the meeting broke up in good spirits, everyone now carrying the mimeographed "suggested" workout program for the summer. (Cassidy glanced at the pitiful amount of jogging proposed and sighed audibly.)

He was afraid that Bickerstaff had heard him, because the coach asked him to linger after the rest of the rowdies had filed out with their general end-of-the-school-year good spirits restored.

Bickerstaff came and sat beside him on the pile of wrestling mats.

"Look, Quenton, I know we've had our differences in the past. I certainly acknowledge my share of the responsibility and I'm hoping you can acknowledge yours. I'm hoping we can put all that behind us now and work together at making this the best basketball team in the state."

Cassidy was unaware of exactly what kind responsibility he might bear for finding himself injured while on Bickerstaff's track team, but he nonetheless replied with a snappy, "Yes, sir!"

"Okay, good! That's the spirit! That's exactly what I wanted to hear! Now, I have a few things I wanted to go over with you . . ."

And Bickerstaff then proceeded to explain precisely how he planned to kill the goose that laid the deviled egg.

CHAPTER 36

WINDING UP

The rest of the school year consisted of that series of anticlimaxes everyone associates with generally winding things up: senior day, graduation practice, yearbook mania. The popular kids would sit on the concrete benches outside classrooms beside a stack of yearbooks, exuding exasperation at the enormity of their burden. Oh, and would you sign mine, too? It's around here somewhere; I think Sandra has it now and Phil is next. Can you get it from him?

The wallflowers searched the passing crowd for people they wouldn't be too embarrassed to ask. Being generally shy with people he didn't know well, Cassidy had a foot in both camps. He was nonetheless assured many times in yearbookese as to his ace personality and limitless future. Stiggs and Randleman took up several pages each, both recounting numerous childhood adventures and silly exploits from basketball road trips, the majority of which seemed to involve water balloons and/or shaving cream.

The three of them triple-dated to the prom, Randleman driving his mother's Volkswagen minibus, whose boxy interior nonetheless could barely contain the elongated tibias and femurs of half its occupants, nor the plastic hoops, bows, sashes, and acres of pastel crinoline of the other half.

Their arrival at the dance attracted a small hooting crowd that was more than entertained by the circuslike aspects of their unloading. The boys had to exit in sections, stepping backward onto the curb while unfolding like jackknives, while the girls popped out one at a time, each suspended in the door momentarily by the compression of her superstructure, springing free suddenly like an orange seed squeezed between wet fingers.

Cassidy of course took the radiant Maria, as it was becoming more and more ridiculous to continue pleading palship. Maybe it had started out that way, Cassidy wasn't sure. Somewhere in the middle of a drive-in showing of *Hush . . . Hush, Sweet Charlotte*, everything had changed. He sometimes intuited that despite what he had been occasionally led to believe, in this particular relationship, he was nowhere near in charge.

Randleman took the dark and beautiful Ruthie Lawrence, one of the tiniest girls in school, who somehow managed to still look diminutive, relatively speaking, in her pale lavender wedding cake of a dress. She and Randleman slow dancing to "Red Roses for a Blue Lady" looked like Paul Bunyan swaying in place with a shin guard made out of a kewpie doll.

Stiggs went with Jerri Frazier, a blond cheerleader he had been dating since halfway through basketball season and about whom he refused to make any locker room comment whatsoever, leading many to speculate that perhaps they had gone most of the way or something like it. This relationship was considered anomalous, as the cheerleaders had been pronounced "solipsistic and frivolous." Cassidy had discovered the wonders of *Roget's Thesaurus*. Besides, they mostly preferred football players anyway. Jerri, a serious, gray-eyed senior, was an exception. She had set her cap for Stiggs early on and the poor dope never knew what hit him.

Dinner at Ronnie's restaurant had been hilarious and nearly irrelevant from a nutritional point of view. Everyone was too excited by what Cassidy called "good old whatever it is" to eat much of anything. On the way to the dance, though Randleman recused himself, the rest of them had a few swigs of Mogen David concord grape wine that Stiggs had filched from what his parents thought was their secret stash. Cassidy was pleasantly surprised to find that an adult alcoholic libation could actually taste almost as good as the kind of beverage he was used to, to wit, Nehi Grape Soda.

They danced beneath the glittering mirror ball. They danced to the Beatles, the Stones, Herman's Hermits. They went out to the hibiscus-scented patio overlooking Lake Formosa, where boys shed their jackets in the humidity and danced to Del Shannon and Petula Clark. They even waxed nostalgic when someone put on some oldies like Buddy Holly, Patsy Cline, and the Big Bopper. Nothing, Cassidy thought, will secure your place in the teen pantheon like plunging to a fiery death in a private plane.

All too soon they were playing "Good Night Irene" by Screamin' Jay Hawkins, and then it was beachward ho, where the junior and senior classes of Edgewater High School were tradition-bound on prom night to exchange their tuxes and crinolines for surfing baggies and polka-dot bikinis and sleep in the itchy sand of Florida's Gold Coast, where, by a time-honored calculus of multiplying a certain quantity of alcohol by a maximum dose of sleep deprivation, followed by a lot of salty romping in the blazing tropical sun, they might eventually achieve the most sustainable teenage high possible without schedule one narcotics.

And, under the circumstances, historically it all went pretty much according to plan, though there was a tiny fraction over the years who really didn't seem to get the big picture, or who maybe got it all too well and ended up like the Big Bopper et al in some flaming calamity out on A1A, their meager passage on this coil now marked only by black-bordered photographs in next year's yearbook and the heart-rending ad hoc plastic flower arrangements scattered all along South Florida's two-lane blacktops that Cassidy called "prom crosses."

But the VW minivan clown car returned to home port with its occupants none the worse for wear, though they were certainly dazed, sunburned and, or so they thought, a little hungover. Actually, they were mostly just exhausted. But they had survived their junior prom in decent order, and there were some who could not say as much.

The next week it was the All-Sports banquet, held annually in the same cafeteria where they consumed their Salisbury steak, mashed potatoes, and vegetable medleys during the week. As befitting a festive occasion, someone had taped up some crepe paper basketballs, footballs, and tennis rackets to the walls, but there really was no disguising the same old lunchroom.

Cassidy, Stiggs, and Randleman sat with their teammates and dates, along with the new coach and his wife. Coach Cinnamon had been invited but sent regrets.

The football team had barely broken even that year, so for once the coaches and players were sincerely humble, if not sheepish, in presenting their awards and rendering their various postmortems and rationalizations. But everyone understood that the whole year had been dominated by basketball and therefore so was the sports banquet.

Despite the stifling air in the cafeteria, the boys all immediately put on their letter sweaters as soon as they got them. Bickerstaff did a nice little sum-up and tribute to that year's team, along with his barely contained enthusiasm for what they would undoubtedly accomplish next year. Stiggs won Most Valuable Player, Randleman was Top Rebounder, and Cassidy was Most Improved.

Cassidy didn't think he'd improved that much, he just got a chance to play is all. But he was happy with his little trophy, which he ceremoniously presented to Maria, who accepted it with a small, sitting curtsy.

As Mr. Kamrad and the other spring sports coaches took their turns at the lectern, Cassidy's mind drifted. In some ways it seemed like a huge expanse of time back to the start of the year, that first hot September morning they reported to their new homerooms. The football team had been doing two-a-days since mid-August, and you could tell them in the hallways by their lean and wan faces: they walked around looking stunned (their coaches were convinced that withholding water would make men out of them—fortunately only a handful across the state died every year).

It seemed like it took forever until basketball tryouts at the beginning of November, and then the season itself had been inordinately long, too. From the first shaky games in early December until the state finals at the end of March, he had to admit that there were a few times toward the end when he had grown weary of it all.

But now that he was sitting here looking back on it, it seemed to have gone by in the blink of an eye. As Bickerstaff went on and on, Cassidy was looking so introspective that Maria gave him a quizzical look. He smiled and shrugged, and tried to pay attention. He didn't really come out of it until a few minutes later as Mr. Kamrad was describing how the Edgewater crew had barely been edged out of second place by Andover at the prep nationals.

"Many times in sports a contest is decided by a matter of inches. In our case it was a matter of about six of them. But that was the difference between first, which is where we wanted to be, and third, which is where we were."

As far as Cassidy was concerned, a twenty-foot jump shot that misses by six inches makes you look like you couldn't throw a Ping-Pong ball into an open manhole.

He glanced down at the mimeographed booklet stapled inside a sad little crepe paper cover. The first page read:

1964 All-Sports Awards Banquet
Saturday, May 23, 1964
Edgewater Cafeteria
6:30 p.m.

- MENU -

FRUIT JUICE

TOSS SALAD

FRIED CHICKEN

BAKED POTATOES   GREEN BEANS

SWEET ROLLS

ICE CREAM PUFF

(Hot Chocolate Sauce)

ICE TEA

Or

COFFEE

As the bowling coach, a lesbian named LizBeth Q. Harlow, yammered on and on about the "near miracle" of her team's third-place finish in the county tournament at Orange Blossom Lanes, Cassidy folded the program in half and slipped it in his jacket pocket.

He figured it would be good scrapbook fodder, though he was fairly sure that in the future if he ever came across it among the desiccated boutonnières and ripped movie tickets, it would be that "TOSS SALAD" that would break his heart.

CHAPTER 37

TRAPPER NELSON, JR.

Having found nothing better, Cassidy thought he might return to his bag boy job at the base commissary, but then the Monday following the last day of school, Trapper Nelson called him from a pay phone at the Pantry Pride.

"You interested in a job this summer?" Trapper said.

"Holy cow, are you kidding me? I hate bagging groceries. I'd rather shovel crap than bag groceries."

"Well, that's about what I'm offering. Come on down to the Jupiter Hilton and I'll buy you a Coke. We can catch up a little and discuss a little business."

Cassidy hadn't ridden his old ten-speed in months, as there was an unwritten law governing the maximum age at which it was still cool to pedal yourself around town. He was well past it, but this was no time to stand on ceremony. It took him less than fifteen minutes to get to the Hilton, where Trapper was waiting on the bench in front of the store, eating four moon pies and drinking from a quart bottle of T.G. Lee milk. Sitting on the bench was an opened Topp Cola waiting for him.

"Youngblood!"

"Hey, Trap. Long time no see. How are the tropicals?"

"All signed, sealed, and delivered, except for one rock beauty. I couldn't bring myself to sell her. She has become a permanent resident. I could swear she recognizes me. When I come into the cabin she swims over to get as close as she can to me. She's amazing."

Cassidy sat, out of breath, and greedily tilted back the bottle. It had been a hot, thirsty three miles of pedaling. After a minute, he could almost talk.

"I know. They have real personalities. But hey, what's this about a job? You're not pulling my leg, are you?"

"I almost wish I was. The jungle cruise business has just about gotten out of hand. Dave Booker brings boatloads of twenty-five to thirty tourists by most days of the week."

Trapper, it appeared, had become a polished entertainer. He donned his Tarzan loincloth, wrapped himself in harmless snakes, and fake-wrestled sleepy old alligators. The crowd never failed to swoon. He would give a little tour of the camp, showing off whatever happened to be in the cages and pits at the time: bobcats, raccoons, lynxes, alligators, turtles. And, of course, Willie the parrot was a great favorite, sitting on low branches and begging potato chips from the kids. ("I tell them to brush the salt off first. It's not good for him.")

"But basically, what it boils down to is that I need help running Trapper Nelson's Zoo and Jungle Garden. That's what I call it now. I even had postcards printed up! Those tourists will buy anything that isn't nailed down," said Trapper. "It pays seventy-five cents an hour and I'll provide lunch. I need somebody to help me work up the trinkets and doodads, clean the cages, feed the critters. I mean, heck, it's getting to the point I don't even have time to go check my traps anymore. I like making money, God knows, but this really is getting out of hand. It's even starting to affect the Thursday night poker game. Last week the tourists barely had time to clear out before Jim Branch's boat pulled up. And he brought Joe Kern and Judge Chillingworth with him. I didn't have a thing ready for them. They joked around about it, but I could tell they were irritated. That ended up being a big night, too. At one point we actually had two separate games going. I didn't think they'd ever leave."

Trapper took the last bite of moon pie and finished off his milk, shaking his head.

"I still don't get why they'd come all the way up there by boat just to play poker," Quenton said.

"Yeah, well, come talk to me after you've been married a few years, Youngblood. You can tell me how much your wife likes having a bunch of your fishing buddies coming around, drinking bourbon and smoking cigars in her house."

"Yeah, but they could find someplace to go closer to town, couldn't they?"

"Sure, but they *like* a little taste of the primitive. My place appeals to their frontier spirit. Why, some of those guys even bring guns with them, pistols. Lay them right on the table in front of them. I think it's supposed to be a joke, but it doesn't seem that funny to me."

"Why don't you tell them to cut it out?"

"Well, I guess because I'm not used to bossing around circuit judges and state attorneys, Youngblood. I'm just the innkeeper. I provide a woodsy refuge from domestic bliss."

Cassidy finished his drink and they sat watching the few boats heading out the inlet for some weekday fishing.

"Hey, Trap," said Cassidy, "you ever been married?"

Trapper sighed. "Not so's you'd notice."

"Yeah?"

"There was a girl, back before the war. We ended up getting married before I got drafted. Lucille was her name."

"What happened to her?"

"Oh, I went off to basic training and left her running the camp. She got bored, I guess. She up and took off. Place was a mess when I got back. I didn't know where she had gone, so I got a lawyer and published a notice in the newspaper and divorced her. I still don't know where she is."

Cassidy was surprised to see him looking wistful for a moment. His name had been associated with a number of young ladies over the years, but if he ever mentioned one, it was always lightheartedly. Lucille must have been different. Several seconds went by before Trapper snapped out of it.

"Hey, so about this job. Can I count on you?" Trapper said.

Cassidy pretended to ponder it for a few moments.

"Do nuns wear sensible shoes?" he said.

The footwear choices of various postulants aside, Cassidy was delighted to be heading out to Trapper's camp first thing the next morning.

On the way over he was thinking about how he was going to deal with his friends' reaction to this. He had already taken a lot of grief over the years, with some people dubbing him "Little Trapper" and "Trapper Nelson, Jr." This was considered quite an insult by a few people around town who still believed Trapper Nelson was some kind of shady character, but Cassidy considered it a compliment.

He couldn't believe how much there was to do around the place. As elaborate as the camp had grown over the years, Trapper had been managing it single-handedly, except for a few weeks during the summers when relatives came down from New Jersey to stay in his "guest cabins," primitive log structures he had built to rent out to hardy souls willing to rough it for a few nights.

This was familiar work for Cassidy. He had often "volunteered" around the place in the past, but money rarely changed hands. He was usually rewarded with gopher tortoise stew, fried gator tail, or some smoked sailfish or barracuda.

Cassidy got to work hosing out the cages of the various creatures. Robert, the bobcat, who looked like a peaceful tabby until he was approached too closely, was content to cower in the back of his cage while Cassidy worked. After cleaning, he filled Robert's bowl with scraps of mullet and turtle from the cleaning tables. Then he fed whole mullets to Stumpy, a ten-foot alligator who would have been twelve feet except part of his tail and most of one foot had been bitten off in battles with rivals. There were a pair of raccoons in separate cages who hadn't been named yet. Fastidious creatures, they cracked freshwater mussels and rinsed them off in the large water bowl Cassidy refilled for them. Trapper arrived as Cassidy was finishing emptying the traps of mice and rats that had been caught overnight, dumping the little carcasses into a zinc bucket for the delectation of the numerous snakes currently in residence.

"Good morning's work, Youngblood. Come on up for some lunch," Trapper called.

Cassidy washed off at the hose by the cleaning station and sat down at one of the picnic tables under the chickee hut, where Trapper had laid out sandwiches, a citrus fruit salad, and iced tea.

"Wow," said Cassidy. "Store-bought! What gives?"

"I splurge on occasion," said Trapper through a mouthful of ham sandwich.

"I guess so. Somebody told me you sold a bunch of land to some developer. It was even in the paper. Is that true?"

Trapper shrugged. "You can't believe everything you read," he said with a mysterious smile.

They ate in silence for a while until Willie the parrot flew over. If he didn't see anything worth begging for, he would fly back up to his limb and scream "cracker!" at them, so Trapper broke off a piece of crust from his sandwich and held it out.

"Cracker?" Willie said.

"Well, it's food, if that's what you're asking. And if you take it and drop it on the ground, that's all you're getting," said Trapper.

Willie snatched the crust greedily and flew back to his limb, where he stood on one foot, holding the bread with the other.

"You're welcome," said Trapper.

"His manners don't seem to have improved much," said Cassidy.

"I've read that mentally they're like two-year-olds. That seems about right to me. And no two-year-old I've known ever read Emily Post."

Cassidy finished his second sandwich while Trapper was on his third. There was one more left and Cassidy was pleasantly stuffed, but with Trapper around no food ever went to waste.

"Hey, Trap, did you ever get a chance to talk to Mr. San Romani about the training stuff?"

"Glad you reminded me. Be right back." Trapper went to his cabin and returned with a handwritten envelope, which he handed to Cassidy. The top flap had been neatly sliced, probably by one of Trapper's fillet knives.

Cassidy took out the two sheets of lined paper. The handwriting was small and very neat:

Dear Vince,

How are things on the Loxahatchee? Sounds like the trapping business is finally beginning to wind down. I hope your other ventures can take up the slack.

I can't believe you actually had Gary Cooper come to visit! Mr. "High Noon" himself! My mom and dad are big fans of his and I sure am, too. I would have given anything to be there!

How did the visit go with Connie and Phil and little Flip? Bet they had a great time, as usual. The new improvements to the irrigation system sound terrific. Bet it's nice to have a real engineer-type guy like Phil Sr. around to help out once in a while.

To change the subject, I've looked over the suggested workouts the coach gave our young friend. As you and I have discussed before, almost any training program can produce results compared to doing nothing, so I want to say first of all that there is nothing particularly "wrong" with anything I saw.

But here's the thing: there is an awful lot of really slow running in there, three- and four-mile jogs and such. It seems like to me if our friend is trying to get ready for basketball, after an initial conditioning phase he'd want to be doing some moderate to long intervals several times a week, then add wind sprints as the season approaches. And it doesn't seem like there's nearly enough weight lifting in there, particularly half-squats. All the jumpers and most of the basketball players I know do tons of them, and your guy hardly has them spending any time in the weight room.

Well, that's my take on it, anyway. I suspect that young Quenton already understands much of this after the program we put him through back in junior high.

I hope he's able to run some cross-country in the fall. It shouldn't interfere too much with basketball. Plus, I'd really like to see him run track in the spring. He might be surprised at what he can do if he sets his mind to it.

Well, that's it from the Midwest. Best of luck with your projects, and let us know if you ever get out this way.

Your friend,
Arch

"Well, that's kinda what I was thinking," said Cassidy, rubbing his eyes. "You know, after last season we all figured this year would be just amazing. Now, I don't know."

"Yeah? Why's that?"

"Bickerstaff hasn't had much to do with basketball since his college days in the forties. He still thinks a jump shot is a show-offy kind of trick shot. Plus he doesn't like the point guard system we had last year. He wants to go back to using two guards, which means I'll be playing with Carroll Morgan in the back court."

"I thought he was pretty good."

"He is good, but he gets in the way when I'm trying to bring the ball up court. That's one of the reasons Coach Cinnamon made me the point guard in the first place. I didn't need the help handling the ball, and it opened another slot for a big man. Plus, poor Carroll can't throw the ball into the ocean."

"Hmm. So what are you going to do?"

"Right now"—Cassidy stood up and gathered plates and glasses—"right now I'm going to go throw a bunch of snake heads and turtle shells into the formaldehyde vat so you can have them ready to foist off on a bunch of people from Wisconsin next week."

"And don't forget . . ."

"I know, stretch the hides, catch some mullet, irrigate the garden, and feed the turtles. Got it. But I gotta be out of here by four so I can meet Stiggs and Randleman at the base gym. I've got to let them know about the new workout schedule I just made up."

CHAPTER 38

ENDLESS SUMMER

Everyone at one time or another should have such a glorious summer.

Stiggs had saved up enough to buy a 1951 Nash Rambler, a little brute of a car that was as unattractive and ungainly as it was underpowered. Much was made, however, of the fact that the front seats reclined all the way back. Stiggs slyly implied that this feature sealed the deal for him, though the $125 price tag undoubtedly had something to do with it. In it, the three of them, with occasional consorts, ranged far and wide. With a few cents' worth of gasoline, no place on Florida's Gold Coast was out of range of the little beast.

It was a good thing that Stiggs and his high-paying construction job had come through because bike riding was all but socially proscribed, and Randleman's parents didn't think he was responsible enough to drive much of anywhere on his own despite what the state of Florida might technically allow. Cassidy was no help. He was rarely able to talk his mother out of her Ford Falcon for anything other than church activities. And there certainly wasn't much chance of playing hooky from God because this was one supreme being with plenty of churchgoing tattletales on His side.

But with Stiggs's intrepid vehicle, they were, as Randleman put it, "Ag-ile, mo-bile, and hos-tile, to quote the great Jake Gaither."

And so they were. They triple-dated to the drive-in to see Steve

McQueen battle a giant flesh-devouring rolling bowl of Jell-O in *The Blob*. They bit the bullet and paid first-run prices to see *Dr. Strangelove* downtown at the Beacham theater. They congratulated each other on their thrift by watching *Blood Feast* from the rear parking lot of a vacuum cleaner repair store near the drive-in, where somebody had rigged up a bootleg speaker with a buried wire that went under the fence and hooked up inside to a real speaker post. (The angle was such that you could barely make out what was going on up on the screen, however, so the biggest thrill came from the mere act of filching entertainment.)

In the rare event that girls were involved in their activities, they always wanted to do dumb kid stuff like roller skate, so they'd head out to the Roll-a-Rama on Dixie Highway and awkwardly stagger around to ridiculously old-fashioned organ music while the really good skaters—the ones you could tell owned their own skates because they didn't have numbers written on the heels—would repeatedly zip by backward, sideways, on one skate, squatting on their haunches, whatever, but barely paying attention and always with exquisitely *bored* expressions.

Or they'd go all the way down to West Palm Beach, where there was miniature golf, batting cages, driving ranges, and many more movie theaters. Or to a go-cart place outside Stuart where they'd get in trouble for playing Thunder Road.

They sometimes hung out at Frazier Ravencraft III's house on Lake Silver, where they water-skied, listened to Frazier's own personal jukebox in a "rec room" converted from his old man's 1950s bomb shelter, played Ping-Pong on the back patio, and tried to decide if they wanted to swim in the lake or the screened-in pool. (Sitting in chaise longues by the pool one day, Cassidy threatened to strangle the next person who wondered aloud what the poor people were doing.)

They went downtown to the telethon at the armory at three in the morning to watch Jerry Lewis blubbering to the TV cameras in front of a line of kids in wheelchairs and a bank of pretty young women answering telephones. Stiggs was hoping to be interviewed on live TV by Jerry himself as he turned over the $52.84 they had collected that night, but the comedian was taking a bathroom break and Stiggs had to settle for a local celebrity, "Uncle Walt" Sickles, host of an afternoon kids' show.

"Sheesh," said Stiggs, "I was on TV with him on my birthday back in the fifth grade."

"I still think we should have kept ten bucks for burgers," said Randleman.

They drove out to Singer Island and dove for lobsters on the reef off Air Force beach, occasionally actually catching one. That was the summer Stiggs taught them how to get them out from crevices using the business end of a plain old floor mop, which, although entirely legal and really quite effective, was nonetheless a pain in the ass because of the hassle of untangling the prickly creatures from the mop's strands.

Mostly, though, they trained. They met at the base gymnasium every day except Sunday, when it was closed. Even on Sunday they were often able to find a set of doors that the corporal who ran the place had chained too loosely, and Cassidy, the skinniest, could squeeze through and open a window for the other two. Then they tried to play basketball "quietly," fearful that any second the MPs would bust in to "haul their narrow asses to the brig," as Stiggs put it.

Usually wearing lead-shot vests and weighted shoes, they would do their stretching, drills, and weights, and play pickup games with the servicemen. They also ran, though Stiggs and Randleman would no longer run with Cassidy at all. Three days a week Cassidy would go home for a quick dinner and, after an hour of "settling," head out to do one of the workouts prescribed by San Romani. At first it was too much, even for him. Stiggs and Randleman pronounced him certifiable. But after a few weeks, he found that he was not only adapting to but thriving under the regimen. It was clever the way the running program alternated between hard days and easy days, and just when he felt he was reaching some kind of breaking point, he would be blessed with a lovely day of respite: light jogging, a couple of wind sprints, and done.

One Saturday afternoon he watched a rebroadcast of a track meet when Jim Beatty ran the first indoor four-minute mile. It was a revelation. There was a guy running a mile at a faster pace than Demski could run a half mile, and doing it on an eleven-laps-to-the-mile indoor track. That night as Cassidy was doing intervals around the playground of the elementary school, he replayed images of that race in his head. He concentrated on Beatty's stride, his determination, his focus, and willed himself not to falter when it got really tough at the end.

Jogging home in the muggy night air while moths worried the streetlights of his neighborhood, Cassidy thought it was the best interval workout he'd ever done. *Maybe this is what it's like, what Jim Beatty feels like when he's running a four-minute mile,* he thought.

He told Trapper Nelson about it the next day, after the last tourist boat left and they were sitting around in the chickee hut drinking iced tea.

"I almost wish track season was going on right now," Cassidy said. "I just feel like I could go out there and run forever. It's like when I got in shape for that half mile, but better. It's not every night, but when it happens like it did last night, it's the most amazing feeling."

Trapper nodded, smiling.

"I wonder how you can really tell," Cassidy said. "I wonder how Mr. San Romani could tell when he was really getting in shape."

"I think I can help you there," Trapper said. "We used to talk about it all the time that summer we worked together. I couldn't really run with him much, of course, but we'd talk about training ideas. This was when he was still trying to break the four-minute mile himself, before

Bannister did it. He said it was a whole different world when you get below 4:10 in the mile, a different feeling altogether."

"Yeah?"

"He said he could tell something different was going on because for the first time in his life, in both training and racing, he didn't want runs to end. Before, he couldn't wait to get to the finish line, to stop, but now he just wanted to keep running."

"Jeez. Why?"

"He said it gave him more time to leave everyone else farther behind."

CHAPTER 39

AT LONG LAST

The Rolling Stones rolled into America and caused a few riots, just like the Beatles had earlier. The Republicans nominated a curmudgeon from Arizona for president (it seemed that after the Kennedy era, politics was reverting back to the same group of old white guys). A handful of college students burned their draft cards and said they wouldn't go to a place called Indochina, wherever that was. President Johnson signed a law saying you had to be nice to colored people, which apparently still didn't include letting them into white schools, certainly not Edgewater.

Football two-a-days started in mid-August and Cassidy wound up his job at Trapper Nelson's. Then he and Stiggs and Randleman went shopping for school supplies, and the next thing he knew, it was September 3rd and Cassidy was sitting in Miss Waldron's homeroom, sweating like a field hand despite being allowed to wear Bermuda shorts for the first time, thanks to a directive from no less an authority than the Palm Beach County School Board.

His senior year had begun.

CHAPTER 40

CROSS-COUNTRY INTERLUDE

In the first assembly of the year, Billy Parish handed Cassidy a thick paperback book called *Catch-22*.

"Read this," he said.

"What's it about?"

"Just read it. You won't believe it."

It was the first grown-up book he read voluntarily. At the time, Cassidy was boycotting anything remotely resembling literature after suffering through *Silas Marner* the year before. It had pretty much extinguished the small spark of interest struck by his summer reading of *Moby-Dick*. But this thick blue paperback with a bomber pilot on the cover rotated his world on heretofore unknown axes.

Right now, though, in fifth-period study hall, he was back to hating literature. He was trying to bear down on *The Scarlet Letter* for a rumored quiz the next day. It was hot in the cafeteria and he was battling the dropsies when Mr. Kamrad appeared at his table. He gestured toward the door with his head. Cassidy followed him out and they sat at one of the concrete tables in the courtyard.

"Jeez, are you still growing?"

"Six foot two and the shortest guy on the starting five," said Cassidy.

"Well, I know you've been running, 'cause you can't possibly weigh more than a hundred and fifty pounds."

"I've been taking these protein pills, drinking banana milk shakes, eating everything in sight. Nothing helps. I can't gain an ounce."

"That's not a bad thing—for a runner, at least. Listen, I know the last time we talked you weren't much interested in cross-country."

"Yeah, two miles seems like an awful long way. Plus, we're going at it pretty hard every day to get ready for basketball."

"I know. I just thought I'd run something by you. We have a three-way meet with Pompano and Palm Beach this afternoon at the Dubsdread Golf Course. Lindstrom and Demski are running pretty well, but after that we fall off bad. We could use a third man to finish maybe in the top ten to have a chance at winning this thing. What do you say?"

"You really think I can race that far?"

"You've been doing the San Romani workouts, right?"

"Three days a week for most of the summer. And some jogging on my own."

"I think you would do fine. You just need to pace yourself. You can't tear out in the first quarter mile like you do in the half. If you get into oxygen debt early, you suffer the whole rest of the way. In crew I have to drum that into our strokes all the time."

"I'd hate to miss our basketball training at the base. We've got less than a month until tryouts."

"It won't take long. We're driving over right after next period. Lenny's taking his car and I'm driving, too. I'll take you over and then drop you off at the gym afterward. What do you say?"

"Okay, I guess so. Sure," said Cassidy. "I can get a ride home with Stiggs."

"You have some shoes with you?"

"Not running shoes."

"Hmmm. That could be a problem," said Kamrad.

"Not really. If it's on the golf course, I'll run barefoot."

*   *   *

Cassidy had never seen so many skinny guys in one place in his life. Not that they all were. Both Pompano and Palm Beach had brought B teams, and Pompano even had a C team that boasted a few asthmatics and one "big-boned" kid. No one ever got cut from cross-country.

Edgewater previously had just five runners, the minimum, though Cassidy made it six. Mr. Kamrad explained that you were allowed seven total, though only five scored. The last two could only push the other teams' runners farther back.

"Where are all the fences and hurdles and stuff?" said Cassidy as he warmed up with Demski and Lindstrom. "I thought that was what cross-country was all about."

"Nah, that's in other c-c-countries. Here we just run around golf courses," said Demski.

"Heck, I think jumping over fences would be cool," said Lenny Lindstrom.

"Yeah, p-plus it would give you a second to catch your b-breath," said Demski.

"Well, I've run three or four miles in training, but I've never raced anything longer than a half mile. I'm not sure I can actually make it," said Cassidy.

"Oh, sure you c-can," said Demski. "You just back off to a pace you can handle. It's not that bad."

But it was. Everyone took off too fast, yelling and screaming like they were having a good time. That, Cassidy noticed, didn't last very long.

Why everyone thought it so important to sprint the first quarter mile he didn't know, because the pace settled down to what felt like a crawl soon after that. They seemed to be in oxygen debt already. Everyone except the Mizner kid from Pompano, who just kept right on going. Cassidy saw him disappearing all alone over the rise at the third hole dogleg and thought, *He's still pretty darned good.*

There was a second group of six—including Demski—trailing

Mizner by a hundred yards, then a bigger group, including Cassidy, another twenty yards back. The rasping all around him made Cassidy feel better, because it told him he wasn't the only one suffering.

The course was marked by an orange plastic tape staked into the ground around the outskirts of the golf course. After what seemed like forever, they reached a group of coaches that included Mr. Kamrad, who was holding a stopwatch. Cassidy saw a handmade paper sign stuck into the ground that said ½ & 1½ It took him a moment to figure out they were running a one-mile loop twice and finishing in the chute he had seen next to the starting line.

As the group passed him, Mr. Kamrad was reading, "Two thirty-*five*, thirty-*six*, thirty-*seven* . . ."

Jeez, they were running pretty close to a five-minute pace. Cassidy remembered that Lenny Lindstrom, their best miler, had won some dual meets the year before in not much faster than five minutes. This was not exactly the nature romp he was expecting.

He didn't see how the group in front could be keeping up that much faster a pace than his group, and sure enough, in a quarter of a mile he noticed that they seemed to be coming back a little bit. He was starting to feel it—for one thing, it was a hot afternoon—but Cassidy had finally settled into the pace and was getting more comfortable with it. When no one else in his bunch seemed particularly ambitious, Cassidy lit out for the group in front, and by the time they got around to the starting line at the clubhouse, he was working his way up through it. He had just caught up to Demski at the front as they passed by Ted Benz, the Palm Beach coach, who was reading the mile times off: "Five *ten*, five *eleven*, five *twelve* . . ."

Cassidy was amazed. He would not have bet a dime that he could run a single mile this fast, and they were only halfway through this race.

Ed looked over and seemed surprised to see him.

"Good pace," he said.

"Should we. Go after him?" Cassidy said. On this long straight-away, uninterrupted by turns or hills, they could see Mizner, still smoothly striding a hundred yards ahead.

"Not yet," said Demski, who seemed to be laboring. Cassidy, on the other hand, didn't feel any worse than he'd felt at the half-mile point.

He remembered this stretch from the first lap—a long row of pine trees, a small pond, a huge clump of hibiscus hedge—and there was something about the familiarity that made it seem a little easier.

They passed Mr. Kamrad again: "Seven forty-*one*, forty-*two*, forty-*three* . . ."

He tried, but he couldn't do the math. He was pretty sure they were on a steady pace and that it wasn't much slower than a five-minute-mile pace. But Cassidy was getting impatient with Ed, who was showing no signs of wanting to run down Mizner. Cassidy glanced back and saw that they had twenty or thirty yards on the rest of the group now.

"Okay, I'm. Going to. Give it. A try," Cassidy said.

Demski tried to give him a smile, but it was weak. He did manage a little wave.

Cassidy set out, trying not to make up too much ground at once, and quickly perceived that Mizner was coming back to him. Mizner had gained most of his lead during the first half mile but then hadn't increased it much. He was running quite confidently, though, not sneaking any looks back.

Good, thought Cassidy, as he bore down all along the backstretch. It was all familiar now, a hole with a long narrow green and sand traps on either side, a big live oak next to the brick road that ran along the back side of the course. Cassidy loved running barefoot like this, like he had as a child playing tag in his grandmother's front yard, or racing the rain down Rosedale Street.

Though he was rasping in the air like everyone else, it did not seem desperate to him. He realized how hardened he had become from his summer interval workouts, and for the first time it occurred to him that he should have been up there running with Mizner all along.

With less than a quarter of a mile to go, Cassidy was twenty yards behind. For the first time, Mizner turned around to see how far ahead he was. Even from twenty yards back, Cassidy could see the surprise on his face. Mizner put on a burst heading around the turn into the last straightaway to the chute, but after that Cassidy gained steadily on him. With a hundred yards to go, Cassidy launched into an all-out kick, but Mizner still reached the chute ten yards in front.

The coaches tried to hurry them through the chute, but there was no need, really. Mizner was bent over at the waist, hands on knees, gasping. He held out a hand limply to Cassidy, who took it, likewise bent over and greedily sucking air.

Mr. Kamrad walked up, holding his watch, looking somehow pleased and puzzled at the same time. Mizner had set a course record in 10:18. Cassidy was two seconds back.

CHAPTER 41

BASKETBALL AGAIN

For the first time in his life Cassidy didn't bother to check the bulletin board in the gym. He was a returning starter from a final-four team. It was a far cry from those awful days in junior high when he'd stand blinking before a posted list that had just dashed his every hope.

"Guess what?" said Stiggs, setting his tray down at lunch. "You made the team."

"Yeah," said Randleman, right behind him. "We did, too, in case you were worrying about us."

"Any other surprises?" said Cassidy, wolfing down his Salisbury steak. He seemed to be constantly hungry these days.

"Nope. Everyone's back on, plus Ramsey Dulin, Jake Stuart, and Ralph Erickson," Stiggs said, naming the three best JV guys from last year.

"I just hope he has some serious drills in mind. It didn't seem like everyone was this far out of shape last year," said Cassidy.

Stiggs and Randleman exchanged a glance. Stiggs was mangling the spout of his milk carton in the process of trying to get it open.

"Just because you're winning the line drills by half a court doesn't mean everyone else is out of shape," said Stiggs. "It only means that you're a freak of nature."

"Yeah," said Randleman.

"Seconds," said Cassidy, standing up with his plate.

*   *   *

Mr. Kamrad didn't badger him about cross-country after basketball started. He kept his powder dry.

On the third Friday in November, he got out his dry powder.

"You mind?"

Cassidy looked up, surprised. Mouth too full to speak, he gestured to the seat across from him. Mr. Kamrad put his tray down and sat. This was unusual. Most of the teachers ate in a separate, elevated area at the end of the cafeteria, with the exception of a few very young and wildly popular male teachers—of which Mr. Kamrad was one—who could occasionally be cajoled into dining at a table full of giggling girls.

Cassidy was embarrassed that his mouth was so full he didn't dare speak. Stiggs and Randleman had already taken their trays up, but Cassidy had gone back for thirds. It was spaghetti day.

"Everything going okay with basketball?" Mr. Kamrad asked. Cassidy swallowed.

"Yes, sir. Well, we've put in a different system from last year, but it's going okay."

"Oh, yeah? Different how?"

"I was the point guard last year. This year we've got a two-guard front. But it's okay. Everyone who started is back but one, so we should be okay."

"Well, I know it's a long shot, but I wanted to mention something to you, just in case."

Cassidy looked puzzled.

"They're having the regional cross-country meet this afternoon. It's on the same course you ran before, at Dubsdread."

"Oh, yeah?"

When Mr. Kamrad saw that he didn't turn it down out of hand, he got a little more animated.

"It's a big meet, more than twenty schools, but the best runner is still probably that kid from Pompano, that Mizner kid. The boy you almost ran down. Remember him?" As if he could forget.

Well, there was no question that he was interested. He hadn't done any intervals since basketball started, but he was running several miles of laps around the court every day before practice, sometimes at a very quick pace, depending on how he was feeling. There was also no question that he would like another crack at that kid, particularly now that he knew not to let him get so far ahead.

Mr. Kamrad could see the wheels turning, so he said nothing and concentrated on his spaghetti.

"What time is the race?"

"It starts at four thirty. You'd have to miss basketball practice."

"What did Coach Bickerstaff say?"

Mr. Kamrad made a little grimace. "I haven't talked to him about it."

"No?"

"I know missing basketball practice is a big deal, so I'm not telling you to do it or not to do it. It's only one practice, but I can't make the decision for you. You'll have to talk to Coach Bickerstaff about it, plead your case. Then just see what he says."

"Wow. I think I know what he'll say."

Mr. Kamrad smiled. Everyone knew that Bickerstaff had mellowed very little over the years, might have gone the other way, in fact.

"Well, I just wanted to present the opportunity to you. You know, we don't keep school records for cross-country because the courses are all different, but as far as I know, 10:20 is far and away the best time anyone at this school has ever run."

Cassidy nodded. Demski had told him the same thing.

"I know how important basketball is to you, but giving up one practice before the season gets under way might be worth it to accomplish something really great."

"Yes, sir."

"Anyway, if you want to do it, the cars leave at three thirty. Talk to Bob, uh, Coach Bickerstaff. If you can work it out, meet us in the parking lot behind the gym."

Coach Bickerstaff looked at him in disbelief. This was going to be worse than Cassidy had thought.

"You want to run what?"

"It's the regional cross-country meet, more than twenty schools. Considering the race I ran earlier, I might be able to do pretty well."

"Well enough that it's worth missing practice? Two thousand kids in this school and you're one of twelve guys who get to play the most important sport in our school. And you want to miss practice to compete in a sport nobody ever heard of?"

Cassidy looked down at his shoe tops. When he put it that way it did sound crazy. Bickerstaff, seeing that his point had struck home perhaps a little too forcefully, softened somewhat. Sitting back in his desk chair, he assumed a magnanimous expression.

"All right, here's the deal," said the coach. "You can do it if you want to. I won't stop you. But if you decide to go ahead and miss practice, you'll lose your place on the starting team and have to work your way back up all over again."

Cassidy thought about it for a second and made up his mind instantly. Springing to his feet, he said, "Thanks, Coach! I won't let you down!"

And with that he cleared out as fast as he could before Bickerstaff had a chance to change his mind.

CHAPTER 42

CROSS-COUNTRY CHAMPION

This time it was different.

He spotted Mizner while they were warming up.

"Th-th-there he is," said Demski

"Saw him," said Cassidy. He had spotted the blue-and-gold uniform with the golden tornado on the chest among the sea of colors all around them. There was no mistaking that stride. He was warming up apart from his teammates, who were all jogging along together.

"Wh-what are you going to do?" asked Demski.

"I don't know. But I know I'm not spotting him two hundred yards this time," said Cassidy.

When Mizner bolted to the lead after the first quarter mile, Cassidy was no more than ten yards behind him. This time Cassidy wasn't worried about what group he was in or who was in it. He only had eyes for Mizner out there sailing along in front. Everyone else could do whatever they wanted. Today he knew where the race was.

There must have been some mistake at the half-mile marker, where Mr. Kamrad was reading off the times: "Two twenty-*two*, twenty-*three*, twenty-*four* . . ."

That couldn't be right. Cassidy was feeling the strain, but this time he was mentally ready for it and it didn't seem as scary. Mizner, like before, ran with that silky stride and did not look back. The second half of the first lap went quickly. Cassidy could hear no runners behind him, nor could he see anyone close when they went around a sharp turn.

The mile splits also sounded crazy, but Cassidy now had to believe them: "Four *fifty*, fifty-*one*, fifty-*two* . . ."

Mizner must have thought it sounded too fast, because he eased up some as they headed down the first long straightaway again. As he reached the long row of pines, he looked back finally but did not seem surprised to see Cassidy ten yards back, running easily. Instead, Mizner motioned to him, as if he had been expecting him.

What's this? Cassidy thought. But he poured it on a little and pulled up even.

Mizner didn't look over, just said, "Work. Together."

Cassidy thought about it. Some kind of trick, maybe? But he said, "Okay."

And so they ran like that, stride for stride, for most of the last mile of the race. Gasping with effort but showing no signs of real fatigue, they went through the midpoint again, where Mr. Kamrad tried to hide his surprise at seeing them together. He read off the times: "Seven *fifteen*, *sixteen*, *seventeen* . . ."

This time Cassidy was more prepared to interpret the in-between time. All he had to remember was that at 10 flat pace they would pass the one-and-a-half-mile point in 7:30. But they were way under that. Was it possible to keep this up?

Mizner ran so beautifully that running beside him seemed to make Cassidy's stride smoother. And running side by side was mentally easier than hanging on from behind or trying to run from the front. Cassidy had not run many real distance races, so he was not sure how this whole thing was supposed to play out. Were they just going to run across the finish line together?

His answer came in another quarter of a mile as they turned for the home stretch. Mizner put on a sudden burst, and before he knew it, Cassidy was ten yards behind again. There must have been some Pompano supporters in the small crowd, because he heard a rousing cheer. But despite the strain and effort of the early going, Cassidy did not feel done in. In fact, he almost wished the race were longer.

On the rare occasions when he peeked back, Mizner always looked over his right shoulder, so Cassidy worked his way up to just behind his left shoulder, being careful not to expend too much energy. Cassidy held there and waited.

When they were two hundred yards from the finish chute, Mizner looked back over his right shoulder to see where Cassidy was. When he did, Cassidy instantly sprinted around his left side and went all out the rest of the way to the finish line. After he crossed it, he turned around and was surprised to see Mizner fifteen yards back.

The crowd had grown silent during that last sprint.

Cassidy had to grab his knees for only a few painful seconds. He straightened up to see Mizner stumbling toward him, hand extended.

"Nice. Race," he said. "Didn't see you. At all there. At the end."

"You, too," said Cassidy. "Guess that's. My last time. Pulling that."

Mizner laughed but stopped quickly, still needing the air.

Mr. Kamrad jogged over, holding his watch in front of him, huge smile on his face.

"Quenton Cassidy," he said, "I hope Coach Bickerstaff doesn't give you too much grief for this, but you are now the south Florida class 4-A regional cross-country champion. And you have run two miles in 9:42."

CHAPTER 43

REPERCUSSIONS

It made the Monday morning announcements.

"Friday was another red-letter day for Edgewater," Principal Fleming said in his gravelly voice. A stir went through his homeroom when Cassidy's name was announced as the regional cross-country champion. Hardly anyone had any idea what cross-country was, but coming in first in a regional anything was apparently a big deal. Miss Waldron, beaming, offered congratulations. People came up after the bell rang and made a big fuss. Through the crowd Cassidy could see Demski sheepishly gathering up his books.

"Hey," Cassidy said, "don't forget *that* guy! Demski finished fifth and ran the best time of his life."

While the little knot of people turned their attention to Demski, Cassidy slipped around them and was out the door heading for first period. He was red as a beet.

Coach Bickerstaff did exactly what he said he would do. Cassidy found himself, jersey turned white side out for the first time since jayvees, playing on the second team. It didn't really mean anything during the warm-up or the drills. But when it came time to run plays in a half-court scrimmage, there he was on the taxi squad.

The second team played defense while the first team ran their zone offense. Carroll Morgan and Drake Osgood were the guards, and since Cassidy knew them pretty well, he was able to anticipate their passing patterns and make a few steals.

When the second team went on offense, Cassidy had a field day. Both Carroll and Drake were under five ten. At six two, Cassidy could shoot over them almost at will. And he knew the first team's defensive weaknesses. Cassidy motioned to his other guard, Dougie Arbogast, to rotate down to the baseline and come up from behind to set picks on the corners; it gave Cassidy easy eighteen-footers. When the first team adjusted and started sending big men up to help out, Cassidy and Dougie Arbogast were able to lob alley-oop passes in to Phil Jones and Jacob Stuart behind them in the key.

The first team was getting frustrated; the three big men started bickering among themselves. Cassidy just smiled and gave Stiggs a quizzical look, which he returned with a bird so quick and subtle no one else noticed. But the first-string guards were also irritated with each other. On the last play, Cassidy brought the ball down, motioned for Dougie to rotate down and take right wing, and for the wing to rotate to the other side. They were essentially in the same 1-3-1 they had used the previous year. They started passing the ball quickly around the outside of the zone, forcing the defense to adjust with every pass. The ball came back around to Cassidy at the top of the key, and as soon as it touched his hands he began the motion to pass it back. The defending guards shuffled quickly to make the next adjustment, so when they shifted prematurely, it left Cassidy completely open at his favorite shooting spot on the court, a little bit to the outside and a little to the right of the top of the key.

He faked the pass, kept the ball, and flexed his knees slightly, going up into a relaxed jump shot, which he buried.

Drake and Carroll were just about to get into it with each other when Bickerstaff's shrill whistle ended the practice. He didn't say anything, but as he was walking toward the stairway, a ball rolled into his path. He took one quick step and booted it into the corner of the gym where it hit the concrete wall with a *thwack*.

The next day Cassidy was back on the starting team, but he knew some damage had been done. He just didn't know how much.

CHAPTER 44

DISASTER

The first game of the season was at Palm Beach High. Their gym was small, packed, and intimidating, and the game went downhill from the opening tip-off.

Stiggs got outjumped by a kid named Bobby Segal who was barely six feet tall. And they pulled the same play that Edgewater usually pulled on everyone else: Segal tipped it to their tallest guy, who immediately flipped it to one of the guards breaking for the basket. It was two–zip Palm Beach and the game wasn't ten seconds old.

They weren't big at all, but they were cagey and well coached. And they kept changing their defense from zone to man-to-man and back again, all on some invisible signal that Cassidy couldn't figure out. Not only that, but they disguised both defenses so that their man-to-man appeared at first to be a zone, and vice versa.

Bickerstaff had not bothered to designate either of the guards to be in charge. The team captains were Stiggs and Randleman, so that didn't help. Whoever brought the ball down was supposed to recognize the defense and start the offense. But Carroll Morgan was especially confused by the shifting defenses and several times started the wrong offense, resulting in total confusion and turnovers before any shots were taken.

Palm Beach also pressured the ball coming upcourt. Cassidy had dealt with that many times the previous season. If it was man-to-man pressure, one of the wingmen threw the ball in and cleared out, and Cassidy brought the ball up by himself. He had practiced full-court dribbling at the base gym until he was blue in the face, and he could shift directions instantaneously by dribbling behind his back, or between his legs, or by crossing over. He could dribble with either hand without looking at the ball and he could control the ball at nearly full speed. He not only didn't mind pressure, he enjoyed punishing teams that tried it.

But Bickerstaff seemed to interpret this as showing off, the product of individual skill rather than teamwork. During a time-out, he insisted that Cassidy and Morgan work together getting the ball upcourt, which gave Palm Beach's guards—who were very quick—opportunities to trap and double-team. When Morgan got trapped for the third time and they lost the ball on a ten-second violation, Bickerstaff called another time-out. Cassidy was amazed when he had nothing tangible to offer in the huddle. He just said, "Work the ball up together. Set screens for each other. Protect the ball." *Basketball wisdom as penned by fortune cookie writers*, Cassidy thought.

At that point they were down ten points only two minutes into the second quarter. Walking back to set up, Cassidy grabbed the side of Carroll's jersey and pulled him over.

"Listen, inbound the ball to me and clear out to half-court. If your guy doesn't go with you right away, look for the pass back. Otherwise just clear out and let me bring the ball up. This is ridiculous."

On the next play, Carroll inbounded the ball to Cassidy and took off down the sidelines. The other guards hadn't seen this before, and his man hesitated before following him. Cassidy hit Carroll immediately with a baseball pass and he sped up the court to take advantage of the four-on-three situation. Stiggs's man left him at the foul line to pick up Morgan, who bounce-passed it quickly to Stiggs, who very nearly dunked it two-handed. The only reason he didn't was that Bickerstaff disapproved of dunking as another example of hotdogging. But the effect was almost the same, as Stiggs held the ball over the rim with both hands for what seemed like several seconds, then simply dropped it straight down. It brought the small Edgewater crowd to life for the first time in the game.

The next time, Carroll's man stuck right to him, so Cassidy began to bring the ball up alone. The smaller guard on him was new, a transfer from Key West named Gonzales, called "Gonzo" by his teammates. Like a lot of guards Cassidy faced, Gonzo assumed that a tall guy playing guard wouldn't be very quick. On Cassidy's third dribble to his right, Gonzo made a lunge for the ball, expecting to get a steal and a quick layup. The ball wasn't there. Cassidy had whipped it behind his back and was now going to his left at full speed, leaving Gonzales flat-footed.

Palm Beach was in a man-to-man, so when Cassidy brought the ball into the front court, several players made lunges at him, but no one wanted to leave his own man completely to pick him up. Gonzales was still scrambling to get back upcourt. Cassidy did a stutter step at the top of the key, and the guard who had halfheartedly picked him up dropped off to pick up his own man, fooled by the stutter step. And there it was, right in front of Cassidy: an open lane to the hoop without a soul on him. Cassidy dribbled straight in and made a plain vanilla, missionary position, right-handed layup whose only distinction was that he was up so high that when he went to slap the backboard on the way down, half of his forearm brushed the glass, too.

The Edgewater fans went wild and Cassidy could see the Palm Beach players exchanging worried looks with each other. It was their turn to be confused. Their lead was down to six points, and the change of momentum was so palpable you could have caught some of it in a butterfly net. Palm Beach called time-out and Cassidy jogged over to the bench, expecting a few high-fives and butt slaps. Instead, he saw downcast, worried looks from the benchwarmers, and a livid coach.

"What did I tell you about how I want you to bring the ball up?" Bickerstaff was jabbing Cassidy in the chest with his index finger. Sweat was stinging his eyes, so Cassidy was trying to towel off, but when he looked at Bickerstaff he had a hard time understanding the question.

"Uh, carefully?" Cassidy said. Bickerstaff slammed his clipboard to the floor. But Cassidy didn't know what Bickerstaff was driving at, or why he was so angry that his team was suddenly back in the ball game.

"Together! You are one member of a team, mister, and there is no 'I' in team."

"Yes, sir."

They went back to the tandem approach and it was a disaster. Carroll kept trying to set screens, but all it did was bring his man closer so he could double-team and trap. They lost the ball three times in a row bringing it up, twice for quick layups. By halftime they were down fifteen points, and the Edgewater crowd was silent again.

Bickerstaff was upset when they lost the ball, but not nearly as upset as he was when they were bringing the ball up successfully using their own technique. Cassidy was baffled.

In the locker room, Bickerstaff paced back and forth, uttering platitudes and generalizations. "We've got to do a better job of protecting the ball" was one. "Keep your hands up on defense," another. There was nothing about dealing with Palm Beach's shifting defenses, nothing about how they were supposed to get the ball up when the opposing guards were trapping and stealing them blind.

The year before, Coach Cinnamon would have had five or six specific things for them to work on in the second half: "Joe, your man isn't hurting us long, so try sagging back to help Randleman out with his big guy—he's killing us in the key," or "Cassidy, your man can't go to his left for love nor money, so overplay the hell out of him."

With a sinking heart, Cassidy began to realize something. Bob Bickerstaff had been successful in junior high school, where the challenge had been to motivate players, develop basic skills, and emphasize organization and teamwork. But the next level up required something else. Everyone was already motivated, already had the basic skills, and was used to working as a team. At this level you had to be able to read different situations and adjust to them. Bickerstaff not only didn't understand this, he didn't even *realize* that he didn't understand it. As far as he was concerned, the problem was that his players were not listening to him.

Bickerstaff's approach was almost the opposite of Coach Cinnamon's, his predecessor. Bickerstaff thought of players as more or less interchangeable, that the important things were running the plays correctly, paying attention to fundamentals and, of course, not hotdogging or showing off. And to Bickerstaff, showing off could mean almost anything that wasn't a fifteen-foot set shot or a straight two-handed bounce pass. He seemed to barely tolerate the most common shot in the modern game because when he played in college in the '40s, the jump shot didn't exist. He wasn't crazy about underhanded layups either, though Cassidy knew for an absolute fact that they were easier to control and far more accurate than the old-fashioned over-hand method.

Now another puzzling thing began to make sense: Cassidy had noticed that Bickerstaff was thrilled that their twelfth man, Dougie Arbogast, still shot an old-fashioned two-handed set shot. It wasn't all that accurate, and he didn't have a prayer of getting it off against an opponent who was half paying attention, but Bickerstaff seemed to light up when the kid was out there practicing this completely outdated, useless shot. Strangely enough, though the kid barely made the team, he seemed to be Bickerstaff's favorite player.

Cassidy had to face facts: Robert Leroy Bickerstaff wasn't a very good basketball coach.

Nothing improved much in the second half. Sensing vulnerability, Palm Beach put on a full-court zone press, so at least Cassidy didn't have to worry about who was going to bring the ball up and how he was going to do it. The whole team was now involved in the process, and since that was something they had had to deal with the previous year, they were fairly adept at it. But the offense continued to sputter until Cassidy had finally had enough. During a break while Stewart was shooting a pair of foul shots, Cassidy pulled Morgan and Stiggs over to him.

"Enough of this shit. Carroll, you go to the wing on Stiggs's side. Stiggs, you go to the high post and tell Randleman to go to low post and roam the baseline. Tell Stewart to stay put."

"Like last year? One-three-one?" Carroll said, brightening.

"Exactly. Clue Stewart in."

The next time up the floor, after studying the defense for a few seconds, Cassidy signaled for a zone offense. He dribbled to the right wing, where Morgan released and went baseline. Randleman came from low post out to the right corner and Cassidy passed it to him, but the zone adjusted and he was covered. He passed back to Cassidy, who whipped it out to Stewart, top of the key. He passed it down to the opposite corner where Stiggs had set a screen that Morgan used to hang up the baseline defensive man. He was just turning toward the basket when the ball arrived. The zone didn't adjust fast enough and he buried the short jump shot.

Bickerstaff immediately called time-out.

"What the hell in God's green earth was that?" The veins were standing out on his forehead, his skin color now approximating his hair.

"Coach, it's just the wheel offense, but starting from one guard in front," said Cassidy.

"The wheel offense is a zone offense. They are in a man-to-man!"

Cassidy could see the looks being exchanged around the huddle, but clearly no one was going to speak up.

"Coach, it's a matchup zone, so it starts off looking like a man-to-man," Cassidy said. "Didn't you see when Carroll released and went backdoor? His man didn't go with him. It's a zone, but disguised. They've been doing this to us the whole game."

Now Bickerstaff was mad for an entirely different reason. He was mad now because he was being shown up in front of his entire team. Cassidy knew this, but he also didn't know what else he could do but point out the obvious. They were in the process of losing to a team they had beaten twice the year before, by twenty-two and twenty-six points, when Palm Beach had been a considerably better team. Edgewater was just plain beating itself. It was the most frustrated Cassidy had ever been playing sports.

Bickerstaff looked around the huddle, still furious. He put his finger back into Cassidy's sternum.

"Run the offense the way we practiced it," he said. "And don't take the fast break if it isn't there!"

Cassidy stumbled back onto the floor, wondering what the hell that meant. How could you tell if a fast break was "there" if you didn't bring the ball up the floor quickly and look for an opening? Stiggs had connected with Cassidy several times for easy buckets by hauling down the rebound and immediately looking downcourt. Cassidy or Morgan would run a post route to the basket and Stiggs would hit them perfectly with a leading baseball pass. But how would they know if that fast break was "there" if they didn't make the attempt in the first place?

Cassidy's head was spinning, and he would have been the first to admit that he played terribly for the next several minutes. But then, so did everyone else. They were used to looking to Cassidy for direction, but he didn't have a clue now. Carroll tried to take over, but he was inexperienced as well as equally baffled by the situation.

Finally, after another confusing huddle before the last quarter started, down by eighteen points, Cassidy threw caution to the wind and just started playing the way he knew how to play. He motioned Carroll down to the wing again and took over as point guard and brought the ball up himself. As soon as the other team put up a shot, Cassidy and Carroll flared out on opposite sides of the floor and took off for the opposite goal, looking for a long pass. They were playing like the team they had been the year before. Everything started flowing naturally as they all reverted to something they knew well.

Cassidy could hear Bickerstaff yelling from the sidelines and he would turn occasionally and pretend to pay attention, but he essentially disregarded everything except playing the game of basketball. Edgewater went on a 16–2 run and closed the gap to four points with 3:24 to play. Cassidy scored ten of those points. They were going to win. Cassidy could feel it.

That's when Bickerstaff took him out of the game.

Stiggs was on the foul line shooting two when the klaxon went off and Drake Osgood trotted onto the floor. Cassidy assumed he was spelling Carroll Morgan, but instead Drake apologetically handed Cassidy his warm-up top.

"Great playing, man," he said, shaking his head. "Sorry."

The Edgewater crowd actually booed. Cassidy had never seen that before, booing a substitution. As he was walking to the end of the bench, still panting from the last fast break, he noticed something else he had never seen before: opposing spectators actually laughing at a visiting coach's unfathomable decisions.

Edgewater lost by fourteen.

CHAPTER 45

GOODBYE TO ALL THAT

Cassidy didn't feel much like company at lunch on Monday, so he opted for the guilty pleasure of the cold lunch line, picking up an Italian sub, a tuna sandwich, a bag of barbecue potato chips, and a couple cartons of orange juice.

It had been chilly earlier in the morning, so he was wearing his red wool letter jacket with a big white "E" on the left breast. He was sitting in the bright winter sunshine at one of the concrete tables in the courtyard, when he spotted Stiggs and Randleman, also wearing their jackets, coming from the cafeteria. They looked dour.

He figured they were going to give him grief about his nutritional habits, but they just sat down and looked at him.

"Okay, okay, you caught me. Cold cuts for lunch. Big deal," Cassidy said.

Stiggs shot a look at Randleman.

"He doesn't know," he said. Randleman nodded.

"It's posted on the gym bulletin board," Stiggs said. "Let us know what you want to do."

Then without another word they got up and left.

Cassidy hadn't finished his second sandwich, but he wrapped it up and tucked his books and sandwich under his arm and headed for the gym.

There were a couple of guys Cassidy didn't know idly perusing notices on the glass-enclosed bulletin board as he walked up. When they saw him coming, they backed away.

The notice was the only thing posted in the varsity basketball section, a single sheet, typed.

Disbelieving, Cassidy read the heading: "The following is the final selection for the 1964–65 Edgewater basketball team."

Cassidy scanned down the list, dread forming a knot of nausea in his gut. It was his basketball team, all right.

But he wasn't on it.

CHAPTER 46

THE SAD TRUTH

Mr. Kamrad looked up from his teachers' planning workbook and took off his reading glasses. He did not look surprised to see Cassidy. He motioned to the chair beside his desk.

"I think I know what this is about," he said. "I heard two of the football coaches talking in the teachers' lounge this morning."

Cassidy nodded. He wasn't sure he trusted his voice yet. He had sat in a numb trance through his last class. Then he was late to his next class because he was talking to Stiggs in the courtyard, not even caring that he was risking detention.

"Mr. Kamrad, I don't get it. Stiggs and I were first-team all-county last year. I played in the state tournament. We missed the finals on a last-second shot. I've gotten letters from college coaches. Sure, things have been screwed up on the team this year, but I just . . ." He sat shaking his head, unable to continue.

"Quenton, if it makes you feel any better, as far as I can tell, a lot of people in this school are flabbergasted, too."

"That's something, I guess."

"Well, I would offer to talk to Bickerstaff on your behalf, but the last time we tried that, things didn't work out so well."

"Maybe I could appeal to . . ."

Mr. Kamrad was shaking his head already.

"There isn't any appeal. Principal Fleming might be sympathetic to you, but a head coach is like the captain of a ship. His word is law. There is nobody to appeal to. I mean, there is always the possibility of a full-blown mutiny by the team, but . . ."

"No, that would make things worse. Stiggs and Randleman wanted to get the guys together to discuss it, but I know exactly what would happen. Even if we could get every single player on the varsity to threaten to quit—which we can't, by the way—he would just play the rest of the schedule with the JV team. They'd lose every game, but he'd do that before he would back down."

"I suspect you're right." Mr. Kamrad still had his glasses off, squeezing the bridge of his nose between two fingers.

"Besides, Stiggs and Randleman have real scholarship possibilities on the line. Their whole futures are at stake," said Cassidy.

"So is yours, Quenton."

"I get that, believe me. I spent the last five years of my life pointing for this season, and it was all working. I started to get feelers from colleges last year—admittedly it was Rollins and Stetson and such—but this year was going to put me—put us all—on the map. Now it's just blowing up in our faces. I don't have a clue what's going on with Coach Bickerstaff. We've been trying to do what he says, but most of it makes no sense."

"Quenton, it's only my personal opinion, but I suspect that very little of this has much if anything to do with basketball."

"You mean that business back in junior high?"

"That's part of it, I think."

"But he said we were all over that. He even put up my time for a school record . . ."

"I'm not saying this is intentional on his part. I doubt he understands it himself. All I know is that when Trapper and I went to talk to him back then, we saw someone dealing with some personal problems, someone not very secure in his own skin. And someone who does not like to be contradicted or shown up. First he told you that you weren't a basketball player, and you proved him wrong about that. He wanted you to run track back then, and you did. Then you got injured while running for him and he refused to acknowledge it. You proved him wrong again. Now he's apparently in over his head in his new job. He wants to come off as a tough disciplinarian, so he doesn't want you to miss practice for a cross-country race. But you go out and win it. Then you play your first basketball game for him and guess what? You're doing it to him again."

Cassidy made a low groan.

"It's just armchair psychologizing on my part, of course," Mr. Kamrad said, "but it seems to me that your whole relationship with this man has been one long process of showing him up."

Cassidy let the breath out of his lungs.

"And the time before, when you two came to an impasse, you had an alternative. You made your point in an all-comers event. Now, though, there isn't any all-comers basketball team to join."

"Wow."

"Right. But, you know, in the Chinese language the same symbol that means 'danger' also means 'opportunity.'"

Cassidy grimaced. He was too young to be an aficionado of silver linings.

Stiggs and Randleman were waiting outside the Temporary Classroom Building as Cassidy left Mr. Kamrad's room.

"You guys are going to be late to practice," Cassidy said.

"Screw that," said Randleman. "What did Mr. Kamrad say?"

Cassidy shrugged.

"Come on, he must have said something."

"Yeah, it was all about this interesting symbol they have in Chinese that can have two different meanings. One meaning is 'danger' or 'caution' or something like that . . ."

"Uh-huh. Yeah?" Stiggs said, wary. Cassidy smiled at him.

"And the other meaning is 'Comes with egg roll.'"

CHAPTER 47

A PLAN

Cassidy didn't even try to talk to his parents about it. He was sure it would just confuse them and then they would probably make excuses for Coach Bickerstaff. They were not big on challenging authority.

He was able to talk his mother into letting him take the car, though, and he drove to the place where the Jeep road left the highway and went into Trapper's camp. Afraid to bury the little car up to its axles in the deep sand, he left it parked on the highway and hiked in.

Trapper wasn't around, so he went inside and got some peanuts and sat out on the deck to play with Willie, who had greeted him by yelling "Cracker!"

"Come on, I won't bite," Cassidy said, holding a peanut up for him to see. "I cannot say the same for you, however."

"Cracker?" said Willie.

"Food, yes."

Willie flew down to the deck rail. "Willie, cut that out!" he said.

"You're just talking to hear your own voice now," said Cassidy, holding the peanut out. The bird walked over cautiously. He tried to snatch it and make his getaway, but Cassidy made him come closer. He had become much tamer with Cassidy over the summer when he was around all the time.

"Head rubbies first," Cassidy said.

"Cracker," said Willie.

"That's right, head rubbies, then cracker."

Willie bowed his head and fluffed up the feathers all around his head and cheeks.

"Good boy," said Cassidy, rubbing the top of his head with his index finger. "Now cracker."

But Willie kept his head bowed, ignoring the peanut. Cassidy kept rubbing the soft little head. He thought he heard something like a very faint mosquito whirring in the distance. It was Trapper's ancient outboard. Willie heard it, too, and lifted his head high and alert.

"Vinnnn-cent!" he squawked.

"Hey, that's good!" Cassidy said. "When'd you learn that?"

"Cracker!" Willie said, snatching the peanut and flying back to his limb, scattering the guinea fowl that had settled there in his absence.

Trapper greeted him as he pulled up to the dock and tossed Cassidy the line. Three large snook and a pile of what looked like green rocks rested in the bottom of the boat.

"Where did he get 'Vinnnn-cent'?" Cassidy said.

"Oh." Trapper laughed, "My sister Lurleen and her brood were down last week. That's what she calls me. He picked it up from when she would call me to dinner. Took him thirty seconds to learn it. I bet you couldn't teach him to say 'Trapper Nelson' in thirty years. Hey, how about hopping up and grabbing the bucket for these oysters while I get the fish over to the cleaning station."

Cassidy got the zinc bucket from inside and hopped down into the boat to fill it with the bivalves. It took two trips to get them all moved over to the cleaning station for Trapper to rinse them off.

"I'm not going to ask you why you're not at practice," Trapper said. "I was at the Jupiter Hilton and a bunch of the old guys were talking about it. Apparently everyone in town is talking about it."

"Yeah, can you believe it?"

"You forget I have some experience in the matter of dealing

with Coach Bickerstaff. I'm only surprised that something like this didn't happen sooner."

Cassidy took the Rapala knife and started filleting the second fish while Trapper rinsed off the oysters.

"So, how are you holding up?" asked Trapper.

"I'm all right," he said. "Nice fish, by the way."

"Good batch of oysters, too. From your favorite bed."

Cassidy nodded.

"I don't suppose you can stay for dinner?"

"Oh, I could be talked into it."

It was good and dark by the time he hiked the Jeep road back to the car. He had a flashlight with him, but the moon was bright enough that he could see the double ribbon of white sand easily without it. He felt a sense of calm, of normalcy that he hadn't felt in days.

He had a tummy full of fried snook and raw oysters.

And he had a plan.

CHAPTER 48

PUTT-PUTT

Maria DaRosa placed the bright yellow ball on one of the dimpled bumps on the rubber mat and assumed a solid putter's stance, feet shoulder wide, rocking back and forth from one foot to the other to settle in, holding the putter straight out, pointing down the course and picking her spot.

Cassidy watched, entranced.

Her tanned legs were set off nicely by a yellow, black, and red madras wraparound skirt, white cotton blouse with a Peter Pan collar, and thin, white leather sandals. She was all concentration as she took a couple of practice swings. Cassidy watched carefully, and sure enough, right before she struck the ball, the little pink tip of her tongue appeared in the corner her mouth. It was outrageous.

Her backswing was short, so it always surprised him how loud the *thwack* was when she connected. The ball flew into the right side of the chute, did a complete loop-de-loop, and shot out the other side heading straight for the angled board in the corner of a sharp dogleg right. The ball hit it dead center, making a beeline for the hole. At first it looked like it would go in, but it was off just a hair to the right and came to rest two inches past the cup.

"Damn," said Cassidy.

"Don't swear," she said.

Cassidy saw that the group playing just ahead of them had taken to watching her shots. It was date night and the place was full of couples. Cassidy and Maria between them knew about half of them.

"I just want to know how the dickens you do that," he said.

"I tell you every time. You don't listen every time."

He placed his ball on the tee mat and knocked it through the loop-de-loop with plenty of force, but it came out crooked and caught just the edge of the angled board in the corner. It sputtered down the green hugging the side rail and came to rest ten feet from the hole.

"Do you mind if I putt out?" she said. "Just so I can be out of your way."

"Oh, sure, why not. Go ahead and putt out by all means. Very considerate of you."

Giggling, she tapped in and watched with feigned sympathy as he two-putted from where he was.

He picked both balls out of the hole and deliberately handed her the wrong one. She waited, hand on hip, giving him the cocked-head look he associated with Willie the parrot.

"Yours is luckier. I think we ought to switch," he said.

"Think again," she said, taking her ball back.

The next hole was a giant clown's head with a big laughing mouth that you had to go through to get to the hole, but otherwise a perfectly straight shot. The Cracker Jack surprise in this hole was that when your ball went through the clown's mouth, a loudspeaker blasted you with maniacal laughter.

"I don't see what's so damned funny about what's going on here," Cassidy said.

"You haven't shot yet either."

She had honors and placed the ball on the center dimple. She addressed the ball, sighted down the club, took two practice swings, stepped forward, and smacked the ball through the middle of Clarabelle's pie hole. The crazy laughter erupted as the ball exited the back of the clown's head and beelined into the cup like it had eyes.

"I don't believe this," he said.

"Believe it or don't, but put me down for a one, Roscoe," she said, smiling. "That's pretty funny, isn't it?"

He fished the little stub of a pencil out of his breast pocket and wrote "1" for her. She was three under par on the seventh hole. He was three over, so it was a symmetrical trouncing.

"How did you get so good at this?"

"I told you the last time. My parents used to drop my sisters and me off here every Saturday morning at eight and would come pick us up at noon. It cost a dollar each and was the cheapest babysitting deal in town. Try to imagine how many rounds of this stuff you can do in four hours. We'd get so bored we'd be wading in the water hazards when they got back."

"Where did your folks go?"

"They said they were going grocery shopping, but I think they went back home for hanky-panky. Ewww, I don't even like to think about it."

"Mine always took a 'nap' on Sunday afternoons. Interruptions for anything less than missing limbs were dealt with harshly."

She laughed, showing white teeth. Next up was the windmill.

As she was placing her ball, Cassidy saw Harry Winkler, one of the football captains, at the next hole over. He waved and Winkler walked over, shaking his head.

"Hey, I heard," he said. "Unbelievable."

"Yeah."

"What are you going to do?"

Cassidy shrugged. "Looks like my roundball days are over."

"Do you have anything lined up collegewise?"

"Not really. A little interest, but I think they were waiting to see how this year was going to go."

"Well, it bites a big one, man. Wanted to tell you."

"Thanks, appreciate it, Wink."

"Hang loose."

"Yeah, you too."

Maria was standing next to the hole and her ball was nowhere in sight.

"Not another hole in one, for crissakes," he said.

"No cussing. And I got a two, thank you. I just went ahead and putted out since you were busy with your big friend."

Cassidy aimed carefully, but his timing was off. His ball whacked the big blade as it swept by, sending it right back toward the tee.

"Do-overs!" he called, and hooked the ball back with his putter. She rolled her eyes but didn't object.

The next shot went through and actually ended up a foot from the hole. He putted in and put himself down for a highly questionable par two.

They decided to take a break before the waterfall hole. Cassidy went for french fries and root beers while Maria grabbed the last available picnic table.

"So what did Harry want?" she asked, picking through the french fries for one that met her standards.

"Just commiserating. Wanted to know what I'm going to do."

"And what did you tell him?"

"I said 'beats me,' or words to that effect."

"Oh, come on. You're the one who's always saying, 'Harumph. Gentlemen, we must have a plan. We have to have a plan, even if it is wrong.'"

"Okay, what we've come up with—"

"We?"

"Trapper and I. What it is, is that I will run track for Mr. Kamrad, but I will be coached by a guy in Kansas."

"Now you *are* kidding."

"Hey, you asked. But it gets better. The guy in Kansas will coach me through a local proxy who lives in a shack in the jungle without electricity."

She looked at him with those big, dark eyes.

"What else?" he said. "Oh, yeah, this guy lives on snakes and turtles."

She studied him closely, looking for any signs of frivolity, but then brightened suddenly.

"Say," she said, making her voice sound hollow and grainy, like a character from a '40s B movie, "it's a crazy idea, but *it just might work.*"

"Sarcasm is the lowest form of humor."

"I thought it was puns."

"Okay, puns and sarcasm are the two lowest forms of humor."

"The one in Kansas I assume is this Archie person, what is it . . . Santorini?"

"San Romani. Santorini is an island off Greece."

"What does he think about this?"

"We don't know yet."

"And Mr. Kamrad?"

"We don't know yet."

She again looked for signs of teasing and saw none.

"I'm just wondering how you come up with these schemes."

"Plans, not schemes," he said. "Schemes connote something sneaky. This is a plan."

"Yeah, and you think it's a good plan because . . ."

Cassidy offered her the last french fry. She shook her head and he popped it in his mouth and smiled.

"Because it worked once already," he said, chewing happily.

CHAPTER 49

WHAT YOU ARE

Cassidy tried hard not to take grim satisfaction from the miserable fortunes of the basketball team.

"There's a word for that," Trapper told him. "It's called 'schadenfreude.' It means taking pleasure in someone else's pain. It's German."

"Of course it is," said Cassidy.

"How bad are they doing, anyway?"

"They lost to Hialeah by eighteen and Lake Worth—who're terrible this year—by ten. Then they went up to Orlando for a tournament and lost to Maynard Evans by thirty-six. But at least Evans is ranked."

They were sitting on the old bench outside the Jupiter Hilton, waiting for Archie San Romani to call on the pay phone. Cassidy had never spoken to him before and was nervous to the point of fidgeting.

"You should really just relax, Quenton," said Trapper. "He's the nicest guy in the world."

As it turned out, he was at least the nicest guy in Kansas, though he told Cassidy he was thinking about moving to California.

"They say the weather is nice in the winter out there," Archie said. "I don't know if that's true or not, but I bet it's better than it is here."

"It's pretty nice down here, too, Mr. San Romani. I hope you can come down sometime. I know Trapper would be happy to see you. And I would, too."

"Call me Archie. We've talked about a visit sometime. Maybe we can work it out."

It turned out that San Romani had just sent his own son, Archie, Jr., off to the University of Oregon on a scholarship.

"He's going to be faster than his old man, looks like," said Archie. "And with the guys Bowerman has out there, he's going to have to be. Heck, we've got a high school kid here in Kansas named Ryun who's under four already. The times are a'changin'. Literally."

"Yes, sir, I've heard that somewhere."

"Now, Trapper tells me you had some trouble with basketball and you're ready to concentrate on track."

"Yes, sir. It wasn't my choice exactly, but that's what I'm doing."

"Okay, I think we can make it work pretty much like we did before. Trapper says Mr. Kamrad is in agreement. You'll run with the team, but Trapper will give you my workouts. Later, after the season starts, Trapper and Mr. Kamrad can switch back and forth with the supervising. Any of the other runners capable of tagging along with you?"

"Ed Demski says he wants to try. He's close to a two-flat half-miler. Maybe one or two other guys."

"Okay, good. It's easier when you've got some company. Now, I understand you did some cross-country this fall. How did that go?"

"Well, I ran a three-way meet early in the season and finished second in 10:20 flat. Two miles, pretty flat. That was my first cross-country race and the first time I ever seriously raced anything longer than a half mile. Then basketball practice started and I had to concentrate on that. But I was able to get out of practice one afternoon to run the regional meet. I won that."

"In what?"

"In 9:42. It was the same course, two miles and flat."

"Okay, good. That was all that summer training you did, I'm sure. Even though you were doing it for basketball, shape is shape. I remember talking to Trapper after you won that second race. And

I'm going to tell you now what I told him then. I know you consider yourself a half-miler like your friend Ed, and I know that when we worked together before in junior high school you had good success at that distance. I also know how dedicated you were to hoops."

"Yes, sir."

"How fast did you run in junior high?"

"It was 2:03.7. That was in the ninth grade."

"Okay, Quenton, here it is: I think I know what you are."

"Sir?"

"I think you are a miler."

CHAPTER 50

THE CHALLENGE

Cassidy, Demski, and Lenny Lindstrom waited by the high-jump pit, making desultory attempts at stretching. Trying to sound non-chalant as they chatted, they were in fact nervous as chickens.

Trapper didn't look anything like a coach, dressed in his usual cut-off fatigues and combat boots with no socks, but he was carrying a clipboard like a coach and was brooking no nonsense like a coach, so they hopped up, shushed, and gathered around him.

"Okay, guys, Mr. Kamrad is not allowed to be here because track doesn't officially start until March. So you're stuck with me for the duration. Archie wants to start off with some nice easy miles for the first couple of weeks. He doesn't want you racing each other in these work-outs, or doing any sprinting at the end of runs, just keep together and keep it conversational the whole way. Any questions?"

"Mr. Nelson, who is Mr. San Romani anyway?" Lenny asked.

"He's a friend of mine who won the NCAA mile and who also ran in the Olympics."

"Oh."

"He also is a person who, when he was eight years old, had his leg mangled when he was run over by a truck and almost had it amputated. Most people didn't think he'd walk again, and most people were wrong."

"Oh."

"He has also helped a number of young runners over the years achieve some great things, including his own son, and he has been kind enough to offer to help us out here."

"Oh."

"Okay, so we've done this before with Quenton and it has worked out very well. Mr. Kamrad and I will stick to the schedules that Archie sends us unless unforeseen things come up, such as injuries and so forth. And that reminds me, we need to know when something like that happens to you, like if you're coming down with a cold, or your knee is sore, anything like that. Don't try to make us guess when something's wrong with you."

They all nodded, jiggling their legs, impatient.

"Okay, today is simple: twice around the lake, as easy as you can. Then do our regular calisthenics routine on the infield, which will take about ten minutes, then a mile of striders on the infield. And that's it, take it in. Cassidy knows the calisthenics routine. What you do today will be your warm-up routine every day from now on."

"That's it? Two point two miles and some jumping jacks?" said Lenny.

"That's right, Len." Cassidy chuckled. "A workout even you can handle. Enjoy it while you can."

"Okay, I'll leave you to it. I have to get back to my camp, so I won't be here when you get back. I'll see you tomorrow, same time, same station, and I'll want a full report on how it went. I'll keep notes on each day's workout to send to Mr. San Romani."

"Uh, Mr. Nelson?"

"What is it, Lenny?"

"I think I have an injury."

"Is that right, Lenny?"

"Yes, sir. My feelings have been hurt by Mr. Cassidy."

"Very funny. Now take off, you characters."

*   *   *

The pattern was familiar to Cassidy. In the early going it was overdistance, usually three to five miles, occasionally longer. There was always an easy two-mile warm-up, which they did around the lake in back of the school, then calisthenics, a mile of striders, then the main workout. After three weeks, just as it was starting to get monotonous, they began doing longish intervals every other day. It started with repeat miles, then three-quarter miles, half miles, and quarters, sometimes in combinations so complicated that Trapper, if he wasn't staying for the whole workout, would have to write it all down on an index card for them. There was always an easy distance day following intervals.

If Trapper couldn't be there at all, Cassidy would find the card tucked into a corner of the gym's bulletin board. On interval days he usually carried Mr. Kamrad's stopwatch, and they tried to follow the program to the letter. Cassidy and Demski usually finished together, with Lindstrom a few seconds behind.

Several of the other runners tried to give it a go. Jarvis Parsley lasted the longest. By that time their long runs were up to six miles, and they were sometimes doing six half-mile repeats on interval days. Jarvis lasted four days.

Never more than a whippet anyway, Cassidy began to lose weight despite eating everything in sight. He had lost the food squeamishness of his childhood and now gobbled even the celery in his mother's pot roast, not because he liked it but because he didn't want to take the time to pick it out. At a little over six feet tall, he weighed 139 pounds.

He still hung around with Stiggs and Randleman, but without basketball in common it was more like the old days, when they were on the bus and he wasn't. This time, though, theirs was not a happy bus. Three fourths of the way through the season, they were 4–14, and two of their victories were by two points. Cassidy listened to their woes and tried not to partake in schadenfreude.

But now he was spending more time with Demski and Lindstrom, whose sense of humor Cassidy had never fully appreciated. It reminded him of the characters in *Catch-22*. The three of them started getting together on weekends to do easy runs on the beach, or on the Jeep trails west of town when the sands were packed down enough from the rain. Sometimes Trapper ran with them, but usually not the whole way.

"You guys are getting out of my league, even on easy days," he said, but with a trace of pride.

As their fitness grew, so did their excitement. They talked at lunch about training theories, workout times, upcoming meets.

"I don't see what the big deal is," Stiggs said at lunch one day. "Basketball players do wind sprints and line drills every single day. Shape is shape."

"It's nothing like that," Cassidy said. "What we do as a sport is considered punishment in other sports."

"Awww," said Stiggs.

"I don't know what line d-drills are," said Demski, "but I know wind sprints, and quarter-mile repeats are a d-different animal."

"Yeah," said Lindstrom. "And that animal is the bear."

"Tell you what, smart guys . . ." said Stiggs.

"Uh-oh," said Randleman.

". . . let's do a little race before practice today," said Stiggs.

"N-n-no way. You can't be serious," said Demski.

"Yes, he is. He's serious as a heart attack," said Randleman.

"Stiggs, don't you want to think this over?" said Cassidy.

"Heck no. I'm tired of hearing about all this interval this and lactic acid that. We've been going an hour and a half every day, plus games, since mid-November. We have it just as tough as you guys and we never say boo about it. I say we do a quarter mile around the track, winner take all."

"Take all what?" said Cassidy.

"Bragging rights. Basketball guys versus track guys. Losers have to shut up about how tough they've got it. Winners can talk all they want."

"Count me out," said Randleman. "Stiggs, you are crazy and you are on your own."

"Fine by me," said Stiggs, sticking out his pointy little chin.

"I still don't believe you're serious, but if you are, tell you what we'll do. You can have Lenny. He's a two-miler and he's the slowest of the three of us, no offense, Lenny," said Cassidy.

"None taken. Only because it's true."

"A quarter mile, one circuit around the track, three o'clock this afternoon, Stiggs versus Lindstrom. Mr. Wind Sprints versus a guy who's been doing workouts written by an NCAA champion miler," said Cassidy.

"Wait. What?" said Randleman. "I thought Trapper Nelson was coaching you."

"He holds the stopwatch. Mr. San Romani sends us the workouts," said Lindstrom.

"San-who?"

"San Romani. He was an NCAA champion in the thirties," said Cassidy.

"Oooooh, scary. Back in the thirties, you say? I bet they were blazing back then!" said Stiggs.

"Stiggs . . ." said Randleman.

"Three o'clock, hoss. Our guy will be there, dressed out and ready," said Cassidy.

"You don't want in on this, Cassidy?" said Stiggs.

"Oh, please," said Cassidy.

"Suit yourself."

"I believe Mr. Lindstrom can represent us adequately," said Cassidy, gathering up his tray.

Cassidy had forgotten that Stiggs, with six and a half feet of elbows and knees, looked hilarious running all out. Though coordinated on the basketball court, at full stride he looked like an enraged waterfowl in strap-on glasses. It was all Cassidy could do to clear the tears of laughter from his eyes so he wouldn't miss anything.

Lenny, too, had always been an unlovely runner. Skinnier even than Stiggs—and a foot shorter—his thin arms and legs were all over the place and his head bobbed on a neck that featured a well-defined Adam's apple. Cassidy called him the Human Sewing Machine. But he had been running track for four years now and had grown more or less comfortable with his awkward style. When in shape, he could run surprisingly close to his top speed for a long way.

And so the race resembled a pair of broken wind-up toys going at each other hammer and tongs, except that Lenny pulled steadily away from Stiggs by running flat out from the start. Halfway through the back straightaway, Stiggs, seeing how utterly defeated he was, slowed to a walk, then jogged across the infield almost in time to be there when Lenny crossed the finish line, arms raised in triumph.

"Sixty-three point two!" called Cassidy, looking at Mr. Kamrad's stopwatch. "Way to go, Leonard!"

Randleman was shaking his head. Demski was jogging along with Lindstrom, patting him on the back as he took a victory lap, waving to the empty stands. A few other basketball players and track guys were standing around the infield, chuckling and calling out insults to Stiggs.

"So, what do you have to say for yourself now, hot shot?" Cassidy said.

Stiggs grinned. "Hey, Cassidy, I was the second-fastest guy on the track today!"

CHAPTER 51

DUAL MEET STANDOUT

Basketball finished with a whimper, though they did manage to win three more games. In the tournament, they lost the first game in their group, ignominious for essentially the same team that had been a hairsbreadth from winning the state title the previous year. Bickerstaff was in trouble and knew it. He was constantly being quoted in the paper on the subject of team unity, discipline, loyalty, and other nebulous concepts that coaches who are losing find paramount and those who are winning hardly ever bring up. Some people not only wanted him gone, they wanted him ridden out of town on a rail. Principal Fleming, however, claimed to support his coach "one hundred and ten percent," a position that softened to one of "unwavering support" when the talk shifted to running Principal Fleming out of town on a rail, too.

Stiggs and Randleman's standing with the college coaches somehow survived, and they began fielding invitations to visit campuses. To his great surprise, Cassidy even heard from a few small basketball schools whose coaches had not forgotten him, but he was too focused on track to think about it.

Mr. Kamrad started coming to regular track practices at the beginning of March, though he also still coached the crew team. Their primary workout of the day was in the morning, however, so he began taking over for Trapper most days after school. Cassidy sensed that Trapper was more than a little relieved to get back to his snakes and turtles, or, as he put it, "I've enjoyed about as much track and field as I can stand."

The first dual meet was at home against Vero Beach, which always had a good, well-balanced team. Cassidy was especially nervous because Mr. San Romani insisted that they "run through" their early meets, so the day before they did a five-mile run. What with the warm-up and striders, it was an eight-mile day altogether, hardly a "rest" day before a meet.

"How are you feeling?" Mr. Kamrad said, throwing his arm over Cassidy's shoulders.

"Good. Not exactly jumping up and down with energy, but not bad, considering," said Cassidy.

"This Jim Lee kid ran under 4:40 last year," Mr. Kamrad said. "He's their best. Ed has it tougher. They've got a 1:57 kid. He's not in the mile, though. He runs the quarter when he doubles. So Lee is your guy. You and Lenny might want to work together, help each other out if you can. Jarvis . . . Well, give Jarvis some encouragement."

Lenny knew he didn't have a chance to win, so he was running for points. He was saving it for the two-mile, but he offered to help with the early pace.

"Thanks, Len," Cassidy said. "But this Lee kid was pretty good last year. I bet he takes it right out himself."

It was a good guess. Lee ran the first lap in sixty-three seconds.

Cassidy was fifteen yards back and worried. Mr. San Romani's only advice had been exactly what he had always said about racing: "Run as evenly as possible, then kick like hell." Simple advice. It had worked for Cassidy before.

Cassidy had never run a mile all out before and was hoping to run 4:40 today, so he figured splits of seventy-one seconds would get him close enough to kick in a good final lap. But now just trying to stay close to Lee had brought him through the first lap in sixty-seven seconds, blowing up his whole plan. Lenny saw what was going on right away and dropped back to the second pack, saving himself for the two-mile.

"Sixty-seven, stay loose," Trapper said as he went by him before the first turn. Lee began dropping back immediately, and Cassidy realized that the guy's first lap had simply been a mistake. Despite Lee's PR, he was clearly not an experienced miler. *Heck, I'm not either*, thought Cassidy, *but I know better than that.*

Cassidy had slowed, too, but despite that Lee came all the way back to him by the 220 post in the second lap. He came back so fast that Cassidy almost ran up his backside. Fortunately, he roused himself out of his midrace torpor in time to see what was going on and pulled out into the second lane to go around the poor guy. Lee looked over at him, surprised, and actually picked it up. He wasn't going to let Cassidy pass!

That was fine with Cassidy. He dropped back behind again and followed all the way through the turn. They came by the post as the timer read off: "Two *eighteen, nineteen*, two *twenty . . .*"

"Right on track," said Trapper as they went by.

Cassidy did the math. He had slowed considerably but was still averaging seventy seconds a lap, a second faster than he had planned. Poor Lee, Cassidy calculated, had gone from sixty-three seconds to seventy-six. *No wonder he came back to me so fast!*

But now Lee was flagging again, and this time when Cassidy went by him there was no fight. Cassidy concentrated on running smoothly and efficiently. And he noticed something for the first time. He didn't feel particularly fatigued. It was a strained feeling, a feeling of effort, but the desperation of running close to his red line wasn't there. It wasn't exactly fun, but it wasn't that hard, either. Most of their interval workouts were harder.

Cassidy had no idea how far ahead he was at the three-quarter mark, but the timer read off: "Three *thirty*, thirty-*one* . . ." Then he went silent. The gun went off, causing Cassidy to jump despite himself. Cassidy listened . . . listened, and then he heard from a distance, "Three thirty-*six* . . ." and he knew he had at least twenty yards on the poor kid.

He concentrated on his form. He was beginning to feel it now, but knowing it was the final lap made it easier to deal with.

Running away with a race like this was a satisfying experience he had never before had in competition. His races had all been such struggles, such long-shot, come-from-behind desperation efforts that he just assumed all races were like that.

It occurred to him that this was what all the training had been about. And this time it wasn't just so he could fly up and down a basketball court; it was to win races. He was doing exactly what he had been training to do.

Mr. Kamrad was at the 220 post, but he wasn't reading out times. He just yelled as Cassidy went by: "Fifty yards! You've got him by fifty!"

Cassidy stretched out and cruised the last 220, not kicking but keeping his stride fast, smooth, and efficient. Guys from other events were rushing to the edge of the track, excited by the size of the margin, urging him on. The handful of people in the concrete stands were making more noise than he would have thought possible as he came out of the turn and sprinted down the straightaway, opening up at last just for the fun of it.

He was sure he had a lot more, but he was still blown out by the effort. He bent over, grabbed his knees, and just stood gasping for several seconds before he could even see straight again. His vision was all hazy. Mr. Kamrad ran up, holding his stopwatch in front of him.

"Four thirty-seven flat! Your first race, Quenton, and you broke Neil Jenkins's school record!"

Cassidy tried to straighten up and smile. It felt more like a grimace. He went back to hands on knees, still sucking air.

Jenkins had been some kind of wunderkind two years ago, a weird combination of nerd and jock, who played in the band and also happened to be the best miler in the county. Cassidy remembered seeing his 4:37.1 on the school record board and thinking, *How can someone run that fast?*

Now he knew.

CHAPTER 52

DUAL MEET BLUES

Demski had cruised to a 2:02 and killed the 1:57 guy, who was not in shape yet. Lenny ran a 10:48 to win as well as to set a PR.

Then they had an endless series of dual and three-way meets all through April, usually two a week. Cassidy managed to win most of his races, but only because the competition was weak. And he never felt as good as he had in that first meet. In fact, he began to feel pretty beaten up by the schedule.

"I want to sleep all the time. I fell asleep at dinner the other night. Just nodded off with my fork in my hand. My mom called Mr. Kamrad," Cassidy said.

"I fell asleep on the b-bus this morning," said Demski. "Do you know how hard that is to do?"

San Romani eased up a little on the intervals but insisted on "running through" all the small meets.

"I asked him again," said Trapper, who drove his Jeep up to watch practice one Friday afternoon.

"Who?" said Cassidy. They had just finished a five-miler and were getting ready to do striders.

"Archie. I told him about your bitching."

"What'd he say?"

"He laughed. He said everyone feels that way and that you'll thank him in the end."

"I'll thank him right now if he wants," said Cassidy. "I just want to run a race without carrying an anvil."

"He says all of this is laying the groundwork for the big ones, for when it really counts."

"Ugh," said Cassidy. "I have to run against Mizner in the distance medley relay tomorrow night in Orlando, and we just finished a pretty hard five-mile run. I feel like I'm sabotaging my own race."

Mr. Kamrad had just walked over and overheard them.

"Don't worry so much. Maybe Ed and Lenny can get you a little bit of a lead and take some of the pressure off," he said.

Cassidy looked dubious.

He should have been. Mizner's teammates handed him a ten-yard lead despite Demski's great 2:00 flat half mile. Lenny just didn't have the speed for a good three-quarter leg, and he lost Demski's lead plus a little more.

Cassidy took the stick and slowly worked on Mizner's lead until he had caught up at the half-mile mark. But then Mizner just ran away from him. Though Cassidy's split, 4:36.5, was a PR, his legs had been dead. He watched helplessly as Mizner pulled steadily away over the last quarter with his silky stride. His split was 4:29. To add insult to injury, a runner from Maynard Evans pulled even with Cassidy and then outleaned him at the tape. He found out later it was a kid named Jack Nubbins and he was only a freshman!

"He's a damn *ninth grader*, Ed. We don't even *have* ninth grade in our school. Apparently they do out in the sticks," said Cassidy.

"Sorry," said Demski, trying to sleep.

It was a long, miserable bus ride back from Orlando.

CHAPTER 53

ONE NIGHT OFF MANALAPAN

"Dammit," said Lucky Holzapfel, who stopped untying the little boat from the dock.

"What is it, man?" Bobby was already nervous. He didn't need any more problems.

"Forgot something. Hang on a sec." Lucky wrapped the line back around the dock post and jogged back over to his decrepit '48 Chevy pickup.

The drunken hubbub from the Crab Pot bar in the distance seemed surreal, as did the weird shadows cast in unlikely directions by the crazy bright summer moon.

Full moon, Lucky thought. *Didn't think of that.* How many other details had he not anticipated?

A burst of laughter from the bar caused an outrageous surge of self-pity to well up from somewhere deep in Lucky's chest. At this moment he wanted nothing more in the world than to be in that bar with the fishermen, barflies, beachcombers, and ne'er-do-wells, all the postwar flotsam and jetsam that flowed in a steady stream from the Republic proper down A1A until it got hung up in Florida's tidal backwaters and mangrove roots.

Lucky, a transplanted Hoosier, was at home among them. He would lean back on his elbows, the small of his back braced against the worn copper-topped counter, soaking up whatever attention was available at the moment. He was athletic, not bad looking, an ex-paratrooper war hero, sunburned from his outdoorsy life, and glib with tales of skin diving and fishing exploits. Wannabe sportsmen and ladies of various ages schooled around him like curious fish.

Instead of having fun, he was out close to midnight in the steamy, rotten-crab-smelling funk with Bobby, plotting mayhem and sweating through his faded khaki Bermudas. He was so wet his salt-encrusted Docksiders made squishy sounds when he walked, and his dirty Walker's Cay T-shirt was sopping.

Where did I go wrong? he asked himself. *I was Terre Haute's Jim Thorpe.*

The driver's-side door had a broken hinge and was hard to close once it was opened, so he leaned in painfully over the sill, feet coming off the ground, grunting as he crunched most of the wind out of his lungs, finally getting his fingertips on the oblong brown paper bag under the seat. Light-headed from the maneuver, he walked back unsteadily to the boat, this time ignoring the gaiety coming from the bar. Some crazy jogger went by up on the Blue Heron Bridge, causing Lucky to shake his head at the lunacy people get up to in the middle of the night.

"Friggin' *joggers*," Lucky said. He had been a sprinter and a halfback.

He handed the bottle down to Bobby Lincoln, who took it impatiently. If Lucky was an intimidating figure, Bobby was more so. He was a huge black man with a weight lifter's build and an intimidating scowl.

"What's this?" Bobby said, tucking the bottle into the top of the equipment bag behind him.

"Liquid courage," Lucky said.

"I heard that." Bobby frowned. "Good idea."

Lucky loosened both dock lines and tossed them into the boat, hopping with surprising agility down into the little skiff and pushing it back from the pier. He sat behind the console and cranked the outboard as the boat drifted slowly in the black water. It was nothing doing.

"Jesus damn Christ on a crutch," Lucky said, turning off the key and sitting back in the seat.

He pushed the yachting cap back off his perspiring forehead and looked at Bobby through the top of his eyeballs.

"Cranked right up when the guy showed it to me. Then it started doing this shit after I paid him and it set awhile. Dollars to donuts he had it all warmed up before I got there so it would crank up pretty for me. *Sumbitch!*"

"Well, you flooded now. May's well give it a minute, let it dry out some," said Bobby.

"I know what to do," Lucky said irritably.

"How much ya pay for it anyway?"

"Hunnert and twenty-five."

"He seen you comin', all right."

"Great mind to take a baseball bat to his skull, little Jew bastard," said Lucky.

"Easy," said Bobby.

"Yeah, well, few more minutes drifting and we'll be right in the lights from the Crab Pot, goddammit."

"Tha's all right if it did."

"You want every sumbitch in Riviera Beach seeing us heading out into the intracoastal in the middle of the night?"

"We got diving stuff. Just doin' a little night dive."

"With no tanks and no lights?"

"Can't nobody see that. You got to relax, man. You gone bust a gasket," Bobby said, standing up to relieve himself over the side. Then he retrieved a dirty hand towel from under the console and used it to wipe the sweat from his forehead.

Lucky heaved a big sigh, sat up to the wheel, and tried the engine again. It caught and sputtered as Lucky goosed the throttle several times, then allowed it to idle raggedly. Blue smoke poured out of the exhaust and floated out across the surface of the warm water.

"Okay, hand me over that bottle and set yourself down," Lucky said.

Bobby picked up the brown bag and pulled the fifth out, holding it up to admire the label in the light from the bridge.

"My oh my, Cockspur," he said, unscrewing the cap and upending the rum bottle, bubbling it several times before hauling it down and holding it up to study it again, smacking his lips with approval.

"Hand it here, goddammit," said Lucky, flicking the running lights on. He eased the throttle forward until the little boat got up on plane, then eased it back until they were making fifteen knots down the middle of the intracoastal.

"Shore, boss, here you go. You don't mind drinking after no Negro, do you, boss?"

"Just don't want no goddamn backwash, black or white," said Lucky. But there was a tinge of humor in his voice, which Bobby took as a sign he was relaxing a little now that the engine was running. Lucky seemed good-natured on the surface, but that belied a vicious streak that had earned him a reputation up and down the coast as far as Titusville in one direction and Miami in the other. It had also earned him some stretches of county time and once almost a bus ride to Raiford, had it not been for a last-minute witness defection. He had been a juvenile delinquent in Indiana before going to war as a paratrooper. He had been decorated for bravery and had seen and done things that he struggled to keep out of his thoughts at night.

Bobby was just as much of a bad boy, but without the surface charm. He owned a taxi company, but his real vocation involved moonshining, bolita, and freelance skullduggery. He was reputed to have killed three black men with a machete one night in Belle Glade, though no bodies were ever found—Lake Okeechobee is a large body of water and more or less full of alligators. If anyone ever had the temerity to ask him about it, Bobby would say that he didn't do it, and if he did, it was in self-defense. But when he said it, it wasn't like he was trying to be funny.

Lucky took a long pull from the bottle and held it out in front of him admiringly while he made little *geck-geck-geck* noises, lips stretched tightly over his teeth in a macabre grimace of a smile. He took a small follow-up sip, then handed it back, wiping his mouth with the back of his forearm.

Bobby stood easily beside the console, his knees absorbing the occasional jolt when they hit a small wave. They could see a few lights from buildings and cars on both sides of the intracoastal but heard no noise at all above the little outboard. Though it was a typical humid May evening, the bright moon and passing breeze made it almost pleasant.

"Where'd you get that?" Bobby pointed the bottle at Lucky's new-looking yachtsman's hat, the only clean article of clothing he had on.

"Part of the plan, me hearty. Lemmee hold that bottle a secont and don't worry about nothin'. White man got everything under control tonight."

"Tha's what I *do* worry about."

Judge Curtis Chillingworth walked barefoot into the small kitchen of his Manalapan beach house, noticing that the linoleum was still sandy from the last renters. He made a mental note to mention it to his wife as he poured two glasses of Johnnie Walker from the new bottle on the counter, one finger for Marge, two for himself. He fetched ice from the small rusty fridge, added a splash of water from the tap to her drink, none for his, and padded back to the bedroom, where she sat up in bed reading a paperback. She looked up and smiled when he handed her the drink, which she placed on a crocheted doily on the bedside table.

The sound of ocean drifted through the curtains along with the pleasant sea breeze. They were just a few scant feet from the ocean at high tide.

"Thank you, Jeeves," she said.

"Yes, ma'am. May I get you anything else?"

Their little joke was to play upper-crust Palm Beachers, though it was hardly the case. Manalapan wasn't Palm Beach, though with his circuit judge's salary and some careful real estate investments, they had raised their three daughters comfortably and were secure in their middle years. Their little beach place made a steady income during the winter months when well-heeled but price-conscious snowbirds wanted a place on the ocean but did not want to pay Palm Beach prices just to be ignored by the Kennedys. It was rented most of the winter and spring, so it was always a treat in the summer when they were able to take a break from their stuffy home in West Palm Beach and steal away for a few nights of ocean breezes. They always brought a bottle of scotch and a couple of steaks for the grill, and treated it as a minivacation, though he had to drive downtown to the courthouse the next day, just like always.

"What is that you're reading?" he asked, putting his drink on his bedside table and pulling back the bedspread and sheet.

"Oh, it's this sort of trashy thing for my book club, *God's Little Acre*. I don't think it's really your cup of tea, dear."

"Isn't that the pornographic one they banned everywhere?" He sniffed.

She giggled. He pulled his own book from the lower shelf of the nightstand, a hardcover biography of Winston Churchill, which he was just starting.

"Well, I'm back to old Winnie myself," he said. "He's got the black dog again and this time I'm afraid it might do him in before he can regain power and deal with the Hun once and for all."

She closed the book on her index finger and regarded him fondly.

"I don't really see the attraction of reliving all that again," she said. "It was bad enough getting through it the first time. Everything you went through over there, and all the rationing and hardship back here, families losing fathers and sons, getting those awful telegrams. I'd think you'd just want to forget it."

"However bad it was for Americans, here or there, it was a hundred times—a thousand times—worse for those poor people over there. I don't know why, but I just find it interesting, getting a historical perspective on it. When we were there, we were much too close to things, too concerned with details. Not just the details of war, but the details of trying to live with all of that going on around you. Sometimes it was a big accomplishment just to get a shower or find a hot meal."

"I suppose. But I'm afraid not even Mr. Caldwell can hold my attention much longer. I was down at the Junior League sorting used clothes first thing this morning, and I haven't stopped all day. I thank you for the drink and I'll leave you and Mr. Churchill to work everything out," she said, kissing him on the cheek and turning her lamp off.

"Not for long, I expect. I had pretrial motions all afternoon and I'm pooped, too," he said.

"I love you. Good night."

"I love you, too, Margie."

Half an hour later when he got up to see who could possibly be calling in the middle of the night, he opened the door to his porch to find a disheveled, nervous man in a captain's cap, saying his yacht had broken down and wondering if he could use the phone to call the Coast Guard. Then he halted his tale of nautical woe and smiled.

"Say, aren't you Judge Chillingworth?" asked Lucky Holzapfel.

CHAPTER 54

DON'T SAY A WORD

The Citrus City main library had once been the home of an early Florida cattle baron, whose grandfather made a living cracking a long bullwhip behind the ears of feral cows. The ancestors of the bedraggled cattle had been abandoned in the swamps by the conquistadors. Cracking those whips was the way they drove the rangy cows out of the swamps and across the grassy wastes of central Florida to Punta Gorda, where they were loaded onto wooden ships and taken north to feed starving Confederate troops. Thus, the term "cracker" came to be applied in a general and mostly complimentary way to early residents of the Sunshine State. It was later appropriated by black people looking for a term derisive enough to apply to white people for all the things black people had been called by *them* over the years.

The library was a grand old structure of two stories, handsome in its day before going to seed in the 1930s. Now it has been lovingly restored by civic-minded Citrus Cityites and put to use housing the town's meager collection of books and magazines. The library had no more reliable patron than "Vincent Natulkiewicz" (as his library card referred to Trapper Nelson), who, every Saturday, rain or shine, would bring in the five books he had checked out the previous week and then troll through the stacks to find five new ones. The head librarian, Marilyn Young, would also save the previous week's *Wall*

*Street Journal*s for him to take back to the Loxahatchee to pore over. The Tarzan of the Loxahatchee was nothing if not well-read.

His weekly patterns were known to Quenton Cassidy, so when he needed to talk to Trapper and didn't feel like making the journey out to his camp, Cassidy knew exactly where to find him at ten o'clock on Saturday morning.

The dictates of the Dewey decimal system had placed the 900s—i.e., most of the books Trapper was interested in: history, geography, biography—in the cattle baron's former master bedroom in the second-floor back corner room of the house, far from Ms. Young at the front desk. That allowed them to talk in normal tones unless she wandered in to shelve books or to find something for a patron. She would then shush them despite there being not another soul in the building. It was the principle of the thing.

"What you got there?" said Cassidy.

"Biography of Churchill. Friend of mine recommended it," said Trapper. He added it to the stack on the table behind them and continued down the shelf.

"Aren't you going to look for anything?" said Trapper.

"This isn't my kind of thing. I prefer novels, like *Catch-22*, or books about sports."

"What are you reading now?"

"Book called *Floorburns*. About basketball," said Cassidy.

"Can't leave the sport behind, huh?"

"I like ones about track, too, but there aren't many of them."

"I'm surprised there are any. What have you read?"

"I liked Bannister's book. And there was a kids' novel called *Iron Duke* and another one, *Junior Miler*, that were both pretty good."

Trapper was engrossed in a book about Africa, trying to divide his attention between that and his conversation.

"So where were you at practice day before yesterday? Kamrad was miffed," he said.

"I know. Lenny was supposed to tell him. We had a forensics meet at another school. I was doing extemp. I told him about it yesterday," said Cassidy.

"Forensics?"

"You know, debate, public speaking, that kind of thing."

"What's 'extemp'?"

"Extemporaneous. They give you a topic and you have to make something up on the spot and deliver it in front of someone, a judge."

"I didn't know you did that kind of thing."

"Well, I wanted to do debate, but they go on trips and stuff and it's pretty hard to do that and sports at the same time."

"Hmmm." Trapper had found a book on Antarctic expeditions.

"So anyway, I got home and took a nap, then went out for my run really late."

"Oh, yeah, you did the seven miles after all?"

"Yeah, I ran across the bridge and along the beach and back. It was pretty amazing. Big bright moon, cool breeze, no traffic or anybody to bother you."

"So you did your workout! I can tell Archie you didn't skip."

"Oh, and I saw your friends again," Cassidy said.

Trapper put the book back on the shelf and looked at Cassidy.

"What friends?"

"You know, that Lucky guy and his sidekick."

"Floyd and Bobby? Where? Where'd you see them?"

"They were doing a night dive, I guess. They were taking off from the dock behind the Crab Pot, really late. It was pretty dark, but I recognized them."

Trapper's eyes widened and he held his hand up to stop Cassidy from continuing. Without a word he gestured toward the door with his head.

"Hey, what's . . ."

Trapper made a shushing sound and led Cassidy out of the building and into a little courtyard under some frangipani trees in the cattle baron's backyard. They sat at a picnic table across from each other.

"Okay, now tell me every single thing you remember," said Trapper.

"I pretty much already did," said Cassidy. "It was around nine or so. Just two guys going out in a boat to dive." He described the boat and the men as best he could, repeating how dark it was.

"What's the big deal?" he said. "I thought you said they were big divers and stuff. Lots of people go out night fishing or diving."

"I'm telling you again: those guys are not my friends. When they're out late at night, it is not likely for any night dives, or night fishing either."

Trapper looked up into the frangipani branches, deep in thought. Cassidy hadn't seen him look so serious since the incident at Moccasin Cove.

"I want you to promise me something," he said finally. "Can you do that?"

"Yes, sir," Cassidy said, puzzled.

"I want you to promise me that you will not breathe a word of what you saw to another human being. Can you do that? This is as serious as it can possibly be."

"Okay, sure. But I didn't really see any—"

"*Not a word!* To anyone. Not your parents, not your girlfriend, not anyone. Okay?"

"Okay, sure."

"Okay, I have to go. I'll probably see you at practice Monday. Remember . . ."

"Right. Not a word."

"Right."

His parents were gone, so Cassidy got to indulge himself for lunch: two banana-and-pineapple sandwiches, made with Merita bread, and one with Hellmann's mayonnaise, the other with peanut butter. He poured a big glass of milk from the wax carton.

When he sat down at the Formica table, he noticed that day's *Citrus City Sentinel.* He hadn't read it before he left for the library that morning.

The front page bore a huge headline: "Circuit Judge & Wife Missing from Beach Home."

Cassidy momentarily forgot his sandwiches and read:

> Manalapan—Circuit Judge Curtis Chillingworth and his wife Marjorie were reported missing from their Manalapan beach home yesterday morning, according to Palm Beach County sheriff's spokesman Dan Holt.
>
> Authorities were alerted when Judge Chillingworth failed to arrive at a hearing scheduled yesterday morning at the Palm Beach County courthouse. They also received a call from a workman who went to the judge's cottage early yesterday morning in order to begin a building project.
>
> Police found little in the way of clues except for a broken porch light, a discarded roll of tape, and a spattering of blood. They wouldn't divulge any other possible clues.
>
> "We ruled robbery out right away. There was money found in Mrs. Chillingworth's purse. And their swimming clothes were found inside, so it is unlikely there was a drowning accident," said Holt. "Right now we are treating this as an abduction."
>
> Family members are in the process of raising a reward for information regarding the case.

Cassidy sat and looked out the jalousied kitchen door to the caster bean tree in the side yard. He remembered seeing Judge Chillingworth at Trapper's, his stern manner and suppressed smile. He remembered the respect with which he was treated in the rough-and-tumble camaraderie of the camp.

Now he had disappeared, along with his wife.

And there was blood at the scene.

CHAPTER 55

RANKINGS

"The state rankings came out yesterday," said Mr. Kamrad. Everyone was sitting on the grass in a semicircle. The coach allowed the buzz to settle down on its own. Finally, he held up a hand for silence.

"Some congratulations are in order. Our own Mr. Stiggs is seventh in the high jump at 6-2¼, despite coming out late from basketball. He's only two inches out of first place, so naturally a lot of people are picking him to finish high—maybe even win state. So, way to go, Stiggs!"

Stiggs, never one for false modesty, held up both arms in triumph, getting a pretty good laugh.

"Uh, Mr. Stiggs has scratched from the 440-yard event, however," said Mr. Kamrad, getting an even bigger laugh. Lenny half stood and took a little bow.

"Okay, that's not all, men, settle down." He waited for quiet.

"Ed Demski is eighth in the half at 2:00.5."

Applause and whoops as Demski, sitting beside Cassidy, grinned and hung his head, embarrassed by the attention.

"And . . ." He waited again. "And, it says right here . . ." He pretended to study the sheet on his clipboard.

"Hmmm, unless there's a typo or something, it appears that our own Quenton Cassidy, at 4:33.5, made the list at number ten in the mile!"

Cassidy was surprised. He hadn't had much competition in the local meets but had run another hard race against Jim Lee, who ran much smarter than the first time.

But Cassidy had run tired in every race and was beginning to think that his physical funk was a permanent condition. He certainly didn't feel like the tenth-ranked miler in the state.

In a good mood, everyone dispersed to their different events, but a few gathered around Mr. Kamrad to study the rankings more closely. Cassidy waited until the coach finally shooed them off to their workouts.

"Yes, Quenton?" he said.

"I was just wondering who's ahead of me in the mile?"

"Well . . ." Mr. Kamrad looked a little sheepish. He studied his clipboard briefly, then handed it to Cassidy.

"Don't let this discourage you," he said. "You haven't begun to peak yet. When you're tapered and rested . . ."

Cassidy found the mile list on the second page. There was his name in tenth place all right. In first place he read: "Jerry Mizner, Pompano, 4:20.8."

"What? Is this right?"

Mr. Kamrad gave him a sympathetic smile, taking the clipboard back.

"Yes, it is. They had a big meet down in Miami and he and this kid in second place, Chris Hosford, from Christopher Columbus, got into it. They both ran PRs." Cassidy took the clipboard back and looked at the list again. The second-place time was 4:21.0.

"I was thinking Mizner's PR was 4:26 something."

"It used to be."

"Third drops off to 4:25.8. At least that seems human," Cassidy said. He was trying not to sound defeatist, but he felt as if he'd been kicked in the stomach.

"Look, Quenton, there's no need to get psyched out here. The regionals are in two weeks. It'll be your first heads-up race against Mizner, and you'll be reasonably well rested for—"

"Reasonably?"

"Archie has you cutting back pretty good two days before. You'll be—"

"That's not enough!" Cassidy said.

"You only have to finish in the top three to go to state. That's all he's thinking about right now."

Mr. Kamrad smiled grimly, pushed his thick glasses back on his nose, and held up his other clipboard, the one with San Romani's schedules on it.

"Don't forget . . ."

"Yeah," said Cassidy. "I know. 'Archie's Axioms.'"

"That's right. And one of them says: 'Train *through* everything until it really counts.'"

"I don't suppose there's one on there that says something like 'Give a guy a break'?"

"You're thinking of Christianity, or maybe Buddhism. This is . . . *SanRomanity!*"

Jogging off to join Demski and the others, Cassidy laughed. *San-Romanity, that's pretty good. Almost rhymes with "insanity."*

CHAPTER 56

REGIONALS—MIZNER REDUX

Two days of easy running wasn't enough rest by a long shot, but it was all he got.

On Thursday they did a short set of 220s. They were specified to be "sharp," for which Cassidy never got a definition. So they ran 30s and 31s, and then Cassidy and Demski battled out the last one, with Demski finishing just barely ahead in 27.8.

On Friday, when Mr. Kamrad announced they were doing a moderate five-mile run, Cassidy felt like walking off the track. He might have actually done it, too, but he saw Trapper's Jeep pulling up.

"Why so down?" Trapper asked.

"The most important meet so far in the season is tomorrow night. Archie—I mean, Mr. San Romani—has us doing a hard five-miler," Cassidy said. He was trying to keep the whimper out of his voice.

"I know. I talked to him last night. He told me this is a crucial time and he's sure you can finish in the top three to make it to state. That's the big thing on his mind right now."

"Top three? Maybe I can, maybe I can't. But I have to run against the best guy in the state tomorrow! I'd kind of like to have at least a chance not to get killed again!"

"Quenton, we've trusted Archie before, and he hasn't let us down yet."

"Maybe things aren't like they used to be," Cassidy said. "Maybe training in the 1930s was different. People are a lot faster nowadays."

"Quenton, you—"

"How fast did Mr. San Romani run, anyway? What was his best mile? Do you know?"

Trapper gave him a sympathetic look, like he used to when Cassidy was just a kid and was messing up.

"Yes, I know," Trapper said.

"And?"

"It was 4:07, Quenton. Less than a half second off the world record at the time."

Cassidy took a deep, resigned breath and looked around.

"Demski! Let's go!" he said.

There was nothing more definitive in their world than their personal black-and-white numbers, their personal records, PRs. The numbers didn't lie and they didn't wear away with time, as even the names on granite tombstones did.

The regional meet was held at Pompano Beach's new rubberized asphalt track. Cassidy couldn't believe how good it felt to run on it, particularly compared to Edgewater's number-two road asphalt.

He also couldn't believe the multihued sweat suits from dozens of schools in the region. He had never been to a meet this big before. What in the world would the state meet in Kernsville be like? If he even made it.

When he saw how fit the other runners looked, he experienced the "what am I doing here?" fears. It was the old self-doubt he always felt at the bigger events. He wondered if this wasn't all some big mistake. But his training log was his security blanket. At Mr. San Romani's suggestion, Cassidy had taken it along with him in his equipment bag.

"When you're feeling psyched out, get out your diary," he told him. "Look back over the last few months of forty- and fifty-mile weeks. Look at the quarter-mile repeats at sixty-four and sixty-five seconds where you and Ed beat each other's brains out in the heat. Then try to imagine any of those other guys working any harder than that."

After getting the feel of the track, he jogged out of the stadium and followed some of the other runners on a path that went around the perimeter of the school grounds. It was a fairly new school, more expensively built than Edgewater. Despite the sun sinking below the horizon, it was still warm and humid. He had left his sweat bottoms in his bag.

Cassidy was used to warming up alone. Demski and Lindstrom's events weren't until later, but the mile was the third event, right after the high hurdles and the hundred. No one else on Edgewater's team had run the 5:00 qualifying time in the mile except for Demski and Lindstrom, and they weren't about to risk doubling in such a big meet.

He was just coming around the tennis courts when he saw the familiar blue-and-gold uniform with the whirling tornado on the chest. Mizner, already in shorts and singlet, looked up and smiled. Cassidy hadn't counted on this. He thought of Mizner as some kind of boogeyman that lived in his daydreams and nightmares and drove him through blistering workouts on the track. He wasn't sure quite how to deal with the flesh-and-blood human being standing in front of him, smiling and offering his hand. Mizner's dark complexion was even more deeply tanned than the last time he'd seen him. With such fine, even features, flashing white teeth, and easy smile, he hardly looked like the ogre of Cassidy's imagination.

Cassidy couldn't help smiling back. They shook hands like it was the most natural thing in the world for mortal enemies to be friendly. Cassidy was skinny as a wading bird, but Mizner's hand felt fragile to the point of delicacy.

"Congratulations on your PR," Cassidy said. "It must have been some race."

"Hey, yeah, thanks. I didn't think I was ready to run that fast, but that Hosford guy didn't give me much choice. I think he's got it in for me for some reason." He laughed.

"What did you do, outlean him at the tape?"

"Pretty much. I thought I had put him away and then he came back on me in the last hundred. That's the first time that's ever happened to me. I'm glad he's in a different region, frankly. I was so blown out I couldn't double back in the two-mile."

"Eight laps after a hard mile, no thank you," Cassidy said. "Sometimes I come back in the half . . ."

"You seemed to handle two miles okay in cross-country." Mizner laughed. "I still have bad dreams about that race."

Ah, Cassidy thought, *I'm not the only one.*

"Well, I'd better . . ." Cassidy gestured at the path ahead.

"Yeah, me too. Good luck out there tonight." They shook hands again.

"Yeah, you too," said Cassidy, and immediately wondered if such a benediction was ever sincere. He guessed he wished him all the luck in the world as long as he was behind.

Mizner turned out not to need any luck at all.

He led off with a sixty-two-second quarter that devastated the field. Cassidy was in a chase pack of three that followed along meekly as Mizner, instead of blowing up and falling back to them as everyone expected, actually built on his lead over the next two laps.

Mr. Kamrad said only one thing every time Cassidy's group went past him: "Top three, Quenton. Top three."

Top three is fine, Cassidy thought, *but this is still a race.*

It was a race to everyone except Mizner, who didn't so much as peek behind him. He strode along with silky strides, far enough ahead that Cassidy couldn't even hear his foot strikes.

Cassidy's pack included the Jim Lee kid he'd beaten twice. There was also a short, very fit-looking blond kid named Brantly. When it didn't look as if they were even going to try to catch Mizner, as the gun cracked at the three-quarter mark, Cassidy broke away and tried to run him down. They had gone through in 3:24, the fastest three-quarter split Cassidy had ever run. He had no idea what Mizner had run. He was too far in front to hear the splits.

Cassidy gained ten yards back by the 220 mark of the gun lap, but at that point Mizner started kicking and ran away from him. Cassidy tried to put together a kick of his own, but that strained feeling in his legs told him that he was right at the red line already. He looked quickly behind him to make sure the other two were well back, then tried to stride as efficiently as he could through the last 220.

Mizner ran 4:23.4 and was so unfazed by his effort that he kept running past the finish line and on to a victory lap. Cassidy finished and stayed in the hands-on-knees position so long an official had to come gently shoo him off the track so they could start setting up for the 440 relay.

Mr. Kamrad came running up to show him his stopwatch, but Cassidy had been watching the scoreboard clock as he finished.

"Great effort! How does it feel to be under 4:30?" Mr. Kamrad said, still excited.

Cassidy just signaled with a wave that he couldn't talk, and allowed Demski to lead him away, stumbling and rasping for air. The post-race fog bank had rolled in, clouding everything in his field of vision, though he knew it was just an artifact of oxygen debt.

"F-f-four twenty-eight one," Demski whispered. Mr. Kamrad had given Ed his stopwatch with the time still on it. "Good f-f-frickin' running, man."

Cassidy just shook his head, still gasping.

Mizner stopped by, smiling, looking like he'd been out for a jog. Cassidy tried to buck up, but he was still just blown out. He could hardly stand up straight. Still, he managed a smile.

"Guess I'll see you in Kernsville," Mizner said, shaking hands.

"You bet!" said Cassidy.

As if he couldn't wait.

CHAPTER 57

CALAMITY

The bus ride back from Hialeah had been raucous, with the major-ity of the team now finished with their season, and it was clear that they were mostly relieved. They wouldn't have to go through the meat grinder of the state meet next weekend like Cassidy, Demski, and Stiggs. But Stiggs was returning with a 6-4¾ PR in the high jump and Demski likewise had realigned his place in the numerical universe with a 1:59.5, his first time under two minutes. Cassidy was taking home a PR, too, but no one would have guessed it to look at him.

The three of them sat in the back of the bus with Mr. Kamrad, talking about the upcoming week.

"Stiggs, you'll do your usual routine Monday and Tuesday. Then I'll have you do tapering workouts for the rest of the week. You won't have to compete until Saturday morning, so your last day of hard jumping will be Wednesday. I'll get you out of class early so you can take a few easy jumps and limber up before we leave for Kernsville."

"Right-o," said Stiggs, still glowing from his PR. He had had one really good attempt at 6-6 and was still riding high from it. There were rumors that Coach Cornwall from Southeastern University had been at the meet. Stiggs would have liked nothing better than to get scholarship offers in two different sports.

Despite their late arrival back at the school, the girls would be waiting for them in the parking lot, and Stiggs would drive them to the Steak 'n Shake, to either celebrate or mourn, depending on how the meet had gone.

Cassidy felt like mourning in either case. He couldn't shake a pervasive sense of dread, even as Mr. Kamrad seemed to grow more animated discussing the coming week.

"You two," said Mr. Kamrad to Cassidy and Demski, "I have a very specific taper program from Archie for you, and we are going to follow it to the letter. Quenton, you have a preliminary round Friday morning. They have to trim the field by a few guys, but I don't expect it will be too bad. The guys from some of the other regions, particularly the panhandle, won't be very tough. Ed, your prelims are Friday afternoon. Same deal. Shouldn't be hard at all. We'll take a station wagon up Thursday after practice. Trapper might come up later."

"Really?" said Cassidy, his mood lifting.

"He said he would if he could get someone to feed his menagerie."

Having Trapper along would be welcome in such an intimidating environment as the state meet, and it allayed Cassidy's sense of dread for a while. But by the time they hopped in the Rambler with the girls and got to the Steak 'n Shake he was back in the doldrums.

Stiggs and Jerri were playing grab-ass across from them in the booth, and Cassidy would have liked to have borrowed some of their energy, but he couldn't even fake it.

"What's the matter, bambino?" said Maria. "You don't look like you just won a big race."

"I didn't win," said Cassidy. "I was second. And not a close second."

A batik headband held her dark hair back prettily and she smelled to Cassidy like some kind of fragrant light dessert, like a vanilla baba. Cassidy thought that if he could just rally a little bit, he would surely be in love with this girl. He took her hand, but she shook it loose and held it against his face.

"Okay, you don't have a fever. You made the top three and Stiggs did, too," she said. "And Ed. So this is a celebration, right? Not a wake?"

"You're absolutely right, bambina. I'll get with the program here any time now, I promise," Cassidy said. His smile felt like it would crack his face.

Cassidy slept like a fourth-dynasty pharaoh.

His mother checked on him several times, standing at his door but not saying anything. He felt her presence, but he was still gliding just beneath the surface, occasionally porpoising up and down for a few seconds and then plunging back into the deep water of real sleep.

Finally, at almost high noon, he dragged himself out of bed and pulled on a clean pair of cutoffs and a T-shirt.

His mother actually looked relieved to see him upright but didn't say anything at first.

"What time did you get in last night anyway?" she said finally. He sighed at this universal parental query. She put a chicken salad sandwich in front of him and a glass of iced tea.

"Just after one. We had to run Maria home and Jerri back to her car at the school."

"Honey, I . . ."

"I was just a little late," he said, going into defensive mode. "It was a long drive back, and—"

"No, it's not that," she said, sitting down beside him, putting a hand on his shoulder. There was nothing in the least bit usual about this, and he was instantly on alert.

"There's some news," she said. He hadn't seen that look on her face since they got the telephone call that told them his grandfather was dead.

He was trying to control his unease, and the recent dread he thought he had slept away was back. He looked at his mother, waiting. He was sure her eyes were glistening.

Finally, she took a deep breath and reached back to the sideboard and retrieved the *Citrus City Sentinel*. She opened the A section in front of him, and the headline caused a sharp, physical pain in his chest.

Trapper Nelson had been arrested for the murder of a moonshiner named Lew Gene Harvey.

CHAPTER 58

CRISIS OF CONSCIENCE

For once he escaped church.

Joe Kern had called and asked if he could come by. His mother greeted Joe and left to attend services herself. His father was on TDY at a DEW Line radar station in Thule, Greenland, where, he often proclaimed, "There's a woman behind every tree." It never got old, that one.

Joe Kern had been "Uncle Joe" since Cassidy's earliest memories. His father and Joe had been childhood friends, little heathens growing up wild back in the Depression. It was Uncle Joe who taught Cassidy how to use a Hawaiian sling, how to shoot a set shot, and how to throw a butterfly net. Now he was sitting in their living room on this Sunday morning, wearing a dark blue flannel suit, which meant he was probably meeting clients later. He wasn't known to be a churchgoer.

"Quenton, you probably know that Mr. Kamrad called me, right?"

"Yes, sir."

"Okay, I'm not here to try to talk you into or out of anything. My purpose is to try to tell you a little bit about what is going on, so that you can make up your own mind."

Cassidy nodded.

"You know, of course, that I'm representing Trapper in this case. First, let me give you some background on what the procedure is.

This hearing on Friday is called a preliminary hearing. Its purpose is just to determine if there is probable cause to require a jury trial. The prosecutor presents a little of the evidence to the judge, enough to convince him that there could be a case against the defendant, Trapper. It's about the lowest standard of proof in the whole judicial system. He doesn't really even have such a hearing if he thinks his case is strong enough.

"Lots of times the defendant will just waive the preliminary hearing if it's a foregone conclusion anyway, but we won't do that because we'd like to see what kind of evidence they might produce later at trial. You understand?"

"Yes, sir."

"So, the first thing is, this part of the procedure is not really very important, okay?"

"Okay."

"The second thing is—and he was very clear about this—Trapper says that the last thing in the world he wants is for you to miss your meet because of that hearing. He understands that you are completely behind him one hundred percent and he really, really appreciates that—Quenton, the man was practically in tears—but he said for you to please go ahead and run the race and he promises that everything will be all right. And Quenton, something else. How long have you known me?"

"All my life."

"That's right. And I haven't ever told you anything that wasn't true, have I?"

"No, sir."

"Okay, I'm telling you this now. You have my solemn promise that everything is going to be okay with Trapper. Do you understand what I am saying?"

"Yes, sir. I know that you are a great lawyer. But I know something else, too."

"What's that?"

"I know Trapper didn't do it. I've heard what they're saying, that Trapper and his brother Charlie never were any good. How Charlie made all those threats to Judge Chillingworth before they sent him off to Raiford, and now he's been paroled and supposedly he came back and he and Trapper are up to their old ways."

Joe Kern sighed. "I know. I've heard that nonsense, too."

"But, Uncle Joe, Trapper would never do anything like this. He just wouldn't." Tears were welling now, and he couldn't help it. He also didn't care. He wasn't bawling, but his eyes were flooding.

Joe Kern brushed his eyes, too.

"I know, Quenton."

"Trapper has never been involved in anything illegal in his life, if you don't count a little poaching. Heck, *I've* taken a crawfish or two out of season, we all have. Trapper's never had anything to do with moonshiners. I've only seen him drink one beer in my whole life! I worked for him all summer long. If he had anything to do with moonshiners, I'd know about it."

"I know."

"Uncle Joe, I just can't imagine Trapper walking into that court-room and looking back and not seeing me there. The man *saved my life*." His eyes filled again. He couldn't help it.

Neither could Joe Kern. He took a deep breath and stood up, dropping a clean handkerchief into Cassidy's lap.

"I told them this wouldn't work," he said, his voice raspy.

CHAPTER 59

TIME TRIAL

"I really don't know why we're doing this. I made my decision," said Cassidy. They were standing on Edgewater's deserted track, with just the security lights from the school providing illumination.

"Come on, no one knows what the future holds. It's not going to hurt anything to follow Archie's program for the last week. Did you sleep okay last night?" said Mr. Kamrad.

"I'm not used to having energy, so it took awhile to get to sleep. Then I had dreams . . ."

"Oh?"

"Yeah, first I dreamed that they announced last call for the mile, and I couldn't find my way into the stadium. It was like someone had hidden the competitors' entrance. I was getting frantic."

"Well, that one's pretty easy to figure out."

"Yeah. Then I dreamed I was in a race and someone was just in front of me in the last lap. I pulled out and started to kick and I just couldn't make my legs go faster. I was desperate, trying to grab on to something and propel myself with my arms instead. It was, I don't know . . . *maddening.*"

"Well, that's another generic athlete's nightmare. The rowers have those, too, if that helps."

Cassidy jogged off to finish his warm-up, a mile of straights and curves. San Romani had been very explicit about these last few days, with this near all-out three-quarter time trial on the Tuesday before the Saturday event. Mr. Kamrad explained that the idea was to get some rest earlier in the week, then stress his body with an almost-race effort so that with a few more easy days his body would be at the peak of its bounce-back from the time trial just in time for the race. But it was a whole tapering regimen that also included some light jogging, some sharp, short intervals later in the week, all carefully thought out to get a runner to his absolute peak for a big race. It seemed perfectly rational to Cassidy, he just couldn't see the point. As important as this race had seemed to him before, it now paled next to the fact that they were trying to send Trapper Nelson to the electric chair.

"All right, I'm ready, I guess," Cassidy said. He was stripped down to shorts and his kangaroo-skin racing spikes, no socks or shirt. His skinny chest was shiny with sweat. He jogged around in circles, nervous as a squirrel, anxious to get it over with. He had never run a three-quarter-mile race or time trial before and had no idea what to expect. Lenny had run his three-quarter leg at that relay meet, but he'd blown up and finished in 3:27. Mr. Kamrad had been hoping for a 3:20 out of him.

"All right," said Mr. Kamrad, "let's run even splits, pretty much as you feel, but Archie thinks you should try to hit sixty-three for the first one and—"

"Sixty-three!" Cassidy almost laughed.

"Remember, it's not a full mile. That makes a big difference. Anyway, just do the best you can. Not one hundred percent sprinting flat out, but otherwise pretty much a full effort. Okay?"

"Well, if I'm not going to race anyway, I might as well get a decent time trial out of it," said Cassidy. He stepped up to the starting post, put his toe carefully on the starting line, and waited for the start commands.

CHAPTER 60

THE NEW PARALEGAL

"What are you doing right now?" Joe Kern asked. Cassidy had answered the kitchen phone because his mother was holding a tray of biscuits with both hands.

"Finishing breakfast, getting ready for school," said Cassidy.

"Okay, never mind that right now. You've got a suit and tie, don't you?"

"Yes, sir, but—"

"Okay, put them on. I'll be over in about ten minutes."

"But I—"

"No time. Just do it. Kamrad will take care of everything at school. See you in ten."

The universe seemed somehow askew wearing Sunday clothes on a Wednesday morning.

"You clean up pretty good," said Uncle Joe, as Cassidy got in the passenger side of his Eldorado. "You tell your mom tonight I'm sorry I didn't come in. We don't have a lot of time."

"Okay. But can you tell me—"

"All will be revealed in due course. Meanwhile, I want you to get your mind back in gear for that race on Saturday."

"Uncle Joe, I've already—"

"I know," he said, opening his hands but keeping them on the steering wheel. "I know, but just do it."

Joe Kern sighed, looked across the seat at him with a little smile, but not unsympathetically.

"When all is said and done, you are going to feel just terrifically sorry for everything you're putting me through right now," he said.

"I already do," Cassidy said, looking down.

"Not like you're gonna. I almost got Judge Beranek to give us a continuance. The prosecutor didn't object, but the judge said no go."

"I don't understand . . ."

"All in due course, my young friend."

They rode in silence down A1A, the car's AC on high. Cassidy was curious but knew better than to ask any more questions. Finally, Joe patted him on the knee.

"Don't fret, son. It might interest you to know that no one thought you'd stick to your guns except me. I told them that they just didn't truly understand the nature of a kid who will hold his breath thirty feet underwater until he passes out."

Cassidy didn't say anything. Hardly anyone mentioned that anymore. He looked around, amazed to see that they were in downtown West Palm Beach.

"I'm not criticizing you. It's actually a compliment," said Uncle Joe. He chuckled as he turned in to the parking lot of the Palm Beach County Jail. Several parking spaces were marked ATTORNEYS ONLY.

"Good morning, Counselor!" said the large bald man behind the barred window. He wore a deputy's uniform with a badge over the pocket and blue jeans. Cassidy thought his forearms might have been just a tad bigger than his own thighs. They were in a small anteroom, separated from the jail proper by a heavy metal door that kept buzzing, opening to let deputies in or out, then slamming shut with a loud clang. *It's a jail all right*, thought Cassidy.

"Morning, Tommy," said Joe, signing the sheet on the clipboard the deputy handed him. "Meet my paralegal, Mr. Cassidy."

"Mr. Cassidy, a pleasure," Tommy said, handing the clipboard to him. "If you would please sign in, sir."

No one had ever called him "sir" for real before. Wide-eyed, he signed the next line, then added the same date and time Joe Kern had.

"They're all waiting for you," said Tommy. "Room three."

The door buzzed and Joe pushed through it, holding it for Cassidy. When it slammed behind him, Cassidy had a momentary attack of claustrophobia, which he suppressed by force of will. There were offices all along the corridor, but then they came to another desk staffed by a deputy, and another heavy door. The deputy looked up from his paperwork and smiled at them.

"Joe," he said.

"Don," said Joe Kern. "My assistant, Quenton."

"Sir," said the deputy. There it was again.

The door buzzed and, with some effort, Joe pushed it open and held it for Cassidy. Inside, Cassidy's senses were immediately assaulted by a greenish glow and a cacophony of metallic clangs, angry curses, flushing toilets, and an odd wailing sound. Cassidy's eyes widened.

They were walking past the green-barred cells now, the inhabitants reminding Cassidy of nothing so much as zoo animals. Some were pacing back and forth, some ignored him, some stared at him with a glazed expression. All wore the same bright orange jumpsuits.

They passed one empty cell and then at the corner Cassidy looked in and was shocked to see familiar faces. In the back of the cell, sitting on metal cots attached to the wall and suspended on either end by lengths of chain, were Lucky Holzapfel and Bobby Lincoln. If they recognized Cassidy, they didn't show it.

"Just a sec," said Joe Kern, going over to the cell. Lucky got up as soon as he saw Joe and came over to the bars. Bobby Lincoln sat on his bunk, scowling at nothing in particular.

"I called him for you and he said he'd look into it," Joe said.

"Hey, thanks, Counselor. I really appreciate that," said Lucky.

"But for future reference, you need to let your own lawyer deal with the bondsman. This was a personal favor. I don't represent you in this case."

Lucky shrugged and smiled, all charm.

"Damn public defenders," he said.

"At any rate . . ."

"Hey, no kidding, I appreciate this."

"Sure, Floyd. And good luck to you," said Joe, taking Cassidy by the elbow and leading him down the corridor.

"What . . ."

Joe held a finger up to his lips until they were out of earshot.

"They're in for running a still out in Belle Glade. That, and a few other things. They are lively boys. They're in the cell next to Trapper. Come on, he's waiting for us."

At the end of the corridor were a series of small conference rooms. Joe went to the one with a number three over the door and held it open for Cassidy.

Inside was Trapper Nelson, dressed in the same green jumpsuit. He sprang up with a huge smile and bear-hugged Quenton Cassidy, who stared at him, flabbergasted.

"Sit, sit," said Trapper. "We've got some stuff to talk about. First, meet Phil O'Connell."

The short, solid-looking man had been sitting on a wooden chair in the corner, talking on the telephone and smoking a cigarette, an ashtray in his lap. He hung up, put the ashtray on the floor, and stood up to shake hands with Cassidy.

"Quenton," said Joe Kern, "Mr. O'Connell is the state attorney for the fifteenth judicial circuit. His office prosecutes crimes committed in this circuit. Phil, do you want—"

"Sure. All right, young man. I understand we have a problem regarding Trapper here and the case he's supposed to be charged with. I'm not sure I understand why you think this hearing coming up Friday is so important that it needs to interfere with your sports program, but I have been told that it is, and I have been importuned to be here today to help do something about that. Now first, everything said in this room is to be held in the strictest of confidence, I trust you understand that?"

"Yes, sir."

"Now, I have a meeting I need to get to, so let me just say that what these gentlemen are about to tell you is in fact the truth and that you may rely on any representations that they make to you regarding this, uh, situation, as well as my role in it. In other words, this is in no way an attempt to fool you or trick you, or anything like that, so pay attention and act accordingly. These gentlemen obviously think very highly of you or they would not have gone to this trouble. Okay, I need to go. Are we clear on this? You know who I am and understand what I have just said to you, right?"

"Yes, sir," he said.

"Thanks, Phil," said Joe Kern, shaking hands. Trapper got up and, to Cassidy's amazement, also shook hands with the man who was trying to put him in the electric chair.

Mr. Kamrad was waiting for him by the high-jump pit.

"Everything okay?" he said.

"Yes, sir."

"So you're all set for this weekend?"

"Yes, sir."

"Anything you need to talk about?"

"No, sir. Actually, I'm not supposed to say anything." He smiled at Mr. Kamrad.

"All right. Easy warm-up and striders. Then a quick set of 220s and a cooldown. That's it. Tomorrow we'll drive up there and get checked into the motel. Then we'll jog some and do a few striders. Then dinner and bed. Your prelim is at eleven in the morning on Friday."

"Okay."

"Archie says don't think about the race until you start your warm-up. Not in the car, not sitting around in the motel. He says that all it does is dump adrenaline into your system and get you worked up and tired out for nothing. He says listen to the radio or read or watch TV, but keep your mind off the race. Okay?"

"Okay."

"Are you feeling okay?"

"I can't *believe* how good I feel."

"You seem distracted. What's on your mind?"

"Just, I don't know . . ."

"Yes?"

"Just, maybe becoming the state champion in the mile run, that's all."

CHAPTER 61

LOOSE LIPS

Trapper Nelson let himself into room 206 at the Mutiny Motel in downtown West Palm Beach. He put the two brown bags on the Formica table by the window, where Lucky Holzapfel was waiting, eyes fixed on the bags.

"George Dickel," he said, pulling out one of the bottles. "Good man!"

"Where'd Bobby go?" said Trapper.

"He got one of his cabbies to come pick him up. I don't know if you noticed, but he ain't that sociable. They don't allow colored in this place anyway," said Lucky, cracking the seal and sniffing the top of the bottle.

He half filled one of the cloudy-looking glasses from the bathroom and immediately started drinking from it even as he filled Trapper's glass.

"You mind if I turn this noisy thing off?" said Trapper, motioning at the air conditioner in the wall beside them. He shivered. "I'm not used to it. Probably get pneumonia." Lucky shook his head, still drinking.

"I don't give a shit," he said, breathless and grimacing from the bite of the bourbon. "I'd sleep in a ditch in a rainstorm tonight. Anyplace but that goddamn jail. I hate that fugging place." He kept the bottle within easy reach.

"I guess you've been in a few times?" said Trapper.

Lucky grinned at him. "You could say that. You?"

"Oh yeah, some." Trapper threw back the contents of the glass and made a grimace like Lucky had. He coughed, looked into the glass like he expected to find something interesting in the bottom.

"I never knew you to be a brown liquor man," said Lucky, pouring Trapper's glass half full again. Lucky was almost finished with his second glass, so in the interest of efficiency he topped it off again.

"Oh, I love it," Trapper said, holding the glass admiringly up to the light. "There's lots of stuff about me that people don't know, and that suits me just fine." He took a big slug of the bourbon without much reaction this time.

Lucky laughed and slapped his knee.

"I knew it! I knew you was up to somethin' out there on the river. *Had* to be up to somethin' to put away the kind of money you do."

Trapper looked surprised.

"It's mostly in land," he said quietly. "I don't live big."

Lucky laughed again. He was starting to perspire, dampening the dirty shorts and T-shirt he'd been wearing when they'd arrested him at the bar of the Crab Pot three days earlier. He glanced at the silent air conditioner a moment, then poured another glass. They drank in silence for a while, then Lucky sat up straight and looked at Trapper Nelson with a big grin.

"How about that moonshiner they say you killed?" he said. "Did you do him?"

Trapper finished his glass and slid it across the table to Lucky.

"Nope, but I can understand how they mighta thought I did. I had some . . . shall we say unpleasant dealings with the man."

"I already knew you didn't do it," said Lucky, pouring another half glass for Trapper, who took it and drank half of it off, wiping his lips with the back of his forearm.

"How'd you know that, Lucky?"

Lucky laughed, swaying in his seat.

"'Cause I know who did!"

Lucky slammed the table with his hand, bent over in laughter, which Trapper joined in. Lucky *liked* this guy. Much better company than that sourpuss Bobby.

"So there's stuff about you that people don't know, either," said Trapper. "Here, let me help you with that. You're spilling."

Trapper took the bottle and filled Lucky's glass all the way to the top. Lucky sat, swaying back and forth in his seat, looking at the glass of bourbon like he was doing algebra in his head.

"Oh, if you knew the half of it, my friend," said Lucky, suddenly looking morose.

Trapper still had two fingers of bourbon in his glass, but he poured another splash in and took a tiny sip.

"What about that judge?" said Trapper. "What was it you were saying about taking care of that judge?"

"People think I got no feelings," Lucky said. He was all but lying on the table, his arm stretched across it, hand on Trapper's elbow. With a major effort of willpower, Trapper left his arm where it was.

"I got feelings, just like other people." Lucky's eyes, bloodshot and yellow, were moistening again. He patted Trapper's elbow. "Where was I?"

"Goddamn engine kept conking out," said Trapper.

"Yeah. Somethin' in the impeller, I guess. Kept overheating. Sumbitch sold it to me musta known about it. We had to stop about a dozen times to let it cool off. And the whole time they're laying there trussed up, staring all wide-eyed at us, knowing what's going to happen."

"That's pretty rough," said Trapper. One of the bottles was sitting empty on top of the air conditioner, the other was between them, one quarter left.

"But I never ever ever woulda made any jokes at a time like that the way Bobby did. Never."

"What'd he say?"

"Mrs. Chillingworth had these weight belts wrapped around her—you know, the cartridge belts we use for diving, lead weights in the pouches—so she's got about forty pounds on her, and Bobby picks her up and says, 'Ladies first,' and throws her overboard." Lucky rubbed his eyes, then giggled. "I guess it mighta been amusin' in other circumstances, but it seemed like it shoulda been a more solemn occasion, if you know what I mean."

He was holding his face in his hands now, half blubbering, half giggling, his tears and saliva puddling on the table. Trapper was relieved Lucky had let go of his arm.

"But before, the judge, he says to her, 'Don't forget, I love you, Margie.' And she says she loved him, too. That got to me a little, I guess. See? I got feelings."

"You saw her go down?"

"Oh, yeah, straight down in the Gulf Stream."

"What about the judge?"

"Oh, we didn't have to do nothin' with him. He sees her going over and he up and jumps in after her. At first it's like he's trying to swim down to her, then he's just treading water beside the boat. God, I don't know how many pounds of lead weights he's got on and there he is, treading water. Tough old bird, I'll say that for him."

"What'd you do?"

"Bobby was gonna shoot him but I said, 'No, Bobby, the sound of the shot could be heard.' By now he's starting to swim away, so I started the boat and chased after him. Bobby grabbed the shotgun and reached out over the side of the boat and hit him over the head with it. I think he broke the stock, but still the old goat didn't go down."

"Tough old guy."

"You can't imagine."

"Yes I can."

"So, finally Bobby grabs him and pulls him next to the boat and I get some rope and tie the anchor around his neck. Bobby lets a go of him, and he went down down down."

Lucky started blubbering again.

"Whatcha cryin' about? Tough man like you," said Trapper.

"It was his eyes. I was shinin' the flashlight down into the water and watching him sinking in those pink pajamas. His eyes just stared up at me the whole way down."

Lucky looked around the room like he couldn't remember where he was. He slumped back in the cheap motel chair, exhausted.

"How'd you let Joe Peel know it was done?" said Trapper.

"Called him when we got back to the dock. Goddamn engine kept overheating all the way back, so we kept having to stop. It wasn't till about dawn we finally made it back through the Palm Beach inlet and over to the dock. Joe wanted us to throw away our clothes, so I had him to bring us something to wear."

"So then you told him all about it."

"Yeah."

"What'd he say?"

"He didn't know Mrs. Chillingworth was going to be there, or so he said. He thought the judge would be alone. But he told us in the beginning that if we found anybody else there, they had to go too, or we'd all get the chair. So that's what we did. So be it."

Lucky got up from the table, swaying, and staggered to the bed.

"Man, I hardly slept a wink in the slammer. I'm going to sleep forever tonight," he said.

"I doubt that," said Trapper Nelson.

Then the door exploded off its hinges, and before it hit the ground seven armed men were in the room.

CHAPTER 62

THE NIGHT BEFORE

The Bambi Motel was south of Kernsville on state road 441, unpretentious and tiny, a little cartoonlike fawn on the marquee just above the NO VACANCY sign.

Demski's snoring had driven Cassidy outside to one of the concrete tables in the courtyard, but he couldn't sleep anyway. He liked Kernsville. It was cooler in this part of the state, with a lot more trees and seemingly more oxygen in the air. *Distance runners,* he thought, *have an understandable affinity for oxygen.*

The preliminary round had been anticlimactic. He almost wished he had had to run harder so that he'd be sleepier. Stiggs didn't need to qualify in his event, but Ed had a tough round, needing a PR 1:58.9 to make it to the final. But at least he was able to sleep. Hell, he sounded like a cement mixer.

In retrospect, all the trouble with Trapper had been a kind of strange blessing. It had kept his attention diverted enough to make those last few days bearable. It was hard to get overly excited about a race you were sure you were not going to run.

But then one little trip to the jail and all of that went away. And now here they were in Kernsville. Mr. Kamrad showed them around the campus—he had taken summer courses there—and their eyes got steadily wider as they took it all in. Southeastern had started in the 1800s as a theological seminary with a tiny student body. Now twenty-five thousand students walked to classes under the moss-draped live oaks scattered around the two-thousand-acre campus. As Mr. Kamrad pointed out the hundred-year-old brick building where he had taken psychology courses, then the cavernous gymnasium, then the awe-inspiring seventy-five-thousand-seat football stadium, the boys got steadily quieter. When they pulled out of Citrus City Thursday they had been something of a big deal in their own minds, regional qualifiers for the state track meet. Now that they were here, they were looking around at a place that could absorb thousands of high school track and field athletes without even noticing them. Stiggs had clammed up completely. They were all feeling pretty insignificant.

Mr. Kamrad noticed and cut the tour short.

"We need to grab some lunch and get checked in to the motel. We'll continue the tour later," he had said.

Now here he was the night before the race, and he had tried everything he could think of to distract himself. Mr. San Romani had counseled him that there would be plenty of time to get his mind in gear when he started his warm-up—they always did a lengthy warm-up. He understood the concept—keep your powder dry and all that—but it wasn't easy to put into practice. In the station wagon on the way up he would willfully put it out of his mind and go back to *The Catcher in the Rye*, but after five minutes of Holden's bitching he would catch himself mentally right back in the thick of the race in his head, pulling up to the leader as they were going into the gun lap, or fighting out of a box before the last turn. His mind was like a puppy, easily distracted but always returning quickly to the toy. Now he longed for sleep just to put an end to his misery.

It should have been a perfect night for sleeping. The pastoral quiet on this side of town was interrupted only by the occasional car hightailing it down 441 to Ocala, and by the ever-present buzz of the motel air conditioners. The place was filled with track guys and coaches, but Cassidy was apparently the only insomniac among them.

He heard a room door opening and figured Demski had awakened to find him gone. But it was Mr. Kamrad, dressed in an Edgewater crew sweat suit and an incongruous pair of flip-flops. He sat down in the lawn chair across from Cassidy.

"How bad is it?"

"Oh, I just can't sleep, is all. I'm not worried or anything."

Mr. Kamrad nodded.

"You know, I remember the first time my little college rowing team went to nationals. Here we were, a bunch of athletes in an obscure sport that no one even knew existed back where we came from. All of a sudden we're surrounded by hundreds of guys like us, except the names on their singlets were famous: Harvard, Yale, Boston College, Cornell. We looked around at these guys and every single one of them looked like an Olympic contender. Nobody said anything, but you could just feel the air going out of us. It didn't matter that we had come through the prelims just fine. We just kept ogling everyone, and by the time we backed into the starting dock, we had convinced ourselves that we didn't belong there."

"Wow. What happened?"

"We finished third. But I've thought about that race pretty much every day of my life since then, and although I'm not a what-if kind of guy, I'm pretty sure we could have won that race. All we had to do is pull from the start like we thought we had a chance. Instead, we hung back, surprised that we were doing as well as we were, not wanting to push our luck. We came on like gangbusters at the end, but we had let ourselves get too far out of it. If the race had been ten meters longer we would have passed both those boats. As it was, they had to look at the photographs, it was so close. But there was no doubt about it. There it was, obvious even in the negatives: we were third.

We were third then and we will always be third. You can look it up in the record books right now and there we will be, third."

"Wow."

"But that's what it means to be an athlete, Quenton. All the civilians see is the triumphant moment, the victory lap, the fulfillment of the dream. They don't pay much attention to the also-rans and the missed-by-inches, the great majority of us who go on with the rest of our lives drawing whatever comfort we can from the fact that we were close. That we were among those who at least tried, were willing to put ourselves at risk. That we would live with the results, whatever they were. But always to try. That is what makes an endurance athlete, Quenton, the contract you make with yourself that you will try and not give up. And if you are lucky enough to be among those that finish at the top, that's a great thing that you get to live with for a long time."

"I never thought—"

"But there's something else."

Cassidy looked at Mr. Kamrad, his familiar horn-rimmed glasses, his sad, empathetic smile.

"There's winning. Don't ever forget that!" he said with a laugh, aware he had gotten pretty solemn. "Hey, wait here a second. There's something I want to show you."

He came back from his room carrying something in his right hand. Sitting on the same bench with Cassidy, he placed it on the table between them. It was his stopwatch.

"I didn't clear it after your time trial. Look at what it says."

"I know what it says."

"It says 3:07.2., Quenton"

"I'm aware—"

"It says more than that, Quenton. It says that—if by some miracle of persistence or training or luck—if you could somehow extend that one lap farther, if you could possibly add a sixty-second quarter to the end of a time like that, you would be a 4:07 miler. You would be as fast as Archie San Romani was at the height of his career, and less than a second from the world record at that time."

"There is no way in the world . . ."

"I know, it's crazy to think such things. That was an all-out time trial, and a sixty-second quarter on top of that is ridiculous to think about. But it's not ridiculous to dream. A little crazy extrapolation like that makes for the best kind of dream."

Cassidy waited. He wasn't really sure what Mr. Kamrad was saying.

"But that 3:07 tells you something else. It tells you that you belong out there, Quenton. Right now, at this moment in time, you belong on the track with Mizner and Hosford and all the rest. You haven't run the times they have, maybe, but you've got those times inside you. You're not some weird accident, some dreamy guy who wandered into a situation he can't handle. It's your race tomorrow. It's yours as much as it is anyone else's."

Cassidy nodded. He had not thought of it that way. He had been more like Mr. Kamrad's poor crew teammates, happy to be tagging along with the real players.

"All right, enough of this pep talk business. This is exactly what Archie didn't want me doing to you before the race. Time to get some sleep. We have a surprise visitor coming in the morning—several, in fact. And then we're going to do a little jog and some striders at the P.K. Yonge high school track after breakfast.

"Who's . . ."

"Don't worry about it. Go back to trying not to think about the race and get some sleep now. Tomorrow, to put it mildly, is a big day, my friend."

"Yes, sir."

Strangely enough, he actually felt a little sleepy.

CHAPTER 63

SPRUNG

The phone blasted them awake at eight the next morning. Demski answered in a voice that seemed to belong to someone else, someone older and less healthy.

"Okay, I'll tell him," Demski said, sounding a little more like himself. He hung up and dove back under the covers.

"Tell him what?" Cassidy was fully awake now.

"Report out front. We have v-v-visitors. And we're gathering for the breakfast expedition. I think I'd rather sleep, but I'm pretty darned hungry."

Trapper Nelson was sitting at Cassidy's table in the courtyard.

He stood, huge grin on his face, and gave Cassidy a bear hug.

"Didn't think I was serious, did you?"

"How in the world . . ."

"I brought something for you," he said, handing him the morning edition of the *Kernsville Sun*. "I wasn't sure if it would make the papers up here, but it did."

The headline read, "Trio Arrested in Chillingworth Case." Stunned, he read on:

By Ron Wiggins
Special from the *Palm Beach Post*
West Palm Beach, FL—A former West Palm Beach city judge

and two Riviera Beach men were arrested yesterday and charged with the kidnapping and murder of Circuit Judge Curtis E. Chillingworth, 58, and his wife, Margorie, 56, from their Manalapan beach home earlier this year.

The former judge, Joe Peel, 36, of West Palm Beach, was arrested at his downtown law office. Floyd "Lucky" Holzapfel, 36, of Riviera Beach, was arrested without incident at a West Palm Beach motel. Bobby Lincoln, 35, was arrested at a cabstand he owns in Riviera Beach, where he also resides. Only hours earlier the two had been released on bail from the Palm Beach County jail in connection with other charges. According to sources close to the case, Peel was not present at the scene of the kidnapping but was charged with conspiracy and first degree murder. Peel had a pending disciplinary hearing before Chillingworth and feared disbarment. He had had several grievances filed against him while practicing law.

State Attorney Phillip O'Connell said the trio was indicted by a direct information filed by his office, bypassing the grand jury. O'Connell said little else at a hastily convened press conference at the Palm Beach County Courthouse.

Police sources close to the case who asked not to be identified said one of the men had divulged details of the crime in a police sting operation involving a confidential informant.

Cassidy sat across the table—mouth agape—and looked at Trapper Nelson, who couldn't suppress a grin.

"Phil O'Connell may refuse to say who snitched on them, but I won't. It was me!" said Trapper.

"I gathered that," said Cassidy.

"It was Peel behind it all along," Trapper said. He took a deep breath. "But I knew the other two were involved. I knew it in my bones."

"I never thought for a second that you—"

"I know, but lots of people were ready to believe I was a real bad guy, including those two. There were plenty of people years ago who thought I had something to do with shooting Dykas, too. That's why it wasn't such a far-fetched scheme Phil came up with after I told him what you saw that night on the bridge."

"Wow. You mean I actually started this whole thing?"

"Well, actually they suspected Peel from the first, but they didn't have a scintilla of evidence against him, and he had set up an ironclad alibi. They also figured Lucky and Bobby were involved somehow, but they had to figure out a way to get me close to them in some way that wouldn't arouse suspicion. Then I'd make friendly with them and supposedly get Joe to help them with their bail situation. They made sure it was late at night when we got out, so I proposed that we get a motel and celebrate being at large. Lucky's a talker anyway, and a bottle and a half of bourbon does wonders for a fella's sociability. I'm still a little hungover, but we got them, Quenton, we got them on tape! It's open and shut."

Cassidy felt light as a puff of down.

"But why did you put yourself on the line like that?" Cassidy said.

Trapper swallowed. "Curtis was my friend. He helped me get my original property on the river. Then he showed me how to get the rest of the land by buying default tax deeds. Even before that, he kept Charlie, Dykas, and me from starving when we first jumped off the train in Jupiter with no money and no prospects." Trapper swallowed again and looked off down 441.

Cassidy didn't say anything.

"I still can't believe what those animals did to Curtis and Marjorie," Trapper said.

They sat in silence for a while, Cassidy reading the newspaper story over again.

"Come on, let's go roust Ed out," said Trapper finally. "We're due at the Flying Biscuit, and your whole cheering section is there!"

CHAPTER 64

THE RACE

The grandstands at the Percy Beard track stadium held several thousand people. Cassidy had never seen anything like it. Nor had he seen so many hundreds of athletes in uniforms of every description, stretching, jogging on the outside of the track, or doing run-ups at the jump pits. Cassidy's race wasn't until three o'clock, and he knew he had to get out of the place for his own good. It was nerve-racking in there.

He followed some other runners who seemed to know their way around. They jogged by the varsity tennis courts and the law school, then entered a little path through some woods that came out in a married students housing area. From there they skirted a small body of water marked by signs that said LAKE ALICE—DO NOT FEED THE ALLIGATORS. Cassidy wasn't sure if they had gators this far north and thought the sign might be some sort of college prank.

Cassidy kept trying to figure out how he felt but finally gave up. He felt restless but blah. He knew that he was truly well rested for the first time in months, but he'd had trouble sleeping for several nights now and didn't feel particularly spry. All the time they had been "running through" races, he had assumed that when he really cut back and tapered for a big race he would have a hard time stopping himself from turning cartwheels.

But he didn't feel that way at all. He felt perfectly fine, but not like

RACING THE RAIN 331

he could leap tall buildings in a single bound. He had almost started feeling better during his prelim race the day before, but Mr. Kamrad told him to run only as hard as he needed to safely qualify. He finished well back in third place, thirty yards behind the Nubbins kid from Orlando Evans, who set a PR.

"Maybe he d-doesn't understand that you don't get extra credit for winning a p-p-prelim," said Demski.

So Cassidy had coasted in with a surprisingly easy 4:35, feeling like he hadn't really even loosened up.

"Don't worry about how you feel," Mr. San Romani had told him on the phone last night. "You might be all over the place. Some of my best races came on days I felt really unexceptional. Just get your usual good hard warm-up and don't worry about it. Halfway through the race is when you want to be feeling good."

So he quit trying to gauge his internal workings and concentrated on the race. He knew Mizner and Hosford were the runners to watch out for. He had thought Nubbins, though just a freshman, might be pretty tough, too, but he probably had taken himself out of it with his crazy prelim race.

Cassidy had almost reached the turnaround point at the end of Lake Alice when he heard a familiar voice.

"I'd recognize that red-and-white flying eagle anywhere," said Jerry Mizner, running toward him, big smile on his face.

"That tornado is hard to miss, too. I wondered where you were hiding."

"Isn't this just the most amazing place?" said Mizner, gesturing around at the campus.

"Yeah, it's kinda overwhelming. I can't really imagine what it would be like to go here," said Cassidy.

"I can. Fortunately, I don't have to worry about it for a while," said Mizner.

"What do you mean?"

"I'm only a junior."

"Holy crap. You've been drubbing me all this time and you're a junior? I didn't need to hear that right now."

Mizner laughed. "Hey, that Nubbins kid is only a freshman!"

"Yeah, and he sure ran like one yesterday."

"Yeah, but he's getting damn tough all the same. I heard he was telling someone he was putting in fifteen miles a day."

"That doesn't sound possible," Cassidy said.

Mizner shrugged. "Well, I need to keep moving. If you're looking for a place to do striders, there's a nice grass field over behind the tennis courts."

"Thanks. Maybe I'll see you over there."

Cassidy watched Mizner's stride as he moved around Lake Alice. It was so silky smooth that it was intimidating just to watch. Cassidy turned and headed back up through the little trail to the law school, passing more and more runners warming up. *So much to be intimidated by,* Cassidy thought. An enormous university with tens of thousands of students, a huge track meet with thousands of athletes. And Mizner with that effortless stride, and him not even a senior yet. And to top it off, a freshman who's in such good shape he can PR in the prelims like it was nothing.

Well, I've got one thing going for me, he thought. *Sure as hell nobody in this race is worried about* me.

Nubbins really was a character. Cassidy heard him cutting up and joking around on the starting line, normally a place of utter solemnity. Cassidy figured he was trying to psych everyone out. From the look of some of the other runners, it was working. Mizner was paying him no attention at all, jiggling his thighs in the second slot in lane one, staring straight ahead. Hosford, a pale, studious-looking fellow, was two runners over, likewise ignoring everything around him, staring into the middle distance. Cassidy had one of the slowest qualifying times and was thus in the inside slot in lane seven. He was most concerned about getting to the rail in one piece as quickly as he could.

The official starter, Walter Welch, wearing an official's striped shirt and a removable fluorescent orange sleeve over his right arm, walked onto the track carrying his starting pistol. He spoke in soft, empathetic tones, trying to soothe anxious runners he knew had been preparing for this race for months. He knew even milers would false-start if they were too tense.

"All right, gentlemen, stand tall . . ." the starter said.

He gave them a few seconds to stop fidgeting and settle down.

"Gentlemen, stand tall while I give you the starting instructions. There will be a three-command start: 'Runners take your marks, set,' and then the gun. All right, is everyone ready? Judges and timers ready?"

After he glanced at all the toes on the curved starting line to make sure no one was actually stepping on it, he began backing away from the starting line and off the track as he raised his pistol arm straight overhead. He looked over to the timers' stand to make sure they were actually paying attention, and said, "Runners, *tuh-ake* your marks . . ."

Cassidy's head was roaring. He looked down at the toe of his white kangaroo-skin racing shoe and thought, *I can't believe this moment has finally come.* It seemed to take a small forever before he heard the second command.

"Get suh-*ehhht* . . ."

Then the gun went off with a loud crack.

Nubbins may have just been clowning around on the starting line, but after the first lap, it was clear he was serious now. He went through in sixty seconds flat.

The heretofore complacent crowd erupted when the split was announced; were they going to get to see the miracle of a high school four-minute mile?

Mizner and Hosford struggled behind gamely and went through

in sixty-two, with Cassidy another two seconds back, so far out of it he felt like he was in a completely different race. The rest of the field had already blown up. Anyone whose strategy had been to run off the leaders' shoulders was in total confusion.

But Cassidy wasn't entirely despondent. He had seen plenty of races where the leaders went through the first lap in a split that was way out of line with their final times. Lots of 4:40 milers would blast out a sixty-three-second first lap, then follow it with a string of seventy-pluses. But Mr. San Romani had been very clear about it from Cassidy's first mile race on the track: run as close to even splits as you can. That's the way you run your best performance, and in high school running your best possible time is the surest way to win races.

"Tactical races might be important later on, but for now the key is maximum efficiency," he had told Cassidy in their last phone call. "There is no way to 'hurry' your way to a good time by getting ahead in the first lap and then hanging on. It's not an efficient way to run."

Cassidy believed him, but here he was after one lap, wondering if he was out of this race already.

Cassidy knew he was not going to run a 4:12 mile. That was nuts. So even his sixty-three was too fast. What he was hoping for in this race was the mid- to low 4:20s. That would mean a PR by several seconds and should put him in contention for a medal.

So he stifled the panic that he would have otherwise felt contemplating the three runners strung out far in front of him. If he was too fast at sixty-three, then these other guys were even more off base. That is, unless they were just that much better than him.

Mr. Kamrad, Trapper Nelson, Randleman, and the girls were situated in the corner of the grandstands just past the finish line so that Trapper, who had the loudest voice, could yell out accurate splits. As he started around the first turn, Cassidy heard his voice booming over the crowd: "Sixty-three four, Cass, sixty-three four!"

Cassidy expected Nubbins to start fading right away, but it didn't happen. All around the first turn he kept up a four-minute-mile pace. Even Mizner and Hosford fell farther behind, though Cassidy didn't lose any more to them.

Now his thinking turned fatalistic: *Maybe this crazy kid is some prodigy like the Ryun guy in Kansas; maybe he is damn near a four-minute miler and we're just the unlucky saps who get to be the also-rans in his coming-out race.*

If that's the case, there was nothing in the world to be done about it but go after Mizner and Hosford and make it a race with them. Let Nubbins run on off and do what he was going to do.

But as they approached the 220 post at the end of the far straightaway, Nubbins began to show he was human after all. Mizner and Hosford began to make up ground on him, and Cassidy—ten yards behind them—went along with them. By the time they got to the starting post at the end of the second lap, the other two had all but caught Nubbins, and all three of them went through in around 2:08. Nubbins had slowed to a sixty-eight, the other two had held on with sixty-fives. Cassidy went through in 2:10, which gave him a sixty-seven for the second lap.

He knew the computations would get harder as the race went along and his brain fogged up, so he concentrated on trying to keep his pace at an average of sixty-five or sixty-six seconds. If he hit sixty-sixes, it would mean a 4:24 mile, a PR, and a great triumph for him, win or lose. Something faster than that would be the stuff of his secret dreams, of course, but not something he would talk about or even allow himself to think about. There are some things you don't put your mouth on. Still, in the back of his head . . .

He was starting to feel it now, as he always did at the end of the second lap: that strained, almost panicky sense of dread of your body going into shock. It seemed impossible that they were only halfway through this, but the next lap would be by far the toughest one. The last lap was a thing apart.

This physical dread was not unfamiliar to him, this approaching gloom. That was what all the training, all those long miles, those searing intervals on the track were all about. They were to prepare him to deal with these few minutes of extreme duress.

But that was what Mr. San Romani had said, wasn't it? The important thing is how you feel halfway through the race. And in truth he felt way better than he could remember feeling at this point in previous races. He was running under control and he was thinking clearly. And his analysis had been accurate from the start: Nubbins had gone out way too fast for his ability. Mizner and Hosford, running in tandem, passed Nubbins in the middle of the back straight.

Cassidy fixed on the back of Nubbins's green-and-white singlet and prepared likewise to overtake the freshman. But he miscalculated. Nubbins tucked in and ran right along behind the other two all through the rest of the straightaway, maintaining a ten-yard lead on Cassidy.

Well, I'm feeling it now, but I'm not dying, thought Cassidy. *Unless my math is off, I've run a lot more efficiently than those three, particularly Nubbins. I've run in the first lane the whole way. I haven't used any extra energy getting bumped or jostled or fighting my way out of a pack.*

He could hear the crowd anticipating a close race, getting jittery and noisy as they came out of the turn. But no one was really pressing the pace now. Mizner on the inside and Hosford on his shoulder seemed content to gather themselves for the final lap, and Cassidy, maintaining the same pace, was surprised to find himself just five yards behind Nubbins as they went by the starting post at the end of lap three.

Now the crowd really was going nuts at the prospect of a four-way race, and Cassidy had a hard time hearing the splits as they swept past the post.

"Three *sixteen*, three *seventeen* . . . three *eighteen*," the official yelled.

Despite the noise, Cassidy heard Trapper's voice booming out: "Three eighteen FIVE, Quenton!"

Cassidy knew that there was a point in every race when a runner senses he can win. It might even be on the starting line. Sometimes it would be in the middle laps when he gets a lead and realizes how strong he feels. But most of the time it is at some point going into the last lap.

With Cassidy, the feeling came as two distinct sensations. One was a sense that the finish line was a reality, that it was a goal he could actually attain. The other was a tingling sensation as the hair stood up on the back of his neck when he realized that he had a kick left, that he could win.

Cassidy was not the only one who felt that way. Hosford jumped ahead of Mizner before the first turn and cut back to the curb, clearly starting his kick and opening a five-yard gap. Mizner responded immediately and ran right back up to his heels. Nubbins began falling away at long last, his insane first lap dooming him. Cassidy stretched out his stride and blew by Nubbins in the middle of the turn. As he did so, it was obvious that Nubbins was finished. It was a three-way race now.

Cassidy was surprised to find himself very quickly coming up on Mizner as they hit the start of the back straight in single file. The crowd could be heard from across the field, and athletes on the infield began running up to the inside edge of the track. As they passed the high-jump area, Stiggs flashed by, screaming his head off, but Cassidy's head was roaring now and he couldn't make out what he was yelling.

Cassidy concentrated on his stride, those long ground-eaters that came from quarter-mile intervals: long, fast, efficient strides. A miler's stride.

Mizner was beginning to strain. He was a pace man, a two-miler at heart, and this kicking business was not his strong suit. He didn't struggle as Cassidy came up to his shoulder and then went around him right before the last turn. Hosford snuck a peek back and looked surprised to see Cassidy there. But he clearly was not flat out yet. He put his head down, dropped into another gear, and began pulling slowly away again.

Cassidy let him go. He let him go even as the hair stood up again on the back of his neck. He let Hosford go because he was no longer worried about him.

All through the final lap, Cassidy had been increasing his speed. It had increased as he passed Nubbins, more as he passed Mizner, and more as he caught up to Hosford. And every time he increased his speed, he was surprised to find more left. It was a revelation. After all the struggles, the stress and frustration of the season, all the times he trained so hard he couldn't eat, when he'd thrashed himself through workouts all week and then run tired in the meets, sometimes being beaten in the process—this was what it was all for.

What was it Mr. Kamrad had said? No one can bench you in track. No one can decide they don't like your attitude, your skin color, the cut of your jib. No one can deny you your due on the track. All you have to do is win.

And Cassidy knew he was going to win.

That was when he felt the presence coming up on his shoulder twenty yards before coming out of the final turn. It was Mizner.

He was obviously flat out, and Cassidy wasn't worried about out-kicking him in the final straightaway, but the problem was that Hosford was directly ahead of them and there wasn't enough room to pull in front of Mizner and pass him. Going into the final fifty-five yards, he was boxed in.

Cassidy tried to remain calm. He knew he had a surge left, but he didn't want to expend it by ducking out the back of the box and then sprinting around both runners, all in the space of half a straightaway. It was the worst possible alternative, perhaps doomed to failure, but it looked like his only option.

Hosford was not slowing and Mizner was not weakening. They were both flat out, and no matter how much run Cassidy had left in him, he could do nothing with it as long as they were locked in place like this.

Just as they were coming out of the turn, Hosford turned to get one more peek and Cassidy understood again why he had been coached to never look behind in a race. As Hosford turned to look over his outside shoulder, his feet had a natural tendency to follow his eyes. He drifted out to the middle of the inside lane, and by the time he turned back, Cassidy had accelerated past him. In his peripheral vision, Cassidy could see Hosford put his head down and dig in, but he had already been almost flat out.

Feeling something almost like elation through the horrific pain, Cassidy kept accelerating, telescoping away down the final fifty-five yards of straightaway, powering away with every stride, as the roar in his head and the roar of the crowd became indistinguishable.

The last few yards felt like slow motion, though he knew this was the fastest he had run in the entire race. If anyone came up on him now, he would certainly deserve to win. No one did. After an eternity of slow seconds over the last ten yards he felt the sweet tug of the yarn parting across his chest.

His hands went right to his knees, but he was at least able to lift his head up and look behind in time to see Mizner crossing the line ahead of Hosford. Nubbins was still struggling midway through the straight, and it looked as if one or two of the other runners might actually catch him before the finish. He had really paid for his fool-hardiness.

Cassidy couldn't hold his head up long, so he went back to concentrating on the rubberized asphalt between his spiked feet, watching the sweat and saliva drip from his chin and puddle on the surface. He felt Mizner's presence, his body heat beside him. Neither of them could talk yet, but Mizner held out a hand weakly and Cassidy hooked pinkies with him, the best he could do at the moment. The crowd was still noisy, but Cassidy couldn't figure out why they started roaring again. He straightened up, looked around the field to see if someone had cleared an amazing height or thrown something a really long way. He didn't see anything.

Then, as he and Mizner started stumbling slowly, arm in arm, down the track, he saw the reason. They had posted the results on the electronic scoreboard at the south end of the stadium:

Mile Run—Div 4-A

1. Cassidy	Edge	4:17.2
2. Mizner	Pomp	4:18.6
3. Hosford	CCol	4:20.0
4. Lee	Rivi	4:28.1
5. Nubbins	Evns	4:28.2

Cassidy didn't know why, but at that point something inside him gave way. He would later think it was just the numbers themselves, the impossible, not-dared-to-be-dreamed-of numerals that did not lend themselves to interpretation. Numerals that couldn't be compromised or politicized or bargained away. Numerals that couldn't be questioned, belittled, or ignored. He had done the training every day without excuses, had run through all the races and had taken his losses and drubbings because of it. He had persevered and remained true to himself and come through it all. And now he had run one mile in 4:17.2, and he would never be the same.

One of the timers walked over, looking at his watch, and whispered, "Your last lap was 59.3. I thought you'd like to know."

Cassidy leaned on Jerry Mizner's scarecrow frame in the middle of the track in front of the scoreboard and just bawled like an infant.

Maria had seen his face and thought maybe he was hurt or ill, and despite his assurances, she wouldn't let him go. This was a maternal side of her he had never seen and he found it mostly comforting. Stiggs had won the high jump and had run out onto the track and lifted Cassidy off the ground. He put him down when he saw the tears, and Cassidy had to make himself smile and insist that he was just happy.

Cassidy thought Trapper would crush him before he let go, and was fairly sure he saw some welling in the corners of his eyes, too. Randleman, shaking his head in admiration, sheepishly bumped shoulders and gave him multiple hand slaps.

Mr. Kamrad was not in the stands when Cassidy got there, and when he finally did show up, he motioned for Cassidy to come down.

He shook Cassidy's hand as they walked.

"I don't need to say anything right now," he said, "except that you did everything I asked you to and that, incidentally, that was the greatest race I have ever seen in my life. We can talk about all that later. Right now there is someone that wants to meet you."

"Who . . ."

"You'll see."

Mr. Kamrad took him to some kind of training room under the stands. It was cordoned off from the other competitors and Mr. Kamrad held up the pass around his neck and indicated Cassidy was with him.

Inside the room, trainers were working on athletes, taping, applying balm to muscles, running whirlpools and ultrasound. But these men clearly were not high school athletes. The big ones were huge, the lanky ones lankier; they were all just somehow more of whatever it is that they were than anyone else he'd ever seen. Cassidy realized with a start: these were varsity university athletes.

Some of them looked up when he walked in, but then they saw his high school singlet and immediately lost interest.

"Hang on a second. I'll be right back," said Mr. Kamrad.

Cassidy sat on the end of an unused training table and tried to make himself inconspicuous. His white singlet with the red diagonal sash and the flying eagle on the breast, the singlet he'd always been so proud of, now seemed paltry.

It was obvious this was just another training day for these athletes. Some of them were maybe a little put out, what with a bunch of high school kids monopolizing their facilities.

Mr. Kamrad returned with a boyish-looking man in a bright blue blazer with a Southeastern University Swamp Dog logo over the breast pocket. Some of the varsity athletes looked up and smiled or greeted him as he walked across the room.

He grinned broadly at Cassidy, and as he approached, hand extended, Cassidy couldn't help being charmed by the guy.

"Quenton Cassidy," said Mr. Kamrad, "I'd like you to meet Ben Cornwall, the head track coach of Southeastern University."

CHAPTER 65

DOOBEY HALL

The hot breath of summer held forth in Kernsville, though it was early September.

Stiggs helped Cassidy with his brand-new suitcase, his brand-new typewriter, and his two army surplus duffel bags. They stood on the sidewalk admiring Doobey Hall, an off-campus dorm that housed scholarship track athletes. Stiggs had two more hours to drive to Tallahassee, where—a legitimate two-sport star now—he would play basketball and high jump for Florida State. He had won the state meet on his last jump at 6-6½. He claimed Cassidy inspired him. Cassidy said it was more likely the three-hundred-pound half-squats.

Somewhat at loose ends, they tried to say their goodbyes while half listening to strange noises coming from the dorm. Finally, someone leaned out a side window and yodeled. They took that as some kind of sign and embraced awkwardly. Then Stiggs drove away.

Cassidy stood watching the ramshackle Nash Rambler disappear up University Avenue, taking with it the last echoes of his earlier life. Randleman was going to play junior college ball back home; Demski, third at state, would be running for Tennessee. So it was also the end of a quartet that Cassidy had been a member of since his earliest memories, since the days when he and Stiggs and Randleman played pickup basketball in Joe Augenblick's backyard, the days when he and Demski raced summer rainstorms down Rosedale Street.

Cassidy suddenly felt very alone. He had no idea what he was supposed to do, so he gathered up his stuff and staggered into the front vestibule. Classes weren't starting for another four days, but a lot of guys were apparently here already.

The first thing he noticed was a large board on the wall with columns of hand-printed Popsicle sticks displaying the names of the top ten varsity performances in each event. Cassidy was dismayed to see that his PR of 4:17.2, the time that he was so proud of, would not put him on the board at all.

Welcome to Division I track and field, he thought.

In the living room, several athletes were watching TV or talking, others were playing cards at a table in the corner. Out on a screened-in porch Cassidy could see a raucous Ping-Pong game in progress. He stood in the doorway with his luggage, looking forlorn, until one of the guys from the card game took pity on him. He bounced over with his hand extended, an elfin-looking fellow with a sharp nose and chin and an altogether winning grin.

"Mahoney!" he said. "Ed. Quarter mile. Bradenton."

"Quenton Cassidy."

"Ah, the miler."

Cassidy tended to think of himself as an athlete in general, or a runner, but usually not specifically a miler. Now in these strange new circumstances it seemed reassuring to know exactly what he was supposed to be. Mahoney, head cocked slightly, studied him closely.

"You play poker?" he said.

"For money? Not often. If I get the urge, I usually just take my cash and throw it in the street."

Mahoney cracked up. He clapped Cassidy on the shoulder like they'd known each other for years.

"Come on," he said. "Let's go look at the room assignments and get you fixed up. I'm sure you're on the third floor with the distance nerds."

On the third floor, they passed an open door where five athletes lounged around inside, the apparent host a freckly-faced kid with a reddish-blond forelock drooping into his eyes and thick horn-rimmed glasses. He got up and introduced himself.

"Atkinson. Steve. You're Cassidy, right? The miler? Saw you win state."

"Cool. Quenton. Or Cass. Whatever."

"Anything but late to dinner? We get that a lot around here. Well, welcome aboard. With Lagotic gone we can use some help out there. In cross-country, too."

"Joe Schiller, prelaw," said a sturdy-looking blond guy in gold wire-rims, offering his hand.

"Godalmighty, Joe, I keep tellin' ya there's no such thing as prelaw!" said Atkinson. "And he's a damn hurdler, by the way. We let him hang around anyway. Over there is Spider Gordon."

He motioned at a lanky, good-natured kid with a head full of tight curls. He was sitting casually with legs crossed Indian style on top of a desk.

"He looks like a runner," said Atkinson, "but he's a damn high jumper. Cleared 6-9 as a freshman last year."

"And a half," said Jordan, with a little wave. "Don't be be-smalling my accomplishments now."

There were two other distance runners in the room who were so shy that when Atkinson introduced them he could barely hear them say hello.

"Come on, Cass, you can hang out with these characters all you want later. Let's get you organized. Atkinson will take you down to your room. It's at the end of the hall. Won't be long until dinner," said Mahoney.

This drew some affirmative rumbling from the group as they left, one saying, "About time, too!" Apparently no one was troubled by a faint appetite. With another handshake, Mahoney returned to his poker game while Atkinson helped Cassidy with his bags.

"Here's your room. Used to be Lagotic's," said Atkinson, putting the duffels down in the hall.

"Lagotic?"

"Frank. Team cocaptain. School record holder, 4:07.2, SEC cross-country champion, other school records out the yingyang. He graduated summer trimester," he said. "Great guy. Great runner, too." Atkinson sounded distinctly wistful.

"Sounds like it," said Cassidy, chagrined to be such a humble replacement.

Cassidy studied the yellowing index card thumbtacked to the outside of the battered oak door. It read:

> *If you can fill the unforgiving minute*
> *With sixty seconds' worth of distance run—*
> *Yours is the Earth and everything that's in it,*
> *And—which is more—you'll be a Man, my son!*
>
> *—Rudyard Kipling, 1892*

"Closest thing to literature you're likely to see around here. Don't know who put it up originally, but Lagotic liked it, so he left it there all four years," said Atkinson. "Anyway, here you are, home sweet home. Key's on the desk inside but nobody uses them. Let me know if you need anything, otherwise see you at chow."

The corner room was clean and bare, with a metal bunk and an oak table with a straight-back chair. There was no closet, but a cheap metal wardrobe would easily hold his meager possessions. Cassidy left the lamp off and enjoyed the orange glow of the setting sun in the blackjack oaks outside his window. The breeze smelled pleasantly of peppery Spanish moss and earthy decaying leaves. He would unpack later.

He felt a pungent mixture of anticipation and nostalgia, with as many chapters in his life ending now as beginning. Maria was going to stay close to home for the time being, going to the same JC as Randleman. She had wept openly as he and Stiggs drove away, barely consoled by their confirmed date for the first football game.

Trapper had held a cookout for them at the river. He was still the Tarzan of the Loxahatchee, but he was now also an acknowledged public hero. Cassidy ceremoniously presented him with his state mile medal, which Trapper wore proudly for a while before handing it back.

"Archie San Romani deserves this more than I do," he said. "But you were the one who earned it. You keep it. I can tell you that he's as proud of you as I am. We'll call him this weekend. He wants to hear all about it."

Cassidy and Trapper sat on the dock, talking about old adventures—some of which actually happened—until everyone else had left. Finally, Cassidy jumped up and swung out on the rope swing and dropped into the chilly Loxahatchee "one last time." It was silly sentimentalism, of course. Cassidy knew he would be back on holidays or during summers to swing on that rope again. But he also knew it wouldn't be the same. Trapper knew it, too.

And now here he was, a scholarship athlete at Southeastern University, sitting quietly in his new room in the gathering dusk, feeling that he was perched at the very edge of something. He tried to sense—however opaquely—what these next few years might bring. Was it possible that he, Quenton Cassidy, might enjoy some moments of glad grace like this room's previous occupant? That he might learn wondrous things here far more revelatory than the exports of South American countries? That the performance ladder in the vestibule downstairs might someday proclaim his name and deeds? Perhaps even that when he himself left this place they would say the name "Cassidy" the way they now said "Lagotic"?

He had no idea. But the prospect alone filled him with an unconstrained joy.

His revelry was interrupted by a deep rumbling in the distance. From the west window he could see a dark storm gathering on the horizon. He had heard that they often rolled in off the Gulf of Mexico up here. Most of the room was now in shadows.

He turned on the desk lamp and rummaged through his duffel bag until he found some running gear and changed into shorts and running shoes. It was still too hot and sticky for even a T-shirt. Atkinson would know of some good five-mile loops from here. An idea struck him suddenly and he double-knotted his Adidas and opened up his most prized possession, the brand-new Smith-Corona portable typewriter his parents had given him for graduation.

He rolled an index card into the platen and typed a few lines, enjoying the snap of the keys, the crisp black pica letters jumping onto the white card stock. No doubt about it, typing had been the most useful course he had taken in high school. Smiling, he pulled the card out of the machine and read it over carefully.

One way or another, he promised himself with a chuckle, *I will leave my name on this place.*

The hall was empty and quiet as he pulled the door closed and thumbtacked his card directly beneath the older one. It said:

Rudyard Kipling was a 4:30 miler.

—*Quenton Cassidy, 1965*

From downstairs, over the distant thunder, he could hear the ravenous hordes gathering at the door of the dining room.

There are seven-foot-high jumpers down there, he thought. There were also seventy-foot shot putters, 4.10 milers. There wasn't anyone in the building who wasn't a state champion, an all-American, a conference champion, a school record holder, *something impossible.*

Yet they were all down there right now, jostling each other on their way to dinner. *What an amazing place I have landed in,* he thought.

Quenton Cassidy would have to hurry to get his five miles in and get back in time to get something to eat.

Maybe if he ran fast enough he could even beat the rain.

ACKNOWLEDGMENTS

I am most grateful to my old friends and teammates, Harry Winkler and Frank Saier, for allowing me to plunder their recollections of growing up wild and free in Palm Beach County, Florida, in the long lost 1950s and '60s—while becoming great athletes themselves.

My fellow ink-stained wretch, Ron Wiggins, was there for me again, as he has been so often in the past, with gentle advice and an occasional wittily rewritten line that was far better than my own.

My old friend Tom Raynor, as always, was a source of encouragement, inspiration, and advice, not to mention the occasional glass of a carefully selected vintage.

Profound thanks to my prescient and tireless agent and friend, Byrd Leavell, and my former editor and friend, Brant Rumble, who ran with this story right from the starting gun.

For years of inspiration, a shout-out to Ray Allen, late of the Miami Heat and the Boston Celtics. In my opinion he is possibly the greatest jump shooter the game of professional basketball has ever seen, and strangely enough, he reads novels about distance runners.

Finally, I am deeply indebted to James D. Snyder for his well-researched and gracefully written *Life and Death on the Loxahatchee: The Story of Trapper Nelson*. I would heartily recommend that little gem of a book to any reader interested in knowing more about the force of nature that was the real Vincent Natulkiewicz, also known as Trapper Nelson, the Tarzan of the Loxahatchee.

Made in the USA
Middletown, DE
21 July 2023

35549871R00217